PRAISE FOR *THE ___* ___ *EL*

"Hilarious and full of heart, S___ ___ ___ce *Hotel* is like a smooth shot of ouzo: surprising, intoxicating, and brimming with Greek charm. Amelia and James are a couple you can't help but root for, and Asteri is an island you can't help but adore—cats, coves, kooky locals, and all. From the very first chapter, Godfrey's writing grabs you by the hand and whisks you away on an unforgettable adventure, one that will make you long for your very own visit to the Ria Hotel."

—Genevieve Wheeler, author of *Adelaide*

"*The Second Chance Hotel* by Sierra Godfrey is a warm, sensory, and voicey novel that transported me from the winter doldrums of Manhattan to the sunny island of Asteri, Greece. While reading this delicious slow burn romance between Amelia and James and their accidental marriage of convenience, I could almost feel the sun on my face and taste the salt of the olives. Escapist yet thoughtful, and ripe with humor, Godfrey's second novel is also a reminder to us all that it is far better to run toward your happiness than away from your fears."

–Meredith Schorr, author of *As Seen on TV* and *Someone Just Like You*

"The perfect balance of quirk and heart, this utterly charming novel is a sun-soaked dream. The food, the people, the scenery—I didn't want to leave the island! Godfrey's talent for creating messy, complex characters you can't help but love and root for is on full display in this enchanting take on how unexpected mishaps can land you right where you're meant to be. Insightful, witty, and bursting with beauty, *The Second Chance Hotel* will leave readers basking in its afterglow like the very best summer vacation."

–Holly James, author of *The Déjà Glitch*

"Hilarious, heartfelt, and utterly transportive, *The Second Chance Hotel* sparkles from the very first page. I fell quickly and madly for Amelia and James's accidental yet moving love story, as well as the quirky cast of locals inhabiting Asteri's shores. Anyone who has ever dared to wonder 'what if' will find themselves swooning over this unputdownable novel, and instantly signing up for a summer at the Ria Hotel. Best paired with a glass of wine and some fresh olive oil, I loved every word."

—Becky Chalsen, author of *Kismet*

"Sierra Godfrey brings together two messy people and an even messier situation in a story that delves into duty, community, and hope. *The Second Chance Hotel* is an ode to the Greek islands, and the many journeys people take to love."

—Lily Chu, author of *The Stand-In*

Also by Sierra Godfrey

A Very Typical Family

THE
SECOND
CHANCE
HOTEL

A Novel

SIERRA GODFREY

sourcebooks
landmark

Copyright © September 2023 by Sierra Godfrey
Cover and internal design © September 2023 by Sourcebooks
Cover design and illustration by Kimberly Glyder

Sourcebooks and the colophon are registered trademarks of Sourcebooks.

Published by Sourcebooks Landmark an imprint of Sourcebooks
P.O. Box 4410, Naperville, Illinois 60567-4410
(630) 961-3900
sourcebooks.com

Cataloging-in-Publication data is on file with the Library of Congress.

Printed and bound in the United States of America.
VP 10 9 8 7 6 5 4 3 2 1

To my mother, Enid, for taking me to Greece.

CHAPTER 1

Amelia Lang was not aiming for Micah's head when she threw the coffee mug. But if he hadn't moved, it would have hit him right between the eyes. Instead, it hit the conference room window behind him with a resounding smack. Tea dripped down the spiderweb of cracks in the glass. The mug, Amelia saw with regret, had broken. It was her favorite one, with whimsical travel illustrations and a gilded rim. Too bad about the tea too—it was a fancy French blend that was hard to find.

Those standing in the vicinity watched in shocked silence.

Amelia's boss, severe on the best of days, looked thunderous. "Amelia. Go sit in my office."

Micah had the gall to smirk as she passed. She closed her boss's office door behind her and sank into the guest chair. And then it hit her. She'd thrown a mug at someone's head. Never mind that it was Micah's head, and that she, still in the flush of fury, thought he deserved it. She'd never done anything like that. Never gotten into a fistfight, never even shoved anyone. She, who gently escorted spiders out of her house and always held the door open for others.

Throwing a mug and cracking a window? That was irreversible, evidenced by being sent to sit in her boss's office like she was five.

The minutes ticked away. She wished she was the type to escape out of the window and briefly considered becoming that person. It looked bad, she could see that. Thirty-two years old, living with her parents again, and about to be fired for throwing a mug at her ex-boyfriend's head at work. The past week had been a one-way ticket to Failureville.

Finally, after a long stretch that suggested her boss and HR were discussing how to handle her, they came in and closed the door behind them.

"Amelia," her boss said. "I'm sure you can appreciate the difficult situation we're in."

Amelia did not appreciate anything, least of all what Micah said right before the mug left her hand, but she nodded.

"Can you explain what happened?" the HR manager asked.

She considered how much to tell them. It had been a terrible morning. She had left home late, and because she'd been running behind, it was a certainty that a traffic incident on Highway 101, running south out of San Francisco into Silicon Valley, slowed her down further. A car fire, no less. And if you were running late, and there was a car fire on the freeway, it stood to reason that your mobile phone would be dead so you couldn't call and let people know you'd be late. Amelia didn't even know where her charger was, because it was that kind of morning.

As a result, she'd missed most of the morning developer meeting. As she slid into the conference room, far from invisible, her boss had pounced on her. In a tone that sounded like he was sucking a lemon, he asked her what the status of the code release was.

"It went out last night, as scheduled," she said. Obviously the code release had gone out. That was the entire point of her job.

There had been a visible shuffling in the room. Amelia looked around, but no one met her eye. Including Micah, but this was no surprise. They'd broken up last week, and he'd done it in the most craven way possible, trotting out the ol' *I need to work on myself* line. She wasn't heartbroken, not by a long shot, but they were supposed to have gone to Paris in three weeks. Amelia had been looking forward to the trip for months. Now, two nonrefundable tickets and a breakup later, and they couldn't even look at each other. Which was a problem considering they worked together.

But there was no reason for the others to avoid her eye. A shiver of horror slid down her spine as she realized that the release had clearly not gone out.

"Apparently there was a problem," her boss confirmed. "Let's take this offline. Amelia, meet me in my office in five and we will discuss. Okay, Standup's over."

Everyone shot out of the room, causing a brief logjam at the door. No one wanted to be blamed for a failed code release, which would freak out the investors and send everyone panicking. There could be restructurings and layoffs, and Amelia, who was the project manager responsible for code releases, would surely be at the top of the list.

She needed something to do with her hands while her boss told her off, so she made some tea. She was almost to her boss's office when Micah rounded the corner. A little spike pounded into her chest at the sight of him. She tried not to picture how they would have settled back into their airplane seats in three weeks' time, getting magazines out for the flight, studying the emergency procedures card, hoping they wouldn't have to use the instructions. Along with not going to Paris, she'd had to move back in with her parents across the bay, a fate worse than death. So it was fine that he wasn't talking to her. She didn't want to talk to him either.

Except he stopped in the hall as she passed.

"I can't believe you didn't get the code out," he said.

The cheek of him. "I can't believe you walk around with that reptile face." She regretted the words as soon as they were out. They made her sound angry. Which she was, but he didn't need that satisfaction.

He shook his head as though disappointed by her childishness. "You're supposed to run the final check before it deploys."

"I did," she hissed. Why was he needling her? Unless there was something… "What are you suggesting?"

"I'm suggesting that it's your job to run the deployment check, and you didn't."

"Nothing had changed since six p.m. yesterday." As soon as she said the words, she knew. Micah had stuck something in the code after hours, knowing her parents' house had terrible Wi-Fi because they refused to upgrade their equipment or plan—it was like living in prehistoric dial-up times—and she wouldn't be able to check after hours. But she had made sure the code was solid before leaving work.

"Your job is to perform a check right before deployment, not leave it the day before and call it good." He blinked and squinted all at once, which looked like a facial tic, but Amelia knew better. It was the same squint he'd used when he was breaking up with her or when he was lying. She's seen that blink-squint a lot in the past few months.

She knew he'd crashed the release on purpose.

Two years with this horrific assface, one living with him. She'd supported him as he took classes to advance at his job, supported him as—wait. Wait, *wait*. That was it. She'd taken a full-stack engineering certification course a few months ago, passing with flying colors. She was proud of it, because it was damned hard. Not that she wanted to become a developer—God, no—but it gave her a deeper understanding of their work and put her in a prime spot for a promotion. Micah, who suffered from a light case of techbro-ism, had decided he needed the certification too. Except he'd failed the final. And he *worked* as a developer.

She was sure he'd broken up with her as a result. Not that he'd said that—never—but his *I need to work on myself* line was suspiciously timed with news that he'd failed the course. Now he was sticking pieces of crap in the code and crashing it on purpose. No one would believe her, of course, and it would be easy for him to make it seem like she was a hysterical, spurned ex. She squeezed the handle of her mug to tamp down the anger.

Their boss's door flew open behind them. "Amelia. Let's go. I need to know what happened with this deployment."

"It's pretty obvious what happened," Micah said loudly, verging on yelling. His eyes were on Amelia's, glittery and mean. "Amelia went home last night and assumed the code was fine. She didn't bother running the final check, so if someone added a piece of code, she wouldn't have known. And it crashed. She always makes developers here feel rushed because she wants to get home to dinner."

———

"That's when the mug left my hand," Amelia told the HR manager now.

"Amelia, we cannot tolerate acts of violence in the workplace," the HR manager replied. She pushed over a folder. "Effective immediately, your employment here at Swinck Software is terminated."

Amelia cringed. "Micah sabotaged me. He let his personal bias affect the work here." Even to her ears, it sounded desperate.

Her boss and the HR manager exchanged a look. To her surprise, a different folder was pulled out.

"We will offer you a small severance in exchange for you signing a paper saying you will not file suit," the HR manager said.

This suggested they might be somewhat familiar with the situation between her and Micah, and that they clearly saw the sexism that ran amok at Swinck despite their official policy opposing it. She signed the paper anyway.

Security walked Amelia out to the parking lot.

In the sanctuary of her car, she let out a breath and took stock. For the millionth time, she wondered if she would have broken up with Micah anyway as soon as they were back from Paris. Part of her had been waiting for the trip to happen to see how she felt about him. She had vague fantasies of ditching him in one of the gardens in Versailles, hiding out in Le Petit Trianon until he gave up and went away. It was ridiculous, of course. She should have just dumped him and gone on her own.

And in fact, now she could.

The tickets were still valid, since they were nonrefundable. She could probably change the flight to a sooner date for a small fee and jet off to Europe by her glorious self, unrestricted by work obligations and unfettered by Micah's whining about French culture, which surely would have been plentiful. The man did not like crepes, which was reason enough to be rid of him.

She clicked around on her phone, and in less time than seemed believable, she found two flight options: one for a few hours from now, and one for tomorrow morning. Both had available seats. She chose the one for tomorrow. She stared at the Swinck parking lot, hardly daring to believe that throwing a mug at someone's head had worked out for the best.

An incoming text buzzed her phone. Her best friend Ella's characteristic to-the-point words greeted her: Celia just texted me that you were escorted out of work. Call me????? Celia was a mutual friend and one of the few female developers at Swinck.

Amelia dialed her as she pulled out of the parking lot. "Celia is right, Ells. I was fired."

"What happened?"

Amelia sighed, letting out some of the upset. "I threw a mug at Micah's head."

There was a long silence on the line. And then, "Shit."

"It's actually fine." Amelia came to a stoplight before the freeway entrance, hoping it was the last time she'd ever make this commute home. The light turned green. Traffic was clear now—it always was when you didn't have to be anywhere on time—and she merged onto the freeway with nary a brake light. "It made me realize I'd been holding myself back in a lot of ways."

"So you threw a mug at his face? I'm not saying he didn't deserve it. But that's—a lot."

"I know." She trusted Ella's opinion. They had been friends since high school, their friendship cemented when their controlling mothers picked them up from swim meets and, with uncanny timing, berated their daughters at the same time for not placing first. Amelia and Ella had supported each other ever since, through things like Ella fighting her strict Chinese parents on everything from attending Chinese classes after a full day of high school to Amelia struggling with her mother's constant attempts to coerce her for Amelia to go to the college her mother wanted.

"I know it's bad and I'm shocked by what I did," Amelia continued. She did feel shocked, but it was beginning to wear off. Now she felt exhilarated about that trip to Paris and excited that it was going to work out. "So I'm taking some time off. Taking a little time out."

"What does that mean, *taking time out*?" Ella asked. "You were fired, right?"

"Yes." Amelia's mind was racing. A freeway sign announcing the exit for the airport loomed overhead. She'd have to drive back over to the East Bay to pack for tomorrow, and her mother would interrogate her as to why she was home early. When she heard Amelia was fired, it would be hand-wringing and screeching and general mayhem, and Amelia could not. It would be so much easier to bypass all that and leave now on that flight today. What did she even need?

Because here was the thing: in the backseat was her brother's old backpack—the one he'd used to hike in Lassen in high school—currently filled with a bunch of clothes that she hadn't yet taken into her parents' house to wash after leaving her and Micah's apartment. Crucially, there was also something in one of the many utility pockets of the backpack: her passport.

"Amelia?" Ella said. "Are you listening to me? What made you throw the mug?"

"Micah stuck a piece of code in the release and crashed it, knowing I'd signed off on the final the evening before." The exit sign for the airport screamed at her, her heart racing. Should I do it?

Ella sighed. "He's an ass. But babes, you should have seen this coming."

Amelia frowned. "Are you saying this is my fault for not predicting he'd do this?"

"I'm just saying that the two of you ended badly, and I know how much you wanted to go on that trip you'd planned. And we also know Micah is a childish loser, so the fact that this all happened isn't overly surprising."

Amelia felt a stab of hurt. "Okay, but I did not expect him to sabotage me professionally."

"It sounds like you did that yourself by throwing the mug."

The seed of hurt bloomed into a full-petaled flower now. *Get off the freeway or keep driving?* Either way, she was leaving. It was a matter of listening to her mother or not.

She chose *not* and took the exit. "Maybe you're trying to be supportive here, but I'm not hearing it."

"Look, I get it. He was a terrible boyfriend. He was constantly staying late at work to play foosball and *Call of Duty* with the other techdouches. He never did laundry and always left you to do the washing up. He never wanted any of your friends to come over, saying it was his sacred space or some nonsense, and what about the time he spent thousands of dollars setting up a saltwater aquarium that took up a whole wall, but you weren't allowed to spend a few hundred on a new sofa when the old one was covered in stains and smelled like feet?"

"Okay, Ells, it sounds like you're angrier at him than I am." Amelia veered toward the sign that said, *Long-term Parking*.

"You should be angry!" Ella yelled.

"I was! I threw a mug at his face. Sorry I missed too." Amelia slowed the car and took the ticket from the machine at the gate. "But all is well. I'm still going to Europe."

"What?"

"I'm still doing it." Amelia's voice sounded calm to her. "Now, in fact. I'm here at the airport."

"What do you mean, you're there at the airport? Did you plan this?"

"No. But I have a backpack full of clothes in my car and my

passport. I got a severance check that's direct deposited into my account. I'm going and I feel great about it."

There was a long silence, which did not come off as supportive or encouraging. And then, "Amelia. I am getting *married* in three weeks."

Amelia felt her eyes go wide. In the melee of getting fired, the swirl of horror that she'd thrown a heavy object at someone's face, and the sweet temptation of going to Paris anyway, she had neglected to remember that Ella was getting married and that Amelia was the maid of honor. Amelia wondered if she'd been lobotomized sometime in the night. It would explain her choices today, including forgetting her best friend's wedding.

"How long are you planning to be gone?" Ella asked. "Because there's the bachelorette party, and my aunt is throwing me that shower, and I still have my final dress fitting."

Amelia pulled into a parking spot. The initial plan had been to go immediately following Ella's wedding. If she went now, it would be longer than three weeks. Why not stay months? Three, even. Three was arbitrary, but she didn't have a job to come back to, and it seemed like a good long time to figure things out.

"Say something, Amelia." A note of hysteria had entered Ella's voice.

"Um, I'm trying to think." Amelia turned off the car.

"What is there to think about? If you're gone for a few days, I mean, maybe okay, but—"

"I can't stay in Europe for a few days," Amelia said.

"People do it all the time."

Like the signs calling her to the airport, Amelia had to make a choice. Only this sign said, *Piss off your best friend possibly forever, next left,* and below that, *Or go to Europe and figure shit out, right lane only.*

Thing was, she might not get this chance again. If she waited until after the wedding, her mother most surely would talk her out of going, and she'd get trapped into looking for another job. She'd forget. Momentum would be lost. She *had* to go now. She and Ella had been friends for years. They could weather this. It was only a wedding.

"I'm sorry," Amelia said.

"You did not just say that."

Amelia got out of the car and rummaged in the backseat. Yes! Passport in the pocket. And enough underwear in the bag to last a week at least. Even better were the four dresses she'd bought for the trip, which she'd shoved in the backpack and had not wanted to look at after Micah had broken up with her.

"Amelia," Ella hissed. "Are you seriously getting on a flight? Are you really doing this?"

"I'm here at the airport," Amelia said. She picked up loose change from her car's console, grabbed her extra sunglasses, and hefted the backpack onto her shoulders. "I have to do this."

"You don't. You're being selfish and dramatic."

Amelia sensed a dent occurring in their friendship. She might not agree with Ella, but she could see that leaving now was hurtful. For that, Amelia was sorry, but she had to leave. Now. "Ella. I know it's your wedding. And I know you're upset—"

"This is the shittiest thing you've ever done," Ella yelled. "It's my *wedding*, Amelia!"

Amelia walked toward the sky tram that would take her from the long-term parking lot to the international terminal. Her body tingled with a mixture of feelings: excitement, fear, and worry.

"Listen. I'll call you as soon as I land, okay?" Amelia said. "We can talk about it and maybe work something—"

"There's nothing to work out." Ella's voice was tight and seething. "Don't bother calling. At all. Ever."

The call ended.

Amelia climbed aboard the tram, feeling numb. She was still wondering if this was the right choice when it deposited her at the international terminal. Before today, there were plenty of reasons not to fly to Paris on a whim, but now there was only one: Ella's wedding. And it just wasn't a big enough reason. Didn't fifty percent of marriages end in divorce anyway? Would Ella even forgive her at this point, if she stayed? The answer was unclear. Amelia felt bad about that, but surely Ella would come to understand in time how important it was for her to go.

The busy chaos of the airport swirled around her. How nice it would be to lose herself in a crowd, sleep in new places, and become someone new.

"Men do this kind of thing all the time," Amelia said aloud as she headed to the ticket counter to get her ticket changed one last time. "They're called brave and adventurous." As though to prove the point, a tall, blond, *very* handsome man walked by and gave her such a nice, interested smile that she almost buckled. Surely that was the weight of the backpack. Pleased, she stepped into the ticket line.

When she got back, she and Ella could talk things through. She would explain that she had to go, that she was at a rare crossroads and unlikely to get this chance again. Upon her return, she'd get a new job—a better one—and an apartment. She would come back stronger and better—an Amelia who made wise decisions, who thought before she leaped, who knew exactly where she was going, and who always landed solidly on her feet.

CHAPTER 2

THREE MONTHS LATER

The moment the ferry bumped against the rotted wood of the small dock, Amelia feared she had made a horrible mistake.

She stepped off the ferry and promptly tripped, falling heavily on her chest with an unseemly *whomp* sound. "Ah," the man said. It was a kind of disappointed noise combined with amusement. "Okay?"

"Okay." Once she got back to her feet, Amelia held out her hands to show that she was fine, thanks, and steady, none of which was true. If she believed in signs, she would read into the fall that Asteri was going to be a disaster.

"*Kala*," the man said. That meant *good* according to the copy of *Learn Greek in 30 Minutes a Day* that Amelia had studied on the ferry to the island.

She had not expected a welcoming committee with a fruity cocktail pressed into her hands—this was Greece, not the Caribbean, but the port was desolate. Ahead, a rental car lot consisted of a small patch of dirt with a few vehicles that looked like they had been around since the seventies. Beyond that, a single dusty road zigzagged up a stomach-turning cliff. Or maybe that was residual seasickness from the ferry.

Amelia had been warned about the island when she booked the ferry from Santorini. "Asteri?" the booking agent had scoffed. "Pah! Not good island. Too quiet. You stay here, you go beach here."

But Asteri it was, partly to shut her mother up. Amelia had been to amazing places during her three months in Europe, but her mother had consistently hounded her to go to Asteri and stay in the "most darling hotel ever," which her parents had stayed in thirty years earlier, in happier times. Amelia agreed to come because she needed a quiet island to reflect on her trip before going back home. And there was work to do—the most annoying kind. The tiresome and possibly unpleasant task of reverting to who she was before she left for this trip. That meant no distractions of bars, clubs, or new people. She definitely had not indulged in thoughtful silence throughout her trip. So, despite the alarming indications that Asteri might offer *too* much contemplation, she booked a ticket.

Her palms smarted, but she dusted them off and hoisted her heavy backpack into the familiar grooves on her shoulders. She walked past three filthy cats sitting beside the water as though they were waiting for something to change. A decrepit kiosk advertising Vespas and cars for rent on a hand-painted sign was ahead. The rental kiosk appeared to be empty. She knocked and yelled, "*Yasoo,*" anyway.

"Yah." A young man sat up sleepily. "Yah. You want car?"

"Yes," Amelia said. "I'd like to rent one for two weeks."

"Two weeks?" he yelled. "No, no, too long."

She was starting to think two weeks *was* too long but, shading her eyes against the fierce sun, she asked, "Why is it too long?"

"You not stay here two weeks." The guy shook his head solemnly.

She hid her eye roll. "A week, then? Can I have it for a week?"

The man's face drooped further. "A week, no."

She sighed, feeling the annoyance bubbling inside her. She was grimy and tired, having flown direct from Rome to Santorini. Then there had been the lengthy argument with the ticket clerk on Santorini about getting the ferry to Asteri, followed by a six-hour wait for said ferry. "Only comes one time a week," he had warned her, indicating that if she hated Asteri, she would have to wait a week to leave again. Amelia had assured him that she was willing to accept the risk. Then the ferry ride itself, which was three hours in choppy water. An archetypal old-world Greek woman wearing a faded black mourning dress had vomited quietly but steadily into a plastic bag the entire way. Amelia badly wanted to lie down and sleep for a while.

"Can I have a Vespa for a few days, then?" She pointed to a scuffed blue moped.

"Ah! *Nay*, sure, sure." The man returned to the kiosk and got keys and paperwork. She could not imagine why this sleepy car rental wouldn't want to rent her a more expensive car for a longer period, but it didn't matter as long as she could get out of this port and to her hotel. She signed, paid in advance, and got directions to the Ria Hotel.

"Far," he said vaguely. "You go end of road." He pointed at the hill, as if there was any other place for her to go but up. Photos of the Ria Hotel showed it was built on the side of a cliff face, hanging on like a whitewashed crab, nothing but dramatically rugged green cliffs and pure blue sea. The island was only eight miles in length and three wide, so she thought she'd easily be able to find the hotel. After navigating her cranky Vespa up the steep switchback road, she came to a crossroads at which she could either go north or south. A small blink-and-you'll-miss-it sign said that the Ria Hotel was up the north road.

It didn't take long to get there. There was nothing else on the road except one dusty dirt road turnoff, and the rest of the way was stepped farmland separated by low rock walls. Beyond that, nothing but blue sky and sea. Despite her misgivings, a zip of excitement ripped up her middle. It was all so beautiful in its simplicity. Occasionally, a single sugar cube of a building appeared, nestled into the green and brown land. She stopped several times to take photos.

The Ria Hotel appeared at the end of the road, a small cluster of buildings so white that they blinded her eyes. Apparently the hotel owners were the most in-love couple her mother had ever met, forming the picture of marital bliss on which her parents had initially based their marriage. This had not worked out, as evidenced by her mother's sobbing call only a week into Amelia's trip with the unsurprising news that she and Amelia's dad were getting a divorce. Amelia had been weaving her way through a crowded Gare du Nord at the time and her response *might* have lacked the sympathy her mother was expecting, but honestly, her mother was insane if she thought no one knew that she and Amelia's dad had existed in a bubble of codependent hatred for longer than anyone could remember. Nevertheless, the Ria Hotel remained a sacred and untouchable beacon of true love, run by the king and queen of bliss, Takis and Maria, who had impressed Amelia's parents enough to prolong their marriage by several years more than they should have.

That it was also dirt cheap was a key reason for Amelia caving to her mother's incessant requests that she come here.

Gray cobblestones with thick white lines separating them lined the hotel's courtyard, pulled together with colorful pots of purple bougainvillea and red geraniums stuck in improbable smidgens of shade. The terra-cotta-tiled roof contrasted gorgeously with the whitewashed walls. Amelia pulled to a stop in front of bright blue doors and cut the Vespa's engine. The silence was grotesquely loud, but then her ears adjusted to the more subtle calls of the wind and the undulating whine of cicadas. The smell of a familiar sweet spice hit her nose, and she recognized it as oregano. It grew in rambling clumps around the side of the road, a visual and olfactory heaven, as though the three months of adventures throughout Europe had led her here, to this quite literal end point.

The wood doors flung open and a stout, mustachioed older man shot out, clapping his hands.

"You are the Amelias, yes? Come, come, welcome to Ria Hotel!" He took her pack from her, giving her that airy feeling that came whenever the thing was off her, like she was floating. "I am Takis!"

"Amelia Lang. So nice to meet you," she said. He ushered her into the building, a cool respite from the afternoon heat. She looked around at the small reception: two uncomfortable-looking chairs and a table covered in piles of paper filled the space.

"Best room," Takis said, rummaging in a drawer. He produced a key attached to a comically large piece of plastic. "Best view." He handed her the key holder and made a tiny check mark in a book on his desk. She had not mentioned the role the Ria Hotel or Takis and Maria played in the canon of her parents' marriage when she booked the room over email. Maybe she should have, but she couldn't imagine Takis and Maria remembering two young newlywed Americans from thirty years ago. He probably got starry-eyed honeymooners all the time.

"Is the hotel busy right now?" She stretched to get the road kinks out of her shoulders and found herself hoping that it was busy. All of her stops across Europe had been a marvelous party, and she had loved it.

"Not busy." Takis beamed as though this was a good thing. "You have whole hotel to yourselves. I take you to room now, you come for a drink later after you have rested, and then dinner. Best dinner."

Amelia put away the worry of an empty hotel in June at peak tourist time in Greece and followed him back outside through the blue doors and across the courtyard. Takis, carrying her pack, wound between white walls and down shallow but steep steps, and then through another set of worn wooden doors and into another courtyard. Down more steps, and it was beginning to feel like she was in an Escher painting, with Greek flair.

"Look." Takis pointed down the worn stone stairs leading to a narrow dirt path, like a sentence that had trailed off. "Path goes to a small beach far below. Is steep, not easy. But private, yes?"

She smiled, delighted at the idea of a private cove, even though the cliff was so steep and the path so narrow that it was almost a deterrent.

Takis stopped in front of a plain door and unlocked it. He pushed it open and stepped back for Amelia to go in.

The room was narrow and long, minimalist, with a white domed ceiling and a simple bed covered in a bright tomato-colored bedspread hugging one wall. In another world, the bedcover would be a charming textile, but Amelia suspected it wasn't meant to be stylish. The other wall had a sink and a table so small that it looked like it had been built for Chihuahuas. Two tightly closed, heavy wood shutter doors stood at the end of the room. She understood the plainness was purposeful because the occupant would be spending most of their time outside, but it was a little disappointing. It looked as though it had not changed since her parents visited. Their brief honeymoon on Asteri was much-treasured family lore, and in their telling, the Ria was the height of luxury and elegance. Amelia might need to tread carefully when she told her mother how it was looking these days.

"Is okay?" Takis seemed anxious. His thick eyebrows knitted together.

"It's great." She gave him what she hoped was a reassuring smile. The past three months had been spent sharing rooms in hostels and even sleeping outside on cots under the stars in particularly crowded places—all of which had been amazing. But a cell-like room was what she needed now. She was not here for a luxury suite with an infinity pool.

"Come and see." Takis pushed open the two doors. Amelia followed him out to a balcony and stopped, astonished.

The small veranda was covered in the same hot cobblestones as the drive, but in front of her was nothing but a jagged green cliff that plunged into the sea. The sky and water were so deeply blue that it hurt her eyes. It was like a screensaver or stock photography, except she could feel a slight breeze on her face, so she knew it was real.

"You like?" Takis asked.

"Yes," she breathed. The four pixelated photos on the hotel's single-page website hadn't exaggerated. This view was everything.

"Okay, you relax," Takis said, stepping back into the room. "Rest, then come up to top. For drinks." He left the room, closing the door firmly behind him, and Amelia turned back to stare at the sea and sky.

After a long time taking in the view, she felt her body let go of the tension, muscle by muscle. It had dogged her throughout Europe, and the best remedy, she'd found, was people and adventures. Without either of those distractions on Asteri, at least there was this view. And this balcony, with its weathered and sagging wood lounge chair. She stretched, arching her back, and slipped off her shoes. This meant leaping over the flagstones to the lounge chair so as not to burn her feet, but it was worth it. She flopped down and closed her eyes. A flicker of memories—the mug, the scowl on her boss's face, the anger in Ella's voice—came to her, but she refused to allow them to take root. The drone of cicadas lulled her from somewhere far below the cliff. Yes. Better. The Ria Hotel on Asteri might actually be perfect. And she should know.

The past three months had been spectacular. Amelia had eaten excellent foods, been ill on her own, had a lover or two, washed her undies in the hostel sinks regularly, and let herself go days without showering. She had felt beautiful in her skin. In Paris, she cut her hair. In Porto, she'd eaten animal intestines and bugs—twice—once on purpose. She had made friends and felt physically stronger with healthier skin. And now, on the last leg of the trip, she had a quiet Greek paradise with the solitude to think about what to do when she got back.

First thing: see Ella and beg for her forgiveness in person. None of her calls or texts to Ella had been answered since Amelia had been in Europe, which was rough. Amelia had tried stalking her but had found herself blocked on all social media accounts. She had a steep road back to Ella's good graces—or if not good, then she'd take a single grace.

Second, Amelia needed to get a job and start repairing the professional reputation she'd detonated.

It was getting into that headspace that required Asteri's quiet. It was going to take a monumental effort to put back on that persona of diligent job hunter and ideal prospective employee—not to mention penitent ex-best friend. She thought about her laptop, which had not been opened once over the past three months. She looked at her battered phone case, itching to call Ella. A familiar feeling.

As much as she missed Ella, she had made friends in Europe. Like Evi in Amsterdam, whose infectious laugh was a delight and with whom she was still texting, and Pau in Madrid, whose chiseled features and low growl had waylaid her until he suggested that she stay and live with him, a commitment she did not want. There was the de Filini family in Salerno, who had taken her in and told her in firm, inarguable tones that she was now one of them, an honorary daughter. They'd had designs on her marrying Alessandro, the handsome son who was older than Amelia but still single, much to his parents' lament. Amelia discovered why after experiencing his propensity for coyote-like howls during sex and shouting instructions to his mother on what he wanted for breakfast, also regrettably during sex. That had been the perfect time for Amelia to give in to her mother's insistence on visiting Asteri. Amelia had emailed Takis and received a fast response, letting Amelia know that he did indeed have a room available for her, and yes, he would be happy to take her payment up front for a two-week stay, and Amelia escaped from the de Filini grasp.

She gave in to the heady drowsiness now, enjoying the complete relaxation of not having to be on her guard. In Amsterdam, she had stayed in a noisy hostel full of drunk Germans who would burst in, gathering volunteers for another of their tiresome hikes. In Prague, two men followed her to her hostel, where she'd locked herself in a closet and stayed until their knocking stopped. In Ibiza, she had lost her head entirely at a rave on the beach and woken up in the arms of a man whose face she had never seen before.

But here, there was only her and that blue.

She woke with a start. A furry tail wound over her shin, attached to the butt of a handsome and enormous white and orange cat who eyed her with open expectation. He looked as though he'd been through a few tough encounters in his time.

"Hey you," she said, her voice a croak.

The cat gave a *prrt* sound and booped his head up under her hand, clearly knowing the drill. She palmed the top of his head, luxuriating in her drowsiness and the touch of softness on her skin. Her palms had grown callused from the heavy straps of her backpack. She was officially tired of traveling, although she wouldn't have changed a thing about the last three months.

The cat meowed again, demanding more attention, and leaped onto Amelia's middle. She made an "oof" sound and shoved him off. She sat up and eyed him, knowing that this guy was likely to try the same tricks if she lay back down, so she stood and stretched. She itched to get into that blue water, but already the heat of the afternoon had waned. A good time, then, for that drink Takis promised her.

She made her way back up the multitude of staircases, stepping over two scrawny cats balled up in the shade of the stairs. Through more indistinguishable courtyards with faded wooden doors and junk piled up in corners. She was considering leaving herself a bread crumb trail to find her way back when she found a set of stairs that looked familiar based on the pots of fuchsia geraniums on them.

"Ah!" Takis boomed when she stepped into the small cave-like den that housed the hotel's bar. An aged Formica countertop that was worn white in several spots separated them. "You like Ria Hotel?"

"It's lovely. The view is something I never imagined."

Takis looked delighted. "Is best place in Greece, I thinks. Good views, the secret beaches cove, good water from spring, best thing in the worlds. You tastes."

"Is—is your wife here?" Amelia asked. It seemed too quiet.

"Ah, no." Takis picked up a wet glass to dry. "No. My Maria dies three years ago."

"I'm so sorry to hear that." Amelia felt as though she knew Maria from her parents' stories. "My parents stayed here many years ago when they were first married and were impressed with you and your wife."

"Ah." Takis turned his face, but Amelia saw the tears fill his eyes. "Ah. That is good. Very nice. Thank you."

An awkward silence settled, and Amelia tried to think of something to say that could lighten the mood. "It's lovely here. Is—ah—is there Wi-Fi?" That would truly make the Ria Hotel the palace of the gods. Being disconnected for the past three months had been glorious, but it was time to plug in.

"Yes, we haves," Takis said, seeming to cheer up. "Two years now. Very lucky. You take drinks, yes?"

"Yes, *efcharisto*." She let Takis guide her to a shady table on the bar's veranda, which was so high above the buildings below that it gave the impression she was floating over the cliff.

Takis slid an enormous glass of amber liquid to her. Amelia could smell the fumes from where she sat. Takis raised his own glass to her and yelled, "*Yamas!*" and tipped the contents back, followed by a satisfied smacking sound. Not wanting to insult her host, Amelia swigged back a hearty mouthful of the stuff and then nearly died. The liquid instantly disintegrated her sinus system. She squeezed her eyes shut as tears streamed out of her eyes and pretended she was reaching down to adjust her shoe so she could wipe them away.

"You like?" Takis asked, his thick mustache wiggling in what Amelia suspected was amusement at her struggle.

She gasped the words out. "What *is* that?"

"Ah, island specialty," Takis said. "I make all island specials for you, no problem. Tonight, we have lamb."

"I hope you're not going to any trouble."

Takis's thick eyebrows moved. "No, no, it is slow time for Ria." He spread his arms wide. "Only one other guest come, later. I am having a hard time to let rooms." He looked comically sad, like an actor in a school play hamming it up for the parents. "You sit here or take walk, and I will cook. Come in two hours."

Amelia smiled. "I'll do that." When her glass was empty, she got up, somewhat wobbly, and decided to explore how far the hotel spread across the cliff. Down one staircase, through yet another courtyard, and up another, she lost track of time gazing out at the Aegean as the golden hour descended—that time of late after-noon when everything was tinged with a shade of orange that had no name. Every courtyard offered Instagram-worthy photos. She couldn't imagine why the place was empty. Then again, she wouldn't have known about the place if her mother hadn't talked about it as the fount of love. She could see why this might not be a hidden gem, seeing as there were no rugged adventures on offer, no significant monuments, and likely no sultry flings with deliciously unsuitable men.

It was far more than two hours later when she finally found her way back to the hotel's bar-restaurant. Male voices greeted her. One of them belonged to a tall man with cropped sandy hair, wearing a light-blue linen shirt and white shorts. His back was to her, and Takis was grinning ear to ear at whatever he was saying. From the back, Amelia could see this newcomer was handsome, but she'd fallen in love many times that way sitting in traffic—a glimpse at someone's ear or neck, and she was his, only to scooch up alongside the car and discover he was a gargoyle.

Takis caught sight of her hovering at the entrance and brightened. "Amelias! Come. We have a new guest. Meet James."

James turned to her, and Amelia's breath caught. What a pleasant surprise. A treasure in the driver's side window.

"Hello, Amelia," James said. He smiled, a dimple creasing one of his cheeks, and it was the cutest thing. He was not Greek; he looked Scandinavian if anything, and by the sound of his two words, American.

"Hi, James." She ignored the pleased look on Takis's face and took the seat next to James. Maybe she could do with one last fling after all.

CHAPTER 3

James was nice to talk to. He was from Portland, Oregon, so they had the West Coast of the United States in common. He too had been backpacking through Europe for a few months.

"Where did you start in Europe?" he asked, which might have been a polite and crafty way of asking why she was traveling alone. It was a question she'd gotten a lot over the past three months, often accompanied by concern that she was a woman on her own. Because he was cute, she was willing to entertain the question.

"Paris," she said. "I traveled around France, and then went over to Scotland, down to England, and over to Ireland. All places I fit right in with this red hair. Then back to the continent."

"The continent," James said in a dramatically proper British accent.

"The *con*-tinent," she laughed, doing hers.

"If you think you fit in great in Ireland and Scotland, let me tell you, when I hit Stockholm, it was like I'd found my people."

"You do look Scandinavian."

"My mother's parents were Swedish, and they immigrated to the United States, but we've lost all connection to the country."

"The old country," Amelia said in her British accent, and then laughed since Sweden had nothing to do with Britain.

"The old country where gnomes linger in the forests. Anyway, from there I did a long wonderful meander through several countries. I probably walked most of them."

Amelia hid her grimace. In theory, meandering through countries sounded nice, but she preferred the excitement of cities and sightseeing.

"After this, it's on to Croatia," he said. "There's this island off the coast, Mljet, that has a place called Odysseus's Cave, which is a beach in a cave where Odysseus is supposed to have shipwrecked. You have to swim to get to it."

"Asteri is my last stop. Time to regroup and figure out my next step." The idea of job searching and writing the dreaded cover letter email made her want to wither.

"I came to Asteri for the olive trees," he said. "It's been my dream for years to have my own olive farm. I read this amazing article about this ancient grove here that was established before Venetian times and how it's still going strong, and I had to come. I can't wait to see them."

"Olive trees," Amelia said, giving a friendly, surface-level smile. "Awesome." She hoped he was more exciting in bed.

He glanced at her like he knew she was being nice. Probably he got that a lot. "I know what you're thinking. Trees are boring, right?" He shrugged. "But I think they're amazing."

"So when do you buy the olive farm?"

"When I get back. I have to figure out how to do it. I'm in finance. Or I was. Before I came on this trip. I quit my job to take the time off."

"Me too." Although in her case, *fired* was the correct word. But that need not enter into this conversation.

James looked dreamy. "I also want to get to Spain and hike some of the Camino de Santiago. Then across to Portugal, maybe over to Morocco, end at Tenerife, where there's supposed to be this amazing rare tree. I nerded out over foliage in every country after I picked up a book called *Trees and Shrubs of Britain and Europe*." He sighed happily.

Amelia tried not to make a face. It was foolish to think she'd find Mr. Perfect on Asteri, no matter how cute he was. A lusty fling wasn't a requirement for her final weeks in Europe.

"I had this epiphany," he went on, "about my own olive farm in Oregon. That's what I'm going to do when I get back. I even know where I'll buy the land. There's a little valley near my parents, and it's been for sale forever. That's my future."

"I get it." It was nice that he had such a firm idea of what he wanted. Her options were more limited. She would have to go back to project management for another tech company where her male colleagues were rewarded for having a penis and she was expected to work twice as hard. She liked the work enough but hated the unending barrage of politics and sexism. "At least you have a passion."

James made a delighted face. "Oh yeah. I've learned so much. Here in Greece, it's all about the minerals and the sea air. Did you see the clumps of oregano outside the hotel? And I love the wild chamomile along the road. And the cypress trees! There's so much here."

A lull came. Amelia feared they had run out of things to say to each other, which was a solid sign that James was a nice man but not a good romantic candidate. Not everyone needed to be a love interest, but after three months on her own, Amelia found that a part of her brain tended to assess men she interacted with as potential lovers.

"And what do you do when you're not taking three months off to travel?" he asked.

"I work as a project manager for a software company in Mountain View." Worked. Worked. She needed to start using the correct tense. "I liked the job, but I did not like the bro culture and the sabotage that went on because people were mad about something."

James raised his eyebrows comically high, a silent comment on this incendiary statement.

"Anyway," Amelia said, making it clear she wasn't going to go into it, "right now, I'm just figuring out my next steps. My mother hounded me into coming to Asteri. She and my dad apparently spent a magical honeymoon here thirty years ago even though they're divorcing now. But it's cheap and quiet, and I needed both of those things."

"Exactly." He nodded. "And no matter what your parents' marital status, it's cool that you have history here already."

But Amelia did not want history here. She wanted to breathe deeply and write a stupid cover letter.

"As for me," James went on, "I want to walk around the island looking at trees and plants without stumbling over someone sunbathing."

"I like stumbling over and meeting new people," she said, lifting her glass. "Cheers, I guess."

"Oh, right." He looked a little uncomfortable. They were definitely not the same kind of people.

"I wonder if we've been ships passing in the night anywhere," James mused. "Amsterdam? Check. Madrid? Check. Stockholm, Prague? Check. Skopje? Check."

"I didn't go to Skopje."

"No, of course not," James deadpanned. "It's billed as the filthiest city in Europe. Absolutely draped in smog. I just threw that in there to see."

He was trying to be funny, and she appreciated that. Takis slyly slid over refills of his drinks.

"Takis," James said, pointing to his glass, "this is delicious. How did you make it?"

"Oh." Takis straightened, looking pleased to be asked. "I take potato. I take honeys. I take the wheat. Special spices. Secret recipe."

"Do you keep beehives here?" James asked, a little too interested. "I read that Asteri has an amazing honey trade. I'd love to learn more about beekeeping."

Amelia lost interest in the conversation and swung her legs out from the bar as Takis and James dove into a discussion of the virtues and intricacies of running an apiary. She wandered out to the veranda, looking up at the stars and breathing in the clean, clear air. It seemed silly to have tables inside when there was this incredible long stretch of balcony to sit on. If this was her hotel, she'd convert the whole restaurant area out here so guests could sit out under the stars. The stars seemed brighter here than anywhere she'd been, probably because there was no other light around to diminish them. The Milky Way had never been so clear, and the constellations stood out in relief from the sky. Of all the places she'd been and seen across Europe, it could be that small plain Asteri was one of the best.

"You like the stars, Amelia?" Takis called. He and James came out to the veranda.

"I've never seen them like this," she answered. "They're... dazzling."

"Ah, when my wife and I build the Ria Hotel, we name this Star Verandas." He looked up dreamily, then coughed deeply. It seemed to consume his whole body as he moved with it. "But now..."

"How did you meet?" Amelia asked. "You and your wife?"

"Ah." Takis brightened and turned to them. "This is good story. I tell you with more retsina." He marched over to the dinner table and poured them all more. James and Amelia followed. "Now. My wife, we hate each other. Like dogs and cats!" His thick eyebrows lowered, making him look ferocious. "I meet her, I think she is most rude person on Asteri! Everything she says, I do not like. Everything I do, she does not like."

Amelia exchanged a glance with James that seemed to agree this was going to be a good story.

"But," Takis said, "my father owns this land, where Ria Hotel is. Maria's father owns land near hotel, where olive grove is. A man without a wife is lonely, my father tells me. A man cannot run a good hotel without a partner, he says. My father, Maria's father, they make a deal. Oh! Po, po." Takis shook his head in exaggeration, swinging it from side to side. "A deal for me to marry Maria. The worst thing possible." Takis slammed his glass down on the table and refilled it. "But, deal is done. Dowry paid. The olive grove given. We marry in small church on south end of Asteri."

"And then you realized that you were in love?" Amelia asked hopefully.

"No." Takis scowled. "We fights like mad, like dogs, all the time. We yell, we nag. I am not happy, she is not happy. But Ria Hotel gets customers, and we have to serve them. Little by little, I think, she is not so bad. Maybe even good."

He refilled everyone's glasses even though they weren't yet empty. "In the end, we are married forty years. Ria, I call her. We name the hotel for her. I love her more than life itself." He downed his drink. "I was fool. I wastes a lot of times."

"That's so sweet," James said, a little unsteadily. Amelia checked his face and saw that he looked as tipsy as she felt, with flushed cheeks and glassy eyes.

"So!" Takis held up a meaty finger. "To have love, you must have patience."

"The patience of *forty years*," Amelia pointed out, her words slurring.

"No, easier than forty years," Takis said. "So many couples come to the Ria Hotel! Not only your parents. I can always tell true love. Some couples come back too. Two ladies, name Sarah and Sandy, they come every year. Once they came here, twenty years ago. They came with their husbands, but I could see—a *fool* could see!—they were in love with each other. I know." He tapped his temple. "I can always sees. I helps them. I tell them, 'You love each other.' And they agree. Now, husbands are gone. I tell them, I always knew they were in loves. This place is for second chances. It is for those who are not sure, or who run, or do not yet know. This place tells them."

Amelia smiled at this sweet story and James did too. Takis broke into a phlegmy, wracking cough, holding up a hand against any inquiries, as though he knew Amelia and James would ask if he was all right.

"Do you ever think about selling the hotel?" James asked.

"Eh." Takis gave that Greek shrug Amelia had seen, a combination of *so be it* and *who cares*. "Only right kind of buyer I will sell to. But no one has come yet." He shrugged, as though perplexed.

"I don't know why not," James said. "This island feels like it's filled with the old ways. It feels less modern than some of the bigger islands. I like that."

"Yes, and plenty still to see," Takis said. "Tomorrow. Go, see. Church of St. Yorgos. Old spring in cave on top of hills. I will make you a map. Many men here on Asteri named after St. Yorgos, you will see." He made vague gestures with his whole arm. "You can see the island in a half day, if you have long lunch."

"What do you say, Amelia?" James asked. "Shall we speed run the island tomorrow? Assuming Takis's brew doesn't give us deadly hangovers."

"I've only got an old Vespa," Amelia said.

"I have a car." James winked at her.

"How did you get a car?" she demanded.

"I sweet-talked the guy," James said. "Had to show a bit of leg though." He stuck out a hairy calf, and Amelia hooted with laughter. "I warn you, the windows don't work. They appear to be permanently down."

"It's hot anyway." She pictured herself zooming along with the wind in her hair. Maybe not a lot of talking, but that was all right; it would be drama-free. The idea of a day with James was not overly terrible, especially if they kept conversation to a minimum. It was only a few hours.

Takis announced dinner was ready: lamb cooked in a nest of vine leaves. Amelia nearly had a foodgasm over it. Afterward, Takis offered a digestif of ouzo, which, while served in a small glass, was stronger than anything Amelia had consumed thus far. James and Takis nattered on about the island's vineyards and wine, which bored Amelia so much that she made the unwise decision to drink more ouzo. If she didn't take herself off to bed soon, the car date tomorrow would be an unpleasant drag. As it was, only the slightest semblance of luck kept her from vomiting.

"I think it's time to put myself to bed," she said, stumbling up to standing. The world slid dangerously.

"*Ohi, ohi, ohi*," Takis slurred. "No, stairs too much." His head drooped down toward his plate, his eyelids heavy.

"Can't sleep in the bar." Amelia held on to the table for stability.

"I will gallantly see you to your room," James said.

"That is exactly what I expected you to say." She held up a

finger. "But no thanks. I have a policy while in Europe: no men seeing me to my room unless invited."

James's face fell. "I didn't mean it like that. But I absolutely get it. Still, I think you should have some help. I promise that is all I offer."

She patted his arm. "You're nice. You can help me down the stairs, but that's it."

Amelia mildly regretted saying he was nice, but there was only so much chatter about olive groves and beehives that she could take. He stood, holding on to the table for a precarious moment, and offered her an arm. He was so tall and lanky—easily over six feet—that her five-four, compact frame probably looked silly hanging on to him. That was fine; it wasn't like they were getting married and would look off-kilter in the wedding photos. Off they went, carefully hanging on to the wood posts that held up the old roof as they went. The stairs were worrisome, but they made a game of it: how many steps could they successfully plant a solid foot on? They shouted out each number.

"Cat," Amelia called out as they stepped over what looked like the large orange and white from her veranda.

"I saw this one earlier. I named it Zorba. Let's christen it now."

"We christen thee Zorba," Amelia said solemnly, patting the cat's head. He was such a raggedy cat.

"Nicely done."

She was pleased in a wobbly way, glad of James's warmth and solidity. The flattering moonlight reminded her how good-looking he was: a long face, a nose perfectly too big for him, and those deep, expressive eyes. A tiny bit of regret that she'd disregarded him crept in. She could ignore a personality that had been dipped in the waters of blah, right? *Don't,* part of her said. *It would be a pity kiss or worse.*

"Look." Amelia waved at the dark sea ahead of them, partly to stop her thoughts. The moon was large enough to cast light on the water, and it was as lovely in the night as it was in the day but in a whole new way. This place was unendingly good. "The moon. The sea."

"The stars," James said, his voice a bit husky.

"The *stairs*," Amelia said, and James laughed. They were almost at the bottom of the steps, but his laugh died away as they turned to each other. He was on the lower step, so their height differential wasn't as pronounced. He leaned his face slowly toward hers, and even in her drunken state, she understood a kiss was incoming. All her hormonal instincts wanted it, but some last vestige of sense that hadn't been muted by alcohol spoke up. She dodged his lips, and his face fell heavily on her shoulder.

"Told you no," she said.

"You did." He shook his head, as though to clear it. "I'm going to bed before I embarrass myself further." He walked over to the first door on that level, which was the room next to Amelia's.

"Remember, you're drunk," he said, turning back and waggling his eyebrows comically. "Drink some water before you sleep, okay?"

She opened the door to her room and gave him a friendly wave. He waved back. She closed the door and fell on her bed, where she slept hard with the vision of dazzling stars over a vast dark sea and a tall yellow-haired man standing beside her.

———

Unsurprisingly, Amelia's skull felt like a lead weight filled with rotten meat that sufficed for a brain when sunlight and the growing heat of the late morning woke her. That, and an incessant and horrible ringing.

It was the sound of her phone, at top volume. She scrabbled around the bedside table. The phone fell on the tile floor and went skittering across the room. Knowing she was going to regret moving, she tried to get up and promptly fell out of bed. The crash to the floor was an explosion of pain to her kneecaps and head, and if only the phone would stop making that noise, she might be able to go on. Stopping the sound was an urgent requirement, so she crawled across the floor and answered the phone, glad no one was here to see this.

"Amelia," her mother said, far too loudly. Amelia moved her head away from the phone. "Amelia, I have been trying to reach you!"

"Is everything all right?" Amelia tried swallowing but found there was no moisture in her mouth.

"You know it isn't!" her mother yelled, and Amelia regretted deeply having answered the call. She was not up for this. Not now. Leaving without so much as a goodbye to her mother had been, predictably, as catastrophic as leaving Ella before her wedding. When she'd finally spoken to her mother (Amelia had been in Toulouse at the time), it had been an hour-long diatribe about how selfish Amelia was.

"I am all alone," her mother wailed now. "When are you going to be back? Divorce is a horror, Amelia. The least you could do is be here for me."

Amelia kept her eyes closed and spoke as though reading from a script. "Have you tried calling Christopher?"

Amelia's father had decided to file for divorce a few weeks into Amelia's trip (right around the time that Ella would be walking down the aisle, in fact). Her mother called incessantly, as though there was anything Amelia could do. She texted her brother, Christopher, to see if he could help, but he'd replied with a terse she's an adult and nothing more. She didn't blame him. Moving to New York hadn't only been about his job; it was about putting distance between him and their mother. Christopher (never a Chris, by some unspoken family acknowledgment) had resisted their mother's remora-like tendencies with an ease Amelia had not figured out how to do herself prior to coming to Europe. "Boys never call their mothers," Amelia's mother would lament, but Christopher didn't call their mom because he didn't have to—she always called him. And also because he didn't *want* to.

The only thing surprising about Amelia's father filing for divorce was that he hadn't done it sooner. Her father was gentle and patient, and her mother was like a teakettle that was almost about to whistle—and then, even though you've removed it from the heat, it whistles anyway, sputtering steam droplets everywhere, burning holes, and making an atrocious mess. Narcissistic tendencies, Amelia knew. She'd read books about it in order to understand how her mother could be so gobsmackingly selfish.

Amelia was privately grateful to her father for doing it now, because the upheaval the divorce wrought in her mother's life had taken the attention off Amelia's sudden departure, which had, before her father moved out, been her mother's greatest focus.

"I need my daughter," her mother said now. She said this so often that it could have been a recording. "I need you here with me. This is so *hard*, Amelia. When are you going to stop running and come home?"

Amelia sighed, both from weariness of her mother and her unsettled gut. She wasn't running—she was having a great adventure. "I'll be home in two weeks. I'm in Asteri now, at the Ria Hotel." This was a cheap deflection but guaranteed to be effective. She forced herself not to add, *And I'm not running.*

"Oh, you're in Asteri. Good. I'm surprised you bothered listening to me about going there." Her mother's tone had lost its wheedling quality and now had that guilt-tripping tone that Amelia despised. "An easy hop over from Athens, of course. I can picture the hotel now. Did you tell Takis and Maria that I remember them?"

"Maria passed away." Amelia didn't want to say that Takis had not asked who her parents were.

"Oh, I'm sorry to hear it. We were close, Maria and I. We struck up a friendship, one of the best of my life."

Amelia did not think this was possible.

"Make sure you visit the south end of the island. That's where the best beach is. Aren't the rooms at the Ria adorable? Oh." Her mother sighed deeply, and Amelia could picture her with her head to the side, a palm over her heart.

"It's great," Amelia said. "I'm getting up for the day now. Listen, as I said, I'll be home in two weeks. I'll see you then."

"Maybe you can—"

"Mom," Amelia said, trying to convey a warning in her tone. Sometimes it worked. "You loved Greece. I get it. Let me experience it myself."

"Right. Yes. All right, darling, I will see you in two weeks." Her mother sounded much brighter than the manufactured whining she'd deployed at the start of the call.

Amelia ended the call over her mother trying to blurt more sentiments, because she knew from experience that if she didn't, she'd never get off the phone. There were moments in her travels, many of them, when she considered never coming back. She could slum it in Amsterdam or get a job as a farmhand in Switzerland. Mine salt in Portugal or wait tables in Barcelona. It was tempting not to deal with the emotional smothering of her mother, the insincere platitudes from her father, finding a new job, or the uphill battle of making amends with Ella.

But she was thirty-two and too old to hide. And it was important to her, more important than anything else, that she go home and take responsibility. She would not be like her mother, blowing up and then assuming everything was fine and everyone else had forgotten, which they most assuredly had not.

Luckily, she had two weeks left, and each day was precious. She showered, dressed, and opened her door to stand in the already-hot cobbled alley. As her door shut behind her, the door next to hers opened and James stepped out.

"Hey, good morning." He sounded and looked bright, which was annoying. Despite her shower and her best attempts at concealer, she felt like something the cat batted under the fridge, forgot about for six months, only to pull it back out and bat it under again.

"Hey." Her voice croaked. "You look like you feel better than I do."

"That was some strong stuff Takis had," James said. He smiled, bright, sunny, un-hangovery, and jerked his head in the direction of the stairs. "But it's a new day. Race you to the top?"

"Ah, ha-ha," Amelia said. "No."

She plodded behind him up the steps but sensed that he slowed down for her. His freakishly long legs could have zipped him to the top much faster.

"This right here," James said, pausing at one of the scrawny cats sitting like a bread loaf on a step, "is an absolute disgrace. I complained already to the cat authority here and was assured that all cats would be removed from the stairs at once."

Amelia stared at him, hoping he was kidding.

"I'm kidding," he said.

"Oh." She smiled, relieved. He was a dry kidder, then. She liked that—when she wasn't hungover. "Yes. I might have to demand to have a word with the Asteri cat council."

At the top, they found the little restaurant. The table where they had eaten last night was now laid with a clean white cloth and transformed by the morning sun. Bowls of thick yogurt sat next to dishes of honey and a platter of fresh bread. Amelia surprised herself by sitting down and digging in, sure that her nausea would have rendered her appetite obsolete. James sat opposite and Takis joined them, bellowing good morning with considerable cheer. In the bright clean sunlight of a fresh day, things were better. Even the murmur of Takis and James discussing the merits of modern-day sheep and goat farming on the island was pleasant, if boring.

After three cups of coffee, her head felt close to normal. James rubbed his hands together and said, "Last night we talked about exploring the island together today. No obligation at all, but my car does have a passenger seat if you want to sit in it."

She hesitated. Her LinkedIn profile was calling her. But it would be there this evening too. It was her first full day on Asteri, after all. She could take advantage of the fact that James had a car to see the island, and then she could be done with the sightseeing portion of her stay on Asteri—enough to tell her mother about. The rest of her time here, she would buckle down on the job hunt. If all went well, she and James wouldn't have to talk much either. "Yes, that sounds nice. Thanks."

"You come for dinner tonight, yes?" Takis asked. "Meze and grilled meats. Special."

Amelia and James agreed they would. Takis presented them with water bottles and a large blanket in case they visited the beaches on the southern end of the island and wanted to sit. They went out to James's little rental car.

"You weren't kidding about the windows," she said, observing the missing glass.

"It's like a race car," he said. "No window, just door. Although there are no actual doors on race cars."

"What?"

"They're decals. So are the lights and radiators."

"Seriously?"

"Yes." James looked pleased. "They have to build them that way. Fewer parts to break away when they crash."

James opened his car door, but she thought, *Why the hell not*, and attempted to climb in the passenger side through the window. The second she slid her waist in, she realized it was a spectacularly bad idea. The window was too small, and even though she was not a large person, she had inherited her mother's curvy butt and had to wiggle inside. She pushed in with a grunt and fell forward onto the seat, her legs sticking out of the car window at an unseemly angle.

"I can't believe you did that." James sounded like he was both amused and horrified.

"I think I'm stuck." She pushed in but there was nowhere to go. Her chest hit the gearshift painfully.

He came around and helped her legs, folding them in at the knee so she could squeeze around and sit in the seat. His hands were huge and warm on her legs and felt nice.

"Thank you," she said, trying for a goofy grin, disliking her body's enjoyment of his touch.

But he wasn't smiling, and she felt like an idiot. Not a good start. She straightened herself and buckled in as he came around and started the car. It didn't matter what he thought, she reasoned. It was only one day.

CHAPTER 4

"Truly, this island is beautiful." Amelia draped her arm out of the passenger window of James's car, catching the air current in her palm as they sped along the narrow road leading away from the Ria Hotel. Sunshine lit up golden hills and thick stands of olive groves as the island rolled down toward the water. Ahead of them, the small *hora* of the island—the main town—loomed, a visual feast of minimalist white squares and blue church domes. They passed several old men riding donkeys. On one side spread a vast nothingness of water; on the other, a cliff covered in impossibly steep rock walls and myrtle bushes. It was everything Amelia had hoped for from the island.

"I've seen so many beautiful places on this trip, but Asteri might be the best," James said. "Maybe because it's the simplest. It's the opposite of home."

"The world is big." Amelia had learned over the past months that there were many possibilities. She had stopped feeling anything at all—wistful or negative—toward Micah, and she had a healthier outlook about Ella, which was that Amelia had screwed up and owed her best friend an apology for missing her big day. But she was still going to head back to a tech job. That was what she did. It was how she lived, made money, ate, had nice things. She inwardly sighed at the thought of sitting at her laptop, typing up cover letters and saying meaningless job-hunty things like *I excel at collaborating with teams to deliver exceptional service. I'm a team player, except when I threw that mug at my ex-boyfriend's head and got fired.*

"What was your impetus for taking this trip?" she asked.

"Ha." He grimaced. "One night I was working late on a huge project that the company was trying to close on. I'd gotten in at like seven that morning, and it was about nine at night. I was beat and we hadn't made much progress. The CEO comes in, surveys what we're all doing, and goes, 'That's all you got? This isn't how you get to an IPO!' And he yells that he wants 'all-night energy' from us and says he was going to lock us in the office to finish. Everyone else had packed up for the night, but this guy wanted us to stay and crunch numbers and give everything we had for him, while he went home and had a nice meal."

"And you snapped?" she asked, a little hopefully.

"I guess I did." He slowed the car to go around a donkey ambling down the road, ears flapping around flies, its owner walking behind it with a long stick. "I had a pressed fern in a small frame on my desk. I'd found it on a hike that I went on with my grandfather before he passed away. He's the one who taught me about plants. We would talk nonstop about trees and flowers and little insects and mammals." His fingers, tight around the steering wheel, relaxed. "Anyway, the CEO sees this fern and picks it up. He goes, 'This shit is why you're not focused. No one leaves this office until dawn tomorrow, and I want to come in and find those numbers finished.' And he tosses the fern in the trash and the frame cracked and he left, and I—was done."

"Did you smash the place up?" She could see this question amused him, which pleased her.

"No. I walked out. I decided there was more to life than typing in numbers on my keypad all night for that guy. I know a lot of companies and CEOs are like that, but I just—I had to remind myself that there's another side to life. So I withdrew my savings, sublet my apartment, and scheduled four months in Europe."

"Yes!" she yelled. "Sublet that shit out!"

He grinned, looking a little shy. "What about you?"

She had given versions of her story throughout her traveling. Plenty of people asked why she had quit a good job to take off for three months. At first, she had hemmed and stuttered and given too many details, or not enough. Then she started giving a summary: "A coworker blamed me for his mistake, and I quit." But James was easy to talk to, and in another week they would never see each other again, so she decided to go with the truth. Most of it, anyway.

"It was a terrible week for starters," she began in a dramatic *It was a dark and stormy night* tone. James laughed, which was a good sign. She gave an abridged account of the day, skimming over the actual mug-throwing part, but divulging how she had hurt Ella.

"I felt like I had to go," she said. "If I waited for her wedding,

I would have chickened out of going to Europe. I would have felt pressured to get another job right away instead of taking the time to decompress and find the right next step. I needed that horrible day as an impetus to go." She shook her head, as she did every time she thought about that day. It had taken her a long time and a lot of travel to realize that she wouldn't have gone otherwise. "I knew that choosing Europe would cost me her friendship."

"But you chose it anyway," James said.

"I did. It was hard. I still feel awful about it, even while knowing these three months have been the most important of my life. But she still isn't talking to me. I don't even have any idea of how her wedding went. I haven't seen photos, and I haven't heard from anyone."

"Both choices had drawbacks," James said. His tone was sympathetic. "I don't think you should feel bad for choosing you."

"I feel bad that Ella was hurt. Her wedding was important, and I was not a good friend." When Amelia had left San Francisco, the plane pulling off the ground and pushing into the sky, she'd tried to reconcile the bad feeling she had about leaving Ella by reasoning that marriage was a silly social construct anyway. Amelia had no plans to marry anyone and couldn't imagine finding someone and settling down. That had lasted all of ten minutes before Amelia had to come to terms with the fact that she'd simply been selfish.

"Well," James said thoughtfully. "You can't change the past. But you can be deliberate about the future."

Amelia liked that. James was all right.

He slowed the car to a crawl as they drove along the main

beach. A taverna with a tattered awning advertised cold beer and fresh fish. "Want to sit and have a drink?" James asked.

They ordered dolmas too. James got a beer, which Amelia thought was brave of him after last night, while she stuck to water.

"You have a family back home?" he asked.

She thought he might be fishing to see if she was attached, especially since she hadn't mentioned Micah in her job-quitting origin story. Plenty of men she'd met over the past three months had employed this method. "I have a brother. He's a lawyer and lives in New York. We're nothing alike." Christopher had been appalled when she'd said she was going off to Europe; his idea of a holiday was a weekend at home with his laptop. "And my parents." The words came out flat. "My mom has been harping on me for years to slow down and find someone to marry. The pressure is probably one of the reasons I escaped to Europe." She rolled her eyes to convey that her mother's nagging was not appreciated.

"I can certainly understand that," he said. "My own family is fairly overbearing too. I have two useless brothers and parents who are eager for me to settle down, and they definitely played a part in my decision to take time off. Among other things."

"Greece is my last stop. Part of the reason I came to Asteri, beyond all my mom's nagging to come here and stay at the Ria Hotel, is to figure out my reentry plan."

"Good place to do it." James nodded approvingly, but a cloud passed over his face. He stared at his beer bottle, picking at the label. "Like you, I can't avoid returning forever. Who knows? Might get lost on purpose on that trail in Spain."

"I would stay forever if I could," she said. "But I have to find work."

"Ideally, you would take what you've enjoyed most in Europe and apply it to work."

She considered how she could take meeting new people and experiencing different cultures back to Excel spreadsheets and Jira tickets. "Haven't figured that out yet. What do you do when you're not thinking about olive trees and traveling?"

"Oh, bird-watching," he said, brightening, and launched into a ten-minute monologue about an old barn in Mount Tabor where he'd seen six barn owls in the rafters. "That's my idea of fun."

"My idea of fun is having dinners with friends, paragliding off Mount Tam, and wine tasting in Sonoma."

"Paragliding," he said, eyes wide. "That's amazing."

It wasn't terribly risky or anything. It was adventurous. But it was clear she and James were different people.

They ambled through the day: simple, uncomplicated, and in easy conversation. There was no angling, no flirting, and no posturing. James was, for his blandness, relaxing to be with. Amelia would have preferred a larger party, more laughter and more fun, but this was fine. It was exactly what Asteri should be.

The day ended with yet another amazing meal cooked by Takis. The three of them sat around the table on the veranda, sipping aperitifs, eating a bouillabaisse that rivaled the ones Amelia had in Marseille, and regaling Takis with tidbits from the day.

It was like this the next day and the days after that. Pleasant conversation, tuning out when James waxed too long about trees or insects, and easy dinners at night at the hotel. She and James took an island drive each day, which always sounded infinitely better than sitting in her room sifting through job listings, and she found herself looking forward to seeing him each morning. They would find a taverna and have a long, lazy lunch during which they would laugh and talk about nothing in particular, followed by a predinner drink and dinner made by Takis in the evening. It was all so easy.

At dinnertime, Takis would ask for stories from the day, and Amelia and James found themselves telling him little nothings that somehow became hilarious in the retelling.

"Then there was the spider," Amelia said.

"Amblypygid," James corrected.

"That sounds like a sneeze, so we'll go with spider."

"What is this?" Takis asked, looking between them. Amelia realized she and James had begun doing that thing that couples or close friends do where they anticipate the telling of stories and finish each other's sentences. She would go with close friends.

"It's a crablike spider insect, although not a true spider," James said. "They've been finding them all over Europe—but they were never known here before, so it's exciting to see one. A graduate student in Athens found one a few years ago in his kitchen."

"And you find this thing on Asteri?" Takis looked vaguely disgusted.

Amelia held up a hand. "He tried. We went through a maze of olive trees, looking for spiders and mites."

"It was a great way to spend a hot afternoon." He'd been so nice about it, asking if it was all right that they went further into the rural part of the island with the incessant waves of cicadas buzzing and heat shimmers. She expected to hate it, but James cracked silly jokes as they went and made her laugh. By the time they found their way back to the car, she realized she had enjoyed it. His interests might not be hers, but she appreciated his childlike enthusiasm every time he found something interesting.

It would go like this:

James: "Ooh! Look at this!"

Amelia: "What are we looking at exactly? I see a stick."

James, slightly perturbed: "It's not a stick. That's a stick *insect*. I didn't know they had them in Greece."

Amelia: "Mmm hmm."

James: "Should I collect it?"

Amelia: "No."

James, laughing: "Okay. All right. I know that look."

Amelia: "Should we try to find a paragliding company here? We can jump off those huge cliffs."

James: "I think we both know there's no paragliding here."

Amelia: "Foiled again."

Takis laughed at this recounting. "You are good pair. I like." He paused to cough. James and Amelia exchanged a now-familiar glance. Takis had been coughing like this every night. It was obvious he wasn't well. But then he would rally, as he did now, slapping his hands on his knees and getting up. "I have announcements. Tomorrow, wedding! You come? I like you to come."

"You're getting married, Takis?" Amelia asked. She hadn't seen any evidence of a lady friend, but what did she know?

"No, my niece Magdalini Zannopoulou gets married. She is my last family here, and I am hers. I am very proud. You come? As my special guests?"

"That sounds lovely," Amelia said, glancing at James to see if he felt the same way. "I don't have any wedding attire though."

Takis waved a hand. "You wear sundress, no one mind. You will eat, drink, dance!"

"I'm in," James said. "Especially if I can wear a sundress too."

Amelia giggled.

Takis launched into a complicated explanation of where the wedding would be held. Given that the island was tiny, it wasn't difficult to place the location. The wedding was in the afternoon, which would give everyone lots of time to party the evening away. Weddings, Amelia worried, were always loaded with intent, and going with James might signal an opportunity to morph from friends into something more. Normally she would be extra vigilant, but James had proven himself a good friend and nothing more. And after the wedding, she resolved, it was time to hunt for jobs in earnest. This halcyon dining and laughter couldn't last forever—and it wouldn't, because somehow the better part of two weeks had melted away and she only had four days left. Asteri was heaven, but waiting on the other side was a life back home that was all too real.

———

Exploring the island with someone with no sexual tension to mess it up was exactly what Amelia had missed going across Europe on her own. No flirting, no pressure, no drama. Well, maybe a little flirting. But nothing more.

Until the next afternoon.

After a swim on the south side of the island near where the wedding would be held, they climbed a hot dusty hill to a tiny taverna with only two tables and fare that was limited but perfect: wine, bowls of shiny olives, thick hunks of feta, and crusty bread. A dish of generously cut tomatoes rounded it out. Amelia and James sat in their bathing suits, letting them air dry. To their back was a grove of olive trees, and in front a hill spread down to the sea, the water so blue that it might be fake, like spilled paint.

James passed Amelia the bottle of wine, and she refilled her glass halfway, even as he ordered a second bottle. Everything was so cheap here. She had been trying to keep her drinking to a minimum since that first night here, and drinking in the afternoon definitely wasn't going to help.

"I can't believe I'm wearing a bathing suit underneath a dress to a wedding later," Amelia said.

"All weddings should be casual," James said. He popped a plump olive in his mouth. "Takes the pressure off."

"Couldn't agree more." Ella's wedding was to be formal and fancy, and she wanted everything to be perfect. Amelia knew this was one of the reasons Ella was so mad she'd left—her leaving was not part of the plan.

"I'm surprised more people don't get married in Asteri," James said. "This place is magical. Nowhere on earth can you find olives like this. Each individual olive is packed with flavor."

Amelia laughed. "I'm not sure tasty olives are a big draw on the wedding circuit, although of course I agree they should be." In France, she had exulted in the easy approach to food that consisted of good things with whole ingredients. In Italy, she had eaten heartily and fully, delighting in flavor. Here in Greece, she loved that she had morphed into someone who could eat a handful of olives and a crust of bread and call it good.

"I barely knew how to feed myself at home." James shook his head at himself. "Everyone should travel. It opens your eyes."

"Gets you out of your rut." She waved a hand to indicate the trees, the view, the wine. "I'm tipsy again. I was trying to be good."

"I never drink this much either." James emptied the last of his wine into his mouth. His face had burnished into a lovely tan since she'd first seen him.

She grinned sloppily and refilled his glass for him. Were they slumping over the table a little? Maybe. Straight lines no longer existed. It was too late to take back the wine, so she filled her glass again too. "Don't get too drunk—we have the wedding to attend."

He rubbed a discarded olive pit, dark and sharp, between his thumb and forefinger. "My grandfather proposed to my grandmother with an olive pit."

She leaned back in her chair, but the movement made her dizzy, so she straightened. "Why an olive pit?"

"My grandfather grew up on an olive farm along the North Umpqua River in southern Oregon. He took my grandmother to the farm and proposed to her under the biggest, oldest tree in the grove. He gave her an olive pit until they could get back to

Portland and pick out a real ring." He smiled. "She had the olive pit made into a necklace. It was pretty weird looking. Years later, my dad proposed to my mother using an olive pit, but she wasn't as charmed by it as my grandmother. Luckily, my dad had her real ring at the ready."

Amelia thought that James's mother must be unromantic. She found herself looking at James, at the freckling on his shoulders, at how the seawater had dried into drops of salt on his skin. He seemed so solid, so present and real. Comforting. Every day with him had been a pleasure, she realized. He was easy and unchallenging. He made her laugh, which was paramount. There were no expectations and no assumptions.

"What happened to the olive farm?" she asked.

"Well." James rubbed the olive pit and tucked it into a pocket in his shorts. "My grandfather hoped my dad would run it, but my dad ending up selling it." He looked out in the distance. "Which was too bad because it was a successful farm. I always wished he'd kept it. Maybe that's why I'm so obsessed with olive trees." He gave a cute smile, as though embarrassed.

It wasn't so nerdy now, hearing about the olive trees. Her eyes went to the salt patch on his shoulder again. Second time. Distantly, in her wine-addled brain, an alarm bell sounded. What was the alarm saying?

She realized what the alarm meant. Because she had the urge to lick one of the salt patches off his shoulder.

Shit.

She tried to sort it out through the haze of inebriation: Was she simply responding to a biological urge wherein a good-looking, half-dressed, lickable man was intriguing? Or was she ignoring something that had been building up over the past week and a half? Had she been totally zombified by the beauty of Asteri and the good food and not noticed a subtext?

How long had that urge been in her? How long had it been simmering while she insisted to herself that he was too boring? While she had already put him in the friend zone?

He looked up, right at her. The air, already thick and buzzing, grew heavier still. Something had changed. It was almost visceral.

"What?" she asked at his look, even though she was pretty sure she knew.

"You—you're beautiful," he said. "Just, with the light on you, coming through the trees. In your hair." He motioned to her hair, which was thin and scraggly and most definitely never looked good wet like it did on some people. No sleek pull-back or sultry tendrils.

"You have salt patches on your skin," she replied.

He looked down at his skin, trying to see, but it was hard to get the right angle on his own shoulder, so she reached over and touched him, which she realized her fingertips had been clamoring to do the moment he removed his shirt. His skin was warm from the sun. She ran her fingers across his bicep, around it, wondering at the shape, the strength, the perfect roundness and solidity of the muscle beneath. He was a beautiful man, with those expressive green eyes and chiseled cheekbones.

Anticipation hammered in her chest. Touching him was exactly what she wanted to do. Somewhere in the last bottle of wine (because there were two empty ones on the table; how had *that* happened?) things had shifted. She pulled herself back across the table and took a large drink of wine to steady herself.

"Amelia," he whispered.

That patch of salt sat there on his shoulder, calling to her. All of his skin did. She knew it would taste good. She found herself leaning toward him, and then he was meeting her, lips first.

It was a good kiss, his lips slightly salty, and he nipped her bottom lip. She drew him in and thought drowsily, *Wow, yes, I think so.* Her body reveled in the sensation of his arm on her back, pulling her closer. In the recesses of her mind where the alarm had sounded, she knew this wasn't wise. She shouldn't do this. No, she wouldn't. It wouldn't end well, even though she liked him, liked listening to his nerdy rants about trees and insects, and liked going off with him each day. Still—they shouldn't. They were friends only. She began to pull back, but then he ran a hand down her arm, sending chills back into her neck. It was a losing battle. She gave in and pushed against him, and the warmth was exactly as she'd hoped: delicious, relieving. He gripped her against his chest, and she *did* lick that salt patch. His skin was every bit as delectable as she'd thought. He nipped her lower lip again and ran a lightly rough hand up her leg, over her hip. She was vaguely aware that doing this in public at a restaurant was probably not the best idea, but she was past caring about mental warnings, and anyway, the owner hadn't been around in some time and no one else was here, not for miles. Their kisses turned from polite exploration to longer, more urgent pulls. Everything about him was scorching hot, and she had not felt desire like this in months. Maybe more than months. Not with Pau in Madrid, and definitely not with Alessandro in Italy. And definitely not with Micah back home.

Her brain was heavy with desire, heat, and wine. Questions swirled in her mind lazily, like flies: What had she been worried about? That he was from home? How long had she wanted to lick his skin?

James pulled her out of her chair, over to his lap. Vaguely, she thought, *We should find a room because I want to get on him.*

"We should—" she started, but a loud "Eh! James and Amelia!" stopped her.

Takis emerged from the path running uphill alongside the taverna, enormous rings of sweat covering his linen shirt from the walk up. "Good, you are here! Wedding is coming!"

Amelia extricated herself from James's lap and tried to pretend her face wasn't on volcanic fire. There was no way it didn't look like she was about to ride him, because she had been about to do just that. But Takis was doing them the kindness of looking the other way, catching his breath from the climb, allowing them to disentangle and pretend nothing was going on. Every one of her nerve endings regretted the interruption.

She became aware of music in the distance, growing louder, clanging through the trees, and echoing off the hillside. A procession emerged, bride and groom in the middle, surrounded by whooping and yelling relations.

Amelia grabbed her sundress from her bag and shrugged into it while James put on a shirt. They joined the tail of the procession and wound through a dense grove of olive trees to a small domed church that sat nestled into the hillside, blindingly white under the afternoon sun. Takis had slowed to the end of the procession, looking pale. His eyes were bloodshot and his mouth slack, and he smelled like he'd bathed in retsina. He did not look well, but who would in a stifling wool suit on a hot day like today? He beckoned Amelia and James into the church.

James put a warm hand on her back, and honestly, she would have gone anywhere he directed. They crammed into the small building, made smaller by the wedding guests.

Inside was a refreshing coolness. The church, little more than a chapel, had no electricity; candlelight reflected off the white angles to provide light along with two small rectangular windows on either side of the small wood altar. Young olive trees in linen bags of dirt bookended the altar, the green and white color palette making the whole thing look beautiful. The wedding proceeded, officiated by a tall black-clad priest with an enormously long gray beard. The ceremony appeared to involve a significant amount of incense and chanting. Amelia might have fallen asleep against James's shoulder and might have jerked awake when a muffled cheer erupted.

The church was empty, and she and James were the only two left, minus the priest who was cleaning up at the altar.

"I think I fell asleep," Amelia whispered.

"We had a lot to drink at lunch."

She was drunk still, because the world was bleary and out of focus and she was relaxed and happy. She turned to his shoulder, which was regrettably now covered in a shirt, and nuzzled it. "I think—"

"I know," he whispered, turning toward her, bending his head and grazing her lips with his. She sucked in a breath and climbed into his lap.

A stream of angry Greek exploded from the priest, who was yelling and waving his arms at them from the altar.

"Oh," Amelia hiccupped.

"I think we've offended him," James whispered. The priest continued to yell, stomping up the aisle toward them.

"What's this?" Takis had stepped back into the church. He and the priest exchanged several angry words in Greek, yelling, hands waving, and eyebrows lowering.

They appeared to reach some kind of agreement, and Takis turned to them. "He says you have soiled his church. With kissing and lovemaking on his bench. I thought you were just friends, but I see now you are making the love, yes? This very nice."

"Oh," Amelia said, unsure how to classify what was happening. "We weren't *making love—*"

"It was a simple kiss," James said.

Amelia sent him a look. A simple kiss? That was all? It was rather more to her—

But the priest yelled and waved his arms, making it clear they had committed the deepest of sins. He and Takis had another extended discussion, which sounded like a negotiation. Takis looked back at Amelia and James in a way that made Amelia think he was evaluating them. He exploded into a hacking cough, and then, when he could speak again, said something to the priest, who nodded.

"I like you are nice together," Takis said at last. "This is good. But Papas says you must have a blessing to wash away your sin. Of course we know it is just love, but he says not in his church. Then he is happy and I am happy, and we are all happy. Okay?"

"Okay. A blessing sounds fine," Amelia said, finding that James's hand was still resting below her breasts and that she liked it. She would also like it if moved further down her waist.

"Totally," James agreed without missing a beat.

Amelia tried to focus on his face. This was the problem with Greek wine, or Asteri wine, anyway. It was inebriating enough while drinking it but positively lethal after it had the chance to sit in your bloodstream.

Takis said, "We do, yes? Now." He pointed to the altar. The priest was already retreating there, setting things up again, lighting his bronze incense holder.

It was all hilarious. Giggling, they stumbled to the altar, where the priest intoned things in Greek, sounding ridiculously solemn.

"Stand there," Takis commanded, gesturing at Amelia and James. They took each other's hands, trying their best not to laugh.

"Stop looking at me, I'm going to lose it," James stage-whispered.

Amelia did her best to make a face that suggested levity but couldn't quite manage it. A burp of alarming acidity made its way up her esophagus. She dropped James's hot hands. The wine was catching up with her.

The priest rocked on his heels and waved the incense around. Its cloying smoke added to her nausea. She closed her eyes and realized too late that this was a miscalculation of the worst kind.

The world spun with a frightening velocity. She stumbled behind the altar to one of the wedding's baby olive trees and vomited her lunch out into the dirt.

James was by her side in an instant, rubbing her back. She hadn't expected that. What a nice guy.

"You are a good one," she murmured.

"You're not bad yourself," he said.

"You're only saying that so I'll sleep with you."

He grinned, but the witty zinger she was hoping he would launch back didn't come. The smile she gave him—or at any rate, the twisted monster face she suspected she was making with alcohol-delayed muscles—faltered a little. But when she offered her hand, he took it. They returned to the altar.

Amelia and James got back into position in front of the priest, who spoke to them in the same sonorous intonation. He appeared to be phrasing a question at James.

Takis yelled, "You tell yes! For blessing."

"Yes," James said.

The priest turned to Amelia and spoke to her in Greek, asking her the same question.

"Tell yes," Takis yelled again, hoarse. He devolved into another of his thick coughs, making large waving motions for them to ignore him.

"Yes," Amelia said. This would make a great story someday, getting a blessing as punishment for almost having sex while drunk in a tiny Greek church.

The priest clasped his hands together and made the sign of

the cross over them. He sang loudly in a wail, and then spread his arms out.

"I think we're blessed," James said, flashing Amelia a huge smile. She laughed in delight.

The priest pulled out a book from behind the small lectern and slapped it open with a thump. He handed Amelia a pen and motioned for her to write in it.

"Put your name there," Takis said, pointing to the next blank line below a long list of names written in Greek. Amelia did, and handed the pen to James, who also wrote his name.

"*Kala, kala,*" Takis said. "Now come eat, drink! *Efcharisto poli!*" He beamed at them.

Then they were allowed to make their way out of the church into the too-bright light.

"That's cute that such a little church in the woods wants anyone getting married or blessed to sign a book," she said.

James covered her hand with his larger one and gave her a wink. "It was like getting married."

Her heart stopped for a slow half second, but her brain couldn't quite catch up. "That wasn't a wedding, was it?"

"Of course not." His green eyes were on hers. "That would be ridiculous."

Yes, that would be ridiculous. James was right.

She laughed and took his outstretched hand, and they joined the festivities.

CHAPTER 5

Music shook the olive grove outside the church for hours after the ceremony. Bouzoukis and gongs and what sounded like people banging on pots surrounded them, and in the middle of it all, the bride and groom dance-walked, laughing and singing with their whooping, joyful guests. Everyone repeatedly wished the happy couple many years of delight and prosperity. And the food! Thick hunks of lamb drenched in the most delectable tzatziki that Amelia had ever tasted, and plenty of wine. Eventually, the bride and groom danced off through the trees to begin their married life, but the guests who were too drunk or too full to move remained in the clearing of the olive grove.

"Should we walk down the hill?" James slurred. "To the car."

"I don't think we can drive." Amelia pointed at Takis, who sat slumped by a tree. "Takis! Takis, time to go!"

Takis, however, was looking pale and drawn and overly sweaty. He waved vaguely at them, and then beckoned Amelia closer with a swollen finger. As she got closer, she could see rivulets of sweat rolling down his face, and his collar was soaked. "Amelia. Come. I tell you."

She scooted across the dirt toward him. "You seem hot, Takis. You should take your coat off."

"I—" He closed his eyes and swallowed as though in pain. "You and James, good. Very good." He waved a hand as though that might illuminate this statement, and then the band started again, making further conversation impossible.

Amelia patted Takis's hand, which was wet with perspiration. She beckoned to James. "Help me get his coat off."

"Okay." James shuffled over. Together they peeled the coat off. Takis did not resist, and Amelia was dismayed to find the entire back of his shirt was soaked through.

"Takis, what can we do to help?" she asked.

"I am dying," he said.

She stared at him. "What do you mean? Should we get a doctor or get you to a hospital—"

"No, no, cannot stop it. Tomorrow, I die. I only want to see my niece married."

"I'm sure you're not dying," Amelia said. "It's hot and there's been a lot of wine—"

"And you're certainly not dying tomorrow." James knealt on his knees in front of the older man. Amelia followed suit and slumped down next to him. "We'll just sit here until you feel a bit better, okay?"

Takis grabbed at Amelia's hand, which she gave him. "No, I die. You take Ria Hotel. My niece, she will only sell it. I want Ria Hotel to continue."

Amelia's head pounded as she tried to digest his words and calculate how much he meant them. "I'm sure she wouldn't sell—"

"She sell," Takis said, wincing as he shifted. "You take."

"Let's get you to a doctor," James said.

Takis tightened his grip on Amelia's hand. "Take hotel."

"Of course," she heard herself say. "Right, James?"

"Of coursh." He frowned, probably hearing himself slur. "Of coursh." He shook his head as though that would get rid of it. "Of course."

That was a great idea. She should have thought of it herself. She couldn't believe it hadn't occurred to her before. "Yes, we'll do it." In the back of Amelia's wine-addled brain, a small alarm bell sounded, but she couldn't be bothered with that now. Maybe after a good long sleep...

"It is a good idea," James said. "Really good."

Takis waved at something—someone—and by the time Amelia could communicate the message from her brain to her neck muscles to turn her head and look, a man had arrived next to Takis. That was a relief. Help was here.

"I'm glad you're here," she told the man. "Takis isn't well."

Takis said something in Greek to the man, who looked at Amelia and James and nodded. She assumed Takis was telling this man that they were his lodgers and that they had helped him tonight. All would be well, and this man, obviously a doctor because now he appeared to be writing something down on a notepad, was going to help.

James slipped down onto the soft dirt next to Takis. Amelia felt for her neck, not entirely sure if her head was still attached to it. She eased herself down next to James. It was cozy and nice. The stars swirled dangerously above her, so she closed her eyes.

"Is a good time," Takis muttered softly. "This wedding. You two."

"It really is," Amelia agreed. She nestled her head against James's chest. His arm was warm, and its weight felt so good and right. There was no stopping now—she slid deep down into delicious oblivion. "It's the very best time."

———

Amelia woke to overly loud cicadas buzzing. It took a long time to open her eyes, which seemed gummed shut. She felt disoriented. Eventually, she opened her eyes to a bright morning in the olive grove.

Her head pounded nastily, and her tongue felt thick and swollen. She needed water. Her brain had transformed into delicate jelly that would slop over at the slightest movement. She could not move, she could not turn, because it would be a disaster for the jelly if she did. Her skin felt stretched thin and would surely rip if she made any fast moves.

Never, ever again. No more alcohol. Ever. It was poisoning her. Her innards were probably already pickled.

It didn't help that it was hot, hotter than it had been so far on Asteri. The flat, heavy heat sat on them with not even a breeze. She looked around, trying to focus. Had there really been a wedding reception here last night? She could smell the heat baking into the dirt: an earthy grain smell. This wasn't helped by lying on James.

He shifted under her. She did her best to sit up and away from him, but the movement made her want to die.

"Hey," he croaked. He was usually so chipper in the mornings.

She felt like a smashed bug on a car windshield, so she was comforted that it wasn't only her.

She tried to remember the specifics of last night. The wedding. Dancing. Laughter. Food. Wine. There was something else significant that she had the feeling she'd done, but it hurt to think. She lay quietly, planning to die right there under the olive tree. A wisp of a memory came of a small restaurant, of the salt patch on James's shoulder that she'd wanted to lick. Had she wanted to lick his skin? Had the wine contained an insanity agent?

"Amelia," James whispered.

The heat and the sun were pervasive. She swallowed unsteadily and uttered, "Can you...give me a minute?"

Sitting up proved a no-go. With every inch of movement heralding the potential for her head to collapse in on itself, she closed her eyes and hoped that she would become one with the tree.

"Amelia," James repeated, more urgently. "Wake up. Look at Takis."

Amelia opened her eyes again, squinting to keep as much daylight out of her eyeballs as possible. She looked over James's chest at Takis, who was still asleep. "What about him?"

"Two flies have landed on him." James pointed to a third. "He's not moving."

Amelia fought back her discomfort and inched her way over to Takis, who lay slumped against the olive tree. "Takis?"

Takis did not move.

"James." She looked at James for some assurance that Takis was only in a deep sleep, but James looked worried. He ran a rough hand through his hair, making it stick up in all directions.

"I think he might have died," James said, his face drawn.

Amelia moved around to get a look at Takis's face. His eyes were open, staring. She reached over and picked up his hand, only to find it unnaturally cold and stiff. She dropped it as though stung.

"Oh my God." She uttered a scream and stumbled back into James. Memory pushed through the horror. "He's dead. James, oh my God. He said this. Last night. He said he was going to die. Who says that? Who tells people that? And then does it! Oh my God."

"Oh," James said, catching her. "Okay. All right. Let's…let's get help."

The olive grove seemed deserted, except for detritus from the wedding: broken glass, soiled plates, wilted flower petals. James made as though to head toward the small church. Amelia scrambled to her feet, ignoring the pain searing in her head. "Don't leave me!" *With a dead body*, she almost added.

They picked their way around olive trees to the church. The door was closed, but James tried it, and then banged on it. "*Yasoo!* Hey! Hey!"

No one answered, but James kept banging. Even the insects stopped their buzzing. Amelia was about to tell him to stop, that it was no use, when the door opened and the old priest from last night appeared, looking displeased at the disruption.

"Takis!" James shouted. "Over there! Come, please!"

The priest shrugged and splayed his hands in the universal sign of *I have no idea what you're saying*, so Amelia grabbed his hand and pulled him. The priest shrieked and snatched his hand back, but James had positioned himself between the priest and the door to the church, so he had to follow.

Amelia led the priest to Takis's body. She couldn't look at him. She wanted to be sick. She might be sick. She was probably going to be sick.

The priest peered at Takis, made the sign of the cross over his body, and then motioned to James to get Takis's feet. Amelia was thankful she was not asked to carry the body. She didn't think she could touch him. It was all horrible. She had seen a dead body before, of course—but properly laid out in a coffin at a funeral. This was feral. This was real.

Her hand flew to her mouth as it occurred to her that everyone was going to think they killed him.

"We slept next to him all night," she babbled. "He said he was going to die. He was sick. We were *with* him."

"Keep it together, Amelia," James called. Takis was not a small person, and James and the priest heaved and stumbled with Takis toward the church. With an assortment of grunts, they got Takis into the cool interior and laid him on the floor in front of the altar. He then shooed James and Amelia out, as though they were soiling his small church. He bent over Takis's body, making a series of gestures.

"Okay," James said when they'd emerged into the olive grove. "Okay."

"I mean," Amelia said. "It's not—I'm not squeamish." That was untrue. "I wasn't expecting that. I wasn't expecting to wake up to that." She smacked her gummy lips.

"We need water," James said. "*You* need water."

Yes. Water. Now that was something that she could get behind. "Is there any?"

"In the car." He looked apologetic. "Down the hill."

"Right. Yes." They began walking through the grove. "I can't believe Takis is dead."

"I can't believe we slept next to him all night."

"Oh, let's not."

James helped her navigate an aboveground tree root, and then they were on the main path heading down the hill. At the car, he handed her a bottle of water, which she cracked open and gulped until it was empty. She looked over and saw that he was drinking a much less full bottle from yesterday.

"Oh—" she started, feeling awful that he had less water and that she'd selfishly guzzled all of hers.

"It's fine. You needed it more. Let's get back to the hotel."

She collapsed into the passenger seat, glad of the car's permanently rolled-down windows so the breeze could blow away her horror. She didn't want to go back to the hotel, where there would be no cheerful Takis waiting for them—ever—but what else could they do? Did they need to tell someone, or would the priest take care of that?

The Ria Hotel was every bit as desolate as she pictured it would be. It was as though Takis had taken the life of the hotel with him. It seemed odd to continue to stay here with no owner. She and James made their way down the stairs to their rooms, nodded at each other, and parted ways. She took a long cold shower as though that would erase the fact that Takis had died next to them, and then collapsed on her bed.

She woke sometime later to knocking.

"It's me," James called from the other side of her door. "There's someone here."

Amelia got up, glad she'd taken a shower, and opened her door. "Who?" As if she needed to ask. Asteri police, obviously.

James gave a remarkably Greek shrug and turned to go up the stairs to the top. Amelia followed, sure they were going to be arrested for murder.

A man in a white suit stood at the top of the stairs as they came up, watching their progress. He seemed vaguely familiar, but everything was too much right now to try and place him. "Ah, *kalimera, kalimera.* James and Amelia."

James agreed that they were.

The man smiled too widely for this time of the morning. "Good, *kala.* Come, come, have coffee. We have much to talk, yes?"

"What?" Amelia whispered at James, but he only shrugged. Was this the preliminary interrogation? Was he going to throw them off by pretending it was a social call? They followed the man to a table on the veranda, where coffee had been set up.

"Please, sit," the man said. "You remember me, of course."

"Sorry, no. Who are you?" James asked.

Amelia poured herself a coffee and sat. The coffee was sludge-like and thick—not the palatable way Takis made it.

"My name is Yanni Papageorgiou," the man said. "I am lawyer here on Asteri. We meet last night, yes? Takis die, very sad, yes? Very sad."

"What do you mean, we met last night?" James asked.

"Ah," the man said. "At the wedding. Maybe you—" He made a drinking motion with his wrist. "Too much, eh?" He took a long, leisurely sip of his coffee. "Now. I have papers. Okay?"

"What papers?" A cold sheen of sweat snaked down Amelia's neck. She hoped the papers weren't an arrest warrant. Or an admission of guilt, typed for them and ready to sign.

"Yes, yes, I tell you," Yanni said. "Because last night when we meet, Takis tell me you will have the hotel. Now poor Takis die, I have papers for you."

"Sorry, what?" James used the same polite tone, as though he'd merely misheard.

The lawyer clapped his hands. "Takis very ill." He rubbed his stomach with wide circles as though this would explain. "Very, very sick. Yes? Here." He patted his chest hard. "Everyone knows this."

"Did he have...cancer?" Amelia asked.

"Yes, yes! Cancer." The lawyer patted his chest again. "Everyone know this."

James glanced at Amelia, and she caught his meaning. *They* had not known this. They had not known he was that close to dying.

"He said he was going to die today," she asked. "Did he—how did he know?"

The lawyer shrugged as though to say, Who *knows how he knew?* And it wasn't his concern regardless.

"So." Yanni tapped the stack of papers. "Last night, you say you will take hotel. Takis tell me to draw up papers today. I have them here." He beamed at them, as though they should be delighted at his efficiency.

"I'm not sure I understand," James said. "We didn't—we were drunk."

"Ria Hotel!" Yanni said, a bit forcefully. "You agree."

Amelia and James shared a moment of stunned silence. Amelia cleared her throat. "That wasn't real."

"Yes, it is real." The lawyer slapped the papers. "You tell, Takis tell, now I have papers. Takis does not leave hotel to niece, Magdalini. He is very clear. You are new owner."

Amelia shook her head as though that would help make sense out of this. "We don't live here. I'm leaving in four days."

Yanni looked at them as though they were stupid. He looked between Amelia and James, and Amelia felt that nervous sliver of trepidation slide down her neck again. "Takis tell me. You get marry, you take hotel. Yes?"

"Married?" Amelia frowned. "No. We didn't get married. His niece did." Yanni was confused. Relief flooded her. Takis had not left them the hotel; Yanni was mistranslating.

Yanni sighed heavily and muttered something that sounded like *vlakas*. "You get marry last night. Priest has record. Now you have hotel." Yanni patted the papers in front of him as though that explained everything.

"No," James said. "That…that was a blessing or something. Not a real marriage."

"Yes," Yanni said, a touch of impatience creeping into his voice, as though Amelia and James were two badly behaved children who didn't yet understand the enormity of setting fire to the school. "Papas Valopoulos, he marry you. In church. He wrote it in register. Takis sign it. You were in church, yes?"

"Yes, but—"

"You married. Now." He licked his thumb and paged through the stack again until he found what he wanted and then shoved a paper over to them. "Sign here."

Amelia thought Yanni had it wrong, that there was a big miscommunication about the blessing, but she was beginning to worry.

"How did he know he was going to die in the night?" James asked.

"Takis long time very sick."

"Okay but," Amelia said, "whether he knew he was going to die soon or not, it was a trick. He tricked us. We didn't agree to get married."

Yanni shrugged. "Sign here."

"He tricked us," James said, his voice rising. "Conned. Hoodwinked. *Swindled!*"

Yanni sighed. "He not swindle you, okay?"

"It was a swindling," Amelia said, arms crossed.

"A professional-level swindling," James said.

Yanni rolled his eyes. "Takis said you are best guests. He said true love. He always knows love, he run Ria Hotel, full of love, many years. This morning I hear from Papas Valopoulos that Takis dies, and also you married in his church. He show me register. You married and you have hotel. Now. Sign, *parakalo.*"

Amelia's mouth opened and shut. She saw a similar mental horror on James's face. This couldn't be happening.

"We were *drunk*," James said.

Yanni smashed his palm on the table, making Amelia jump. Another nervous sweat flushed up her neck, wrapped in the horrible suspicion that this might, in fact, be real. "You drunk, this not matter! You marry here—Takis give hotel. Sign here." He shoved the papers at them with the force of someone whose patience had deserted him.

"Fucking A," James spluttered. Amelia saw a flash of anger in his eyes. If he'd displayed that look from day one, she might not have pegged him as such a softie. She might have enjoyed a passionate, breathtaking affair with him rather than relegating him to the Nice Guy bin.

Never mind all that. Amelia felt ill.

"I think we need to ask his niece," Amelia said.

Yanni tsked. "Magda want to sell hotel, and Takis does not want hotel to be sold. This is why he gives to you."

If Amelia hadn't felt like a piñata after being whacked open by aggressive six-year-olds, she might have taken James's irritation and added her own, but instead she shook her head at the lawyer. "We're tourists here."

"We're not even EU citizens," James said.

Yanni gave another Greek shrug. "You are here? Now? On Asteri? Then you are to our law. EU will support. You are married, Papas Valopoulos wrote it in book. So. You are now new owners."

"Are you sure it wasn't a blessing?" Amelia whispered.

Yanni fixed her with an eye that was half-obscured by a bristly eyebrow. "I am sure. It is marriage, not blessing. I think maybe you and James not know this, and I am sorry, but this is still the case. Takis was sure about you two. He says true love. Now, please sign."

Desperation rippled through Amelia's wracked body. "Can we have it translated to English first?"

Yanni appeared to consider this, and James leaped on his hesitation. "She's right. We can't possibly sign something we don't understand. A full English translation, and then we'll talk."

"Okay," Yanni said, pulling the paper back too easily. "I get translation."

Amelia and James exchanged another look, but this time it held tentative relief. They had bought themselves some time.

Yanni straightened his stack of paper by tapping it on the table. He glanced at Amelia. "You need rings."

"What?" she asked.

"Wedding rings. You must go back to church, have Papas Valopoulos bless rings." He turned to James. "Where your rings?"

"Why on earth would I have rings? We weren't getting married!" James yelled, which, on the whole, was not the way Amelia had envisioned starting a marriage. She had not envisioned marriage at all, because she did not want to be married, no matter how much her mother had cajoled and begged and hinted. To anyone. It was something that Ella always teased her about. Ella. Oh God, Ella would have enjoyed this debacle.

Yanni raised one eyebrow as though this was incredible incompetence on the part of the groom. "You buy good Greek gold, take them to the church, have them blessed."

"Oh yes, another blessing," James seethed. "Because the first one went so well."

"Is this happening?" Tears of frustration and pain leaked out of Amelia's eyes.

"It can't," James said. To Yanni, he said, "Look. This is all too much, too fast. We need—we need to speak to the American consulate."

Yanni laughed. "You can do what you want. I get translation, then you sign." He stood, pushing the contract into a battered leather bag, and left the restaurant. The silence in his wake was punctuated by the start of a car engine, and then the sound of it retreating down the drive.

After a long moment, Amelia lowered her forehead to the table. "Do you think he's telling the truth?"

James ran a hand through his hair. He sat staring, his eyes wide and vacant in the manner of someone who has received a large shock. "I don't know, but I don't know enough Greek or about the island to know. I mean, we were *drunk*."

"How did Takis know he was going to die?" She stood with the intention of finding the kitchen. "We're still guests here." What she meant was, *Who's going to feed me?* But that sounded awful. "Who gives a hotel to someone for free?"

"I guess we're no longer guests." James stared out at the sea. "There has to be a catch."

"I'm supposed to go back home in a few days. This is...." Amelia pushed through a door to find a small kitchen in a state of absolute filth. A single tiny workspace was next to an old range covered in an assortment of burned lumps and crusted spills. Brown grease drips coated the walls. A large refrigerator that might have been there for thirty years stood making a cantankerous rattle. She pulled it open to find a glass jug of milk that smelled fresh, at least, a container of dolmades—rice-stuffed grape leaves that were Amelia's idea of heaven—and a larger container of olives. She rummaged in a cabinet and was relieved to find a bag of coffee grounds. There wasn't much else. She stood in the kitchen for a long time, trying to wrap her head around all they'd been told.

The sound of a motor came from outside, and she hoped it was the lawyer returning to say he was sorry and he'd made a mistake. She stepped outside the kitchen.

"*Kalimera!*" An older woman came through to the restaurant, holding a basket of three huge bread loaves. The smell was heavenly. Amelia was not sure anything she ate would stay down, but she might make an exception for that bread. "Po, po, po." She said something and Amelia caught the name *Takis* in it as the woman made the sign of the cross.

"*Kalimera,*" James said from where he sat at the table, sounding dazed.

"*Psomi,*" the woman said, holding up the basket. "*Agorazeis?*"

Amelia wished she'd picked up more Greek over the past two weeks. But then, she hadn't thought she'd need to use it to run a hotel that she owned with her new husband. She wondered if her *Learn Greek in 30 Minutes a Day* book had suggestions for when your hotel owner died on you and tricked you into taking over the place. That might take *60 Minutes.*

"Bread?" Amelia asked the woman.

"*Nay!*" The woman smiled. "*Psomi.* Bread."

Psomi was *bread.* Mental note made.

"Yes," James said, pulling his wallet out. "Nay. We'll have *psomi, s'il vous plaît.* Shit, that's French. Um, ah, *por favor.* Shit, that's Spanish."

"*Parakalo,*" Amelia supplied, pulling the word for *please* out of some deep mental pocket. James pulled out several banknotes and held them toward the woman.

She waved away James's money. "*Ohi, ohi.*" In halting English, she said, "Nice. Nice. Take. Good."

"*Efcharisto,*" Amelia thanked her. She pointed to her chest. "I'm Amelia, by the way, and this is James."

"Apparently, we're the new owners of the Ria Hotel." James sounded deeply sarcastic.

"Ah," the woman said. She pointed at her chest. "*Enai* Katarina. Katarina Yagapololis."

"Katarina." Amelia nodded, and James joined in. His smile did not reach his eyes.

Katarina took out all three loaves of bread and a parcel of something that felt like a brick wrapped in parchment paper and tied with twine. She nodded and backed out of the restaurant, smiling as she went.

"I think she may be our bread supplier," James said.

Someone's bread supplier, anyway, Amelia thought, because she certainly wasn't going to be theirs. She unwrapped the parcel to find two thick blocks of feta cheese.

"This is insanity," she said, more to herself. But that cheese looked amazing.

James sat back down heavily. Amelia got them cups of coffee and brought the container of dolmades out. She tore off a hunk of the still-steaming bread and shook her head. "How did this happen?"

James played with his mug. "Takis is a piece of work, I guess."

She wanted to cry. "But how did he know how close to death he was? And why us? Why give us a hotel? His family has to want it. Why would he *give* us this place, for *free*? What are we supposed to do with it?"

James shook his head angrily. He didn't have the answers either.

They fell into a silence, helped along by Amelia stuffing her face full of the freshest, most excellent bread she'd ever tasted. There were a million things to say, and she didn't want to say any of them. Like, how long did they have to stay married? Could this be sorted out in three days before she took the ferry back to Santorini and flew home? She was beginning to worry it might not, but there was no way she wasn't getting on that ferry. Worse, what kind of person was James? Who had she tied herself to? He was nice, and yes, she would definitely have had sex with him yesterday, but that was then. A mere blip in time. They'd had a little over a week together, not months or years. That was not enough time to know if he was trustworthy or a big snake. It had taken her nearly two years to figure out that Micah was a horse's ass, and by then she'd moved in with him. Had James ever cheated on a partner? How many partners had he had? Maybe he had a venereal disease.

Maybe he'd absconded with a ton of money from his employer and that was why he'd taken a (rather convenient) three-month trip across Europe. Maybe he abused his partners. Maybe he was deeply, deeply broken inside. Maybe he wasn't broken, but he was immature. Had he murdered small animals as a child, portending future serial killer traits? So many possibilities! Spending a pleasant ten days with someone who was, conceivably, on his best behavior, with the expectation of nothing, and knowing she would be leaving soon, was not the same as shackling herself to a stranger.

The reality of it was horrifying. Tears slid down her face. She turned so he wouldn't think it was about him personally. Even though it kind of was.

He sighed, obviously seeing her distress. "Listen. We don't have to stay here. We can walk away. I don't care what that lawyer said. We can get on a ferry and go home. No one even has to know about the marriage part."

She sniffed loudly. "Yeah."

He stood and shoved his hands in his shorts pockets and stalked out to the little reception area. At last, the jelly that had fought so bravely in the face of shock gave way, and Amelia's breakfast came roaring up her throat. She leaned over into a pot of geraniums next to the table and let go. It was a relief to have it out. She wiped her mouth and sat up slowly, hoping this wasn't a sign of things to come, but when she allegedly married a stranger and came to own a hotel in another country all in one fantastically ruinous evening, it probably was.

CHAPTER 6

Amelia sat at the table on the veranda, staring at the sky for a long time. The view was Instagram-worthy perfection, and the warm air should have been relaxing. Unfortunately, accidentally getting married to a stranger and being saddled with a hotel in a foreign country weren't relaxing activities.

If she moved, it would upset the progress she'd made in terms of not being sick again. Her mind sped, trying to find a way out of this horrifying situation. The best she could come up with was simply leaving Asteri. She couldn't see a better solution.

She badly wanted to talk to Ella. Ella had a huge laugh that made everyone who heard it smile, and she would have found this hilarious, if they were on speaking terms. She would have made some jokes to put Amelia at ease—and then gotten down to business and suggested a way out.

She pulled out her phone, as she'd done so many times over the past three months. She wouldn't be surprised if the screen was worn in the pattern of opening a text thread to Ella. There was never any answer. Every time Amelia had arrived in a new city, she'd texted

Ella, and sometimes in between too. At first she had typed every form of "I'm sorry" she could manage. It ranged from short text to essay-length. She took photos of herself in front of monuments, holding a sign saying, *I'm sorry I wasn't there on your big day* and *Forgive me, Ella Wu.* In front of Stonehenge, the Colosseum, the Eiffel Tower, La Sagrada Família, St. Peter's Basilica.

Ella never replied.

Amelia had started texting her little updates instead. You won't believe this little cafe in Bern, she typed from Switzerland. Thinking of you at this museum in Lyon, she texted from France. I am an asshole, she sent from Genoa.

She typed now, I know you're still not talking to me, but I did a thing in Greece. I got married and now own a hotel. Now we are both old married ladies.

She hesitated before sending it. It was blatantly leading, the kind of text that, in Amelia's opinion, was pathetic in its need for attention and response, but she had tried everything: short apologies, long-form essays on how sorry she was and how she had learned her lesson, and texts begging Ella for a chance to talk. Nothing. Amelia wasn't surprised; Ella never questioned herself. If you hurt her, you were dead to her.

Amelia deleted the message. What use was there in sending it?

Then she retyped it on the theory that if she was dead to Ella, she may as well send it. She pressed Send before she could delete it again.

Almost immediately, her international call app rang.

Holy crap! Had it worked? The caller was an unknown

number—a Bay Area 415 area code—but maybe Ella had dropped her phone in the bay and only now gotten a new one with a new number.

"Ells?" Amelia said, heart in her throat.

"Amelia? This is Celia Garcia."

Amelia blinked. Celia. From work. Ex-work. But she had Celia's number, so it was weird the numbers didn't match. She hadn't heard from Celia in the wake of her inglorious departure from Swinck.

"Celia, hello," she said, trying to sound smooth. "So nice to hear from you. How are you?" She hoped her tone wasn't noticeably fake.

"I'm well, thank you. I had to get a new phone, so sorry if this number took you by surprise. I dropped my old one in the bay. Anyway, I heard you've been backpacking across Europe."

Amelia smiled and said, "That's right." Celia had a penchant for getting right to the point. Some people (office gossipers who fed off the emotional damage of bitching about people) thought Celia was rude, but Amelia thought Celia was confident and direct.

"And how is your back?" Celia asked. "From the backpack."

Amelia paused and laughed. "Not in terrible shape, although my shoulders do have indents."

"Listen, I'm calling because I left Swinck. Your former boss told me in a staff meeting that if I were a man, he might listen to me more. So I left and started a new company. We make a similar software package, better of course, and in no way a violation of intellectual property at Swinck. I've taken my code and applied it the way it should have always been applied if it wasn't for stupid decisions and even stupider egos."

"That's—wow. Congratulations. That's great news." Amelia had no doubt Celia would tear the tail off Swinck in terms of functionality. But Celia wasn't in the habit of calling and chatting about news like this, so Amelia wondered what the point was.

As though she could hear Amelia's thoughts, Celia cleared her throat in a way that sounded like a purposeful prelude. "I wanted to know if you have secured new employment yet, and if not, would you be interested in interviewing with us?"

Amelia's mouth fell open. She hadn't expected that. "Even after..." Celia had seen what she did.

"Yes. Even after that."

"And Ella..." Celia was also a friend of Ella's and had been on the guest list for her wedding. She would have heard about Amelia going on the run. She would have seen the lack of a maid of honor.

"Ella? Well, she's doing okay, I guess, considering."

"Right." Amelia felt that familiar deep weight against her heart. She didn't think Celia needed to say *considering* like that. Way to twist the knife that Amelia had abandoned her best friend, but she guessed she deserved it.

"Anyway, my company is still in early stages, but I know I'll need a kick-ass project manager, and that's you. We don't even have an office space yet. But I have solid funding, a board, and a structure that's friendly to women and rewards us for hard work. Generous vacation policy and lots of flexibility. Are you interested?"

Amelia pulled her attention to Celia's words, letting them sink in. "Yes. Absolutely. Wow. Thank you for thinking of me. After that day—I don't usually, um—" She tried to think of a way to say she didn't usually break the way she'd done, that she'd never done that before, but Celia cut her off.

"You can still manage projects, right?"

"Yes."

"I need someone who can do that for me, as well as you did it at Swinck."

Amelia could barely believe this was real. "I'd love to."

"Good," Celia said. "Where are you now? Are you back in the U.S. yet? Can you come interview?"

Amelia looked out at the turquoise water, the rugged green cliff, the stretch of blue nothing beyond. "I'm in Greece."

"You'll be back soon?"

"My plan is to return in a few days."

"Call me then when you're back. Glad we spoke. Hope you found good things on your travels." Celia hung up.

Amelia continued staring out at the water for a moment. That had been so *easy*. Oh, to not have to submit to the dreaded interview cycle, trying to earnestly convey how she would meet and exceed key responsibilities and be the best team player! No anonymous applying for jobs and getting a "Thanks, if your skills match the job posting, we'll be in touch" followed by "We've decided to go in a different direction," when the job posting was written as though it was a biography of her!

This was so, so good. She was golden. And even more of a reason why she could not possibly stay in Greece and deal with this hotel.

James strode onto the veranda in a purposeful way that Amelia had not seen in their relaxed week together. "Good news and bad news."

She put her phone away, trying to clear her head. "I thought we already got all the bad news."

"There's some more."

She held her stomach as though it might spill out of her mouth again.

James sat in the chair next to her. "I'll give you the good news first, which is I got on Takis's computer. Super old, but at least the password was easy to guess—it was *Maria*. And the keyboard is in English. I was able to get into his email for the hotel."

"That's what you consider good news?"

"Everything on it is in Greek, so it literally told me nothing. That's not quite true. Hotel bookings are in English. I found yours and mine, for example."

She nodded, impatient for him to get to the point.

"And…a new one."

"What?" She turned to look at him.

"That's the bad news. Apparently, we have two guests coming in on tomorrow's ferry. Two British women named Sarah and Sandy, who booked three nights. Paid in advance."

She stared at him in horror. "Shit. They're the couple Takis was telling us about. Who fell in love here."

"The way I see it, we have two options. We can try to meet them off the ferry when they get here and tell them that we're sorry, but we can't host them and they'll have to find something else." James looked beaten, tired. It was only nine in the morning.

"Or we can host them," Amelia finished.

"Yeah."

"Obviously, we can't host them."

"I know."

She sighed and dropped her head against the back of the chair. "I don't know what to do."

"Neither do I."

Amelia tried to turn over possibilities, but her brain refused to cooperate. Instead, she wondered about James again. She couldn't stop. How had he voted in the last two elections? Did he have a criminal record? How much did he tip at restaurants? Did he want children? Did he listen to crappy music? These were important basic questions to know about someone you had married. But she didn't want to be married to him, even if he was a nice guy. And she certainly didn't want children with him. Her confusion made her tired.

"You doing okay over there?" he asked.

"I'm trying to both not barf again and also wrap my head around this situation."

"I hear you. What I do at work when I'm conflicted with tough things is—"

"Are you mansplaining to me?" The words came out harsher than she intended. They came from a place of not wanting James to be the type to mansplain. Too late, she realized that accusing him of doing it was not the same as him doing it.

James said slowly and carefully, "I was simply sharing what I do in tough situations. Not telling you that my worldview is the only view."

"I'm sorry. I'm on edge. I feel like crap, obviously, and I don't know what to do here. Don't take this the wrong way, but I wasn't ready to get married, you know? At all. I never saw myself getting married. Or having kids. None of it. It isn't you, although it could be you, but I wouldn't know because I've only known you for ten days. This is…ridiculous. I can't be here, I can't stay here. I'm leaving in a few days." She shook her head, tears springing to her eyes. "And my best friend isn't speaking to me and…" She hiccupped a sob.

His face, which had tightened in defense, softened. "Yeah."

She didn't want to sit here with him, searching and stumbling for things to say that would make this more comfortable or overcome the questions and the worries. "I'm going to go back to my room and clean myself up." And feel sorry for herself in private.

James nodded.

She was on the third staircase down when the words surfaced in her mind: *I just walked away from my husband.* Followed by: *No, God! Stop thinking that.* He was not her husband. A husband was a partner. A friend. A companion. Okay, those were bad terms— because in the past week, James had been all those things. A husband, then, was a world and a future. Or should be, in Amelia's view. She felt terrible that she was searching for words that he couldn't possibly fit, but then, this was not a situation in which she knew how to behave or think.

She got into the stifled heat of her room and sank down onto the bed, where everything felt a bit better. Maybe when she woke up, this nightmare would be only a dream.

———

Of course it was not a dream.

In the afternoon, James was at her door again, calling her name. This day was officially the worst, longest, most awful day ever.

"Amelia! Let's go. We need to go to town and get supplies for tomorrow, for our guests."

She stifled a groan. "I thought we decided not to host them."

"I called the two other hotels on the island, and they're booked. There's nowhere else they can go."

Amelia was not ready to transform from guest to proprietor; she had not ever considered a life in which she would be doing the hosting of the hotel she stayed in. Then again, her vision of life had also not included soulless, mind-numbing commutes, blatant sexism in the workplace, hurting her best friend to the point of no contact, and being thirty-two with depleted savings.

She got up, defiantly decided not to take a shower, and slipped on shoes. She looked around her room, trying to see it with the eyes of the new guests. Was it sufficient? That was a clear no, but when she'd checked in, she hadn't cared about decor or amenities beyond noting that they were out of date. There was no time to do anything about it now anyway.

When she opened the door, James was not leaning fetchingly against the doorframe, nor did his face light up when he saw her like it had every other day they'd been here. This time he looked resigned and tense. And not altogether pleased to see her.

"Can't we just get Katarina and her bread?" she asked.

"We need milk. Meat. That kind of thing." James threw his hands in the air. "We have to feed these women when they get here. I don't want to do this either, but I also don't want them to arrive and feel totally abandoned."

She knew she was being grouchy. "Let's give them yogurt and honey for breakfast, and a Greek salad for lunch, and we can do lamb shanks for dinner."

He eyed her as though trying to decide what she was saying. "And are you volunteering to cook all that?"

"I guess we have to, don't we?"

"Cooking for people is going to get old fast." He shook his head. His shoulders were almost touching his ears. "This is ludicrous."

She put a hand on his arm. The touch reminded her how much she'd wanted him yesterday around this time. It felt like a lifetime ago. "It's only three days that they're here. We can fake it that long."

He relaxed a little, and she was pleased she'd had that effect. "Yeah. We can." He turned and quietly led the way back up the cliff. There was no arm offered, no jokey jostling on the narrow steps. At the top, he zoomed off through the restaurant and out to the office; she had to jog to keep up with him.

"Wait up," she grumbled.

"Speed up," he replied.

She shot him a glare to let him know he was being a jerk, but he wasn't looking.

They had always chattered in the car, but now they were silent. She focused on the landscape: a stepped hillside of rocky terrain separated by low rock walls, set off by blue sky and the occasional single white domed building. Sitting next to her *husband*.

"I can't believe this," she muttered. "I can't believe I've given my mom the one thing she wants from me in one fell swoop."

"What?" James turned and looked at her, eyes wide.

"I told you my mom has been demented about me finding someone and marrying them, as though marriage is the end-all answer to a person's woes. Which she should know is not true."

"No—I mean, did you…" James's fingers gripped the steering wheel so tightly that she thought he might crumble it. "Did you *plan* this? Did you and Takis plan this?"

"Marrying you and having him die overnight and giving us the hotel?" She barked a laugh. "Yes, excellent detective skills, James. You've found me out! And I would have gotten away with it too, if it wasn't for you rascally kid."

"Be serious."

"Why on *earth* would I plan it?" she yelled. "*You* be serious!"

A silence fell, during which Amelia hoped that James was berating himself for opening his giant jerk mouth, but feared that they were both only stewing in mutual irritation.

He pulled the car into the small main town.

"Look," he said. "I agree that owning a hotel or getting married was not what I'd planned when I arrived here. I don't want to be married either. If it comes to it, we could leave Asteri and the hotel will just…I don't know, revert to Takis's niece. But right now, we have two women coming that will need food and care. While you were snoring your head off, I was checking to make sure there are even decent rooms."

"I wasn't *snoring*." She glared at him.

"You were." A hint of a smile played at his lips.

She opened her car door and slammed it closed. He got out at a maddeningly sedate pace. With a significant space between them, they walked together into the town's *plateia*—town square. Olive trees and stalls surrounded the expanse of cobblestones. Old men sat at small tables with thimble-sized coffee cups, tossing and clacking dice on backgammon sets. Lazy loops of sausage hung from shop awnings. Amelia counted six dirty and unconcerned cats lounging.

"I'm going to check in at the bank here," James told her, pointing to a building with a small metal sign.

Amelia nodded and wandered among the stalls. Old Greek women smiled at her and gestured to their food for sale. Amelia bought a jar of quince jam jar of honey with a thick wedge of honeycomb inside, and a packet of butter.

"Hey," James said a few minutes later at her elbow. "The bank is closed, so I can't ask if Takis had an account. Have you noticed everyone is looking at us?"

Amelia looked around. It was true. The old men playing backgammon side-eyed them. The women running the stalls kept their eyes on them too. Young men walked too close as they passed. Two boys ran past, giggling and pointing.

"Hallooo?" A tall blond woman, deeply tanned and wearing a flowing sarong, marched toward them across the *plateia*. Her hair was shorn in a pixie cut, and Amelia admired her long, perfectly fit legs with calf muscles Amelia wished she had. "Aha. You must be the two."

"We're two, anyway," James said.

"You are *the* two. I am Birgitte. I live up the road from the Ria Hotel." She spoke with a Scandinavian accent.

"Up the road?" Amelia asked. Apart from that single dusty turnoff on the way to the Ria Hotel, there was nothing.

"Nearby, whatever." Birgitte tossed her head. "I am here to translate."

James frowned. "I'm not sure—"

"The document, whatever, whatever." Birgitte flapped her hands impatiently. "Yanni has me translate. My Greek is perfect."

"The papers for the hotel, you mean?" Amelia asked.

"My Greek is perfect," Birgitte repeated. "It was an obvious choice. Mind you, I wanted to see the two idiots for myself. Who gets married while drunk? And Takis manages to rope you into taking the Ria Hotel, and then he dies? Oh my. *Fånig.*" Her nose went in the air in a caricature of snobbery, and she scoffed loudly.

"We'd love it if you could translate with your perfect Greek," James said, with scant emphasis on the "perfect." Amelia liked him for that. "Do you have the document? The lawyer took it back with him."

"Of course. If I did not have the document, I would be unprepared, and I am never unprepared." Birgitte produced a crumpled set of papers from her voluminous bag. "Get me some wine and olives, and I will translate."

James indicated a cafe across the square. "There?"

With a dramatic sigh, Birgitte flounced across the square to the little cafe with three minuscule tables outside, separated from the square by a fence made of pots of bright pink flowers. Birgitte sat down and leaned backward, reaching one long arm behind her and snapping her fingers. Amelia thought she was doing a stretch, like maybe she'd slept wrong; Amelia got those kinks all the time in her shoulders and neck. But a deeply handsome, raven-haired man a little older than Amelia came out, wiping his hands on a towel.

"Ah, Birgitte," he said. "*Tikanis.*"

"*Kala,*" Birgitte said. "Kostas, these are the two *malakas* Takis gave the Ria Hotel to."

Amelia didn't know much Greek, but she knew *malaka.* "I mean, I wouldn't classify us as—"

"Ah, Takis," Kostas said, making the sign of the cross. "*Anápafsou en eiríni.*" He focused intense brown eyes on Amelia. "I am happy to meet you." He held out a huge hand, and his grip was warm, strong, and assured. He kept her hand in his for a beat, staring into her eyes. He was sexy and magnetic and—wow. She could not have named a single person she'd ever met who she would describe using those terms (Ella always seemed to be the one meeting those types) until now. Suddenly she thought maybe she'd been missing out most of her life.

"Amelia," she told Kostas, maybe a tad breathlessly.

Kostas briefly lingered on her fingers as though he was reluctant to let go, and then turned to James. He shook his hand with a single perfunctory pump.

"Nice to meet you, Kostas," James said, maybe a touch loudly. Not unlike a jealous toddler. Amelia shot him a look. "I'm James."

"I will bring you wine," he said, winking at Amelia and going inside.

"Lovely man, Kostas," Birgitte said. "Make sure you befriend him. He will be helpful as you get started running that hotel. He knows all the builders and suppliers on the island."

Amelia could tell from James's sour lemon face that he did not find this idea appealing.

"Let's see if we can get out of the situation," he said.

Birgitte shot him a *Don't hurry me* glare and slowly unfolded the document. Instead of reading it or whatever would be needed for translating, she threw her head back and closed her eyes. Amelia and James watched, waiting. After a long uncomfortable moment, during which it was unclear if Birgitte was going into a trance, she opened her eyes. "It says Takis left the hotel to you. This seems clear. So you are the new owners."

"But we don't want to be," James said. "We're only visitors here."

Birgitte studied him. "Are you Swedish?"

"What?" James asked.

"You look Swedish. Obviously, I can tell a Swede." Birgitte raised an eyebrow.

James and Birgitte did share some similarities, Amelia thought. They were both tall and Nordic-looking.

"My mother is Swedish," James admitted.

"Ha!" Birgitte said. "I knew it. Now. Let me see here." She scanned the document. "Yes, that's about it. You both own the hotel and Takis's small car. The lawyer has added that Takis intended the hotel as a wedding present."

Amelia and James exchanged a wary look. Amelia shook her head. "Why would you give someone a hotel for a wedding present?"

"About getting married," James said. "That was a mistake too."

Birgitte eyed him. "What do you mean, a mistake?"

"Takis swindled us," Amelia said.

Birgitte gave them both a calculating look. "*Swindled* you? Takis *gave* you the hotel. He knew he was going to die soon. He loved that hotel, and I know he wanted someone to run it with the same level of care he gave it. He wanted someone to continue its success."

"But he *didn't* care for it," Amelia pointed out. "The rooms are out of date, and the whole place needs updating."

"And the hotel isn't successful," James said. "We're the only guests there."

Birgitte scoffed. "Takis hasn't put in the effort since his wife died. You can make tons of euro if you try, and you'll be helping to keep the island healthy. Many people here rely on the Ria Hotel. Did you meet Katarina the bread supplier? That's how she makes her living, by supplying the Ria Hotel and a few tavernas with bread, and there are plenty more people who do that. The Ria is the end of the road away from the town, so it all comes to you. In the busy summer months, Takis hired extra hands from the town to help."

"What does that have to do with giving strangers a hotel as a fake-wedding present?" James asked.

Birgitte studied them. Amelia had the feeling she was deciding how much to say. "Listen. Maybe you are illiterate in Greek— not everyone is as fluent as I am—but you did get married. So first thing, stop saying it was a fake wedding. And these papers clearly say you are the new owners of the Ria Hotel. Now. Takis's funeral is tomorrow. You must be there, of course. Even though you are typical rude Americans and have not thanked me, you are welcome for my work. Of course, I am the only person they go to for excellent translation services."

"You haven't translated everything," Amelia pointed out.

"I did the important parts. The rest is legal nonsense that says you're the ones who will accept ownership." Birgitte closed her eyes against the sun as though this was a casual social outing. "When my Spiro was alive, no one even knew about Asteri. Now it's a stop on the ferry circuit and everyone knows. Outrageous." She tapped the contract with a long fingernail. "Look, I don't like to speak ill of the dead, but Takis didn't have much time. Everyone knew it. No one blames him for finding a perfect pair and taking his chance. He loved that hotel, and he wouldn't leave it to you if he didn't think you would run it well for him. And he wanted you to be married because that way, people here would trust you. They do not trust unmarried sinners, of course."

"Seriously?" Amelia asked. "This isn't 1950."

"Asteri is very old school still," Birgitte said, sighing dramatically.

"Why didn't he leave it to his niece?" Amelia asked. "I don't understand why he chose strangers instead of family."

"Perhaps he did not view you as strangers," Birgitte said. "And everyone knows Magda would sell the hotel. Especially to pay for Takis's burial."

Amelia frowned. That seemed a macabre thing to use the hotel proceeds for. She wondered if Takis's funeral would be a grand, expensive affair.

"What about the marriage?" James asked. "We only met each other a week ago."

Birgitte snorted and barked a laugh. "Call it a lesson learned to not get drunk and marry someone."

"How do we know it's legal?" Amelia asked.

Birgitte waved a hand. "The Greek Orthodox Church is not to be trifled with."

But, Amelia wondered, if they left the island, who would know? The Church wouldn't chase them to the United States.

"Can I ask what your story is?" James asked.

Birgitte brightened. "Of course you are interested in my background. Although I am Swedish, I have lived in Greece for fifteen years. I married a Greek man, and for him, I learn to read and write Greek. I like to live here. I do not want any more expats though." She said this in a stern tone as though James and Amelia were planning some sort of mass migration of fellow Americans.

Kostas appeared with a large carafe of red wine and a dish of dolmades glistening in oil with a block of feta. To Amelia's surprise, he pulled over one of the other small chairs and sat down with them. He poured wine for them all, including himself.

"*Yamas,*" he said, tossing back half his glass.

"*Yamas.* Excellent wine," Birgitte said. "Always can count on you, Kostas."

Kostas laughed heartily, and Amelia found that his smile was gorgeous. "Amelia, from where do you come to Asteri?"

"The San Francisco Bay Area," she said. "But I've been

backpacking across Europe for three months. Asteri is my last stop." She glanced at James, but he wasn't looking her way.

Kostas raised an eyebrow. "Most people go to Naxos or Mykonos or Santorini, especially for a last bit before home."

"I wanted quiet." Amelia shrugged. She didn't want to get into how her parents had told her fairy tales of the Ria Hotel and the amazing time they'd had here. It all seemed like a big joke now that her parents were getting divorced.

Birgitte barked a loud, short laugh. "Instead, you marry this fool and now own a hotel!" She beamed around the table, and Kostas joined in with a ready smile.

James did not.

"I'm leaving in a few days, so we'll be sorting all this out before then," Amelia said. James glared at her, so she kept her gaze averted. One of the town's stray cats surreptitiously approached the café, probably to see if there were any handouts. Amelia lowered her hand and made little beckoning motions at it. The cat sauntered over.

"You find good food here, simple life, and beautiful island." Kostas spread his hand around. "It is better, because this way, you see real Greek life, eh? Eh, James?"

"That's why I came here," James agreed, but he looked distinctly dour.

"Now, you stay," Kostas said, nudging the bowl of dolmades toward Amelia. "Please, Ameliaoula, do not feed the cats."

She snatched her hand back above the table, surprised Kostas had been watching her closely enough to see her below-the-table cat petting. She peeked at James and saw him looking away, out past the square, all broody. He had every right to be upset at their predicament, but she wished he could be pleasant to Kostas and Birgitte. They were only trying to help.

"That is beauty of Greece," Kostas said. "We are here, always. So." Kostas addressed James. "You run the Ria, you get visitors, eh? Better than poor Takis." He made the sign of the cross again.

James had sunk down in his seat like a surly teenager. "We have two guests coming on the ferry tomorrow. But apart from that, it appears business was down."

Birgitte drained her glass and stood. "Yanni is expecting you to sign those papers. And remember what I said about going to Takis's funeral."

Amelia had forgotten how tall Birgitte was while sitting and was surprised all over again by her statuesque height. James, Amelia noticed, saw this too. He followed Birgitte with his eyes. She felt a pang of something—jealousy, yes, fine, it was—and stamped it down. They were both allowed to gawk at others. It was a marriage in name only.

Kostas sat back down after seeing a butt-sashaying Birgitte off. "Well, it is not so bad to stay, eh? We have good food, good drink, the sea." He spread his arm wide to indicate that the island was paradise. "Not many tourists."

"Yeah, that's the problem," James said. "Not enough tourists to sustain a big hotel like the Ria."

"You said the other two hotels on the island were booked," Amelia told James. "There must be tourists, if that's the case."

Kostas gave a dismissive bark. "No, no. They each have only

one or two rooms to let. Not real hotels. Usually they don't want to clean the sheets, so they say they are full."

"That bad, eh?" James asked, looking around the square as though expecting to see a tumbleweed blow by.

"Well." Kostas refilled their glasses with the rich dark wine. "It only takes one good resort, and the rest will follow. People here will follow the money and cater to tourists." He waggled his eyebrows with a smile. "The Ria Hotel used to be a big hotel, many guests, but then business dried up." He shrugged again. "You can make it nice again."

Amelia thought she could see why business had dried up, given the decidedly unluxurious state of the hotel.

A small boy ran up to their table, shouted, "*Vlakas!*" and ran away shrieking with laughter.

"What did he say?" James asked.

"He called you stupid." Kostas did not sound concerned. "When the Ria was full, we have more ferry service to accommodate tourists. But it went away before Asteri had a chance to be well known. So did many other things. Young people left to go find work in tourism on bigger islands. The rest of us were left here with our sheep and little cafes. If you can help the hotel, it has effect on the rest of the island."

Amelia exchanged a look with James. That was what Birgitte had suggested.

"We can barely feed the two guests we have coming tomorrow," James said.

But Kostas waved that away with a word that was a combination of a shrug and *eh*. "Everyone will help. You pay when you get money from your guests. It is the Greek way. You are neighbors now. Go see Markos in the meat shop, he will give you."

Amelia could see James turning this over in his mind. "We could do that for these guests, maybe."

"Yes, and everyone is happy." Kostas turned his blinding smile on Amelia, and she felt herself blush. She chanced a glance at James and saw him roll his eyes.

"We should go," James said. He began to stand, and Amelia was tempted to tell him to go on ahead and she'd find her way back to the hotel later. But they still had to get supplies.

"Thanks so much for your help and advice," she told Kostas. She stood too, and Kostas reached for her hand, placing a kiss on it.

"A pleasure. I am here. I help. Okay?" To James, he pointed down the square. "Go to Markos there, he give you meats. I come in a moment and tell him."

"*Efcharisto*," Amelia told Kostas.

"*Parakalo*." Kostas smiled. A little too widely.

James rolled his eyes again and began moving into the square. He was officially being a grouch. Kostas noticed because he widened his eyes comically at Amelia. She pursed her lips to keep from giggling (giggling! honestly!) and followed James up the square.

"James," she called. James slowed but did not stop, making her scurry to catch up.

"Are you always going to be an ass about Kostas?" she asked.

"What are you talking about?" He stopped suddenly.

"You know exactly what I'm talking about." She stared him down.

"That meeting was not how I expected it to go, that's all. And now we're going to go into debt with people here. I don't have time to be an ass about people." James looked, and certainly sounded, cold. "But you do you."

There was so much she wanted to say to him—that he could drop the petulance for starters. But she didn't want to get into it here on the square with everyone watching. They would need these people and their support. It was bad for the hotel brand to publicly argue. Also, she was willing to extend a modicum of credit for this being an unprecedented stressful situation, and therefore he had responded poorly. But that credit had a short shelf life.

Kostas appeared again, saving her from having to come up with a suitable reply to James that would combine compassion with a steely warning not to say, "You do you," ever again. They followed him into the meat shop.

In moments, via rapid Greek and many hand gestures, Kostas had fixed it with Markos that Amelia and James would have supplies on credit.

"Ameliaoula, good luck with your guests." Kostas touched her briefly on her shoulder. To both of them, he said, "I come up to the hotel soon, yes? We can eat, drink, talk more. Smile more." He sent Amelia a saucy grin.

"For fuck's sake," James muttered.

"Sounds great," Amelia said loudly, irritated by James's nonsense. Kostas waved and disappeared back down the *plateia*.

"Ah, *yasoo*," Markos greeted them. "Takis, *anápafsou en eiríni.*" He made the sign of the cross over his chest. He held up various items—lamb shanks, a whole chicken, a container of ground lamb— and raised a pair of bushy eyebrows by way of asking if they wanted them. At last, when they'd gathered a feast's worth of food, including cheese and a veritable vat of olives, they headed back to James's car.

The late afternoon sun had begun to wane as James navigated the car through the maze of streets. Amelia tried to think what their evening might look like. Last night, obviously, she'd been getting drunk and getting married and obtaining hotels, like an absurd game of Monopoly. Tonight, she wanted quiet and reflec- tion. This might not go over well with James, since they were the only people at the hotel.

"I can make us some dinner," she offered.

"Appreciate the offer," James said. "But I think I'd like to be on my own tonight."

She felt secretly glad, given his performance with Kostas. "Fine."

He said nothing until they were on the main road. And then, "Besides, it looks like you have all the dinner companions you could want here."

Ooh, that was it. "Look. We barely know each other, you and me. You have zero claim on my attention."

"That's true. Absolutely. And thank goodness for that, since you seem to be giving it all over the place."

She was so furious that she didn't trust herself to reply right away. It took several minutes of driving before she was calm, but by then they were back at the hotel. They got out and took the load of groceries in, dumping it on the single work top in the small kitchen. Once it was all put away, he washed his hands and said, "Okay, then. Have a good evening."

"Yep. You too."

He stalked out of the kitchen. Her fury burned. He wasn't going to get away with saying those things. "James."

"Yeah." He stopped in the restaurant.

"After the guests leave, we can leave Asteri and go our separate ways, but until then, you can keep your weird jealous bad moods to yourself. We don't owe each other anything, and we don't belong to each other. You don't get to comment on where you think my attention is going. We just have to be civil for our guests. Got it?"

James stared at her for a long, tense moment. Tight lips, clenched jaw muscles visible. "Sounds great to me."

He turned and left the restaurant.

She poured a small glass of red wine and cut a wedge of cheese and took them out to the veranda. She would sit here and watch the tangerine sunset and eat cheese and wallow. First thing tomorrow she'd see what she could do to get out of this mess. The lawyer, the embassy—all of it. She'd be a busy bee on the internet. If she had to, she'd ask her brother, Christopher, whose law contacts could maybe help. Whatever it was, she fully intended to no longer own the Ria Hotel or be married to that man by the time she left Asteri by ferry in a few days, even if it meant simply walking away.

CHAPTER 7

Amelia felt bad about the way she'd left things with James last night, even though he'd been ridiculous with his jealousy and there was no possible way she could allow that to carry on. No, it was *envy*, because that word referred to something you wanted and didn't have, as opposed to *jealousy*, which referred to something you already had and were afraid of losing. And James most certainly did not have her.

But it was a fresh new morning, oven-hot again, and she had work to do. She left her room and looked around at the white buildings clinging to the cliff face. The place was all blue sky and savage cliffs with dramatic edges. It boggled her mind that Takis hadn't taken advantage of this vista to market this place better.

She thought about going upstairs for coffee, but she wasn't ready yet to see James.

So, she took the steps down.

The next level down held a few utility rooms and some smaller, narrow rooms clearly intended for hotel staff. The dirt path spilled precipitously over the cliff, but there were a few steps to the left.

This must be the way down to the private cove Takis had told her about. The idea of a refreshing swim against this heat felt like it might prepare her for any unpleasantness from the day—and there was sure to be a lot of that. She picked her way down the worn stone steps, taking care not to let herself slide.

It took ten minutes of careful, goatlike descent before she reached the cove. The final zag of the path turned around a huge boulder, and a beach made of pebbles greeted her like a surprise. It was a small cove protected by huge outcrops of rocks and couldn't be accessed from anywhere except this path. It was large enough to lie out on and not feel claustrophobic, but small enough to feel personal. And in front: nothing but clear turquoise water.

Her first thought was how much James would like this.

Her second was *Pah*.

She didn't have her suit with her, but there was no one around—obviously—so she stripped and dove in. She had never in her life swum naked or gone to a nude beach, but as soon as the water slipped over her skin, she knew she'd been missing out. This was heaven. She felt free and daring with her unconfined bits bobbing and floating.

Her body began to relax. Floating in a private cove in water so blue that it didn't seem natural, far away from the churning unhappiness that had defined much of her adulthood, she could see so many other possibilities in life. She had loads of advantages—she was educated, without a significant amount of student debt, and had gotten a job right out of college that enabled her to pay rent in the Bay Area. It was her own fault that she'd chosen to work for a company that valued men over its female contributors, but she'd accepted the trade-off of having healthcare and a 401k. Being fired for throwing a mug at Micah's deserving head was the first time she had lost a job. And even with all that, she had an interview waiting for her with Celia already. Things were on the up. And this experience in Asteri with James would strengthen her. Somehow.

When she got out of the water, she reveled in the freedom of standing naked in public. To dry off, she lay on the huge flat rocks. Another first: spread-eagled in public. Yeah, she was doing all right in life.

"Oh, God. Sorry. Sorry."

Amelia yelped and sat up in a hurry, realizing in an instant that there were good reasons for not being a nudist.

James stood at the bottom of the path, shielding his eyes. It was ridiculous given their smoldering lunchtime session the other day, but probably the only polite response. She grabbed her shirt and struggled to get it on, the fabric catching and dragging on her wet skin. She pushed and moved and got the shirt on and grabbed for her shorts.

She glared at him once she was dressed. "What are you doing?"

"Coming down here for a swim. Same as you."

"Water's great. Have at it." She moved to reach the steps, but he stayed where he was, blocking them.

"I saw nothing."

He was totally lying, but she didn't want to start another argument. "Okay."

They stared at each other. She looked for yesterday's disdain in his face, the petulant teenage boy hurt, but that wasn't there. This time, there was something else.

She only recognized it because she felt it too: a little bit of thirst.

She tried to keep her eyes from noticing the outline of his biceps under his T-shirt and the curved lines of his pecs. She'd seen his chest several times when they'd gone to Asteri's beaches on the south end of the island. It was a nice chest.

"Okay," he said pointedly. "I'd like to get in the water."

She stepped aside. He moved too close as he passed, and his arm brushed her shoulder, burning it. He traipsed down to the water and kicked off his shoes. There was no way to know how long he'd been standing there watching her.

He turned to see her looking at him. "What?"

"Nothing."

"Good." He made a little shooing motion with his hand. She headed for the stairs, not looking forward to the climb. For one thing, it would negate the effects of the cooling swim. For another, she wouldn't be able to watch him swim.

Not that she *wanted* to.

There was, she conceded halfway up the cliff, something about him. It might be his charming self-deprecation. It might be his tall awkwardness, like he was one move away from stumbling. And in fact, he had stumbled a few times when they'd been out. Maybe it was simply being the antithesis of Micah and his ilk. Yes, fine, there was something about James. He was handsome and dorky and had a great body, and those chiseled cheekbones—

"Ah, Ameliaoula."

Kostas stood on the whitewashed steps directly above her, looking casually fresh in khaki shorts and a chambray shirt.

"Hi," she said, wishing she had not hiked up a mountain and gotten all sweaty. "*Kalimera.*"

"Were you swimming in the cove? Is nice, no?" He skittered down the steps to her and took her face in his hands, kissing her cheeks fast, European style. He looked great: put together, confident. He had a great body too, but there was something different between him and James. Kostas looked slightly feral, like he lived for the hunt. He wasn't a man to marry and have children with. He was a fling, a lover.

"Yeah, the cove was great," she said, shoving away the lingering whisper of the word *lover* in her mind, sung in a Taylor Swift voice, because her mind was a sneaky devil.

"Takis liked to tell people to swim naked there," Kostas said, one eyebrow raised.

She blushed furiously, heat consuming her face like a wildfire. "Um. Um hum. What can I do for you?"

His eyes met hers, and they were so intense, so communicative, so clear as to what he could do for her that she blushed anew.

"I come because I have news and I have idea. Which one you want first?"

"The news." She led him up the steps toward the restaurant at the top level.

"I give you idea first. It is about hotel. There is option for you."

"Oh?"

"There is man, he investigate for a resort. He has come to

Asteri before and met with Takis. His name is Stavros. He call me last night after he hear about Takis death."

"What did he say?" She went behind the bar to put the little kettle on the single hot plate to make coffee. Kostas sat down at one of the creaky tables and watched her, one leg casually balanced over a knee. He looked like an animal tracking its prey.

"He has idea to make Asteri the new Santorini. He likes idea of the Ria to be big resort." He lit a cigarette and sat back, arms spread over the back of the chair. "Takis did not want this, did not want a company to take the hotel. But *you* could sell to him."

Amelia raised her eyebrows. Now, that was interesting. She poured two coffees into little thick cream-colored cups and brought them over to the table.

"He ask who you were, and I tell him you are travelers. He is interested if you could sell to him."

"This place is almost begging for cash and to be turned into a luxury resort," she said. "I can see why he's interested. Almost everything needs updating, not to mention the marketing."

"You can do all of that, you know. If you don't want to sell." Kostas eyed her over his coffee. "You are smart. Maybe even James is a little bit smart." He made a clicking sound of derision. "There are many fine builders on island. They can make bigger. You need hire help, cooks, cleaners, it is no problem."

"But *paying* them is a problem."

He smiled, playing with his now-empty cup. "They know that when the hotel becomes successful, so do they. Besides, I can negotiate a good rate for you."

She noticed he was looking at her with a lascivious squint, and his tone had definitely lingered on the words *good rate.*

Kostas leaned forward and took her hand. "We can do a lot." His thumb caressed the top of her hand in a featherlight touch, sending a shiver down her back. Okay. Now there was no doubt what he meant.

She pulled her hand back slowly. "I'm married. Apparently."

Kostas did not take this as much of a rebuff. He sat back and did another *eh* shrug. "You love him?"

"We just met."

He spread his hands out as though to say, *No worries.* "Then you can take lover. No one will mind."

If Amelia had arrived on Asteri and met Kostas first, she might have been charmed long enough to visit his bed before leaving. But she knew his type. He would give her sneaky winks and sultry little smirks and say all the right things. But after, he would get her out of his bed as soon as possible.

"*Kalimera,*" James said. Amelia turned. James had come up the same way she did, from the open cliffside entrance. His hair was wet and his shirt stained with water.

"Ah, James," Kostas said in what sounded to Amelia like a falsely cheerful tone. "*Kalimera.*"

"Kostas came by to let us know of a possible way out of our situation," Amelia said. "He says there's a developer who was sniffing around, looking to see if Asteri might be the new Santorini."

"If you want to sell." Kostas gave another shrug.

"Sure, I'd like to hear all the options." James sat down at the table. He gave Kostas a smile—but Amelia saw it was frosty and lost any hope she had of him getting over his dumb jealousy nonsense from yesterday. "Any ideas how to get out of this marriage too?"

She shot him a look. He met her look with a defiant tilt of the head.

"I cannot help you with that," Kostas said. "You talk with Lawyer Yanni."

"Great."

There was a tense silence, so Amelia said, "Kostas, you said you had news too?"

"Ah." Kostas rubbed his hands together. "Yes. Takis funeral. His niece Magda needs suit for Takis. I have come to get one."

"Birgitte mentioned the funeral yesterday," Amelia said. "She said we had to go."

"Yes, you must go, you talk to Magda. This is expected." Kostas stood. "I look in Takis's apartment, okay? I find suit. Funeral is at one this afternoon. Same church as the wedding." Kostas gave an imaginary tip of the hat, said, "Ameliaoula," and went through to the front of the hotel. Amelia and James sat, saying nothing.

"*Ameliaoula*," James said quietly, picking at a scratch on the worn table.

"That's hardly equivalent to humping right here on the table, which is what you're ascribing to the word."

"I find it interesting that you would bring up the image of you two having sex."

"Can we not do this again? It was unattractive yesterday, and today it's downright gross."

"I'm pointing out that his flirting is slimy."

"You are not the Flirt Police," she snapped. "I'm perfectly capable of determining whose flirting is slimy. I'm a woman. I've heard *all* kinds. And for your information, even though you don't deserve to hear any right now, I am someone who takes vows—even those made while drunk—seriously. I'm not going to go hop in other people's beds."

His face went tight and closed. "This is not a real marriage."

She stared at him for a moment to get her anger under control. "All right, James. No worries. You won't be disturbed or expected to act as a husband in any possible way."

He glared at her; she glared back. They seemed at an impasse. She was furious with him and herself for going right back to this nonsensical exchange. She'd wanted to be better today, back to their easygoing friendship. She pushed her chair back and went into the kitchen to get breakfast. Yogurt, honey, and one bowl. He could fend for himself. When she came back out, he had not moved from the table and sat with one hand tangled in his wet hair. He looked adorable, which was irritating. Amelia could not take him looking adorable right now.

He sat while she ate, and she looked up to find him watching her, but she couldn't read his expression. It seemed like a mix between frustration and something else she couldn't identify. Moments later, the loud clatter of a moped engine started and receded.

"What?" she snapped.

"I think," he said slowly, "we need to make an effort to be civil at the funeral. And when we pick up the guests coming today on the ferry. Those women have a history here. We don't want them thinking that they're in for an awkward stay."

Amelia looked around as though the small restaurant was filled with guests. She put on a hideous (so she'd been told) English accent. "Terribly sorry, Mrs. Chives, if our bickering has put you off your soup."

There was a flicker of a smirk on his face, but he controlled it. "Right."

"Yeah, so. Truce." She pointed her spoon at him. "All you have to do is stop accusing me of wanting to sleep with Kostas."

James tapped his finger on the table again and sighed. "You know what, I'm sorry. You're right. I'm acting like a donkey. I'm—I've never been in this situation before. I was being rude. Will you accept my apology?"

His maturity surprised her. She studied him for a moment. He hadn't shaved this morning, and his blond stubble was coming in. She wanted to run the back of her hand down his cheek and feel the burn on her skin. It was such a mad urge that she could almost feel the sensation.

"What?" he asked.

"Nothing." She concentrated on the last vestiges of her yogurt. "Yes, I accept your apology. I'm sorry too. We'll have to work together to get through this mess."

"Are you still planning on leaving in three days?"

"I have to. I have a nonrefundable ticket and no cash to cover changing it, and I have an interview waiting for me. I don't want to leave you to deal with this, but I don't have a lot of options. My plan today is to start investigating what we can do. We can't afford to waste any time."

"Okay." He ran a hand through his hair again. "I agree. Let's see what we can find out. And I'm sorry about being a jerk. I want us to be friends."

"I do too. Years from now, we'll look back on this, and it'll be one of those stories you tell at parties."

He nodded, but he wasn't smiling. He looked glum. She sensed this was not the answer he wanted to hear, but what else was there to say? She had a life to live, and it wasn't on Asteri. Inheriting a hotel or marrying someone wasn't going to change that fact. At least they seemed to be past the silly jealousy and were back to being friends.

———

Amelia had nothing to wear to a funeral. She ended up wearing a gauzy black shirt that required a cami, which she didn't have. So she wore her red bathing suit underneath. The ensemble was suitable for clubbing in Ibiza, which she had in fact done, but not funeral appropriate. James wore a white button-down shirt with a little red crab stitched on the pocket.

"What is that?" she asked, pointing at the crab.

"My mom gave it to me for this trip. I don't know what she was thinking. I haven't worn it." He looked sheepish, as well he might.

"You have literally nothing else?" The crab had a smiley face and looked like it was dancing. "Nothing black?"

"I have a dark blue shirt that I got in Munich advertising a biergarten."

"Surely that's better?"

"It has a picture of a buxom…ah, serving lady."

Amelia pictured giant boobs hanging out of a milkmaid outfit. "Really."

"I didn't buy it. It was pushed on me by the biergarten."

She gave him a look as though to say, *Sure*. "All right. Crabs over boobs."

"I mean, personally I'm boobs over crabs any day, but maybe not this day."

She suppressed a smile. He made her laugh, and this was a problem. Just three more days though, and she would be out of here.

They drove across the island back to the church where Takis's niece—and Amelia and James, ha-ha—had gotten married. The little church was packed tight like sardines. People moved aside for them. It was hard to say whether they saw them as Takis-killer pariahs or just newcomers. Kostas waved them over. He was nicely turned out in a formfitting button-down black shirt that curved over his body, not that Amelia was noticing, except of course she was.

"Do you think they hate us?" James whispered.

"I think they're wondering why you're wearing a jaunty white crab shirt to a funeral," she said.

James hid a smirk, which made her smirk, and because smirks were inappropriate at a funeral, this made her smirk more. She covered her mouth with her hand and bowed her head, hoping she appeared to be deeply moved and prayerful, and not on the verge of laughing.

The priest who had married them and helped with Takis's body was waving incense again. A fog of piney frankincense covered the back of the chapel, making it difficult to see and Amelia suspected, given the heat outside, smell. The priest sang and chanted and yelled for an interminably long time. The incense made time slow and brain function difficult. Amelia felt drowsy but forced herself to stay awake. This chapel had gotten her in enough trouble already.

At last, it was over and everyone pushed outside to the fresh air of the olive grove. Kostas led Amelia and James to a couple standing in the middle of a small crowd, accepting condolences. "You remember Magdalini and her husband, Yorgos Andrianakis." Magda was dressed in black, her face tearstained. Her husband, Yorgos, however, looked furious. A clenching-fists-and-jaw-tight level of furious.

"Hello again," Amelia said. "I'm so sorry for your loss."

Magdalini looked to her new husband. "My wife does not speak English," he said. His face was red and scowling, and his whole posture was like that of a young bull, ready to fight but uncertain who or where or even quite what. "Of course, you will fix our sadness. With hotel."

"I hope you don't think we're trying to *take* the hotel," James said quickly. "Because—"

"Takis should have left my wife the hotel," Yorgos said. "This is very wrong."

Amelia glanced at James, mortified. "Oh—I'm sure we can—right, James?"

His eyes were wide with horror too. He nodded. "I'm sure, yes. We'll talk to the lawyer."

"We do not want hotel," Angry Yorgos—that was how Amelia now thought of him—said. "You pay us instead, is okay."

"Pay you?" Lawyer Yanni had not mentioned payment. Payment had absolutely not been mentioned at any stage.

"Payment." Yorgos took a step toward James, his fists clenched. White-knuckled and ready, in fact. "We need €150,000."

"But Takis left us the hotel," James said. "He didn't ask us to *buy* it from you."

Because if that was the case, Amelia thought, they could have the bloody thing.

Kostas gently pushed Yorgos back. "You don't buy the hotel. You already own it. What he mean is all of this, the burial for Takis, is expensive. It can be a lot for a family. You have Ria Hotel now, so you can pay."

"Yes," Yorgos said. Magdalini smacked his arm to get his attention and issued a stream of Greek. Yorgos listened and then said, "Since her uncle did not leave her hotel, it is only right you pay."

"This funeral is €150,000?" Amelia asked, glancing at the shoebox-sized chapel behind them.

"The grave," Kostas explained. "In Greece, on all islands, there is not enough land to bury body. So it costs a lot of money. If you want to keep the body buried."

Amelia's mouth fell open. "What do you mean, *keep* the body buried?"

Kostas sighed. "It is the law in Greece. You must pay for permanent grave or else rent it."

"What about cremation?" James asked hopefully.

"The Church does not like cremation." Kostas shook his head. "And there is no facility to cremate. You can take body to Bulgaria to cremate. But taking a body is difficult."

"This all seems—" Amelia started, unable to finish.

"What happens if you don't have that kind of money?" James asked, his tone aghast.

Kostas grabbed Amelia's and James's arms and turned them away from Magda and Yorgos, as though facing them in the opposite direction would hide the conversation. He whispered, "Magda and Yorgos are a young couple. They cannot pay for the grave, okay?"

"Why didn't Takis sell the hotel before he died or give it to his niece to sell?" Amelia asked. "Why bring us into it?"

"I told you," Kostas said. "Takis hope you can run the hotel instead. He is not thinking of his grave."

James exhaled a long, noisy sigh. He turned back to the young couple. "I am sorry. I would like to help you. Takis was a good friend to us, and we want to see him buried…on a permanent basis. But we don't have that kind of money. Not even in savings. Not in America, not anywhere. We can't help."

Yorgos looked almost cartoonish in his sudden fury, like steam might come out of his ears. "You give money at end of olive harvest time."

"What is that?" James asked. To Amelia, he whispered, "Is that some old-style farm way of telling time?"

"Olive harvest is November," Kostas said. "At olive harvesting time, you shut hotel. Have nice winter here or somewhere else.

Takis always stay. In the meantime, you make money, give to Magda and Yorgos."

Amelia widened her eyes. They had literally two guests coming, no one else, and she had no idea what the hotel even made. "James."

"Okay, we will take money you make from guests," Yorgos agreed, looking slightly less murderous.

"Ah, *kala*," Kostas said, beaming at the resolution. He nodded at Yorgos and Magda and pushed Amelia and James away from them.

Amelia hissed at James, "I'm *leaving* in three days."

He splayed his hands out. "Okay, but I don't know what to do."

"They should get some cremation facilities."

"Maybe there's a special dispensation for young couples who don't have that kind of money."

"There is no dispensation," Birgitte said from behind them. She wore spiky black heels and a dress that left nothing to the imagination. "It is a burden on families. When my Spiro died, I had to sell my summer house in Stockholm to pay for his permanent grave. It is a terrible thing."

Amelia grimaced. "How do people do it?"

Birgitte's mouth made a kind of smile, her teeth white in her tanned face, and tottered past them. "If they have a hotel, they make money with it. Welcome to Asteri."

CHAPTER 8

"Should we tell them we're only temporarily running the hotel?" Amelia asked James as they waited by the hot empty ferry dock.

"No, it's best to care for them as any guest would expect." He leaned against the car, long legs crossed in front of him, slightly slouched.

Amelia's head was still reverberating from Takis's funeral. Yorgos's red face, screwed up in impotent anger. The revelation of that impossible sum of money. She hated leaving these people on the hook for something like that, but Takis wasn't her relative, and all she'd done was come here for a vacation and to reset her life. And taking on a hotel, a husband, and the responsibility of making sure someone stayed buried was *not* what she had in mind for a life reset.

"What?" James asked, seeing whatever expression was on her face.

"Ugh. The whole thing with Magda and Yorgos and Takis's grave and the money."

"I know." James shook his head.

The second they'd driven away from the funeral, they had agreed that it was not possible to pay for the burial. The only thing to do, they agreed, was see Sarah and Sandy off after their stay, and then get off Asteri. The Ria Hotel would not and could not be their responsibility.

The ferry came into view, followed by the sound of its gentle chugging. The aged ferryman, who'd been languishing with a donkey under an umbrella, got up slowly and hobbled to the planks of wood that served as a dock. The heat was relentless; two donkeys and a dog hovered in the scant shade offered by the awning of the car rental kiosk.

"I hope these women don't want wine," Amelia said. "I didn't see a lot of it at the hotel."

"We can't serve them that retsina that Takis gave us."

"Maybe if we serve it, we can trick *them* into taking the hotel."

James snorted back a laugh. "Maybe Takis was one of a long line of people swindled into taking over the place. The curse must continue forever with each set of guests."

"I would have left a letter of apology, myself," Amelia said. "And a stern warning that my burial will bankrupt the new owner."

The ferry was close enough now that they could see people on it. Several were lined up to get off.

"Are two of them British women?" Amelia asked.

"Definitely." James squinted. "Well, maybe. I can't see details yet, but probably."

After an interminable amount of time during which the boat seemed to bump up against the dock and steady itself a lot, the passengers disembarked, helped off carefully by the ferryman. Indeed, two white women with blond hair made their capri-clad way over the dusty space.

James waved. "Ria Hotel! Right here!"

"Takis definitely didn't do this for his guests," Amelia muttered.

The women, Sandy and Sarah, looked past them and, not seeing Takis, reverted to Amelia and James. Their expressions fell almost in unison as they took in James's small car.

"Welcome," Amelia said. "To the Ria Hotel. I mean, Asteri— and the Ria, but—"

"Shh," James murmured.

"Where's Takis?" one of the women asked.

"Ah," Amelia said. "We'll talk about that on the way to the hotel." She gestured to James's car.

The other woman stared at it in horror. "Are we expected to fit in that little car?"

"It's like a TARDIS," James said cheerfully, referring to the time machine police box from *Doctor Who*. He tossed their bags in the minuscule trunk. "Much bigger on the inside."

They all piled in. Amelia ignored the grunts of the women squashing themselves into the small space.

"I'm Sandy," the first woman said, with cheer that even Amelia could see was forced. "And this is my partner, Sarah."

"Charmed," Sarah said in a tone that suggested the opposite.

"We're Amelia and James," Amelia said. "The new owners of the Ria Hotel."

"What?" Sarah asked. "What happened to Takis? I'm not going any further until you tell us."

"Quite right," Sandy said, despite the fact that they weren't the ones driving.

"I'm sorry to say that he passed away two days ago," James said.

Sandy made a sharp intake of breath. Sarah clutched Sandy's arm.

"How did you get the hotel then?" Sarah asked. "How do we know you haven't killed Takis and taken it?"

Amelia sighed to herself. She was not cut out for this. She loved meeting new people but not like this. James was the quiet, introverted one, and she supposed she could step in and help him out with Sarah and Sandy.

But James raised a devilish eyebrow and said, "You never know these days!"

Amelia realized she might have underestimated him.

It worked, anyway. Sarah's stern expression vanished as she realized James was kidding. "I'm sure there's a whole story here."

"Definitely," Amelia said, glad they were on more even ground and no longer murder suspects in the eyes of Sandy and Sarah, at least.

"Good old Asteri," Sandy said as James drove up the switchback road.

"But without Takis," Sarah said. "Really, it's very upsetting."

"We're all sad," James said. "It's been a rough few days."

"Oh, you poor things," Sandy said. "Of course, if you're the new owners, you must be absolutely *reeling*. Tell us all about it over some tea when we get to the hotel."

"And maybe a biscuit or two," Sarah said.

"Of course." James sent Amelia a look that said, *We are so screwed.* They had no biscuits. And what would they say? He pulled the car into the Ria's round drive.

"Hm," Sarah said, her tone resigned, "I must say I'm concerned that an American couple owns the place now…"

Sandy looked doubtful too. "I hope you aren't expecting us to eat hamburgers and the like."

"Ugh. Hamburgers." Sarah made a *blughh* face.

"Do you order your tea in from Athens? Takis always did that before we arrived every year."

"Takis mentioned getting air conditioners in the rooms last time."

"Have the rooms been updated? They were always so out of date. You know, charming for a small island and all, but Takis promised he would update them this year."

Amelia and James tried to answer, but the women marched into the small reception area. James picked up their bags and followed. He grabbed a set of keys and led the way down to the third level. Amelia did not want to follow, but abandoning James seemed wrong, so she trailed after them and waited as James opened the door to their room.

"Well." Sarah stood, hands on hips, looking disappointed. "Hasn't changed any."

Amelia cringed. "I'll make you tea. Give me five minutes and come up."

"Oh." Sandy looked stricken. "Up those steps again? Are there no kettles in the rooms?"

Amelia and James exchanged a panicked look. "Did Takis provide tea in the rooms?"

"No, but we had hoped he would someday," Sarah said. "This summer, in fact."

"Actually, we just put in an order for all new systems for the rooms," James said smoothly. "Our apologies that they haven't arrived yet. You know how shipping to the smaller islands can be."

"Oh. Yes, that's true." Sandy turned from the view. "We'll have a quick nap, and then we'll be up for tea in about an hour."

Amelia and James left them to it, climbing back up to the restaurant and office.

"Shit," Amelia whispered.

"I know," James said.

"If this is what running a hotel is like, it's no wonder Takis chose to pop a clog."

"I do not want to laugh at that," James said, laughing anyway.

"As soon as these two are off the island, let's hightail it after them."

"Agreed."

James went to the ledger at Takis's desk. Amelia stood in the entryway to the restaurant, viewing it in the critical light of Sarah and Sandy. Only that view and the huge veranda saved it from utter hopelessness. There should only be a counter for food serving in the restaurant, and the rest of the tables—there were only four—could be moved out onto the veranda, which had more than enough space. Even simple, colorful pots of flowers would improve it. Thank God no one could see the kitchen from here.

She went to the kitchen, disheartened again by how dirty it was. At least Takis had some cleaning supplies for the rooms—she'd seen them in a closet off the reception area. She went to it now and pulled out gloves, sponges, some caustic-looking bleach mixture that she suspected would melt skin on contact, and went to work on the countertop and the stove. The stove took a lot of work, but after hard scrubbing, it no longer looked like savages had used it as an altar for human sacrifice.

Exhausted, she took a big glass of water out to the restaurant's balcony. James sat on a lounge chair with the ledger.

"Oh, that's nice," she said. "Sitting out here while I'm scrubbing away."

"You were in the zone." He offered a weak smile.

"Learn anything?" Amelia nodded at the ledger.

"You smell like a chemical bath. I did learn something, in fact, although it's not a revelation. This place is deeply in the hole." James closed his eyes. "I don't know how Takis was surviving."

"We paid for our rooms in advance, that was probably how, just as Sarah and Sandy did."

"There's nothing to give to Takis's niece and that angry husband of hers, that's for sure."

Amelia was touched that he was trying to think of a way to help them. "Is it wrong to walk away from this place? Kostas said there was that developer who was interested. Maybe he can just take it."

"That guy is looking for profit. He certainly won't give Magdalini and her husband the money for Takis's grave. He'll destroy what's good about the hotel and make Asteri into some gross commercial thing."

"What exactly is good about the hotel? Because those rooms are outdated and sad. The restaurant is terrible. And I'm shocked we didn't get food poisoning from food made in that kitchen."

James shrugged. "The location is beautiful. The architecture is amazing. When I arrived, my impression was that it was a little run down, but otherwise gorgeous. It's all cosmetic."

Amelia looked out at the cliff. In the distance, she could see a white speck in the blue expanse of sea: the departing ferry, on its way back to Santorini. James was right. This could easily be a chic, modern hotel with some design updates. She pictured a few well-placed accessories that matched around the room, bringing in the island's rich olive wood against metal. Yes. A few rearrangements on the veranda, some flowers, and some candles, and it wouldn't look half bad out here.

Never mind. In two days, she'd be on that ferry, on her way home. "It's not our problem. We're not hoteliers. It isn't our concern that a developer will destroy it."

James sighed. "Yeah."

Amelia went back to the kitchen to get the tea started. After some random cabinet-opening, she found beautiful hand-painted teacups with a lemon motif that Takis had certainly not used with them. Amelia washed the greasy film of dust off them that had come from sitting in the back of a cabinet for a long time.

"Did you find any tea?" James asked at the door to the kitchen. The space was too small for two people, and even in the doorway, he felt close.

"I found these pretty cups. And some old-looking tea that will have to do." She turned off the singing kettle. James stepped in to help, pulling the tea tray away so she had room to pour. He was still too close. She could smell him: oranges and sunblock and *him*.

She opened her mouth and needed to inhale him all of a sudden. *He smells so good.* She looked at him, and he met her eyes. There was something—some understanding that they both felt—that the passion from the day of the wedding had not gone away. It had only burrowed out of sight. *I want you.* She tried to shut her lizard brain up, but it had already said the words.

But he blinked and turned away.

A little smidge of hurt pinched her. Whatever might have happened the night of their blessing-wedding, that was gone now for him. Amelia took a breath to reorient herself. She would not be humiliated by pining after someone who wasn't interested. She would not pine, period.

Sandy or Sarah called distantly, "Yoo-hoo! Anyone around for that tea?"

James called, "Tea's on its way!"

Without a backward glance, he went out to the veranda. Amelia put a little pitcher of milk on the tray and some slightly crumbly and likely old chocolate tea biscuits. She could hear Sandy and Sarah chatting and the timbre of James answering. She could feel her blood pumping a little harder and hoped he hadn't noticed the flush she felt on her cheeks.

"Ah, Amelia," one of the women said as she brought the tray out. "Oh, tea—wonderful. James was telling us that you can serve dinner tonight?"

"We have some lamb shanks in." Best not to tell them that she had no idea how to cook them.

"Good," Sandy said, sipping the tea and making a face. "My

goodness, this is awful. Tastes like soap. Can you get something else in tomorrow? Now, we want to hear all about poor Takis and what happened."

Amelia felt exhausted. The weight of all that had happened—the shock of Takis dying and the visit from Lawyer Yanni and the funeral—was finally catching up to her. "Apparently Takis was sick. We didn't know that though. We went to his niece's wedding—"

"Magdalini!" Sarah exclaimed. "Oh, that's fantastic to hear she's married. I imagine it was lovely."

"Bet it was," Sandy agreed.

"Anyway we—um, had a lot to drink and—"

"We got married," James said. "It was a spur of the moment decision, and it was entirely wonderful."

Amelia glanced at him to find a determined look on his face. He had apparently decided that a happy front was the correct move.

"Oh, that's lovely!" Sarah said.

"Fabulous," Sandy agreed. "Young love. No better place than Asteri."

"No—" Amelia started, not wanting them to think she and James were an item.

But James patted her arm and said, "That's right. We couldn't be happier."

It was so at odds with the quick turn in the kitchen that she sent him a *WTF* look. He sent her back a look, and she thought she understood. He didn't want them to have the idea that he and Amelia were dumb enough to marry each other by accident.

"Unfortunately, Takis passed away that night," Amelia said, patting James back a little harder.

"He'd been sick for a long time," James said. His arm pat turned into a smack. "As you no doubt know, he's a wonderful, friendly host, and we grew close over our stay here."

"On the night he died, he asked us—"

"If we could run the Ria Hotel for him," James finished. "And then he passed away. His niece doesn't want the hotel. So here we are."

Amelia grinned so wide that it probably made her look like the Joker and gave his hand on her arm a hard squeeze. "It's a sort of a wedding and honeymoon all in one. Of course, we're devastated about Takis, but we're also *so* in love."

James shot her a look and removed his hand from her grip. *Don't overdo it.*

"This makes the terrible news about Takis a bit better," Sarah said. "I like that you two have a lovely story here. We've always felt there was something special about Asteri for a couple. Sarah and I realized we were in love here too."

"What made you choose Asteri to visit?" Sandy asked.

Amelia said, "It was cheap," at the same time James said, "The olive trees."

Sandy shot Amelia a knowing smile and turned to James. "Olive trees?"

"They're fascinating," James said. "Especially the ancient variety here on Asteri. In Greek mythology, Athena and Poseidon competed to be the patron god of Athens. Poseidon gave the people some saltwater no one wanted, but Athena gave them an olive tree, which produced oils and food and wood. She won. So now the olive trees are the symbol of peace. Of course, they're amazing because they've evolved to be incredibly drought-resistant. The ones here on Asteri were supposedly planted by the Venetians, who were amazingly—"

Amelia could see the eyes of their guests glazing over. "Anyway, as you know, it's a lovely place."

"*Yasoo!*" A voice trilled from the reception area. Birgitte appeared, filling the space with her height. She wore a bright yellow sundress and stiletto heels, which only added to her goddess appearance. "Sandy! Sarah! I heard you arrived!"

"Darling Birgitte!" Sandy and Sarah got up, and there was much cheek-kissing and hugging. Amelia hoped Birgitte was only here borrowing a cup of sugar, but who wore an outfit like that to walk up a dusty road and ask for sugar?

Birgitte sat down at the table. "It's lovely to see you again. I heard you'd arrived and had to come. I expect you heard the terrible news about Takis." (There was much sighing and nodding.) "Did these two *vlakas* tell you how they accidentally got married and then agreed to take on the Ria all in one fantastically drunken night?"

"They didn't say it quite like that," Sandy said.

"Oh, let me tell you all about it," Birgitte said.

"We've already told them," James said quickly.

"Did you tell them how you thought you were getting a blessing instead of getting married?" Birgitte turned to Sarah and Sandy and hooted with laughter. "What did they think 'I do' meant?"

"We were *told* to say yes," Amelia growled. She shot James a look. They should have known Sarah and Sandy had friends here if they'd been coming for over twenty years, and that those friends would include Birgitte.

"These two have only been on Asteri two weeks, can you believe it?" Birgitte tittered.

"Fascinating," Sarah said. Both she and Sandy gave James and Amelia stern looks.

"Let me tell you the worst part," Birgitte said. "You know how the Greek burial laws are? Remember when I had to bury my Spiro and pay all that money?"

"Oh yes," Sandy said. "Terrible. Just terrible. So much money. A terrible law."

"Magda's new husband wants these two to pay for Takis's permanent grave." Birgitte smiled happily to herself, clearly delighted to impart this bit of gossip. "They have to stay and run the place and give them €150,000."

"We don't *have* to stay," Amelia said.

"Oh my," Sarah said. "They didn't mention that part."

"This one was asking me what to do because she thinks she's *leaving* in a few days!" Birgitte said, patting Amelia hard on the arm and cackling.

"You're not seriously planning on leaving?" Sandy said, her voice sharp. Amelia looked back and saw a kind of warning in her face. "You can't abandon the hotel."

"We don't yet know what we're doing." James's voice was quiet but firm, and Amelia was grateful for the support. "It's been a shock. We didn't plan on getting married. We were drunk when we agreed to take the hotel. But we did form a good friendship with Takis, and his death was upsetting."

Sarah and Sandy exchanged a look. "*We* might as well run the place. We've a much longer history here than you two."

"You should!" Amelia said, hoping this suggestion was serious.

Sandy gave her a look that suggested she was an imbecile. "We're longtime guests. Not owners."

"A fresh perspective and a younger eye could do wonders for the place," Birgitte said, pointedly looking at Amelia.

On the whole, this first experience with hosting guests was not ideal.

"Whatever the status of your relationship," Sandy said in an admonishing tone, "you can't expect Magda and her new husband to come up with money for Takis's grave on their own. That's cruel."

"What happens if they don't pay?" Amelia asked. "Has anyone…not paid?"

"People don't pay all the time," Birgitte said. "In which case, the body is exhumed after a period of time and the bones are thrown into a mass pit. It's horrible. Even worse is the family has to be present to watch."

Amelia swallowed. "What country puts its citizens in this kind of predicament?"

"That isn't our problem," James said. "It's not—I mean, that's awful, but it's not our problem."

There was a moment of silence among the group, during which Amelia could sense the disapproval coming off Sandy and

Sarah and Birgitte in waves. But it *wasn't* their problem. They could dislike it all they wanted, but it didn't change the fact that she and James could—and should—walk away from the Ria Hotel and Asteri, however temporarily Takis might be buried.

"You know," Birgitte said, her tone careful, "maybe it's best if you see it."

"See...it?" Amelia pictured the stiffness of Takis's hands and shuddered.

To Sandy and Sarah, Birgitte said, "Do you remember Yorgos who owned the Blue Tavern?"

"Of course," Sandy said. "Blue Tavern Yorgos, right?" She must have caught Amelia's frown, because she added, "There are so many Yorgoses on Asteri. So we differentiate them depending on what they do."

"Blue Tavern Yorgos had cancer," Birgitte said. "He passed away and the tavern closed. His family cannot pay for a permanent grave. They had many debts to pay off. They were able to afford a three-year rental, but the time is up."

Sarah and Sandy shook their heads in unison.

"They are out there now," Birgitte said, a little gleefully. "I passed them on the way here."

"Ohh," Sarah said in understanding.

"What?" Amelia asked, feeling she was going to regret hearing the answer.

"I think it's better if we show you," Birgitte said.

Amelia shot James a panicked look. His eyes were wide too. "Show us?"

"It's what happens if you can't pay," Birgitte said.

"I have to start preparing the lamb for dinner," Amelia said. "I don't have time. I don't think I need to see."

"It'll only take a moment," Birgitte said, unfolding her unending legs and standing. Sarah and Sandy stood too.

"We can't all fit in my car," James said.

"We can walk," Birgitte said. "It's just down the road. It'll only take a moment. Now come."

And with this ominous promise, she led them out of the Ria Hotel.

CHAPTER 9

They took a short walk across a field and through a barren, dead olive grove. They could hear the wailing before they saw anyone: a long, thin keening like a bird or the wind whistling through a hole in a rock. The noise belonged to the black-clad widow of Blue Tavern Yorgos. The crying widow huddled next to an open grave in a small cemetery with crooked and weathered stone crosses, a pile of dirt next to it. The form of something that might have once been her husband lay next to an open and worn wood casket, still clothed in what was probably a burial suit. Two gravediggers stood leaning on shovels while a priest chanted over the remains. Amelia looked everywhere but there.

"Why on earth do they have the casket open?" Amelia said, her voice slightly shrill. "Why does that poor woman need to see his body? And me—why do *I* need to see it?"

"They have to remove the body somehow," Birgitte said. "They ask that the family witness it."

James offered an arm and Amelia grabbed on to it, grateful for his comfort.

She peeked back once to see the widow fall to the ground in her wailing. "It's awful."

"This is how it is," Birgitte said, not without sympathy. She and Sarah and Sandy weren't looking either. They stood with their backs to the scene. "The law says the family must be present. They have to do it."

"Doesn't she have anyone to help her?" Amelia asked. She didn't want to add, *Should we help her?* They should have, of course, and if she was a better person, she would. But there were several lines of separation here. She was not Greek, she was a stranger, and she would only be doing it to assuage her own non-Greek, privileged feelings about it. After all, Amelia would surely never be in a position where she'd have to dig up a decomposing loved one. These lines of separation were buffers against doing what they should all do: go help. And she would use those lines. She disliked all these thoughts, all these realizations about herself, but she was not going to leave the solidity of James's arm.

"Ideally, their children would be with them," Sarah said.

"Blue Tavern Yorgos and his wife had no children," Birgitte said. "Have you seen enough?"

"More than enough," James said, his tone cold. "We shouldn't be watching this poor woman in her grief." Amelia liked him for that. James was a good egg.

They walked back through the dead olive grove to the hotel.

"None of that was necessary," Amelia told Birgitte. Even Sarah and Sandy looked a bit green.

"It *is* necessary," Birgitte said. "Because now you will see that it is the right thing to do to give a little money to Magda to help pay for Takis's burial. He decided to leave the hotel to you, hoping you would run it. Magda would only sell it outright and use the money. Now, you can do both—run the hotel the way Takis wanted and help his niece with the money. It is win-win."

"Not for us," Amelia said defiantly.

"Well," Sandy said in a change-of-tone voice. "It's lovely to see you, Birgitte, of course. But this has been quite an eventful first day back on Asteri what with the news about Takis and this…walk. I'm rather tuckered out."

Amelia understood that *tuckered out* meant *Watching someone get exhumed was not the way I envisioned my first night in Greece.*

"Maybe if we could just get a small bit of bread and cheese for dinner," Sarah said.

"Of course," James said. "We can do that. I'll bring it to you in a few minutes."

Amelia was glad to be free of having to make lamb because she definitely had no appetite. She turned to Birgitte. "Seriously."

Birgitte did not look sorry in the least. "You needed to know. Sarah, Sandy, lovely to see you." Without her ostentatious display of cheek-kissing or anything else, which suggested to Amelia that Birgitte knew she'd gone too far, the woman toddled away from the hotel in those ridiculous heels.

Sarah and Sandy made their way down the steps to the lower levels. James headed inside, presumably to get bread and cheese for them. Amelia took several long, restorative gulps of fresh air. Birgitte's field trip had, unfortunately and irritatingly, had the intended effect: Amelia felt guilty now about leaving Asteri. Walking away from the mess required smothering a lot of feelings, particularly guilt. She was supposed to have spent her time in Europe expunging guilt and fixing herself, and while not a huge amount of progress had been made, this didn't help. She might know herself better now, but she still had the same problems as when she'd left San Francisco. God, that was maddening.

With her head in turmoil, she went inside to help James.

In the kitchen, James was slicing the morning's fresh bread and putting it on a platter. "Bad news. I checked the computer again. There's another booking. A young couple from Denmark."

The news made something sink in her. This could not go on. "James. I think we have to tell them no. That the hotel is closing."

He arranged cheese slices on the platter, preciously nudging them into perfect formation. "The thing is, I don't have to be back in the United States. I don't have a job to go back to. I sublet my condo. I was planning on doing more traveling after Asteri. But I could stay here and see if I can help make some money and give it to Magdalini and her husband. It might not be much, but it could be enough to extend the grave rental period beyond three years. And there are the suppliers we owe money to. Katarina for bread and Markos for meat. Kostas said a lot of people rely on the hotel for work. Someone should make sure they get paid."

He was giving her an out. He was offering her the chance to walk away, without too much guilt.

She appreciated it more than he would know.

Amelia thought about Ella, and about that promising job

opportunity with Celia. She thought about leaving Europe, leaving Greece, and the inevitable slide of disappointment she would feel as her plane touched down on the tarmac at SFO. Of making her way to baggage claim, amid fellow Californians and Bay Area residents all arriving home from somewhere. Of those last few moments inside the airport where she might cling to the idea of still being away, abroad. The moment she exited the doors, that would all disappear. She would make her way across the bay to her mother's midcentury home that was worth a fortune despite its 1960s wood paneling hideousness because it had a full view of the city and the Albany Bulb. The house would smell comfortingly, but also dismayingly, of childhood. She would set her battered and stained backpack down in her childhood bedroom, the backpack's filth and wear not belonging in the sterile room. She would pry open her laptop. Press the power button and sigh.

Her eye fell on the ugly room key tags. The kernel of the idea that she'd had before, when they'd handed the keys to Sarah and Sandy, took form now. She could see it, blooming in a circle of color.

"This place needs an update," she said.

"True," he said.

"I bet we could get some paint. Hire a local builder. See about getting in some nice textiles and updated accessories."

"We could." James sounded cautiously hopeful.

"I've worked as a project manager my whole professional career," she said. "I'm good at it. I imagine hotel running is a little like that. Make a master list, then many small lists, set it all into motion, and then check on everything repeatedly to keep it spinning."

James studied her. "I'm not sure how Takis managed the finances of this place, but I can certainly look into them and see where we can do better."

People would help, Kostas had told her. If they wanted them to. She thought about a small green pot she'd seen in the town at a stall, which would look beautiful on the tables on the veranda. "There's a pottery seller in town who has some pieces that would be gorgeous in the rooms."

"I have a friend who's a freelance web designer. He owes me a favor. He could make us a nice website, maybe get some digital ad campaigns going so people can find us."

"You have a friend?" she asked.

This earned her a small smile.

If Celia wanted to interview her, then other companies might too. They would wait if she was a desirable candidate. The chance to stay on Asteri and see what happened was very attractive. "Are we crazy if we do this? We're trained to do professional work for corporations, not run hotels that no one's heard of on an island that no one visits."

"I prefer the term *visitor challenged*."

"*Guest deficient.*"

He laughed, sounding a little giddy. The kind of laugh someone give when they're about to jump.

"We might regret it if we didn't try," she said. "Regret is bad." A swell of excitement bloomed in her chest.

"At least until the end of this tourist season." James's face was serious. She liked this look on him, this careful, thoughtful look. It was the kind of face Micah never had because everything was a party to him.

"Olive harvest time," she said. "Also known as November."

The smile again from him. The nervous, heady smile. She matched it with one of her own.

Were they crazy? They might be crazy. Recent evidence was not in their favor, what with the getting married and agreeing to take this place. It was the kind of problem she never would have imagined being hers. It was the kind of story you read on a tabloid website, like the *New York Post* or the *Daily Mail*, full of clickbait and long headlines with inflated emphasis like *Couple Gets MARRIED and BUYS Hotel So Family Can BURY FORMER OWNER and Keep Him Buried!* It was not the kind of thing that happened in reality.

"I don't even know if this place has a laundry facility," she said.

"It's on the fourth level," James said. She threw him a surprised look. "I went exploring last night. There are a bunch of little rooms down there, smaller than the regular ones, probably for the nonexistent staff. There's a big laundry room, and the machines look serviceable."

She raised her eyebrows. "That's something."

"What if we—" He looked around, hands on hips, thinking. "What if we did what Takis couldn't?"

"What if," Amelia said slowly, "we asked Sandy and Sarah to write us an amazing review in exchange for a free meal or something?"

"We're already giving them a free meal." A natural crack in his voice made her meet his eyes. He held her gaze and that electric snap happened again, the one that had been there in the kitchen earlier.

"Okay," she whispered.

"All right," he agreed. If Amelia was reading it right, she'd swear he was forcing himself to look away and break the tension. Then he picked up the dinner tray for their guests and went downstairs to deliver it.

At breakfast the next morning, Sandy and Sarah were in much better spirits. It was a lucky thing that they had fresh bread delivery. In addition to still-warm bread, Katarina Yagapololis brought them yogurt and a pot of honey.

Amelia asked Katarina if she could recommend someone who could help her paint. Between her poor Greek and Katarina's poor English, Amelia feared she had asked Katarina about goats, but Katarina nodded vociferously and smiled a lot, so maybe she understood.

"We're really sorry about that strange interlude with the grave yesterday," James said, setting down tea in front of Sarah and Sandy. Already the dining area looked far cheerier than when it had all been crowded in the dark bar area. Amelia had filled an old jug with pink germaniums to brighten the tables. The veranda, she and James agreed, would be the new restaurant. "But we hope we can make your stay here as wonderful as it's been over the years."

"Asteri will always be lovely," Sandy said. "But we appreciate your effort. You two have gotten yourselves in quite a pickle here, but you seem nice. And I appreciate the tea, even though it's disgusting."

"I'm going to see if I can pick up some better tea today in town," Amelia said.

"Maybe we could get a ride down to the port so we can rent one of those ancient cars?" Sandy asked. "I swear we've rented them before."

"Probably have," Sarah agreed. "All three of them."

"You can rent this one again," Amelia said. "We have Takis's now. We'll take it back to the port and swap it out."

"Yes, absolutely," James said. "We want your stay here to be as nice as possible."

"That'd be fabulous," Sandy said.

"I think you two will do all right," Sarah said. "We were discussing it. You have an interesting story here. Keep your guests away from exhumations and improve your tea offering, and you should be fine."

Amelia got the sense that they had passed a test of sorts with the couple. She and James had tried to pretend all was well and had been proven disastrously wrong, but Sarah and Sandy appeared to appreciate them trying. And the truth. The truth was always good.

Sarah and Sandy went to gather their bags for the day, and Amelia went out front to Takis's car. James jogged out after her. "Hey. Thought it might be a good idea if we exchanged numbers. In case we need to get hold of each other about guests or something."

"Right." Or something. "Guess I should have my husband's number in my phone."

He arched an eyebrow. "Right." He read off his number, and she kicked herself mentally five hundred times in a row for calling him her husband.

"What are you going to do today?" she asked. He'd shaved this morning, and Amelia couldn't stop herself from noticing that he cleaned up nicely. As in, the misbehaving portion of her brain whispered, "Mmm, *wow*," while the logical part of her swiftly told the misbehaving portion to shut it. They were going to be partners in running the hotel—nothing else—and she would train her brain to believe it.

"I'm going to reach out to my website designer friend and see if he can help us," he said.

"You said he owed you a favor." She was hoping he would tell her what. Probably it was something boring like James spotting his friend a coffee, not hiding his friend because the Mafia was after him or paying his bail bond. Not that she wanted James to have friends that required bail bond favors or safe harbor from the Mafia, but she was worried, she realized, quite a lot of the time, that James was too mild mannered. Too boring. Because she was married to him now.

"He does owe me a favor. It involved tiki torches and grass skirts." James raised his eyebrows at her dramatically. Her expression must have given her away because he laughed. "You so badly want me to be wild."

"Not true; you're very useful as a boring finance guy." For a moment she thought she'd gone too far saying he was boring, but he didn't seem upset. "Anyway, your friend. Will he do all the fancy keywords and SEO and things?"

"All that and more."

Sandy and Sarah emerged, expansive straw tote bags in tow. James nodded at them and went inside.

"You two make a cute couple," Sarah said, accepting the rental car keys from Amelia.

"Oh—that's not—" Amelia started.

"We know," Sandy said. "You just met each other. But still."

"That's how it works," Sarah said. "It starts that way."

"It definitely does."

"We're just friends," Amelia said, thinking of his apparent reluctance to go further. Which was fine. Especially now that they were business partners.

"Oh, by the way," Sandy said. "We were thinking that tonight we would love moussaka for dinner if you can arrange that. Thanks so much!"

Amelia's heart pounded. Moussaka? She hadn't the first clue how to make that.

She drove them to the port, and they switched the rental, and then Sarah and Sandy dropped Amelia off in town. She found a little shop selling an assortment of dry goods and some British-looking tea, which she bought, along with some laundry detergent and dish soap, none of which she'd found at the hotel. Emerging back into the square, she wondered what else she might need, when she saw the blond cropped head of Birgitte disappearing into a shop. Amelia decided to get out of town before she spotted her, but as she was crossing the main square, Birgitte called after her.

"Ah, my loud American friend," Birgitte trilled.

"You're the one doing the shouting," Amelia said.

"Come now, don't be upset about yesterday." Birgitte pulled her lips down. "It proved the point, did it not?"

Amelia did not want to rehash the exhumation in any way, so she put on a falsely bright voice and said, "I was hoping to run into you. I could use some of your excellent translation skills."

"I *am* an excellent translator," Birgitte agreed, without a hint of humor.

"Our hotel guests have asked for moussaka. I don't know the first thing about it. Can you help translate with ingredients around here?"

"But Amelia!" Birgitte laughed, putting her head coquettishly to the side. "I make an excellent moussaka. You can come to my house. I will show you."

"No! No, I don't want to inconvenience you." The idea of being trapped in a house with Birgitte was alarming.

"Yes, it *is* a bit of an inconvenience, but it is all right." Birgitte wound her arm through Amelia's. "Come."

"But ingredients and things?" Amelia asked, scurrying to keep up with Birgitte's long strides. She didn't want to do this, didn't want to spend a second more in Birgitte's company, but the woman had her in a death grip.

"I have it all, whatever." Birgitte didn't slow down. "Come before I change my mind. You will drive with me."

Birgitte didn't allow room for consideration, and anyway, Amelia was without a car. Slinging her groceries, she hopped into a tiny red clown car that barely sat the driver, let alone a passenger. It was a convertible though, and Amelia's hair streamed pleasantly behind her as Birgitte sped along. The air was delicious, clean, and smelled of lemon trees and rosemary.

"How is your James?" Birgitte asked.

"He's not my—argh. He's fine. He's looking into the hotel website today."

"Yes. Takis was not much for such things. He thought the Ria Hotel's beauty would draw tourists by osmosis." Birgitte made a clucking sound and tapped the steering wheel with beautifully manicured fingers. "And you and James will make a go of love too, eh?"

Amelia felt her face heat. "No, um. No. We're just friends."

"Mmm. Don't delay too long. He is enormously good-looking, even for us good-looking Swedes." Birgitte said this without a hint of irony. "It is only amazing that he was single. Why was he single? Is he broken?"

Amelia both liked and disliked that Birgitte got right to the point. "I don't know."

"Hmm." Birgitte turned the little car onto the single dirt road that Amelia had noticed before on the way to the Ria Hotel. "You both are in your late thirties, are you not?"

"I'm thirty-two!" Amelia realized with a deep stab of alarm that she didn't know how old James was. She had assumed he was near her age, but how could she not know that? It didn't matter, but it was a detail she would like to know if she was married to him.

"When you have figured out the way he is broken, tell me so I can watch out for it."

"What do you mean?"

"I don't like broken men." Birgitte flashed her a devilish look. "If you are done with him, it is possible that I will take him. I like to know the ways people are broken before I get to them."

Amelia rolled her eyes. "Right, well, if it comes to that point, I'll be sure to let you know his deficiencies."

Birgitte pulled the car in front of a low daffodil-yellow house, the shock of color a surprise after the overwhelmingly white-washed buildings on the rest of the island. From the outside, it was a simple structure: two large, blue, and weather-battered wooden doors served as the entrance. No windows from this side. Amelia hoped Birgitte didn't live in a dark cave.

"Okay. Moussaka." Birgitte led Amelia to the blue doors. As soon as she was over the threshold, Amelia's breath caught.

A large indoor courtyard welcomed them, featuring a fountain with a small naked male statue sporting an enormous phallus pouring water into it. Intricately patterned blue tiles surrounded the floor around the fountain, followed by mosaics made of tiny black and white rocks, forming a design of sweeping circles. In every corner and against every wall stood a rich green plant in an azure-blue container. French doors on the other three sides of the courtyard led into other wings of the house. A long-haired black and white cat lounged lazily and precariously on the thick edge of the fountain, its tail flicking. It was a lush feast of color and sound.

"This is...gorgeous." Amelia could hardly speak for trying to take it all in.

"Yes. This is why I live here. Who could give this up?" Birgitte spread her arms to indicate the fountain. "It is, essentially, my living room." Large benches and a table and chairs completed the space. "Come through to the kitchen."

Amelia followed, and the kitchen made her squeal inside too. It was long, clean, and modern. "This looks like a professional setup."

"I love to cook." Birgitte opened the industrial-grade fridge and took out an assortment of ingredients. She grabbed a bottle of red wine from a large rack that reached to the ceiling. "Spiro ordered in all this equipment for me. No one else on the island has a stove like this. I am a gourmet. My father wanted me to be a chef when I was young, but I only like to cook for myself and friends. I love a dinner party. These days, there aren't many on the island for dinner parties, and even fewer who will come all the way out here for it, but still I love it."

Amelia wondered if Birgitte, for all her flouncy puffery, was lonely. A stab of sympathy hit. It was obvious that she was an entertainer and that there was no one to entertain.

Amelia stepped over to the large window at the end of the kitchen. Outside was an untouched cliff, which, like the one in front of the Ria Hotel, plunged dramatically to the sea. It was glorious. Amelia wondered why the Ria Hotel hadn't taken advantage of a window like this for its kitchen. It would have been easy enough, had the kitchen been a priority for whoever built it.

Birgitte assembled the ingredients for the moussaka: ground lamb, gorgeous, plump tomatoes, spices like cinnamon and cloves and allspice. She pulled off a bulb of garlic from a huge braid hanging in the window and plopped a sack of small white potatoes on the counter.

"This dish is traditionally made with eggplant," Birgitte said. "But we will be using potatoes because eggplant is appalling. It is bitter and the texture is like that of a—never mind. Mind you, while my cooking is excellent and you cannot find a better cook on this island than me, using potatoes is not very Greek. But I have had several Greek friends to dinner, and they all loved it with potatoes, probably because they had eaten it all their lives with eggplant and secretly hated it and are now liberated. So, we will accept that my moussaka is superb, although not usual, but this dish honors the Greeks and their beautiful land."

Birgitte sighed and leaned her arms on the counter. Her eyes were unfocused, and she seemed to be far away.

"Everything okay?" Amelia asked.

"Yes. Yes." Birgitte shook her head as though to clear herself. "Now we will chop onions. Onions hurt my eyes, so you will do that." Birgitte slid two onions over to Amelia, followed by a gorgeous olive wood cutting board and a professional-looking knife. Amelia peeled and cut the onions, weeping, while Birgitte had the nicer job of slicing the potatoes into thin coins. They both chopped garlic and tomatoes, and Birgitte showed Amelia how to make the meat mixture: sauté the minced lamb and onion and garlic, add the tomatoes and an assortment of spices including salt, pepper, cinnamon, bay leaves, allspice, cloves, and, of course, great quantities of wine.

Birgitte kept her and Amelia's wineglasses filled as they cooked, and by the time the meat sauce was simmering, Amelia was loosened and relaxed enough to laugh at Birgitte's outrageousness.

"Spiro was an absolute bull in bed," Birgitte said. "Huge down there." She made a hand gesture. "I cooked every day for him." She sighed. "I miss him, but it is not every day a woman can take a man that big, if you know what I mean."

"I'll take your word for it."

Birgitte gestured for Amelia to pay attention to another sauté pan, in which she heated butter. "How is James in bed?"

Amelia stirred the butter, avoiding Birgitte's eyes. "As I said, we're only friends."

"No sex? What is the problem? Is he—you know?" She made a downward drop motion with a finger.

"We just met. We didn't mean to get married, so we're not hopping into bed with each other." And it appeared that James had decided he was no longer interested, so there was that.

"Ridiculous," Birgitte scoffed. "I met my Spiro. Two nights later he proposed. We knew."

"Well, we didn't know."

Birgitte gave an elaborate shrug. "Have sex, then you can see what he's like." She added flour to the melted butter, whisking with an impressively perfect quickness. "Then you can make your decision." She shoved a basket of potatoes over to Amelia. "Peel and slice more, please."

Amelia pulled the potatoes toward her. "My decision won't hinge on sex."

"Of course not." Birgitte poured milk into the flour mixture, still mixing with that expert flick of her wrist. "But sex is an easy way to tell you if he is broken. If he is a considerate lover, then there is less chance of broken. If he is a selfish lover or a rough one, broken. If he comes in thirty seconds and leaves you wanting, end it immediately because there is no hope of repair." She guffawed loudly.

The béchamel sauce thickened, and Birgitte showed Amelia how to add nutmeg and egg yolk. It was a lot to remember. They fried the potatoes in a frying pan. "James isn't interested in having sex. It's not that kind of partnership."

One of Birgitte's eyebrows rose. "Oh? He said that?"

"Not so much. But he doesn't seem…interested." She wasn't sure how to articulate it except that since the blessing-wedding, he didn't seem to want to revisit the lust. In the shock of what had happened, she hadn't been consumed with it either, but if she had sensed continued interest from him, she might have thought about it.

"Broken," Birgitte pronounced.

"No, I just think there's a lot of life change going on, and we were never meant to be together anyway. Have you not wanted another relationship, after your husband passed away?"

"Of course!" Birgitte scoffed. "I have many lovers. Layer the potatoes in a scalloped pattern in the baking dish, see, like fish scales."

"Is that a Greek way?"

"It is Birgitte way. I will never marry again, Amelia, understand. When you find the right person, you cannot stomach anyone else."

"Life isn't always that intense," Amelia said.

"Yes, it *is* intense." Birgitte refilled their glasses and began to layer the casserole in the baking dish: potatoes, then meat mixture, then potatoes. "If it is done right." She regarded Amelia over the rim of her glass. "James is nice. He is certainly handsome. Why wait?"

"For sex?" The wine had reduced her overall irritation with Birgitte. She poured the béchamel sauce over the top of the casserole.

"For sex, for anything." Birgitte waved her glass around.

"I agree sex will tell me a lot, but some men hide things." Amelia thought of Micah. "They're on their best behavior at first, and then they let their guard down. Once that happens, you find out whether they're a keeper or not."

"No." Birgitte put her glass down and slid the ready casserole into the oven. "You train them."

"Some can't be trained out of bad behavior."

"*You* are worth him being trained," Birgitte said. "You have to believe it. I take no lovers who aren't willing to give me everything. Even those who, as a rule, do not give much. They can have it back when I'm done with it. But they must give it freely."

Amelia wasn't sure what *it* was in this conversation, but she thought she understood. "Like demanding transparency up front?"

"Yes, of course. If a man wants into my bed, he must accept the terms. There can be no hidden agendas." Birgitte sniffed haughtily. She got out a little blue and white dish and filled it with fresh olives. She gestured for Amelia to follow her out of the kitchen to the main courtyard where they sat among the lush plants and gentle gurgle of the fountain.

"I think it's too early to have this conversation," Amelia said. "James and I don't know each other well."

"It is never too early. You are in the situation, so you must address it. You will demand from James transparency, you will investigate his body, and you will see what he is like."

"And, somehow, get the Ria Hotel to be successful." Amelia laughed.

Birgitte waved her hand. "Takis had no passion for it. But the two of you, you are vibrating with it. I can see. This is why I ask about the sex. It's going to be good." She sipped from her glass. "And, now you know how to make moussaka. I think things are looking up for you."

"Okay, well, it's a pretty steep climb. We have to do so much with the hotel. Refresh the decor. Structural renovations. Food. A shuttle service." Amelia shook her head. Two weeks ago, she was merely a visitor. Now she was googling *how to run a hotel*.

"You can do all that." Birgitte nodded, her eyelids a little droopy. "I will teach you many more dishes. You'll see. You'll be happy and you won't even notice it."

CHAPTER 10

Sarah and Sandy left Asteri, showering Amelia and James with compliments for a great stay. Before they left, Sandy took Amelia's hands in hers and said, "You have a good thing here. Keep at it. We'll come back and see you next year."

Amelia felt pretty good about the way she and James had hosted Sarah and Sandy, even with all the missteps and scrambling at the beginning. Admittedly, the island did most of the heavy lifting. It was hard not to be relaxed here, hard not to have a lovely time when the warm wind ruffled your hair and the sea offered the perfect amount of refreshment. It was Greece, after all.

"So." Amelia stretched after the ferry carrying Sarah and Sandy departed, arching her back. "That was different from sitting in an office all day."

"Morning meetings that could have been an email." James got back into their little car.

"Misguided HR directives."

"The power jostling."

"The KPIs and the aligning. What happens when we get more guests?" Amelia wondered.

"No worries. I spent the morning reading up on hotel management."

"Oh, we have it covered then."

James laughed. "I found good info. Like, we have to make sure we don't burn out. Changing laundry and cleaning a room is supposedly the worst of it. We shouldn't offer to cook dinner for guests. Maybe just breakfast."

"We need Birgitte's kitchen." She had told James about Birgitte's magical courtyard and the beautiful, fully equipped kitchen. The Ria's kitchen had a single battered saucepan and a roasting pan that looked like it had seen a lot of action in the war.

Birgitte, perhaps to atone for the horrific field trip she'd dragged them on, had made several wonderful dinners for Sarah and Sandy and, along with the food, brought plants and little trinkets she said she "had extras of." Amelia had placed these things—a mirror, a star-shaped metal wall hanging—in different areas and rooms, and already the infusion of texture and metals and wood began to change the dated look of the hotel. Amelia was thinking of asking Birgitte to give more ideas for the rest of the rooms. She could already hear her saying, *I am an excellent interior designer.*

"How's the website coming along?" she asked as James swung the car into the Ria's main courtyard.

"Looking good, from what I've seen. Pedro's been working hard."

"That's some favor he owes you." This was a regular joke now between them.

"The biggest." James turned off the engine. "Have you decided what you want to do with the reception area yet?"

"Lots of plants," she said. "Poor Takis just had no style. I wonder where he stayed and what his place looked like."

"His apartment is on the top level, over from reception."

"What? Really?" She hadn't considered this. But then, she hadn't expected to look further than her own room during her stay here.

"Yeah. It's a nice space."

Would they need to move into the owner's quarters? Give up their rooms? Sleep together? Amelia's mind whirled with the possibilities. "If we start getting a lot of guests, we may have to vacate our rooms."

"Well, the apartment's waiting for us. Come see." They made their way inside to the minuscule reception area. Amelia paused to give it a critical eye. She could work on this right away. Use one of her masterful Excel files to manage it all, with cascading color-coded lines and categories and unnecessary but cool macros. Was she nerding out? She might be.

"Through here." James went down the short hallway off the reception area and opened a door onto a small, depressingly brown sitting room with a few basics: a square uncomfortable-looking couch, a chair, and a table (all brown). There was nothing on the walls and no personal effects that would suggest this was the owner's apartment. A door opened to a little bathroom. Another door led to a surprisingly large bedroom with a neatly made double bed, but the entire space was shrouded in darkness. Through the gloom she could make out two framed photos on the bedside table. One was of a woman in a flowery dress, which Amelia assumed was Maria, Takis's wife, and the other was Takis and Maria on their wedding day looking dour and unhappy, as Takis had described.

"Is—are his things still here?" she asked.

"Yeah." James opened a drawer to reveal neatly folded clothes. "We can box it all up and give it to his niece and her angry husband."

The place felt desolate and sad. Takis had not taken any joy living in these rooms. Amelia felt horribly sad for him, for the grieving he had been doing over the loss of his wife and falling ill. He had responded by curling away from the light like a pill bug.

Amelia tried to picture living in here. The space was fine but would be greatly improved with plants and sunlight. She pulled open heavy wooden shutters that revealed an unfettered view of the plunging cliff. "Wow. I can't believe these were closed."

James came to stand next to her. "Oh yeah. This is beautiful." He turned and his arm brushed hers, leaving an electric trail where their skin had touched. She turned to look at him and wondered if—

"Anyway." James ran a hand through his hair and stepped back from the window. "I guess we should talk about this. Would living in here be—would that—"

A conflation of feelings hit her: Regret. Irritation. Anticipation. A zip of excitement over the fact that he seemed flustered too. "Assuming we have enough guests to warrant vacating our rooms, I think the best answer is that we share this suite. As business partners."

His shoulders sagged. "As business partners. Yes. Absolutely."

Amelia had no idea what would happen when it came to

deciding who would sleep in the bed, but they'd face that later. "Why don't I make a spreadsheet tomorrow of all the things we need to do and all the people we need to talk to. I'll list the big things, like when we have to make the first payment to Magda and Angry Yorgos, and what we owe to the vendors giving us credit right now." She could feel herself sliding into project management mode and then sinking as the enormity of taking on a hotel hit her. "James. How are we going to do all this?"

He met her eyes for a long moment. "Let's just take it one step at a time. We're here until the end of the season, and we'll take it bit by bit."

Amelia pursed her lips. When she had agreed to stay until the end of the season, she hadn't counted on how they'd actually do it. "Okay."

"After that, we can go back to normal life."

Normal life. What was that, even?

James expelled a truly impressive collection of flotsam from his pocket onto Takis's long chest of drawers. Amelia peered over to see bits of shells, sprigs of flowers, olives, change, a small length of rope, and black Asterian beach pebbles.

"You're right at home here," she said, trying for a jokey tone that she didn't feel. What was home? What was real?

But he seemed pleased. "Let's go see what cleaning a hotel room is like."

They crept down the steps to Sarah and Sandy's room and peeked inside, worried they'd find chaos on the scale of a college frat house. But the beds had been stripped and the sheets neatly piled with the towels in the corner. Sarah and Sandy had left €10 on the small table, as though the Ria Hotel employed a maid service.

"Ten euro is not to be scoffed at," James said.

"No, it is not." When you only had a trickle of money coming in, it was something.

They gathered up the laundry, and Amelia swept the room. They threw the sheets into the massive washing machine on the fourth level. They would be dried in the unending sunshine on a line strung between two poles that were stuck into the cliff below.

"The bathrooms look okay, right?" James asked, peering into the bathroom.

"Bathrooms should be cleaned after each guest, same as you would in a normal hotel." Amelia pointed to water spots on the mirror over the sink.

"God, I'm such a fumbler." James shook his head. "I have no idea how to do this."

"Hey." Amelia straightened. "Washing sheets and sweeping floors and wiping mirrors is not difficult. The difficult parts are marketing and booking guests. And we're making steps toward that."

"Yeah." He looked out at the sea. "It's funny to say this, but even though we didn't want this, if it fails, I'll be disappointed."

"I get it. And yet, if we don't invest ourselves in this, how can we succeed?" She didn't want to fail either.

"There's the being married part too." James grabbed one of the clean sheet piles and began folding. "I never wanted marriage to be a casual thing. I wanted to be married for life."

Amelia stiffened. When they left Asteri in November after this season, they would inevitably go their separate ways. James would go back to Portland, and she would go back to the Bay Area. They would carry on as they had been before this strange interlude. It was unlikely that the Greek Orthodox Church would track them down, although she pictured opening her mother's door to find a black-clad, gray-bearded priest issuing a stream of furious Greek, waving papers in her face.

She didn't even want marriage or kids, especially not after watching her parents' marriage dissolve slowly over the years like a horrible chemical bath. What was it they said about boiling toads? Put them in hot water and slowly turn up the heat so they never knew they were being cooked until it was too late. That appeared to be marriage, and Amelia couldn't stand the idea of realizing one day after thirty years that she was boiling and did not like her spouse.

"Let's focus on filling this place with paying guests," she said.

"All right. I'm going upstairs to work on blog posts about the olive trees for our website."

"That's a great idea," she lied, not wanting to be discouraging.

He rolled his eyes, clearly hearing the doubt in her voice, but it was a teasing sort of eye roll, the kind that didn't carry a *You're an idiot* agenda behind it. That was what Micah had done—given her eye rolls with a whole commentary behind them.

She applied herself to the laundry, throwing a sheet over the clothesline. There was a satisfaction in the physical part of this work and in knowing that she was cleaning the hotel well. In the afternoon, when it got too hot to work, she would take a dip in the clear, delicious sea down at the cove. She was considering doing that now when her phone rang.

It was her mother. Amelia knew this was coming. She'd sent

her mother a message earlier saying she was staying on in Greece but didn't explain why. But if she didn't answer, her mother would assume the worst and alert the consulate or something.

"Hey, Mom." Amelia stifled her sigh.

"Amelia, I'm really very concerned. You said you had to stay on in Greece for a while, but I need to know why now. Are you in trouble? Have you done something embarrassing? I tried so hard to raise you and your brother not to do something stupid."

"It's all fine."

"No, it isn't. Tell me what's going on. What is so interesting in Greece that you have to stay on, with no departure in sight?"

Amelia sat on a whitewashed bench that was built into the wall and sighed. "Actually, Takis died. I…am staying on to help out with the hotel."

There was a pregnant silence—one Amelia knew well. She braced herself for the deluge. Sure enough, long wails of dramatic lament came across the line, shrill keening that made Amelia cringe and pull the phone away from her ear. "Mom, stop. It's—" *Weird and gross.* "Difficult. Okay? It's hard for everyone—"

But her mother increased the volume of her wails, a feat Amelia didn't think was possible. She was going to have to make a decision: hang up on her or find something to stop her.

"There's more," Amelia said, the words mostly getting drowned out. "I, um, was gifted the Ria Hotel."

The keening stopped.

"What? Did you say you *were gifted* the Ria Hotel?"

"That's right."

There was a long silence, and this was one Amelia was also familiar with. It would not be followed by an explosion. This silence was used as a tactical weapon. It would go on—indeed, was dragging into minutes now—to suggest shock. And then—

"Takis left you the hotel? Why? Why would he do that? Why you? Did you sleep with him? He's old enough to be your father! And you *slept* with him? Amelia! I can't tell people that! What are they going to think? They're going to think I failed as a mother, that you would go off to Greece and—"

"I didn't *sleep* with him!"

"Well, why else would he leave a pretty young woman a hotel if you hadn't debased yourself and climbed into bed with him?"

"He didn't leave it to just me," Amelia said, regretting every word she was about to say. "There's someone with me. James. I met him here. Takis liked us both and left it to us jointly."

"Why? Who is this James? Why leave it to two strangers? That doesn't make any sense!"

"We got married, okay?" Amelia squeezed her hands into fists. Giving this to her mother was like handing a serial killer a knife.

The signature long silence launched again. Amelia leaned her head against the wall and waited for the victimhood to rear. Sure enough, after almost three minutes (Amelia timed it on her watch), her mother started in.

"My only daughter. The baby girl I held in my arms and dreamed of her wedding day. I just cannot believe this. The number of friends whose stories I had to suffer through of their experience as mother of the bride, and I can't even share my story now? I even went on dress shopping trips with my friend Caroline! Never, ever in my wildest dreams did I think—not when you were a baby, not when you were a toddler who everyone said was my mini me, not when you were a teenager whose good behavior I made sure of—never once did I ever think you would turn your back on me like this in one of the biggest moments of our lives. My heart is truly broken, Amelia, shattered, just in a million pieces right now, and I feel alone. So, so alone, and I—"

"Mom! There's a scorpion!" Amelia yelled, sitting up straight. "It's in my room! I have to get it out! Bye!"

She hung up.

Normally, there were severe consequences for hanging up on her mother, but this was a special case. She shuddered to think what introducing James to her mother would be like. Luckily, that wouldn't have to happen.

Up on the level above, James shouted, "Amelia! Pedro's done with the website! Come see."

Amelia got up, glad for the return to reality, and started up the stairs. She did her best to shake off the emotional blanket her mother had tried throwing on her. Her time in Europe had given her practice at pushing her mother's dramatics off by dint of the distance, and she was better at it now than ever. By the time she reached the top, she was able to disassociate enough to cheerily ask, "Does the website play sappy piano music over a montage of sunset photos?"

"Yes, and it flashes neon colors in at least six different fonts."

"That is my kind of website."

He smiled, sunshine lighting his face. "Come look."

THE SECOND CHANCE HOTEL 173

She followed him through to the reception area. Takis's old computer whirred and coughed like it had emphysema. Amelia made a mental note to bring up her laptop as soon as possible. James jabbed at buttons until the screen came up and the most beautiful, simple website appeared. Amelia's mouth fell open.

"That looks amazing." A sleek splash image with *A 5-star hotel with a 10-star experience* written over it greeted them, which was some excellent lying.

"And look." James clicked over to a button that said *Book now.* "An online booking system. That way people can book ahead, choose all their own things, and pay online. We got an email confirming the test booking."

"Oh, that's really good." Amelia studied the home page. James had taken decent photos of the island and rooms and restaurant balcony—and of course, the view—with his phone. He even got one in of the private beach at the bottom of the cliff. "It makes us look like we're a real hotel."

James laughed. "We *are* a real hotel."

Amelia took the mouse and clicked around. Pedro had done a wonderful job. There were nonsensical claims about a *serene stay in spacious, comfy-chic rooms* and how each room provided a "perfect escape from your busy life" with a veranda and coffee/tea service. Comments from supposed guests appeared at the bottom of the page in script font, proclaiming things like *A fabulous stay!* and *delicious food, amazing hospitality from owners James and Amelia!*

"Holy shit," Amelia breathed. "Those lies are going to do us in."

"They're not lies," James said. "It is delicious food, so far, even if Birgitte made it, and we did our best to provide hospitality to our guests. Sarah and Sandy were really happy when they left."

She pointed to the social media icons on the upper-right corner of the page. "Click on one."

James did, but they didn't go anywhere. "They're not live. Takis didn't have any social media accounts."

Amelia opened her phone and within a minute had a new Instagram account set up, @theriahotel. She posted the photo from her first week here, of a church tower with two bells, added a few hashtags like #Greeklife and #islandliving and #vacationdeal and #Asteri and hit Post.

"What's all that?" James asked.

Amelia showed him her phone, setting the cover photo for the account. They already had a few likes.

"That was fast," he marveled.

Amelia's thumb hovered over the Search button, debating whether to send the new account to Ella to show her. She wanted to. Surely a quick text couldn't hurt. *What I'm doing.* And she included a link to their new Instagram account.

"We need an owner photo." Amelia grabbed James's arm and pulled him to the window. They posed, the view of the mountain behind them, and she snapped the photo. She punched in another load of hashtags and posted it.

The computer emitted a sonorous ding, dignified and loud, and several seconds later, a pop-up on the screen announced a new email. James clicked over and they read in wonder that someone had booked a room for a week.

"Um," Amelia said. "I thought the website was a mock-up."

"There's no way social media could have worked that fast?"

"Unlikely." Amelia peered over his shoulder to see the booking. It was a man named Adam from North Carolina. He had put in the notes field *honeymoon*.

"How did he find us?" Amelia asked.

The computer emitted another reticent ding. A new email.

"I think the site might be live," James said. "Oh my God."

Amelia stared open-mouthed at the new booking. A woman named Cynthia from Chicago, who explained in an unnecessary manifesto in the notes section that she'd booked herself a trip to Greece to celebrate her divorce from her cheating husband.

"Where did they find us?" Amelia clicked the social media button for Tripadvisor, which led to the Ria's entry. They had one five-star review. *Amazing owners, amazing place. Incredible views. The Ria Hotel is actually the reason why you go to Asteri. It's quiet, peaceful, and you still get incredible beaches. Highly recommend. —Pedro P.* It had two hundred likes.

"I mean," James said. He typed in *Greek island hotel* into the search bar and the Ria Hotel came up as the tenth result. "Wow, he's good. He said he was going to do some kind of ad-word trial program. Look here—he got us included in a Tripadvisor list of ten best hotels in Greece!"

"We are *not* one of the ten best hotels in Greece," Amelia pointed out. They had twenty-four guest rooms in terrible shape.

"No kidding."

The computer dinged again. "Oh God," Amelia said.

James clicked over to email, and after a tortuously long moment of buffering, another booking appeared. This time it was for two rooms, a family of four, and a two-night stay. All of these new guests had paid in advance.

"What does this mean?" Amelia shrieked.

"It means people want to stay here. It means we have money." James met her wide eyes with huge owl eyes of his own.

"How much?" She clicked around the email, trying to add up the tallies in her head, and failing.

"This is €3,900," James said in an awed, hushed voice.

"Ahhhh!" Amelia danced around the small area, screaming. "Oh my God! We can pay our vendors back!" She grabbed James and he danced with her. His hands were so warm on her arms as he pulled her into a hug. She landed heavily against his chest, aware suddenly of his nearness.

"Okay, yeah," he said, releasing her and pointedly focusing back on the computer. His forehead creased in his classic tell of consternation. "There's so much to do. We have to provide tea and coffee in each room!"

"We need fresh, new bedding," she said. "I'll see if I can order some from Athens."

And paint. She needed paint. She looked at her phone. Ten new followers in the past five minutes for the Instagram account. Fifteen now.

"We should go arrange for the car rental place to provide transport for people coming off the ferry to stay at the Ria." She opened her phone's notes app and started making one of her patented

Amelia lists, with a priority column and a space for how it related to other tasks. Later, she'd reorganize it all into one glorious table.

"Okay. We're doing this," James said.

"We're totally doing it." Amelia jotted down notes. There was a stall in the *hora* with beautiful blue and white bowls that were made here on Asteri. She could get a few of those, plus a few jugs. She would watch hotel renovation shows for ideas. She would ask Kostas to recommend someone who could help cook part-time. Kettles! Coffee trays! "I should go down to Birgitte's and ask for some help."

Suddenly there was so much to do, and the right amount of excitement behind it. Amelia jotted disjointed notes to herself on her phone: *Arrange limes on table with a stone bowl. Pink cushions to match bougainvillea. Can Pedro link to ferry tickets or schedule on site?* She made a mental note to study the websites for other luxury resorts on the bigger islands.

She strode out to the veranda in the restaurant and looked around before closing her eyes against the light breeze. This was insane, and yet it appeared to be working.

They didn't have a single television in the hotel. The computer had to be replaced with Amelia's personal laptop. They didn't even have their own mailbox (it was a poste restante system), and if she wanted to buy a book in print, she'd have to wait four to six weeks for delivery. Running the Ria Hotel guaranteed her a life of hard work changing sheets and cleaning up after people. Birgitte was her only friend here, apart from James, and that wasn't saying much. Would she ever have sex again? With whom? Would she fall in love? Could this small island be enough for her? Staying here kept her from the amends she needed to make at home.

And yet, the sunshine with a light lemon-scented breeze over her face was delicious. When she opened her eyes, she would see nothing but blue sea and minimalist whitewashed buildings, whispering of a simple life with good food and fewer stresses. Whispering, like a siren, that they could do this, if they wanted to. Could they compete with established luxury hotels, some of which charged exorbitant amounts per night? They could. They definitely could.

CHAPTER 11

A week later, Amelia and James vacated their rooms and moved into the owner's apartment.

It was a significant move because it meant that the entire second level was now booked, along with three rooms on the third level.

"Home sweet home," James said, slumping his ragged backpack on the floor. Amelia stood in the doorway, her adrenaline racing. There was a ginormous elephant in here: the bed.

As if reading her mind, James quickly said, "You take the bed. I'll sleep on the floor."

"What—for as long as we're here? That could be a few months. Won't you be uncomfortable?" She took a deep breath, as she always did when confronted with the dilemma of their marriage.

He shrugged, which wasn't much of an answer.

Out of the corner of her eye, a flash of brown movement: a gecko, slinking around the leg of the bed frame.

There were loads of geckos running across the floors and along the walls. They weren't harmful, but their little splayed feet could be off-putting if they ran across your face at night.

"Listen," she said, noting that James had seen it too. "Sleeping on the floor might not be good. The geckos. And scorpions. And there's literally no sleeping bag or anything. We could share the bed until we can get a cot or something. As friends."

James appeared to consider this, although she could already see that the lack of forehead creases or an anxious hand through his hair indicated he was not opposed. "As friends. A line down the middle."

"Yeah. Exactly."

He rubbed his chin. "We should have rules."

"Right. No hanky-panky."

"No spooning," he said. "None."

"Absolutely not." She started to laugh but morphed it back into a serious face when she saw he was not laughing.

"No stray legs crossing over other legs."

"Nope."

"No cold toes trying to warm up on my skin."

"My toes don't get cold," she lied. "But none of that. Friends."

"Friends," he agreed. He stepped over to the little veranda that opened off the bedroom. It was big enough for two chairs and a table, and she could picture them sitting with a glass of wine after a long day of directing guests, providing extra towels, and cleaning up questionable fluids. He stared out for a moment and turned back. "It solves some problems."

"Just until we can find a cot," she said.

"That sounds doable."

It *was* doable.

She looked over at James, who stood looking out of the huge

window in the bedroom. A little flutter of panic went through her chest at living in here with him in tight quarters. She remembered how very little she knew about him. "How old are you, James?"

"What?"

"I never asked. I realized I don't know."

"Oh." He ran a hand through his hair. Telltale nervousness sign. "I'm thirty-four. And you're thirty, right?"

"Thirty-two. Obviously still thirty if you round down."

He sat on the bed. "Anything else you want to know? My middle name is Anders. After my mother's Swedish father."

"Anders. Nice. My middle name is Brynn. After—I'm not sure."

"Brynn. That's pretty."

"Thank you."

"What else can I answer for you? I know—I know it's not easy, and if we're sharing living quarters, I want you to be comfortable with me."

She was not comfortable with him, but also very comfortable. They had been ready to have sex, so ready, the day of the wedding.

"Do you have close friends back home?" she asked.

He looked up, away from her. "I have two good buddies from college who I'm close with."

"That's it? Did you drive most of your friends away because you're super weird? Do you collect glass eyeballs or human teeth or something?"

He laughed. "Yes, absolutely. That's why I had to get drunk on a Greek island and marry someone I'd just met."

She smiled, pleased that he was able to make a joke. (She hoped it was a joke.) "Well, I mean. My best friend isn't talking to me, and I had to block my mom on my phone." Which she'd done after her mother's freak-out over the news about James. She probably couldn't keep her mother blocked forever, but it was sure nice for the moment.

"We all come with issues, I guess."

She waited, because this wasn't quite the response she wanted, but he didn't elaborate.

"All right," she said after an impatient pause. "Tell me more. Where did you go to college?" She knew he'd grown up in Oregon. They'd gone over limited origin questions their first fun week together.

"University of Oregon. Undergraduate in finance. Graduate degree in, again, finance. You?"

"Mmm, *master's* degree, okay." She said it like he was a smarty-pants, which she already knew he was. "I went to Sonoma State and got a degree in business administration, which propelled me to a thrilling life of project management."

"College, check. Siblings? You already told me you have a brother. I have two, and they are both awful."

"I bet they say the same about you."

"They would never. They worship me." He laughed, and she was reminded how much she liked it when he was delighted.

"Are you the favorite?" she asked.

"By far. If you ever meet them, you'll see why."

It was said so casually, but it suggested that they might have a future in which meeting family happened. Amelia felt her face heat. She couldn't even begin to think it.

"Okay." She clapped her hands to punctuate those thoughts.

"I'll get some plants in here, and maybe we can look for a nice picture over the dresser."

"That would be nice." He picked up his bag and began unpacking. As he did before, he turned out debris from his pockets onto the small dresser.

"How do you fit all that in your pockets?" she asked.

He gave her a wink, as though to say it was a mystery, and walked into the little bathroom, putting his toiletries in the medicine cabinet. She stared at the pile of treasures—maybe *treasure* was too strong a word, since it seemed to be trash too—and tried to ignore the feeling deep down that was creeping up no matter how much she tried to suppress it. It was cute. The pocket mess was cute. But cute pocket flotsam did not make for a good marriage. She was tempted to ask her mother whether she found her father's habits cute when they began their marriage. Somehow she thought not, because she couldn't imagine a time when her mother admired anything of her father's, but it must have happened. And look how they had turned out. Anyway, asking would require talking to her mother, and that was a no-go.

She did her best to tamp down the affection over the pocket junk and went out to the reception area. There was work to do, and mooning over inconsequential things like that would not do either of them any favors.

As soon as she got into bed that night, Amelia knew this bed-sharing thing was a bad idea. It was the closeness and warmth of him. The depression of his body on the mattress. He was too *near*.

James must have been thinking the same thing because they both lay still, not moving as though afraid of illicit skin grazing. How far they'd come since the wedding. Sometimes when she thought about that lunch, about climbing into his lap and how aroused she'd been, she felt her stomach tighten with excitement. Thoughts like that would upset the delicate equilibrium of their friendship now.

How easy would it be to reach out a hand? Or a leg? What if they committed to being partners in running the hotel during the day and bed partners at night? No, that was insane. (What was insane was lying next to her accidental husband in bed at a hotel she accidentally owned.) The problem was that James was undeniably handsome and she liked his face. And his body. And he was nice, and she liked that too. And he made her laugh. Damn it.

"Why aren't you sleeping?" he asked into the dark.

"How do you know I'm not sleeping?"

"You answered me, for one."

She gave a fake snore. He laughed.

"Because. It's weird sleeping in a bed with you," she said.

"I know."

"We were ready to absolutely get it on the day of the wedding." She held her breath in case she'd gone too far, opened the floodgates by even saying the words.

"True. But we didn't know we'd be in this situation then."

What was that supposed to mean? She stared into the dark, wondering what to say. "Can we do this? Sharing a bed? Living in here together?"

"I think we can. Are you suggesting you're finding it difficult not to ravage me?"

Her eyes went wide in the dark. *Yes.* Yes, she was suggesting that. She wanted to cross the imaginary divide and wrap her arms around his neck, breathe in his scent (which was an entrancing elixir, so male and delicious). She wanted to be on top of him; she wanted to straddle him and feel every inch of his skin against hers.

Slow down, Amelia. Think.

Wait—was he fishing? Was he hoping for a yes? He was so hot and cold—one minute brushing against her or holding her eyes, the next turning away quickly like he'd caught himself out. Having sex would bring problems, no matter what nonsense Birgitte said. They weren't going to be together in a few months.

"I can practically hear the internal struggle right now," he said with a laugh.

She laughed too, relieved. "You're lovely, James. You know I think so. But I don't want to ruin what could possibly be a great partnership here."

"Oh, I agree. I think we've done a great job of being friends."

"And a superb job of talking it through like adults."

"Absolutely." He sounded like he was in a corporate meeting: decisive, pleasant, professional. "And as long as we don't go any further, this isn't a real marriage."

"What do you mean?"

"Not consummating it."

"Oh, right. Yes." She felt annoyed. Was he worried about this being a real marriage? Of course he was. And she should be too.

Yes, she was. Right. Even with that logic in front of her, she still wanted to feel his arm over her middle, cuddling her, wrapping her against him. "Are we dumb to think this could work?"

"Which part?"

"All of this." She stared at the wan moonlight through the half-shut slats of the shutters.

"I think we can do it. Sleeping in the same bed is honestly my biggest hurdle right now."

Shit. She wished he hadn't said that. A thrill zipped along her spine. He was fighting off attraction too.

"We're going to have to be careful," she said. She did not want to be careful.

"We can be careful."

She was probably overthinking this. Birgitte would certainly agree. Her time in Europe was the first time she'd let loose and slept with random people, but even then, she'd spent a fair amount of time with each of her lovers. Sometimes she tried to picture herself as a free hippy-style chick who wore flowing dresses and rarely had shoes on and got her pleasure where she could.

But she was not that person, as much as she wanted to be. One thing she had learned throughout her travels was that even though she had escaped things at home, she was still Amelia. She was someone who wanted to know her lovers and laugh and be adored by them.

The sound of deeper breaths, and then light snores, came from his side of the bed. He'd gotten over the temptation quickly enough then. She tried to push herself toward sleep, but she was too attuned to any slight movement from his side of the bed.

And when she woke up sometime later, 4:00 a.m. according to her little travel LED clock, he was up against her, spooning.

She didn't move an inch.

Cautiously, she put a hand over the top of his, featherlight, alert for any movement on his part. But he was out. She reveled in the warmth of him against her back, the solidness of him. She chanced moving her hand over his, feeling the muscles beneath his hand and forearm. Here, she could admit that she wanted him. For this moment, in this bed. It made no sense for them to pursue things, and it would assuredly be messy, but this moment was bliss.

CHAPTER 12

The olive trees had begun to produce emerald-green fruit, shiny and plump. It was the start of August, and Amelia drove to the town for supplies. Going to town was almost a twice-weekly trip now, given the number of guests. Vendors and shopkeepers presented her with trinkets and blankets and rugs, eager to contribute to the Ria's makeover. They offered her strange pieces of materials that looked like scrap, because word had gone round that Amelia wanted pieces of trash—which was not quite what she'd told Kostas originally, but it had worked out. She was slowly morphing the rooms into spaces people living in today's time might actually want to stay in. And she and James were getting better at making food too. They had a regular fishmonger in addition to the daily bread delivery, and often the butcher Markos came up the hotel to deliver.

Her first stop was always to cross the *plateia* to say hello to Kostas.

"Ah, Ameliaoula!" Kostas yelled. "Please, come, sit." He brought her a seltzer and sat with her. He lit a cigarette and blew the smoke out with his face turned away. It was gross, but he managed to make it look sultry. "I hear you are able to pay people for supplies. You see? I say it will work, and it works."

"It is starting to work." Amelia couldn't agree it was a huge success yet. "We're giving people work, and we may be able to make a payment to Magda and Yorgos."

"*Kala*," Kostas said in a kind of growl. "Stavros, the developer? He called. He asked me about you."

Amelia had almost forgotten about him in the melee of guests and fixing up rooms and playing house with James. "What did he say?"

"He said he is still interested in speaking." Kostas shrugged like it was no big deal.

"I think we are," she said, but she wasn't sure. They were making this work, but *this* was still temporary.

Kostas waved a hand. "You can think about it. And you and James? You have fallen in love now?"

She smiled. He was fishing. He did this in some variation every time she saw him. "As I said the last time you asked, we're friends. And as I *also* said the last time, no, I am not interested in taking a lover."

Kostas did his Greek *eh* shrug. "Friends are boring, yes? Someday you will decide this, and you will think of me."

She rolled her eyes.

He laughed, apparently unoffended by her eye-rolling. He was never a jerk about being rebuffed, which was one of the things she liked about him. "Ameliaoula, I have a favor to ask. My sister is coming from Athens on the ferry today. She will have many bags.

Can you please to pick her up? I only have a moped, and you have a car."

Amelia couldn't say no after everything Kostas had done for them, and since this wasn't, for once, sexual in nature, she felt comfortable saying yes. "I'm happy to."

"I think you are very alike. You will get along. She speaks English very good, although your Greek is not as bad as it was. She is maybe a good friend for you."

That was sly of him, Amelia thought. She had mentioned once a few weeks ago that one of her concerns about staying on Asteri was that she lacked girlfriends, apart from Birgitte. Amelia tried to chat with Katarina every morning when she made a bread delivery, and she always made sure to visit Eleni in the Traditional Olive Shop. But the language barrier was fierce, and both Eleni and Katarina seemed overly shy. Kostas had explained that this was due to the still-present patriarchal island culture where women were not supposed to be seen or heard out and about until they were married, and after that, their primary concern must be their families. Based on the bright smiles and nods she and Eleni and Katarina exchanged, Amelia didn't think this was entirely true. These women were perfectly capable of having friendships, but she lacked the Greek to crack the outer shell and find out.

"I'm happy to meet her," Amelia said. "Oh—before I forget, I wanted to ask you about bathrooms. Some of our rooms have some seriously crumbling plumbing. We got marked down on Tripadvisor because of it. Can you recommend some builders or contractors who can help us?"

"Of course, Ameliaoula. I send Yorgos up tomorrow, okay?"

"Which Yorgos?" she asked in alarm. "Mover Yorgos? Feta Yorgos?"

"Plumber Yorgos. You know him."

"Do you think he'll work first and be paid later?" she asked, knowing the answer was yes. These people put so much trust in her and James not to screw them over.

"For you, anything." Kostas grinned as though legends of Amelia had been told far and wide.

"*Efcharisto poli.*" She stood, accepting his double-cheek kiss, escaped his attempt to leave his lips on her cheek longer than a half second, and headed over to the Traditional Olive Shop, where an assortment of capers, jarred grape leaves, olives, every imaginable olive oil derivative, and handcrafted copper trinket plates and bowls were on offer. She and James had come up with the idea to offer a cheese and wine hour on the restaurant veranda for an extra fee, and it had been incredibly popular. *The wine hour on the top level at sunset was truly divine,* one guest wrote on Tripadvisor. *Owners James and Amelia made us feel like celebrities.* Amelia was especially pleased about that review because she had spilled a dish of olives in that guest's lap. It wasn't the first time she had dumped olives in a guest's lap, which was perhaps not a great track record given it had only been three weeks since they'd become really busy.

She paid for the olives and chatted with Eleni in their limited way, which involved much nodding and smiling and gesturing, but with the understanding that both of them liked each other and wanted to be friends. She went back out to the *plateia*, feeling good, closing her eyes a moment to bask in the sunshine and the moderate breeze that was strong enough to whisk away the unpleasant edge of the day's heat. It might have made for a choppy ferry trip though. She got into Takis's little car and headed down the windy switchback road to the port as the ferry was docking.

Leaning against the car as she waited, she eyed the ferry struggling to line up with the little dock in the waves. At last, a stream of islanders got off, including a young woman with a long magnificent cape of dark hair, carrying four unwieldy bags and almost falling into the water. Who, even at this distance, looked strikingly familiar.

She looked like Ella.

It was her posture and the way she marched down the ramp as though she'd done it five thousand times before. Amelia squinted. It couldn't possibly be. Her chest seized. It was somewhere in her throat. Her heart began to race. Her body was obviously saying it was Ella.

Amelia called, "Ells?"

Ella did not respond. As she came closer, Amelia felt foolish. This was not Ella. Not even remotely. Ella was Chinese, and this woman was not. But her posture was like Ella's, and the hair was the same. As the woman approached, Amelia could see a slight resemblance to Kostas. Amelia didn't know how she could have mistaken her for Ella. That was some serious nonsense her eyeballs had played on her.

"You must be Kostas's sister," Amelia said, trying to cover her still-racing heart.

"Yes! I am Alexandra," the woman declared proudly. She looked around Amelia's age, dressed in a tank top with spaghetti straps and short shorts. Her gorgeous long hair was straight and glossy. Amelia's own red hair was a frizzy nightmare of curls that could only be tamed by keeping it short and in a ponytail. "*Yasoo*, you must be Amelia." She shook Amelia's hand. "Kostas talked a lot about you. It is nice to meet you, nice to have someone on the island to speak English with who is not Birgitte or my tiresome brother."

Amelia laughed before she could stop herself. "It's nice to meet you too."

"I hear you have taken the Ria Hotel," Alexandra said. "That is amazing. I say before that Takis should sell."

"Guess he was waiting for the right people."

"I think maybe he find them! Okay! I pile bags in." Alexandra opened the small car's trunk and shoved her luggage in.

As soon as they started up the switchback road, Alexandra began talking.

"No need to take me to the town. I do not want to see my parents. You can drop me off at Birgitte's. Anyway, it is on the way to the Ria, yes? I am so glad to be back. Ah." Alexandra dropped her head against the headrest dramatically. "My parents named me after one of the greatest kings of all time, Alexander the Great, and yet I have not pleased them by getting married and having lots and lots of babies. My mother wears black when I visit." She pealed with laughter. "Kostas said you are mare?"

"What?" Amelia glanced at her.

"Married." Alexandra floated her bare arm out of the car window in the breeze. "I like to save time from saying the whole word. I want to know these things because I am a very good matchmaker. The whole island comes to me for matches. Kostas says your husband is very nice but that you married him too fast?"

"I'd say it's more of a partnership than a marriage."

"Ach." Alexandra laughed. "Well, don't run to my brother's bed. I would not match you with him. You are too nice. He wants you, of course. He has already said as much."

Amelia made a face. "I know. Not interested."

Alexandra gave a huge infectious laugh. "You have not fallen for his charms. I like you! It is nice to have another English speaker here. I like to speak it every chance. My oldest brother, Spiro, was Birgitte's husband. Is she still as awf as ever?"

"Awful? Yes. But Birgitte has her helpful moments."

Alexandra slid a sly glance at Amelia. "You must take a heap of the bad with the good, eh? I like to see Birgitte because her house is very beautiful and because even though *I* am the matchmaker here, my parents will want to introduce me to young men in town. I introduced Spiro to Birgitte, you know, many years ago. I was a little girl and my brother was fifteen years older than me, but even then I had the gift. Anyway, Birgitte is Birgitte."

"Birgitte is definitely Birgitte." She and Alexandra exchanged a look of understanding.

"There is nothing like driving up this road when I am first back to Asteri." Alexandra spoke cheerfully. "It is always full of anticipation. You never know what you will find. Did you know, one year a shepherd's entire flock of pregnant sheep packed this road for days? You could not get around them. They just stayed here, on the road. They blocked everyone from getting through. The sheep mamas had their lambs on the road! We all had to hike through the land to get around them."

Amelia slowed the car as they approached Birgitte's house. The cicadas burst into their heavy drone as soon as she cut the engine. Alexandra got out and extracted her bags from the trunk and slumped them on the ground, then waved. "You are a darling, thank you for the ride! I like you. Kostas was right about that. I come see you at the hotel soon, okay? I want to meet James."

"That would be great." Amelia decided she liked her too. It was hard not to. Alexandra was like a burst of sunlight.

Moments later, Amelia parked in front of the hotel. James came striding out of the small office, looking great doing it with the sun lighting up his face. He seemed so confident here, so in his element. She envied it, because there wasn't a single day that she didn't question whether they'd made a mistake by staying here and giving the islanders hope that the hotel would be a big money-maker and boon for their local economy.

James leaned into the driver's side window. "Bad news. We have an unhappy guest in room twelve. She said she did not care for the, as she put it, 'modern, cheerful decor,' and she says she did not come to Asteri to stay in a place that looked like the pages of a design magazine."

Amelia laughed. "I'll take that as a compliment to my room renovations."

"You should." He pushed off from the car and she got out. They walked into reception together, which was looking pretty modern too, Amelia thought. And they had instituted a welcome wine, where newly arrived guests were ushered to the veranda for the full effect of the stunning view and a retsina. By now, too, they had fallen into a comfortable rhythm where James did the checking in and seeing guests to rooms, and Amelia handled the checkout process and wine and cheese gatherings.

And with the exception of the cranky guest in room twelve, the feedback had been great. It seemed they were finding the sweet spot between luxurious and accessible, offering extra experiences that guests loved but at an affordable rate. Maybe that was why Takis had not been more successful—he'd been trying to cling to the idea of a resort. But their younger professional holiday-goers, especially from around Europe, wanted a fresh, modern vibe without paying a million euro a night for it.

"I picked up Kostas's sister, Alexandra, from the ferry today," Amelia said as they walked to the bar area with the supplies. "She's really nice."

James grinned.

"What?" She tried to hide the pleasure of him smiling at her by unpacking the milk.

"Just you. Making friends."

"Well, yeah." She needed friends if she was going to survive living in a small place.

James kept up that smile, the one that made him look adorable. "That's good. I like to see it."

She didn't know what to say to that. She poured them both a glass of wine, and they went out to the veranda. Rough circles of olive wood served as little side tables next to woven seagrass deck chairs. Birgitte had mysteriously sourced bright orange pillows for the chairs, and the whole setup looked sophisticated and inviting.

She and James didn't usually have time in the afternoons to sit and enjoy the view, so it was nice now that he plopped into one of the chairs next to her.

"Kostas told me he heard from that developer guy, Stavros, again," she said.

His smile disappeared. "Olive Grove Yorgos told me he heard from him too. Sniffing around, trying to see if we might be willing to sell."

Amelia sensed James wasn't pleased. "We should probably hear what he has to say. We have to leave eventually."

James opened his mouth as though to say no, they didn't, but he didn't say it.

"*Yasoo!*"

Amelia and James turned to see Alexandra breezing through the bar.

"I am here!" Alexandra said. She stopped in front of the view. To James, she said, "You must be the James. I am the Alexandra."

James stood and politely cheek-kissed her. "Amelia was just telling me about you. It's so nice to meet you."

"And you. Now this is how to run the Ria Hotel, no?" Alexandra plopped into the chair opposite Amelia and took Amelia's glass of wine for her own.

"Was Birgitte not home?" Amelia asked.

"Oh yes, she was there. I say hi, drop bags, and come here. I wanted to see James and the hotel. Birgitte says both are very handsome. So far, she is right about the hotel."

Amelia snorted. James looked bewildered, but Alexandra shot him a high-wattage smile and he laughed too.

"Birgitte said you are Swedish and handsome, but she did not say you are Alexander Skarsgård," Alexandra said. She nudged Amelia. "Isn't he, Amelia?"

Amelia had to admit there was the barest hint of a vague similarity, if you squinted while doing a headstand. "No?"

James looked a little pink in the face, as though he didn't know how to take any of that.

Alexandra sighed dramatically. "I miss this view. Poor Takis, eh? I heard all about the funeral, and how Magda's new husband Yorgos shouted at you about money." Alexandra waved a dismissive hand. "Ignore him. He is an idiot."

"We want to do the right thing and help with Takis's burial costs," Amelia said.

Alexandra laughed. "I would have been on the next ferry out of here if it were me."

"We considered it," Amelia said.

"But then we started getting bookings and providing work to people here," James said. "It got harder to walk away." He glanced at Amelia with a look she couldn't decipher. "For a lot of reasons."

"Ah." Alexandra nodded gravely at them. "Yes. You stay here permanently now."

"For this season," Amelia corrected.

"What do you do in Athens, Alexandra?" James asked.

"I am between jobs at the moment," Alexandra said. "Whenever that happens, I come home to Asteri. I am a matchmaker here. I make wonderful matches." She shot a knowing smile at Amelia. Her eyeteeth were longer than her other teeth, giving her a slightly wolfish look that complemented the rest of her tousled appearance. "But it is unpaid. Do you need help here at the hotel? I am good at cleaning. I was hotel maid for a while on Naxos."

A hotel maid was the one position they did need to fill, but paying anyone was a challenge. "We need someone who can help strip the beds, wash sheets, and clean rooms. It's a lot of work, and it's fairly gross. You never know what you'll find in a bed."

"And the pay is terrible," James said. "But we can offer you a room to live in and food from our kitchen?"

Alexandra squealed. "I will take anything. After the season I will go back to Athens, so it is summer pocket money. Working here means I don't have to work with my brother Kostas."

"Surely working with your brother is better than changing sheets?" Amelia asked. James shot her a look. She stuck her tongue out at him in case he had ideas of her being jealous. He nudged her with his elbow in a move that might have hurt had he applied any real pressure. She found herself smiling. They were playing. She loved playing with him.

"No, no. My parents want me to be there to attract a husband." Alexandra pretended to spit in disgust. "Sitting there every night, batting my eyelashes. As if I don't know how to match people."

"Well, we could use the help here," Amelia said.

"Done." Alexandra did her impression of a fox who is pleased with herself. "So. Now. Tell me the story. Kostas tell me you married at Magda and Yorgos's wedding."

"We were a little drunk," James said.

Alexandra threw her head back and cackled. "You were only here for a holiday?"

"I was supposed to go home over a month ago," Amelia said.

She peeked to see if James was looking like he might agree with her, but he was staring at the wine bottle, running a thumbnail over it. "I like it here a lot," he said in what she recognized as his careful tone. He used it when he was trying to placate a complaining guest. "We—we've been able to do some amazing things already with the hotel. We're updating it and trying to offer guests different experiences. They seem to love it."

"I see already the transformation," Alexandra said. "Everything was old and ugly. Takis did not update." She wrinkled her nose in distaste but made the sign of the cross over herself, as many people did when mentioning Takis. A passing prayer for his soul, even as they insulted his business practices.

"It's been fun to redo everything," Amelia said. "I can't believe the amazing materials on this island."

"I always think so too," Alexandra said. "Many things to love here. Many artists here. Sometimes I see things in expensive shops in Athens and think, pah, Elena Papachristodoulopoulos makes these blue bowls here on Asteri and sells them for nothing! You know?"

"Yes." Amelia did know. She had been buying those bowls.

"So, you have everything you need." Alexandra spread her arms out wide to the view. "This view, that sea, this wine, good hotel. You have guests! You have each other! Running a hotel on a beautiful Greek island isn't the worst thing to happen to two silly Americans. Didn't Meryl Streep do that in *Mamma Mia*?"

James snorted.

"I hated that movie," Amelia said. "Too much singing. Terrible plot."

"Yeah," said Alexandra, refilling her pilfered wineglass, "but everyone else *loved* it."

———

"Alexandra seems nice," James said as they were getting ready for bed that night. This was a deceptively domestic ritual in which they engaged in a dance of carefully turned backs and excessive politeness about the bathroom. ("After you." "No, after you.") These ablutions were followed by a delicate entry into bed that did not suggest fervor or excitement. It didn't always work. Amelia often snuck peeks. She'd seen him quickly look away several times too.

And he spooned her almost every night. Even if it was unintentional.

"I like her," Amelia agreed. "I thought she was Ella at first, coming off the ferry." Even saying the words hurt, right at the top of her chest. Alexandra had been incredibly helpful over the evening, lending a hand unasked with the sunset wine and cheese service and going to get extra towels for a guest on the second level. "It kind of threw me. My heart was pounding so hard that I believed what my senses were telling me."

"I'm sorry. That would have been great if Ella showed up. She still won't answer your texts?"

"No." Amelia sighed and sat on her side of the bed. "Nothing." The shame still felt appalling, but at least now she could look it in the eye.

James sat next to her. "You can't keep beating yourself up about it. We all have different reactions to pain, right? She wanted her best friend at her wedding, but you had to go. It was a terrible choice. Believe me, I know."

She turned to look at him. "How?"

"After I walked out of my job, I called off my own wedding."

Amelia's mouth fell open. "What? I—I didn't know you were going to get married."

He had the grace to look embarrassed, and she knew it was because he hadn't told her this morsel, this little nugget of interesting intel. "We were engaged. But then my fiancée expressed doubt about us, about me. I called it off. Then I booked this trip."

"Wow." Amelia tried to do the calculations quickly in her head as to how long ago that was. It couldn't have been long. Was he over his fiancée? Why hadn't he told her? Kind of a big thing to keep from your wife, even if she wasn't really his wife. "Joke's on you, I guess, since you're married now anyway."

"Right." A half smile, tinged with sadness.

Worry sparked in her that he wasn't over his fiancée. "Are… are you okay?"

"I'm fine." He got under the covers on his side. "Best decision I could have possibly made. She wasn't fully in it, and I consider myself lucky to have gotten out of something that obviously wasn't right."

"You hear yourself, right?" she asked. "Because you jumped out of the kettle into the fire."

He gave a short humorless laugh. "Yeah. Believe me, I know."

It wasn't quite the answer she wanted, but if he'd protested and said this was the best, most unexpectedly wonderful thing to happen, she'd have questioned that too. She got into her side of the bed—carefully—and turned off her light.

But as his breathing turned into deeper, relaxed sleep breaths, she had to wonder if he considered himself lucky because he was out of a clearly unhappy relationship, or because of her and the Ria Hotel. And whether both things could be true.

And whether she wanted them to be true.

CHAPTER 13

Early September was hot and burnished, the golden fields now a deep brown, but the nights were increasingly crisp. Olive Grove Yorgos told James that they would begin to see a drop-off in bookings.

But tonight, they were having a dinner party.

For the first time, they had friends to dine with: Alexandra, who fit right in at the hotel, Birgitte, Kostas, and Olive Grove Yorgos. Eleni from Traditional Olive Shop and Magda and Angry Yorgos were coming as well. It was a good time to have the dinner, because there was a two-day lull between groups of guests, and tomorrow a large group was due—a couple and their two kids, four French women on a bonding trip, and two half sisters who had discovered each other through a DNA site and were now taking a special trip together.

Amelia cut a swag of fuchsia bougainvillea for the middle of the table and used round woven seagrass place mats. In an old stained box in a high cabinet in the kitchen, she found dusty crystal goblets that had clearly been in vogue in the prior century and were now chic again.

"This looks great," James said, coming out to the veranda with an air of inspection. That he was inspecting at all suggested he was just as excited as she was. The night before, he'd hung a string of lights atop the veranda, which looked so festive that Amelia couldn't believe Takis had never put them up before.

"Thanks."

He stood, hands on his hips, looking too long at the table.

"What?" she asked. "Is something off?"

"Nothing. You've done an incredible job." He had a look on his face, that little smirk he seemed to use only for her. His eyes traveled her body. A flush of goose bumps ran down her legs.

She thought he might turn and escape. He typically did whenever there were awkward moments between them. But he held her eyes. On the rare occasions when this happened, she invariably remembered the entrancing salt patch on his shoulder and how she wanted to lick it, and how if his shirt was off right now, she might not be able to resist licking it, salt patch or no. And that the urge to lick had not, in fact, faded one bit, and she was going to be in danger of losing herself if she continued along these lines.

It was good, then, that Birgitte came yodeling her customary "Yoo-hooo" in a startling imitation of a Sigur Rós song. Amelia snapped out of James's Svengali gaze and went to greet her friend.

Birgitte had made her moussaka. Alexandra had volunteered to show Amelia how to make *koupes*, a Greek meat pie made of bulgur and minced lamb. They also made stuffed bell peppers, filled with lamb and bulgur and tons of feta.

They had a Greek salad, and Kostas brought calamari caught that afternoon. There was mouthwateringly fresh bread. Eleni brought a dessert called halva, a dense, lovely pudding-cake thing made from semolina topped with slivered pistachio nuts and honey, and Magda and Angry Yorgos brought a beautiful platter of *loukoumades*, deep-fried dough balls smothered in hot honey, as well as a huge crate of wine. Amelia didn't think a crate was necessary, but Kostas assured her it was.

Magda told Amelia in Greek, "The hotel looks very nice. Much nicer than before." Her tone was quiet and admiring, and it made Amelia's heart twinge. She couldn't imagine this shy young woman having to watch as they dug up her uncle in a few years.

"I am selling more products this season than any other," Eleni said in Greek. "The Traditional Olive Shop is having a good year, thanks to James and Amelia!" She held up her glass, which obliged everyone to stop and yell, "*Yamas!*"

"Congratulations to Ameliaoula and James for making Ria Hotel successful!" Kostas called, signaling another toast.

"We couldn't have done it without your support," James said in English, which Alexandra translated for him for the benefit of Eleni and Magda. "Amelia and I are grateful for the help we've received from all of you." He put his glass down and his pinky finger brushed Amelia's hand. A shiver ran up her arm. Had he meant to touch her?

"We are still waiting for the burial money," Angry Yorgos growled. Birgitte passed him a glass of wine and motioned for him to drink up. Amelia was worried he would spoil the vibe, but no one seemed to pay him any mind, including his wife.

"Eh, Eleni," Alexandra called in Greek. "Any husband yet? I will fix you up."

Eleni let loose a stream of scolding Greek, which was the correct answer.

"I see Eleni looking at Fisherman Yorgos," Kostas said.

Eleni must have understood, because she turned beet red, which was a sure giveaway.

"*Ela*," Alexandra said. "I will fix it."

"*Ohi! Ohi! No!*"

"Fisherman Yorgos already loves you. I saw him look in your direction in the *plateia*."

"You eat him tomorrow," Amelia told Eleni in her terrible Greek. Everyone dissolved into howls of laughter.

"Never mind," Alexandra said. "Consider it done. I'm good at this." She looked at Amelia and James. "What about you two? Papas Valopoulos wants to bless your wedding rings, I hear."

James gave Amelia an amused smirk. She wasn't sure how to take it. At least he didn't look as embarrassed as he usually did when their marriage was mentioned.

"Can't. We have no rings," she said.

"You still don't have rings?" Angry Yorgos yelled. "It is a sin to remain here without them. Get Greek gold. Of course, you cannot pay for them because first you must pay for Takis grave."

"Oh, would you stick a cork in it," Birgitte said. "No one's going to dig Takis up. The only reason anyone wants Amelia and James to get blessed is so they can throw a party and roast a lamb, and you know it."

James leaned back in his chair, a picture of relaxation. *Aragma*, they called it; Amelia loved how the Greeks had words for that state of being. "Everyone likes a feast."

"I agree," Olive Grove Yorgos said in his quiet, serious voice. "A feast makes everyone happy."

"So?" Angry Yorgos made several wild gestures. "You get blessed, then. Since you stay here, you must do this."

"We've always been clear that we won't be here after this season," Amelia said. She didn't like to remind their friends of this, as evidenced by Alexandra's immediate frown in response, but there was no point pretending.

"We will have no more of this talk of leaving," Birgitte said firmly. "Amelia and James, you belong here now." She held up her glass. Amelia's glass was empty, so James filled it from a bottle that was going around. Everyone toasted and yelled, "*Yamas!*" Amelia took a giant swig of her drink, and then spluttered into coughing and choking.

James patted her on the back, laughing. "All right there?"

"What is that?" Amelia pointed at the bottle. "That's evil stuff. Reminds me of what Takis served us."

"Eh, I brought it," Angry Yorgos yelled. "My father makes it."

Amelia vowed not to take another sip. She didn't want to repeat the hedonism of their early weeks here when they'd done all the damage.

The party surged all around her. There was laughter and more food and storytelling. Birgitte told the story of how a nine-year-old Alexandra saw Birgitte in the *hora* one afternoon and grabbed her hand, pulling.

"She forced me to come meet her older brother Spiro, who was home for the week from his job on Crete where he had a shipping

business. She was determined that she had found him a wife."
Birgitte sent Alexandra a fond look. "She was right."

"I always know," Alexandra said, laughing. "I matched Magda
and Yorgos last summer."

Amelia was careful to avoid James's eye during this matching
talk, which was a sure sign she was tipsy. Kostas began to refill her
glass as part of the never-ending passing of dishes and bottles, but
she held up a hand.

"Had enough," she mouthed.

"You can never have enough," Kostas said in a sexy growl that
made it clear he was saying something else.

James cleared his throat loudly and passed Amelia the water
pitcher.

"I was thinking we should have a picnic," Birgitte said. "A
women's-only picnic."

"That's not fair," Olive Grove Yorgos said quietly.

"You can be an honorary woman," Birgitte told him. "It's a
generous offer."

"Then we all go," Kostas said. "Eh?" He sent James a raised eyebrow.

"Sure." James sounded uptight, the way he got around Kostas.
Amelia, definitely feeling a little tipsy now, tried to kick him lightly
under the table but ended up rubbing her ankle on his calf.

In response, he gently pressed his whole leg against hers.

Wow, that felt good. Every nerve in her body seemed to tingle.

"It will be a mysterious picnic," Birgitte was saying.

"Mystery picnic!" Alexandra whooped. "Yes."

"When?" Amelia asked, trying to sound normal. All of her

senses—her entire being—were focused on the warm pressure of James's leg. What the hell was happening? Was he doing this because Kostas was flirting with her? Whatever, she was relaxed, and it felt good. Really good.

"I won't tell you when the picnic is," Birgitte said. "I will simply appear."

"What if we're busy with guests?" James asked, as though he weren't doing things under the table.

"Oh, don't worry," Birgitte said with an air of knowing. "I will come when you aren't busy."

"We hope you are always busy though," Eleni said. "Now the Ria Hotel is a primary employer on Asteri. All the cafes have more demand from more tourists. Agnes Faragolis is putting her beehive honey in little bottles and selling them in my shop. Everyone wants to take a souvenir, so now people make them. I hear that Kiln Yorgos is making photo frames with *Asteri* written on them. It is nice, yes? Everyone benefits."

"And if the hotel goes away...so does everything else," Amelia said, thinking aloud.

Birgitte shrugged. "This is why you do not get drunk and get married and take hotels."

"Oh Birgitte," Alexandra said in a scolding voice. "Do not be so...nose in the air. They have already done more than Takis did."

"I know this. It is as good as when my Spiro was alive," Birgitte said, her voice wavering a bit. It was the wine. An incredible number of empty bottles littered the table—possibly the whole crate Angry Yorgos had brought.

"It was very sad," Alexandra said. "The whole island mourned not only my brother, but also their love."

"The best love story there ever was," Birgitte said. "Ever."

"That is the love I want," Alexandra said. She gave Amelia a side-eye. "And possibly, what you have here."

Amelia widened her eyes at her and shook her head, trying to tell her to zip it. But James applied gentle pressure to her leg again, and she stiffened. What did that mean? Was he telling her he loved her? That was too much—that was too large a thing. Especially to say with leg pressure.

"Amelia, have you figured out the broken part of James?" Birgitte called.

James gave Amelia a look. "What broken part?"

"Nothing," she said, sounding unconvincing even to herself.

"What is this broken part?" Olive Grove Yorgos asked.

"Well," Birgitte said, looking like she was settling into a story. "I told Amelia that everyone is a little broken, and she must figure out how James is broken."

"I'm not broken," James laughed. "And I'm right here, you know."

"Of course," Birgitte went on, ignoring him, "I was willing to believe you are not broken because you are Swedish, and Swedes are typically unbroken. I am brokenhearted because of my Spiro dying. Alexandra here is broken because she is not married—"

"I don't *want* to be married," Alexandra protested.

"And Kostas is broken," Birgitte continued, "because he wants love but cannot stop being a lover." She sent him a triumphant look. To his credit, he merely shrugged. No denial from him.

"As far as I know, I'm not broken," James said.

"Neither am I." Angry Yorgos banged the table.

"You are broken into angry pieces," Birgitte told him. "We are all broken. Amelia, you run away from things. And you—" She pointed at Olive Grove Yorgos. "You will not commit to anyone."

"I don't run away," Amelia said, even though she fully knew she did, and Olive Grove Yorgos said, "I commit to my trees."

"This is ridiculous, Birgitte," James said. "What you call broken is just being an imperfect human."

Amelia applied pressure to James's leg to show him she agreed. She used her whole leg, sending shivers up her spine.

"Yes," Birgitte said, seeming to run out of steam. She sagged a little over her empty plate. "Yes. We are all imperfect humans."

"It may be time to head home," Olive Grove Yorgos suggested in that soft way of his.

There was a murmur of agreement, perhaps because the dinner had been long and satisfying, perhaps because an entire crate of wine had been drunk, or maybe because Birgitte was getting a little too real.

With regret, Amelia left the scintillating touch of James's leg and helped people get themselves together, assisting with dishes and boxes and bags.

"We will have a dinner," Angry Yorgos shouted in English. "Soon. Magda will make a lamb."

Magda slapped his arm and made him translate, and then slapped him again when she heard she'd be cooking. But in Greek, translated by Alexandra, she told James and Amelia that she would be happy to host them.

As the last of their guests departed—Birgitte being helped down the road by Olive Grove Yorgos, both of them weaving across the road and singing.

"Are they going to be okay?" Amelia asked James.

James snorted. "I don't think it's the first time either of them has stumbled down a dark road at night."

Amelia breathed the perfect night air deep into her lungs, looking up at the incredible array of stars in the sky, bright even with the moon at three-quarters full. The idea of running in and clearing the table wasn't appealing, so she breathed in deep again. She felt contentment from their friends and the evening. She had never sat around and blathered with friends over a leisurely meal before like this, where the feeling was one of relaxed enjoyment rather than eat and run, as her friends tended to do in San Francisco. There was something else too. The contentment of having James to sit next to, to partner with. Even if they weren't lovers—no matter what the leg rubbing was about—it felt right sitting next to him. It felt…well…something deep that she wasn't willing to admit to herself. She swayed a little, cocooned in the feeling of happiness, eyes unfocused at the moon.

"Waxing gibbous," she said, more to herself.

"What's that?" James asked.

"The moon. I think that's what you call it when it's almost full."

She became very aware of how close James was, standing there with mussed hair and glowing in the moonlight.

"Amelia," he said, a tad too softly and with the hint of a question.

Desire surged through her, setting her lower belly on fire. Was this inevitable? It was insane, thinking they could pretend to go on as they were without admitting they wanted each other. She let the wine remove the objections that a sober Amelia would have, and she went for it, wrapping her arms around his neck. The comfort of being held by him made her soul sing.

His lips met hers with a speed that said he'd been wanting this too. Their mouths opened, searching, and she let herself feel his face and touch his neck, giving in to the things she'd wanted to do for months.

He breathed in, pulling her tight to him, and it seemed the under-the-table leg hanky-panky had been a prelude to the desire that was crashing over them now. His hands found their way to her butt, then back up her sides and to her breasts. She arched her back to give him full access. He slid a hand under her blouse and under her bra cup to find a nipple, running a rough thumb over it and making her gasp into his mouth. She wrapped a leg around his as their mouths got hungrier. She was ready to do it out here in the driveway circle if need be. In fact, she reached for his shorts, running a hand over him, and he breathed deep into her in response.

"Do you have any idea…?" he whispered, working her skirt down her legs. It was all happening so fast. They raced to get their clothes off, desperate to find more skin. With her skirt off, he grabbed her butt and pulled her to him. "Holy mother of—are you wearing a *thong?*"

"Yeah." She laughed into his mouth. His hands explored the skimpy material. She wanted him inside her, needed to get his shorts off, and was about to slide them down when a scream came from the front door.

"*Oh*, oh my God, I'm so sorry!" Alexandra squealed.

Amelia and James sprang apart. Alexandra's mouth was an O of shock, which was understandable given that Amelia was standing skirtless in the driveway of the hotel. "I am sorry! I go inside now!" She turned and scurried inside.

The shock of being interrupted stunned Amelia. She looked at James. "I—"

"We—" He sighed like someone who'd just woken up. "I'm—I don't know what to say."

"How about if you suggest we go inside to bed?"

He gave a half smile, but it wasn't saucy or flirty. "Believe me. I would like nothing more than to do that. *Nothing* more. But I don't...We agreed not to consummate this, and I...It's complicated."

"I know we agreed that," she said, accepting her bunched skirt from him. She was suddenly aware of the cool night air on her rear. "But that was before—I mean. I was into it."

"It's complicated," he said again, running a stress hand through his hair.

"What's complicated though? We're here. We're single. I mean, apart from being married to each other." She gave a short laugh. "I think it's pretty obvious—"

"Amelia." To his credit, he looked like he was regretting his words. "If we do this, it's going to mess everything up."

"What is there to mess up?" She stopped, because the last thing she wanted to do was try to convince someone to sleep with her when they didn't want to. Obviously. There was some reason he didn't want to go forward, and pushing would only make things worse. "Yeah. You're right. I'm sorry."

"Don't be." He gave her that hungry look again, and for a moment she thought he would kiss her, and that would be it—they'd *have* to go inside, and they wouldn't stop this time. The line between stopping and not stopping was as thin as the thong between her butt cheeks. But he turned away and went inside, leaving her standing by herself on the driveway, bewildered and frustrated under the stars.

CHAPTER 14

James never came to bed.

It was just as well, Amelia thought the next morning. She was pretty sure that if he had come to bed, it would have been *on*.

He must have slept in one of the small rooms on the fourth level, where Alexandra had her room. Amelia felt unreasonably jealous of this, even though the James she knew (and the Alexandra she knew, for that matter) would not jump someone else's bones simply because he was horny. Maybe, she tried not to think, this unreasonable and obvious manic jealousy was what James felt when Kostas was around.

Being rejected hurt. She tried to tell herself that it wasn't personal, that it wasn't *her* but the *situation* he was rejecting, but it was difficult to believe it, especially as the day went on.

Since there were no guests until later in the afternoon, Amelia used the morning to do busywork, zipping around so that she was never in one place long. James appeared to employ the same strategy, giving her a bland smile in passing, never stopping to talk.

Late in the afternoon, Amelia went down to the fourth level

to drop some towels in the laundry. She looked at the doors to the small rooms, wondering which one James had taken, wondering if she had the guts to open the doors and peek. She pictured him coming upon her snooping and quickly closing the door behind them and kissing her again. This time, the bed would be right there (the rooms weren't much bigger than a cell) and they would not stop.

She fanned herself a bit. *Get a grip, Lang.*

"Amelia," Alexandra called from the bottom step. "I know you are not thinking about which room James took last night, eh?"

A furious blush exploded on Amelia's face. "No."

Alexandra *tsk*ed. "I am very sorry to have interrupted you last night. Then I was annoyed when I saw him come down here and go into a room because I knew he was avoiding you! I was going to bang on his door and yell at him, but I hope he comes to his senses on his own. Anyway, come down to the cove below with me now. We can swim and sun ourselves, and you can tell me what happened."

"I think you saw what happened," Amelia muttered, but she agreed to go get her bathing suit and meet Alexandra back on the fourth level in a few minutes. They were between chores, and she could definitely use the time down on the beach to wrap her head around what had happened.

"What I want to know," Alexandra said moments later, as they navigated the steep trail to the cove, "is how have you and James not had sex before this? You broke apart last night like two peeps who have not yet done it. If you had, you would have had the sense to go inside."

"We've been trying to run the hotel as friends and business partners only. We didn't want to consummate a marriage if we were only going to leave the island."

"And *are* you leaving the island?" Alexandra sent her a thoughtful look.

"We can't stay here at the hotel forever. You know that. We have lives and plans to get back to. It just seemed easier to friend-zone each other. Less chance of entangling ourselves that way."

"Okay, sure." Alexandra didn't sound convinced.

"We only knew each other a little over a week before getting married, and neither of us wants to pretend this is something that could work based on a week, you know? And James has his heart set on running an olive grove at home." An ache twinged somewhere deep in Amelia's chest, as it did every time she thought of James running his olive grove. Why not here? In literal olive grove country? Why not…? She didn't even know what, couldn't articulate the thought.

Alexandra gave the Greek shrug. "I do not know if you know this, but you are already those two things, the love and the partner. He loves to help you."

Amelia thought about how she and Alexandra had gone to Birgitte's one evening to have wine and snacks. Alexandra and Birgitte had teased her when she said she needed to get back to help James with the evening service. It was undeniably true that when she got back to the hotel and James had greeted her with the information that there was a "bit of a mess in room eighteen" that she didn't bat an eye, not even when it transpired that the mess was barf from an eleven-year-old who was apparently allergic to shellfish.

Amelia had gone to the closet where they kept the Gross Spills Kit and pulled on gloves. She and James had lifted the bucket and mop and other supplies down the stairs to the lower level. Not once had she considered what she'd left behind at Birgitte's house.

Instead, she had snapped on her gloves and prepared to be horrified. "All right. Let's do this."

"We might not smell the same afterward."

"I accept the consequences."

"We'll have to flip a coin to see who showers first."

She laughed. "Open the door, James."

He did and they went in. She was still smiling behind her mask. They went to work (and it was bad).

"I like that you were having wine with Birgitte and Alexandra," he said, as though they were strolling through a park with umbrellas on their arms and not sopping up vomit. "I like that you're making friends."

He pulled the bucket of dirty water into the bathroom and dumped it, something she appreciated because she would have hated to do that. He often took the nastiest parts of the job. Maybe it *was* a little weird that she'd prefer cleaning barf with James to sitting in Birgitte's Eighth Wonder of the World courtyard. But Amelia hadn't missed being at Birgitte's at all.

"We have a good working relationship," she told Alexandra now. "It's a partnership. He does a lot of the heavy lifting, but I run to town and pick up supplies because he hates driving Takis's little car. It's too small for him. And that's how we work. We each have things we like to do, and we compromise on the other stuff."

Amelia felt proud of this, and was glad Alexandra was commenting on it, because she wanted someone to notice how well it was going.

"Sure." They were at the cove now, stepping off the trail and around the huge boulder to the small strip of beach. Alexandra put her bag down and removed her top. Amelia was not innocent to the bare-breasted preferences on European beaches, but she hadn't yet adopted the custom.

"Ah," Alexandra said, stretching out. "This is so nice. Asteri is much better than some of the other islands. I never could see why more people didn't figure that out. Even the smell of Asteri is nicer."

"The smell?"

"It stinks of sulfur on Milos and Nisyros. Too much volcano. I like to smell the oregano along the road to the Ria Hotel, and every time I go to my brother's taverna I smell anise, in the ouzo, you know, and I think that I am home."

Amelia had not been in Greece long enough to develop a fondness for the scents and tastes, but she knew about the sounds. "I like the tinkle of sheep bells and the ring of church bells. Maybe it's the lack of cars and buses and airplanes." When she left, she would miss those things.

"Ah, we have Wi-Fi, that's important." Alexandra laughed and patted her phone. "We would all still be sheep farmers without that. Did you know Birgitte campaigned to get Wi-Fi on the island? She showed how younger people are leaving Asteri and going to bigger islands or Athens for jobs, and we had to move with the times."

"Wow." Amelia had not known that. She wondered if she stayed longer whether she, too, might contribute to Asteri in a permanent way.

"There is a special flavor here too," Alexandra said. "Each island has its own, but I love Asteri best. On Santorini you must eat *tomatokeftedes*, because the tomatoes there are grown in the volcanic soil and taste special. Here our olives are sweet, and our honey is spicy with thyme." She lifted her sunglasses and peered at Amelia. "I am sorry to have interrupted last night. You shouldn't have stopped because of me. You are too uptight. I mean this in a nice way."

Amelia gave a loose shrug, trying to show that she wasn't uptight even while knowing Alexandra was right. "I tried to chip away at being uptight over my travels, but I'm nearing on six months in Europe, and I still can't take my top off down here." Apart from that time she'd gone naked and James found her. And last night about to have sex in the driveway.

"Do what is comfortable. But if I were you, I'd take your top off."

Amelia didn't need anyone telling her how to feel, but Alexandra wasn't wrong. She reached around and peeled off her bikini top. It felt weird, and then not weird.

"Good!" Alexandra laughed, lying back on the rocks again. "Next step is have sex with James."

Amelia laughed.

"It is inevitable," Alexandra said. "Someday he will want kids. Or you will. Or you will simply want some afternoon sex. I know these things, because I am good at matching people."

"Yes, but it isn't forever, remember? We're leaving in November, so there's no point getting involved with each other. Anyway, how about you? How's that husband hunt of yours coming?"

"Okay, yes, yes, you are sounding like my mother, sure. But not finding the right man is a different problem than not sleeping with your husband, especially when you like each other."

Amelia sighed. "You are incorrigible."

"What does this mean?"

"Stubborn without stopping."

"Oh yes, I am that." Alexandra laughed. "I am only twenty-six. Plenty of time to find a husband. I have not liked any of the prospects so far. But back to you. You had a boyfriend before you came to Greece?"

"I did, but he was inconsequential." She told Alexandra about throwing the mug at Micah.

Alexandra thought it was hilarious. "I love this image of you throwing a mug at this *malaka's* head!"

"It got me fired, but it sparked this trip." Amelia cracked a smile—the first ever on this subject.

"This is a fiery Amelia I am hearing about. Like last night."

"What do you mean?"

"Last night, you let it all go with James. You moved on."

Amelia had not thought of it that way. She had trouble thinking about it at all without the cloud of desire. "I had moved on before last night, but I see what you mean. I moved on overall."

Alexandra laughed, the sound echoing off the giant boulders that formed the beach. "You married him! You are married now! And it is obvious, Ameliaoula, you are in love."

This was so exactly the type of thing Ella would say to her, in exactly the same tone, that Amelia's heart seized with grief. Alexandra was fun and blunt and delivered her truths in a way that was loving—exactly like Ella.

"Being attracted to him isn't the same as being in love," Amelia pointed out.

"I think you will find love is there too." Alexandra made a dismissive *tsk* sound. "You like being around each other. You like talking. You are friends. It is a good foundation."

"Anyway," Amelia said. "I was thinking: Are you up for helping with some of the Ria's social media accounts?"

"You know how I know James is in love with you?"

Amelia laughed at her refusal to allow the subject change.

"Because he does not look at me," Alexandra said. "I do not mean to sound bad, but men look at me. That is why my parents want me to sit in my brother's bar and get a husband. I do not have to do anything and men look. When I wave, I have a boyfriend. When I raise a finger, I have a lover. But your James does not look. Never once."

"Maybe he's asexual." A patently false statement.

"He looks at *you* that way."

"Okay. Can we not talk about this?"

Alexandra shrugged and got up, picking off small black pebbles that had stuck to her skin. She stepped into the water, kicking sprays of water up with her feet.

"He didn't look at you at *all?*" Amelia asked. "Maybe you didn't see it."

"A woman sees it when a man gives her a once-over."

This was true. "Maybe he's just being polite."

"We can talk about this, or you can pretend you do not want to talk about it."

Amelia studied her cuticles.

"Your idiot boyfriend in San Francisco wasn't right, and the men you found in Spain and Italy were not right. But now you have found your guy, and you freak out because it is not the way you thought it would be. He looks at you not only with lust, Amelia. He looks at you with *attention*. You must come to terms with it soon. And get in the water, by the way. It is *amazing*."

CHAPTER 15

The next load of guests arrived and were dispatched to activities on the island, served breakfast, and given extra towels, and still James did not return to their apartment.

Something, perhaps irrevocably, had shifted. Their relationship was no longer the easygoing hotel partnership. There was a layer of caution between them now, noticeable in the extra care they took not to bump or brush against each other.

And it hurt.

"After you" was said often in an overly formal tone. It was maddening. Amelia's rational brain knew they were never supposed to be a thing. The problem now was that her feelings were confused on the matter.

The following week, at the start of October, Angry Yorgos and Magda made good on their threat to hold a reciprocal dinner party.

James knocked on the apartment door as she was pulling on a blouse. "Okay to come in?"

"You don't have to knock." She turned so he wouldn't see her face. She didn't want him to see her disappointment that this was where they were now. Excessive politeness and boundaries, and it stunk.

"I wasn't sure if you were getting dressed," he said, as though he hadn't taken off her skirt the week before. "I need to get a clean shirt."

"Don't wear the one with the dancing crab on it."

"No, that's my funeral shirt. Inappropriate for dinner parties."

She laughed, noting for the first time, perhaps, how effortlessly he made her laugh. He often did—she had been laughing since their first week here, exploring the island together. She thought about how Alexandra said he paid attention to her. Previous boyfriends, most especially including Micah, had not laughed with her. They hadn't known how to. Not that they weren't capable of it. They hadn't *known* her well enough. It was an interesting realization.

Together with Alexandra, they crammed into James's car. They stopped to pick up Birgitte, who stuffed herself in the backseat with Alexandra like a praying mantis folding her limbs in.

"I must say, I haven't seen any of you three since your dinner," she said. "What's been going on?"

"Nothing," Amelia said, shooting Alexandra a look to keep her mouth shut.

"Just dealing with guests," James said lightly.

It was funny, Amelia thought, how interpretation of words changed whether or not your core was on fire for someone. *Dealing with guests* would have been fine a week ago, but now it was so much more—avoidance, pining, frustration.

"Ah, October," Birgitte said, thankfully oblivious to the mood.

"Now is the time when people begin to make their plans for the winter. Stay here or go to Athens? It is always a consideration."

Again, no one said anything. They were lucky that Birgitte was especially consumed with Birgitte tonight. She nattered on about the olive tapenade she had brought and her moussaka and her Swedishness, all of which were superior.

Angry Yorgos and Magda lived on the north side of the island in a tangerine house with white shutters, festooned with flowering pink bougainvillea. The windows and doors were all open, and the smell of delicious sizzling lamb floated out to them like an arrival carpet. Angry Yorgos gave fewer scowls, seeming more relaxed in his home. The last of the day's sun, doled out through chunky clouds in bright columns, filled the courtyard in the back of the house with golden warmth. A huge table stretched across a whitewashed patio, covered in colorful pottery holding delicious-looking food. The same guests who had been at Amelia and James's party were there tonight, with a few more friends, and the wine (three crates this time) flowed freely.

Amelia made sure to sit as far away from James as possible. There would be no illicit leg rubbing and resulting rejection for her tonight. Instead, she sat next to Calamari Yorgos and a man in a heavy wool suit she didn't know on her other side. A halting conversation in half Greek and half English ensued with Calamari Yorgos. She thought they were talking about boats, but then he mentioned doors and she was confused.

The dinner was lovely. She didn't speak to the man in the wool suit, as he seemed engaged in conversation with Telephone

THE SECOND CHANCE HOTEL 229

Pole Yanni on his other side, which was too bad because she had exhausted her linguistic possibilities with Calamari Yorgos. A moth flew past Amelia's face, attracted by the candles on the table, and she batted it away. Wool Suit also batted it, and they caught each other's eye and smiled at their flailing hands.

"You are Amelia, yes?" he asked. "You have the Ria Hotel?"

"Yes," she said.

"And that is James, over there?" he asked. James, despite sitting next to Magda and Olive Grove Yorgos, did not look like he was having a great time. And pointedly not paying attention to her at all. Maybe Alexandra was wrong.

"I am Stavros Ioannidis," Wool Suit said. "I work for a development company in Athens."

Amelia pulled herself away from staring at James and focused on Stavros. This must be the developer Kostas had mentioned months ago. "*Tikanis.*"

"*Kala, kala.* Of course when I saw you, I knew I needed to sit next to you. You are a smart woman, so I wanted to meet you tonight." There was a tinge of oiliness in his tone now.

"Why is that?" She glanced over at James to send an alert— about what, she didn't know—but he seemed deeply engaged with Olive Grove Yorgos.

"Because," Stavros said, "Kostas, he told me about how Takis left you the Ria Hotel. I tried to buy the hotel from him before, but Takis wouldn't sell."

Again, she tried to catch James's eye, but there wasn't even a hint of awareness that she existed to him. *Ass*, she thought. There was no way she didn't know where he was or what he was doing at all times, because she—

Because she made it her business to be focused on him. *She* was the one who paid attention.

And he simply did not feel the same way.

It hit her, all of it. He'd kissed her in the driveway because she was there. He'd spooned her at night because she was warm. Not because he wanted her. Not because he might feel a lot more for her than simply being fake spouses. It felt awful. And she felt stupid for believing it might be something else.

She turned to Stavros to keep from going down this unhappy mental rabbit hole. "What can I help you with?" She already knew what he was going to say.

"Ria Hotel is not as successful as you would like, and season is ending soon. Good time to sell. My company is interested in the hotel. We give it an infusion of cash, which it badly needs, yes? It needs renovations to kitchen, apartment, driveway. We can do all that. Let me ask you, what were your three-year plans for the hotel?"

"My—" She hadn't thought further than the end of the season. She, a project manager, whose forecasts stretched in color-coded, cross-referenced perfection, had never once thought that far.

"We have a good three-year plan," Stavros said, clearly sensing her failure to plan for the future. "And a five-year plan too. In fact, we see so much potential for the Ria that we made a ten-year and twenty-year plan."

Amelia didn't think that was even possible, but sure. She got it. They were looking ahead and planning.

"Let us take this burden from you. You and James, you are travelers, your visas have expired, and you—"

"What?"

Stavros gave her a closed-lip smile, looking like a fish. "You are here longer than ninety days, no? If so, you must have a visa. And you do not have visa. I ask this my friend Michalis Siskiadis in immigration. No visa. This will cause trouble. Easiest way is to sell and avoid authorities."

Amelia stared at him as he casually refilled his glass. She had no clue that they needed a visa for longer than ninety days or whatever. She felt stupid again, because she should have known this detail or thought about it, even though this was her first time out of the United States. It would be great if James could pay attention right about now or pick up on some telepathic distress signal from her. But if anything, his back was turned even more.

Birgitte cleared her throat loudly and boomed at Stavros, "We are enjoying a dinner, not talking business."

Now people stopped and looked. Including James.

"Just talking about the future, no?" Stavros put out his palms in the classic *What? I wasn't doing anything* pose.

"It does not sound that way," Birgitte said. For once, Amelia was grateful for her friend's volume. "It sounds as though you are trying to do a transaction at the table while making my friend uncomfortable."

"Everyone knows Amelia and James want to leave," Stavros said.

"What?" James asked. Amelia glared at him, annoyed that he was two steps behind, and annoyed that she'd been right about his attention.

"So I offer," Stavros went on. "For Ria Hotel. Yes? €800,000."

There was a collective gasp. Now everyone at the table was listening.

Layers of feelings swirled in Amelia. Fear. Anger. Hope. Rising to the top, slowly but surely, pressuring all the other feelings out, she felt something like relief: here was their ticket out in one fell swoop. She could go home, interview with Celia, find a way to make amends to Ella, deal with her mother, and get on with her life. James could go buy his olive grove land in Oregon and open a nerdy farm shop where visitors could dip bread into his different varieties, and he could extol the healthy virtues of his oil.

They would be absolute fools not to entertain the offer. It was so much money.

"And this way," Stavros was saying, "you can pay money to Yorgos and Magdalini for Takis grave. Ria Hotel has big renovation, tourists come. Everyone is happy."

"Yes," Angry Yorgos said. "That is good. We will be happy. Everyone gets what they want."

"Is there a deal being done about the hotel?" James asked, still looking as clueless as before. "Amelia?"

"No," she said, but Stavros said, louder, "I have come with a generous offer. It is your only out, and you have visa issues. So, we talk." He took a swig of wine with a flourish, as though he had just made an irrefutably brilliant point.

"I don't appreciate not being included in any talks about the hotel," James said, his tone uppity and tight.

Amelia glared at James. "You're down at the other end of the table!"

Stavros shrugged. "The offer does not last forever, of course."

"I would appreciate it if we could discuss this elsewhere," James said in his most pissy tone, one Amelia had only ever heard one other time: around Kostas. The only thing missing was him running a stress hand through his hair and—oh no, there it was.

"No one wants a large company owning the Ria Hotel and turning it into a luxury resort," Birgitte said. "You will destroy the land around it."

Stavros shrugged. "That is for my company to decide. How about November fifteenth, yes? That is a good day to have decision."

"When did you decide on a date?" James fumed.

The warm atmosphere around the table was less warm now. But because no Greek wanted to end a party, Angry Yorgos pulled out a bouzouki and called for songs. Stavros seemed to get the message. He hauled himself to his feet.

"We will be in touch, yes? It was a genuine pleasure. I think when everyone calms down, you will see it is not only a good plan, but the only plan."

Clearly, Amelia realized, Stavros was a man used to volatile discussions because his jovial attitude had not wavered. Whereas James's face was white and drawn. He watched Stavros make his way to Angry Yorgos and Magda, kiss them, and see himself out.

"That *malaka*, coming in here and making offers!" Birgitte

said, but Angry Yorgos played louder and shouted in song, possibly to drown her out.

Tears pricked the corners of Amelia's eyes. The week of blatant rejection from James, the neat and sudden offer from Stavros, and now James, sitting over there fuming at her for something she hadn't done, was too much. She pushed back her chair and excused herself.

She wandered through the house, looking for the bathroom. Tears blurred her eyes. She found the kitchen, then the lounge, then a bedroom. No bathroom. The hurt came in waves now, and she stopped and leaned against the wall, letting the tears crest and spill. The worst part about it all was that it was her own doing, as usual. She was hung up on James, and she needed to get herself un-hung up, stat.

"Ameliaoula." Kostas said her name gently behind her. She briefly debated trying to hide her tears, but there was no point since her cheeks were wet. He held out his arms, and the comfort was too great to ignore. She dove into them.

"How did he know about our visa status?" she asked.

Kostas smoothed her hair. "He has friends in the right places, which benefits his business. Do not cry. Please, we will figure this out."

She had forgotten how comforting a warm hug could be. Her tears let loose as she sank into him. Accepting comfort from Kostas was probably not a great idea, even though he was a friend. His arms and his warmth felt so good. It felt like ages since she had been held, eons since anyone had hugged her or even touched her with comfort—last week with James didn't count because that was uncontrollable lust. Neither did illicit middle-of-the-night spooning count, because she didn't get to lean into it or respond, or even wake up half the time. Simply being held? She was starved for it. And Kostas was being a good friend.

Except, and oh no, yes, there it was. A hardness between him—*his* hardness. Poking her hip. Jabbing her, in fact. She began to pull away. Kostas could be a friend, but he could also be a weasel.

As she tried to pull away, he moved his hands to her face and brought her forward, toward him.

"Ameliaoula," he whispered, his voice husky.

She made to pull away fully, but not fast enough. His lips—warm, sensual lips—landed on hers and some traitorously animalistic part of her responded. Responded! Unbelievable! Her lips kissed back, even as her brain fought for control over what was happening, and pushed through, triumphant, to yell, *Stop! Stop this now!*

"Seriously? Fucking seriously?"

She ripped away from Kostas and turned to see James.

Kostas let her go and, with the practiced ease of someone who has been caught in furtive embraces before, offered a sheepish but unapologetic smile and backed off down the hall and out of sight.

James stared at her, his face tight and angry—with unmistakable hurt in his eyes. He walked away.

What—was she was going to say all the things now like *It wasn't what you think*, or *It didn't mean anything*, or the classic *James! Wait! I can explain!* But those were such clichés and those lines never worked. The damage was done, so she took a deep breath and hoped he would figure out that it wasn't her, she didn't want Kostas, she wasn't like that. After a long moment, she dried her eyes and went back out to the table.

CHAPTER 16

The ride home was wretched. No one spoke, not even Birgitte. Her shoulders ratcheted up so high that she looked like a Scandinavian Babadook. James gripped the steering wheel as though the car was falling apart and only the steering wheel could save them. Alexandra, who had sat up front so Amelia wouldn't have to sit next to James, stared out the side window, closing her eyes into the night air.

Everyone went their separate ways with little more than a grunt. To Amelia, James said nothing at all.

In the morning, Amelia threw herself into the morning service. She busied herself serving a Belgian couple and a British couple with their young son on the restaurant veranda. The end of the season was on their doorstep. There was one last batch of guests coming, and that was it. Amelia's head swirled: They had been handed the solution. They could leave.

And yet.

James appeared as breakfast was ending, breezing onto the veranda as though he'd been out gallivanting in the hills. His blond hair was mussed from the wind coming off the sea, and he smelled like the outdoors: oregano and grass and sun.

"Hello!" he called.

She thought—her heart leaped in hope—that he was talking to her, but she realized he was speaking to their guests. "Have you been enjoying this gorgeous morning? Weather's getting a bit cooler, but that makes for amazing walks in the fields."

"Ah yes," said Mr. Peeters appreciatively. "A bracing walk is exactly what I like too."

"If you'd like a suggestion, I'd be happy to draw a map for you." James was so bright and sweet—Amelia could almost believe last night hadn't happened.

"That would be fantastic," the man said. "I'd like that, if it's no trouble."

"No trouble at all!" James was always nice to guests, but this enthusiasm was too much. He turned and bounded into the reception area. Amelia followed.

"Hey," she said.

"Hey yourself." He rummaged in the desk drawer for a pen. Was he rocking a little on his feet? He was. He was *bouncing*.

"Sure could have used your help this morning."

"I was over at Olive Grove Yorgos's," James said, still in that stupid golden retriever tone. "Anyway, it's just two couples and a kid. You had it handled."

She wondered if that was supposed to mean more but couldn't tell because of his ridiculous upbeat tone. "James."

He met her eyes, and his green ones, full of brooding fury,

did not waver. "Let's not get into it right now, okay? I want to talk about it, but now's not the time. Not during the morning service."

She couldn't disagree, especially because the shout of a small child had just come through from the veranda. It belonged to the five-year-old who had upended his orange juice, which he had done every morning of his family's stay. Amelia went through to get a rag. It never seemed to stop after that. More messes and requests and four rooms to prepare for their very last arrivals who were all coming in on today's ferry.

Amelia wasn't an idiot. James was upset or weirded out at the offer from Stavros, had an existing and sizable stick up his ass about Kostas, and that kiss probably had not appeared to him the way Amelia had experienced it. Which was accidental and not romantic. But really, what did James care? Hadn't he rejected her and then moved out of their apartment? She could be screwing Kostas every night for all it mattered.

In the early afternoon when things had died down, she escaped to the balcony in the apartment. Here she could gaze at the big sky and try to make sense of everything. She was frustrated and felt a tightness in her chest that felt suspiciously like heartbreak.

A heavy sigh came from the doorway. She turned to see James leaning against the doorframe and felt a surge of hope or delight. Whatever it was, she hated it because *he* was certainly not feeling hopeful or delighted with her.

"Will you come walk with me?" he asked.

At least he was talking to her and making the effort. She would take it. "We don't have much time. The ferry will be here soon."

"A short walk. I want to talk."

I want to talk were four of the worst words in the English language, and in response her soul dropped out of her body and floated away. She swallowed against a dry throat. "All right."

In moments they were walking down the road away from the hotel, shading their eyes against the sun.

"The sun's at a different angle now than it was a few weeks ago this time of day," she said. "The light is different." She lifted her face into it. "And it's less intense too. Season's changing."

"Yeah, into the dreaded off-season."

They headed away from the hotel to the derelict olive grove with dubious ownership. The trees were withered and gray, and Amelia knew James hated to see it. He'd mentioned a few weeks ago that the trees would have to be razed and replaced by saplings, but the money and time and labor would be enormous. And anyway, who would pay for it? No one knew who owned the grove. In silence, they followed a narrow goat path through fields and hillsides, past the small cemetery where they'd seen the unfortunate exhumation, and through tall strands of golden wheat.

When she couldn't stand it any longer, she asked, "You going to talk at all?"

James didn't answer. He cut through the fields like he'd been doing it all his life. She envied it. Feeling at home here wasn't something she'd yet experienced, and she wondered what it would take for that to happen. They crossed a long stretch of pasture into the dappled and striped shade of another olive grove, this one healthy and heavy with fruit. The air here was still, the sounds of the sheep bells slightly muffled. They stopped, and James pulled out two bottles of water from his pack and handed one to her.

"So," he said. He picked up a shriveled olive pit from the ground and played with it between his fingers.

"Shall I start with my opening statement?"

He shrugged and leaned against a tree. "I imagine it will go something like this: Kostas kissed you because he is an opportunistic pig. And you kissed him back."

"That sums it up. Except you're missing key evidence."

He arched an eyebrow. "What would that be? A condom that Kostas had in his pocket?"

"You're getting close."

"Don't fuck with me, Amelia."

She huffed air out. "Why would that upset you if he did? You and I are friends. Partners. Not lovers. Not real spouses. You made that clear last week in the driveway. You didn't want to do anything because it's complicated, you said. So how are you seriously jealous?"

"Why wouldn't I be upset? He took advantage of you, finding you in the house like that." He was getting angry. Angri*er*. She could see it in his rigid shoulders.

"I am a grown woman who can look after herself. I don't have a problem with a friend comforting me when I was upset about Stavros—and *you*, the way you tried to make it out like I was conducting nefarious deals behind your back."

He shook his head. "Look. Let's stop. Let's start over, okay?"

"How?" Her own annoyance had gathered steam, rising up like a geyser. They'd already gotten to the heart of the matter. Delaying the discussion about his jealousy would only extend this conversation. "I was crying. Kostas offered a comforting hug, and you know what? It felt *good*. It felt good to be held."

He ran a stress hand through his hair, leaving it in an alluring mess. "This is extraneous detail."

"It isn't. Because, apart from that moment last week, for three months I haven't had the contact of another human, particularly a man, preferably you, and when he hugged me, my body responded. Okay?"

"You're saying that you need to have sex with someone in order to not have sex with me?" He put on an exaggerated and snarky confused face.

"If you choose to see it that way, that's your problem," she snapped. "It was a hug. He misinterpreted it for more, which I should have seen coming but didn't. He made it clear that he was hoping for something else, and then he kissed me."

James strode around the grove. "Your Honor, counsel does not understand what she means by 'He made it clear and then he kissed me.' Did Kostas say, 'Amelia, I would like to have sex with you?' and then you kissed him anyway?"

"Wow." She glared at him. "Are you really trying to introduce evidence that you're making up in order to support your silly claim that I wanted to kiss him?"

He flipped out his hands. "You tell me."

"He was obvious in his interest," she said. "Let's leave it at that."

He shook his head in disgust. "So basically, you fully knew where he was coming from and went for it anyway."

"He pulled me into the kiss, you idiot!" she yelled. Her voice echoed in the grove. "You saw us kissing, because *he* kissed *me!*"

"I didn't see you push him away."

She could feel her heart pounding. "Who cares, James? You and I are not together! You moved out of the apartment!"

"I care because we're married." He crossed his arms tight against his chest: a shield.

"*Now* we're married? How convenient. Besides, it's only according to some archaic Greek Orthodox Church record in a tiny church on a small island that literally *no one* will ever check."

"According to the fact that everyone on this island thinks we're married and if you start fucking around, they're going to know it. Not like it matters if you do, but it matters to the hotel."

"No." She shook her head. "No. That's so dumb. Don't pretend you're concerned about the hotel's brand being tarnished. And really, it's okay for me to fuck around, as you say?" Her voice had gone regrettably screechy, but she couldn't stop. "Really, James? Is that what you think? That I would do that?"

James stared at her, his face tight and angry, but she thought she saw a glimmer of realization there. She hoped it was recognition that he'd gone too far.

He ran his hands—both hands, she noticed—through his hair, which was utterly messed up now, and then rammed them into his pockets and took a few steps away. A surprising surge of affection washed over her. What on earth were they going to do with themselves? Would he say that they were both right, and he was sorry, and she would say she was sorry, and they would resolve to be nicer? Would things go back to the way they were, sleeping in the same bed, spooning that he didn't know about, and pretending that was all? Or would they make declarations about each other here in the olive grove that may or may not be true, and then watch to see how that played out? She couldn't see a good outcome from any of it. There was too much at stake, like their egos and the rest of their lives.

After an interminable time, James turned and walked back toward her.

"I'd like to make a closing argument," she said, holding up a hand to whatever he was going to say.

A half smile crossed his face before it was gone again. "Yes?"

"I did kiss him."

He frowned. "That's your closing argument?"

"He kissed me, and I did not invite it, but when his lips touched mine, my lips went *yahoo*. They responded without authorization from my brain. In fact, my brain was appalled. It has instituted swift discipline to my lips."

"Is that so?"

"Yes. The only reason my lips gave in their defense is that they had been untouched for so long, not counting last week." She held up a hand against him interrupting. "My brain cannot see how on earth my lips could have done such a thing, when my brain is secure in its belief that kissing Kostas is not now, nor has it ever been, what it wants."

He nodded, but it was a tight, angry movement and not necessarily understanding. "All right. Can I make my closing argument now?"

"You may."

He inhaled, his chest puffing out, and let out the breath slowly. "I'm sorry."

She waited for the *but*, but he didn't continue. "Good."

"And of course you can screw other people."

"Um." She scrunched her face up, trying to work out how that was an apology. "You could have stopped at *sorry*."

"What I mean is, it isn't up to me to place any limits on you, especially since we're friends and business partners. That's all. We decided that months ago, and we're living it."

"Right. Yes." She felt confused and a little hurt. It seemed like he was bowing out of having to admit he was jealous. "You could have phrased it another way though."

A wry grin crossed his lips. "I probably could have. You're right. What I was trying to say is that while I don't think you were seeking it out, and I believe that you didn't want to kiss him, it's not for me to get pissy about it."

She *wanted* him to be pissy about it though. That was the thing.

"Are you calling this case closed?" she asked. She ignored the kernel of growing hurt in her heart.

He looked at his wrist, where there was no watch. "Yeah, I am, because that ferry's going to be here and we will have to greet guests. Let's—let's pretend this never happened, if you're willing."

She sighed and pushed herself off the tree trunk she'd been leaning on. It was a weak truce, but it *was* a truce, and it would get them back to civil footing. She couldn't help feeling disappointed. All that anger and frustration. What did she want from him? A passionate kiss?

Maybe. Yes.

It wouldn't solve anything. Their relationship was doomed to be platonic. It was a disappointing truth that she'd tried to skirt around over the months here with him. She had wanted it to turn into something more. There were so many little hints that it was turning—or so she'd thought. There had been nights when it would have been easy to turn to him, to whisper, to run her hand down his side and feel him respond.

Sometimes, things didn't happen that way.

They trudged side by side through the olive grove back toward the hotel.

"This grove is a lot healthier than the other one, yet they're next to each other," she said.

"That's because this one belongs to Olive Grove Yorgos. Blight killed the other one. He said it would be incredibly expensive to replant the old grove, not to mention the water requirements, so no one's done it."

Amelia looked up at where the olives hung green and shiny, their weight pulling the branches down. James had gained a lot of knowledge about the trees.

"You know what we should do," she said, "is arrange an olive grove farm tour with Olive Grove Yorgos for guests. Like a kind of rugged day out. They'd get a free bottle of olive oil. Maybe even a picnic."

James rubbed his chin. "That's a fantastic idea, actually. What do they call it? An agri-cation?"

"Yeah. That's how little farms survive. You know what else?

You should write down all you've learned about the olive groves, or even the landscape here. Add adoring mentions of the Ria Hotel, of course. Like a travel guide for tree enthusiasts." She forced her tone to be light.

"Also good." To his credit, he sounded a little forced too. "Got any more?"

"Not right now." She didn't want to chat about marketing. She wanted to get lost in the hillside with him, with no one around and nothing but the breeze. But things were precarious, and probably would be for some time, and they had to get back to check those guests in. Alexandra couldn't do it on her own. When she got flustered or overwhelmed, she started speaking in shrill half words that nobody could understand.

They walked back to the road that led to the hotel. Lizards scuttled across the hot asphalt in front of their steps. Their time to clear the air was ending.

"I guess we should discuss Stavros at some point," she said.

James sighed. "I know."

"It's an incredible offer."

He nodded.

"Are you thinking you don't want to take it?" She stopped walking as they came up to the hotel's driveway, forcing him to stop too. "He wasn't wrong about our lack of visas. We're going to have to resolve that, and it might not be clear cut."

"I don't know. I want to think about it, I guess."

She waited, but there was nothing more. "Do you...do you want to stay here?"

"My plan is still to buy land in Oregon. I just—it was a surprise, I guess. I felt attacked. I don't know." He stared at the front of the hotel, hands on hips. "I mean, we probably should sell to him. I just didn't like the way he sidled up to you and tried to get the deal done like that. He was a snake. The whole evening was full of snakes."

"I thought that case was closed."

He opened his mouth to no doubt fling back a retort, but Alexandra stepped out of reception and called to them.

"Guys! The guests are here, and I need a little help! There is a problem!" She used her screechy, panicked voice, the one she'd used last week when a frantic guest had come upstairs to report that one of the stray cats had brought a dead rabbit into their room, its head chewed almost completely off. "Hanging by a thread!" were the exact words. The guest had wanted a refund, but they'd talked her out of it and promised that the cat would be severely reprimanded.

"Is it one of the cats again?" Amelia asked Alexandra.

"And two geckos." Alexandra darted inside and out of the heat of the sun. Amelia and James followed. They were going to let this whole thing sit, Amelia could see. But for how long? Time was ticking here. She could feel the movement of clock hands. This could not last forever. She hoped it wouldn't hurt too much when it ended.

CHAPTER 17

Amelia was woken out of a restless sleep by a noise. Usually James opened the doors to the little veranda to let in a breeze, but he wasn't here to do that. Again. She glanced at the clock and saw that it was 11:15 p.m., which meant she hadn't been asleep for very long—maybe a half hour. Her phone had woken her up with an incoming email ping.

She pulled it over to her, hoping as always that it was Ella.

It was another email from Celia, checking in with the usual *Still in Greece?* subject line.

> Amelia. Checking in again, with some urgency this time. I have office space, management in place, and investors with seed cash. The position I had in mind for you is no longer for a project manager. Instead, I need a C-level who is meticulous and organized and who can oversee the whole deployment operation. I'm now recruiting for Chief Operations Officer. I know that's you because I've seen you do it. So, can you please get back to San Francisco? We'll fly you home—the interview is more of a formality, to be honest. Let me know when you're ready to come and

I'll have my assistant book the flight. First class, the works. You need housing? I'll get you housing. Big office with views of the bay. Let's do this, Amelia. —Celia

A C-level position? No toiling away at Excel charts with part numbers and code? A thrill went through Amelia, from her toes to the top of her head. The salary was probably fantastic. Her own office with views. This could be the exact reentry to her old life that would make it all bearable. This was the job she'd wanted. *This* was reentry, baby!

She did a quick time difference calculation and dialed Celia.

"Amelia!" Celia answered. "I take it you got my email? Can I book you a flight home?"

"I did get it," Amelia said. "It's really tempting."

"Then let's do it. C-level. Great salary."

Amelia knew she would be a fool to let this go. She could buy a condo, have an actual savings account for once. Her future rolled out in front of her. If her salary was as great as it sounded like it might be, she could send money to Magda and Angry Yorgos to help pay for Takis's grave. A token amount, but it was the right thing to do.

"I hear you thinking," Celia said. "I know Greece is amazing, but what's holding you back? You told me you needed to come back to the Bay Area and you needed a job."

"I do." Amelia sat up, turning her palm in the moonlight.

"Then what is it? Is it the whole thing with Ella?"

"That's part of it." Amelia realized that was true. If Ella hadn't answered any of her attempts at communication thus far, then things were friendship-over bad. Amelia had no idea how to fix that, and the thought of trying while living in the same city as Ella and getting silence in response was scary.

"You've got to get over that."

"I know."

"It was bad for a while, and she even quit her job, but things are much better."

Amelia could only imagine the freak-out Ella must have had trying to find another maid of honor, but quitting her job seemed a little rash. "She quit her job over me leaving?"

There was a long pause, and Amelia felt confusion rising like a mist. She was missing something here.

"You don't know? Ella called off her wedding."

Now it was Amelia's turn to leave a long pause as she tried to process this information. "Because—of *me?*"

Celia huffed a laugh-snort. "It was something else, something to do with her fiancé. I don't know all the details, but it was a huge deal. She called everything off, returned the gifts, and hid out for a while. But I had lunch with her two weeks ago. She's better. But she could use her best friend."

Amelia was truly shocked at this information. "I had no idea."

"Well, now you do. So, can I book you a ticket?"

Celia had seen Amelia throw a mug at someone's head and clearly knew that she'd abandoned her best friend during what must have been the hardest time of her life, and she still wanted to hire her. It was amazing. And it probably wouldn't happen with anyone else.

And James?

The longer Amelia stayed here, the more nonsensical their sham of a marriage was going to become.

James could manage the sale to Stavros. He didn't need Amelia here. They would part as friends, like they wanted to, and still tell people about the crazy summer when they married a stranger and bought a hotel. *What was that?* They would ask. Yes, it was an insane three months, and then it ended. He married some lady in Oregon and had six children. No, he never saw Amelia again.

The idea of never seeing James again was too painful, too searing to look at even out of the corner of her mind's eye.

She gazed at the moonlight pushing its way into the room through slats in the shutters. Beyond those shutters was that beautiful plunge of cliff that spilled into the sapphire sea. The thought of leaving it all made her heart flutter.

But there was no way staying here would work. Especially not with Stavros waiting like a vulture with piles of cash, and not with James's rejection.

"Yes," Amelia said, feeling her heart sink a little. "I'd love it if you booked me a ticket."

Celia sighed in relief, and Amelia felt she'd made the right choice. Even if it hurt. "Good. I'm excited. I know I've chased you, but this is—you're going to love what I've built here."

Amelia thought she might understand part of the reason why Celia wanted her—she wanted to show a colleague what she'd built. A bigger, better version of where they'd previously worked. "Celia, I know it's going to be amazing. *You* are amazing. You're brilliant and talented, and investors gave you gobs of cash. You're a star."

"Ah well." Celia sounded bashful. "Thanks. Keep an eye on your email."

The call ended and Amelia put the phone on the nightstand. She lay back, head swirling, sure she wouldn't be able to sleep. She couldn't stop thinking about Ella and whatever horrible thing she must have gone through to call off her wedding.

But she must have drifted off, because again, she awoke. This time the clock said a few minutes past midnight.

A different sound had woken her. There. Again. A thump, too big for one of the cats, followed by voices. A sinking feeling occurred at having to show drunken guests back to their room or cleaning up yet another unsavory expulsion. The sides of her face hurt from clenching her teeth in her sleep. She eased out of bed, rubbing her temples. She crept along the dark hall between the apartment and reception.

"Shhh!" Laughter. Women's voices.

Amelia saw shapes now, recognizable ones: Birgitte and Alexandra were huddled, giggling and jostling and arguing about something.

"Guys," Amelia said. "What are you doing?" Her voice was craggy from lack of sleep.

"Midnight picnic!" Alexandra said in a loud whisper. Birgitte held up an enormous basket as proof.

"Put on shorts and let's go," Birgitte said. "I told you I would come when you weren't dealing with guests."

"Hurry up!" Alexandra laughed. "The basket is heavy."

Amelia didn't have it in her to argue or ask more questions.

She went back to the bedroom and slipped on shorts and a shirt and shoes and rejoined them.

"I'll be along in a moment," Alexandra said mysteriously. Birgitte motioned for Amelia to follow her, and they went out of the hotel and down the road to a small goat track. They traveled across a vineyard and past a group of sleeping sheep, and then through another olive tree grove. Finally, Birgitte stopped.

"Here." She pulled a blanket from her pack and spread it on the ground. They were in a perfect circle of open space. Amelia looked up at the clear night sky, agog at the spread of stars above.

"Stunning, isn't it?" Birgitte handed her a thermos and laid out a feast: tins of sardines in golden olive oil, puffy pita bread as soft as pillows, flaky squares of spanakopita, a container of tzatziki, and an enormous chocolate cake.

A crashing of footsteps came, and James and Alexandra appeared. Amelia's sleep-deprived brain had trouble figuring out how she should feel. She settled for a mixture of confusion: glad, attraction, annoyance, sadness. It wasn't an unusual combination to feel whenever she saw him and thought about their complicated relationship.

"See? Midnight is perfect time for making up," Alexandra said, motioning for James to sit. Birgitte poured thick red fruit syrup into little glasses and added champagne. "*Yamas!*"

"I hope you don't mind my intrusion," James said to Amelia. "Alexandra was insistent."

"Of course, we are all friends." Birgitte motioned for him to sit. She handed them cups of the fruity champagne and passed food around. The spanakopita was cold and, with a hefty dollop of tzatziki on it, divine. Amelia shoveled little squares into her mouth, savoring the crunch of the crispy phyllo.

"This is ridiculously good," she said.

"My mother used to do this during the summer in Sweden," Birgitte said. "We would pack enormous feasts and take boats out onto the lakes and pull up at these little uninhabited bits of land, usually no bigger than this space here. We would sit for hours laughing and eating and watching shooting stars. Always we had cake."

"It's such a good idea," Alexandra said. "I can't think of a single instance when cake isn't welcome."

"We will have midnight picnics every summer," Birgitte promised. Amelia busied herself with her food. They might have them—but Amelia wouldn't be here.

"Stars and cake are also good for love," Alexandra said, winking at James.

"Alexandra," James said. "Come on."

"What! You know I am a matchmaker. You two, you must make up and be in love."

"Is that what this?" Amelia asked, realization dawning. "Another of your matchmaking schemes?"

"Please no," James said. "Alexandra, your matchmaking is not good."

"It *is* good!"

"It is not, *sötnos*," Birgitte said. "Look at Tailor Yanni and Agnes Faragolis. They hate each other. Look at Oyster Diver Yorgos and

Small Groceries Connie. Disaster. Their families still aren't speaking to each other."

Alexandra tried to look offended. "I matchmake you and Spiros. Greatest love story ever."

"I would have found him regardless." Birgitte sniffed.

"Anyway, can you not try?" Alexandra asked Amelia.

Amelia downed her glass. "It's a fake marriage, and us being here at the hotel is not forever." She didn't look at James.

"No, no." Birgitte shook her head. "You cannot say that."

"We're here because of circumstance," James said. "Look, I love this cake"—he held up a piece—"but the reality is, we're going to have to sell to Stavros."

"Well at least you are not bitter and silent anymore," Alexandra said. "I cannot stand the tension at the hotel."

"That dinner was a bit unhinged," Amelia allowed.

"Especially after," James said in a wry tone.

Birgitte's eyebrows raised in a question. "And what happened, exactly?"

Amelia sighed. No point hiding anything from Birgitte. "After you left dinner the other night, Kostas kissed me. James had some concerns."

"I mean..." James said.

"Ach," Birgitte said in understanding.

"My brother is a terrible flirt," Alexandra said. "He has wanted to have you the moment he saw you, Amelia, everyone knows this. But we all know you are with James."

"Oh no—" Amelia said.

"Not quite true," James said.

"Hmm," Birgitte said, but for once, that was all she said.

"I arrange tonight so you can admit it," Alexandra said. "Look!" She pointed up at the sky. "A shoot star."

"Shooting," Amelia said.

"I say *shoot* to save time."

Their laughter provided a way to turn from the ridiculous matchmaking topic. They talked instead of constellations and the coming olive harvest in November and how young people from all over Europe looking for an easy job would descend on the islands to work the harvest. It was how the farmers managed to pick the abundant olive crop. The quiet winter period would follow, during which the islanders would strengthen bonds with one another because they were all they had. Very few tourists visited during that time.

"It gets a little lonely," Birgitte admitted.

"I come see you at Christmas," Alexandra pointed out.

"Yes, true, but there are so few people. Many will leave Asteri and go to Athens to stay with family for the winter. And you two? Where will you go?" Birgitte directed this at Amelia and James.

"The Bay Area," Amelia said. The heaviness of it, even though it was unavoidable, felt unbearable. "I have to leave."

"And you, James?" Birgitte prompted when he didn't speak up.

"I guess—" He sighed. Amelia wondered if he was truly thinking of staying. "I have my olive farm plans in Oregon. I've learned so much here from Olive Grove Yorgos, and I want to see that happen. That's my next big life step."

It was clear Birgitte was expecting something else. Her face slumped, and Amelia saw grief and disappointment there. She reached out and touched her friend's hand, and Birgitte leaned into her for a moment.

They changed subjects to lighter matters: the on-again, off-again boyfriend Alexandra had in Athens, but also the few nights of surprising passion she'd had recently with Olive Grove Yorgos. Birgitte said she had called a former lover on Santorini and told him she would spend the night with him again if he would steer tourists toward Asteri and the Ria Hotel. She admitted that it wasn't a hardship on her part.

They toasted several more times than strictly necessary, and by the time they cleaned up the picnic, it was almost three and Amelia was pleasantly fizzy but exhausted.

"I matchmake you and James," Alexandra slur-whispered into her ear.

"You didn't though," Amelia whispered back. "I keep telling you."

"We will see," Alexandra said.

"You're silly," Amelia whispered. "It won't happen now."

"I always know these things," Alexandra murmured.

They waved goodbye to Birgitte on the road to the hotel. Alexandra went down the side steps from the main courtyard to the lower levels, and Amelia and James went inside the front door of the Ria Hotel.

She made to go to the apartment, but James hesitated, which made her hesitate and, if she was being honest with herself, hold her breath, waiting for what might happen next. He stepped over to her and kissed her quickly on the cheek. "Good night, Amelia."

She stood still, shocked by the kiss. "Good night."

He turned and disappeared down the steps, too fast and sure on his feet for someone who was supposedly drunk—and she would know since she'd seen him at his most inebriated. She carefully made her way along the hall to the apartment, holding on to the wall to steady herself. If he came back here right now, she would absolutely sleep with him. She debated making her way down the treacherous stairs and knocking on the door to his room. What would he do? Would he let her in? No one wanted to make their way up four flights of stairs and through numerous courtyards to see her back to bed. What if that was all it took to bring them back together?

Not that they were ever really a thing.

Yes. She would go down.

But she found herself at the door to the apartment, and she remembered the call with Celia and the news about Ella. If she went down to James now, her decision to leave would hurt even more. So she lay down in the bed and closed her eyes, thinking that she could still go down there if she wanted, and she might, but after she rested her eyes for just a moment.

CHAPTER 18

Celia moved fast. Her assistant had Amelia's first-class flight booked the following day for six days later. The assistant had even taken into consideration the reduced ferry times from Asteri to Santorini, which had now been set to a fall schedule of twice a week. In November it would go down to once a week. All around the island, there was a sense of closing down and packing up. Their bread delivery was set to reduce, and Fisherman Yorgos had suggested they let him know if they needed fish rather than him automatically bringing any up. Alexandra had little to do and had started to make noises about returning to Athens. A wind picked up and blew a chilly breeze off the water. Green olives pulled down their branches, plump and ready for harvest. Workers began to arrive from Bulgaria and North Macedonia to pick the trees.

Amelia tried to find a good place and time to tell James she was leaving, but they were busy cleaning rooms after the last of the guests left. Maybe he wouldn't care that she was going, since that was the eventual plan for both of them, but she knew that if he were the first to go, she'd feel a mixture of sadness and hurt.

Their painter, Stephanos Spinoglou, delivered a note to them from Stavros. Amelia had the suspicion that Stavros had timed this to arrive just when things were starting to wind down for this reason. Amelia opened the envelope, which was addressed to her and James in overly fancy handwriting, and read it on the empty veranda, the wind whistling through the space and blowing her hair into a mess.

Dear Amelia and James,

My company's offer stands to purchase the Ria Hotel for €800,000. I come back November 15.

She handed James the note when they passed each other on the steps. He read it and put it in his pocket.

"James," she started.

"We have to get the second-level rooms packed up," he said.

They were trying to pack away the bedding and towels, making notes on any furniture that needed replacement or repair. It seemed pointless when they were going to have to leave, but it was the kind of thing that seemed like it needed to be done.

Somehow, several days passed like this. A kind of limbo of inaction and pointless busywork. She had to tell him.

She found him running up the stairs from a lower level.

"Hey," he said, a little breathless.

"Hey yourself," she said. There was no good place to have this conversation. On the stairs, his arms full of sheets, seemed imperfect. But where else? She'd wasted five days not telling him. Avoiding it.

"Excuse me," he said, trying to go past her.

"James."

He stopped, turning slowly, and stepped down a few stairs. "You're going to tell me something, and I'm not going to like it, am I?"

She sat down on a step. Zorba roused himself and came over to stand with his two front paws on her lap. She ran a hand down his silky length. He looked so much healthier and fatter now that he was getting regular meals from her and James. Who would feed him when they were gone? Who would look after the stray cats at the Ria Hotel?

"My former colleague in the Bay Area," she said. "The one who contacted me about a job? She has an executive position for me. She's flying me home to interview. First class and everything." She attempted a little hop of a laugh, to make it sound like it was surprising and unbelievable and therefore something to be laughed at together.

He did not smile. "I see. So you're going."

There was something petulant in his tone, and she couldn't blame him. She'd feel the same way if the roles were reversed. "There's something else. Ella called off her wedding. She's been heartbroken this whole time, and I didn't even know."

James furrowed his brow. "That's terrible."

"I want to be a better friend to her."

"I know." He looked at his fingers, callused from the work. "I like that about you."

There was a silence, and in it, Amelia thought she heard what kind of person James was—the type who knew her faults and wanted her to do and feel better, not because it mattered to him, but because he knew it mattered to her. A true support.

"Thank you," she whispered.

He nodded, his expression unreadable. "November fifteenth is in a few weeks."

"Yeah." The few remaining cicadas surrounding the hotel, one or two, called out in a lonely and probably fruitless rattle. They had missed the mating season. "What are you going to do?"

"I don't know." He looked up, into the sky. "I don't really want to leave, but running this place on my own won't be fun either. Look at Takis. He was miserable on his own. He had to swindle tourists into taking the hotel."

She gave a wan smile. "But you won't have to. Stavros is ready to buy."

"Right," he said. Zorba, tiring of her lap, crossed over the steps to James. He scratched the cat under his chin. The afternoon sun, beautifully warm in that way that made her drowsy and delighted, tried to lull her.

"When do you leave?"

She breathed in. "Tomorrow."

"That's—what? You're telling me now?" He looked around at the hotel, as though it was full of tasks, and not made-up ones.

"I didn't have a chance to tell you. I mean—I did, but it was hard."

He nodded, the movement tight and quick. This was why she

was leaping at the chance to go—because if he left first, she might not get over it.

"I guess that's it then." He stood and turned to go up the steps. "I wish you well."

I wish you well? That was it? She hated to play this game of false cheer and goodwill, but all right.

"Thanks," she said. "I wish you well too."

He glanced at her. "Good. Yes. It's an easy goodbye."

Easy. Nothing about this was easy. "Okay."

He turned and ran up the steps. She and Zorba watched him go. That was fitting, she guessed, because that was what she was doing: leaving and making him watch her go.

As though they'd been listening and waiting to see the outcome of the conversation, two lonely cicadas sent out a shrill call.

Amelia sighed and stood. There were people to see, to say goodbye to. There wasn't much time. She plodded up the steps. The last cicada fell silent.

———

Birgitte was furious.

"Everything can be overcome!" Birgitte yelled. "You are so stupid, Amelia; do not do this. Leaving solves nothing!"

"It solves a few things. The big things. And now that I know my friend Ella is all heartbroken, I need to go."

"Amelia, please," Birgitte said, and there were real tears in her eyes. "*I* am heartbroken."

Amelia sank into her arms and they held on tight. It was

unbearably sad. Amelia never would have imagined she'd become close to Birgitte, and here she was, clinging to her.

The goodbye was similarly difficult with Alexandra, who tearfully told her, "I know you do not want to, but please say goodbye to Kostas."

As if she wouldn't. No matter what Kostas had done the night of Angry Yorgos and Magda's dinner party, he had been a friend here. She would miss him. Amelia walked the whole way to town. It was a good walk, the wan sunlight warming her but not enough to make it hot. She counted scuttling lizards on the side of the road, trying to impress every detail of this place into her mind so she could feast on it later when she was home and needed it.

In town, she said goodbye to Markos the butcher and Eleni at Traditional Olive Shop. They both seemed to have heard about her departure already because they had sad looks on their faces when she came in. She headed across the *plateia* to Kostas's taverna. He came out immediately, wiping his hands on a towel. "Ameliaoula."

"I guess you already know."

He held his big arms out and enveloped her, rocking them together slightly. She was on high alert for nonsense, but there was nothing suggestive this time, no inappropriate poking, no trying to turn it into something else. He released her. "You are sure?"

She nodded. "I have to go." She would be on the ferry the next afternoon.

"And James? What will he do?"

"He has to deal with Stavros, I guess. The rest is up to him."

Kostas made a dismissive *Ach* sound and shook his head. "He can get visa, it will be fixed. He has time. He has us on his side. Everyone here will make statement for James for keeping the Ria Hotel. Our fortune has all increased. You, you could have *ypomoni*."

"What does that mean?"

"Patience."

She studied her shoes, willing herself not to cry. "I have to go."

"Will you ever come again, Ameliaoula?"

A tear that she'd worked hard to corral spilled out of her eye. "I don't know."

"*Ypomoni*," he whispered, and she wasn't sure what she should have patience about, but she nodded.

He released her from his arms. "You have good travel, Ameliaoula."

"Thank you, Kostas."

She turned to go, moving among the raggedy cats that haunted the *plateia*, stepping over cobbles, wondering what it would be like to twist her ankle on things that were not cats or cobblestones, and whether it would hurt more or less.

"You know, he love you," Kostas called. "I think you do not know this."

Amelia shook her head. James had rejected her—twice—and was letting her leave without a fight. "It doesn't matter."

She wasn't sure who she was trying to convince.

CHAPTER 19

The ferry to Santorini took three long hours. The wait to board the flight from Santorini to Paris was interminable. By the time Amelia boarded the flight from Paris to San Francisco, comfortably enclosed under a blanket and stretched out in a pod, she was exhausted.

At least flying first class was nice. Champagne and tasty meals and high-end snacks. She slept for a lot of the flight with a privacy curtain drawn around her pod. When they landed in SFO, she did not look bleary-eyed and crumpled like other passengers did, even though it was around three in the morning for her, Asteri time. She was glad she was too tired to react to how busy it was in California, how everyone rushed around.

Every iota of her being wanted to be back in Greece. This was not a new feeling. When she ran from something, there was always a sense of disappointment and pull to the thing she'd left. When she left San Francisco the first time all those months ago, she had felt plenty of pull to stay, to make Ella happy. But as soon as she landed in Paris, she had not looked back. This time, she looked back constantly. She considered doing a runner and getting back on the plane. Anything was possible.

But Ella was here, and Celia was waiting.

At baggage claim, a man held a sign with her name on it.

"Oh," she said, surprised. "That's me."

"We have a car waiting for you, Ms. Lang," he said. "I'll take your bags for you."

Her worn and stained backpack was a little embarrassing—as was that she was the type of person who had a limo waiting for her at the airport. Everything had a surreal quality to it, as though real life was back on Asteri and the Bay Area was a fever dream. As they merged onto the freeway, she was glad of the comfort afforded by the car, because they immediately slowed, stuck in traffic.

"Rush hour," the driver said apologetically.

Amelia used to sit in parking lot–like traffic every day on Highway 101 to get to work. She hadn't thought about it in months. Her stomach churned a little at the idea of sitting in this over the next hour across the Bay to her mother's house in El Cerrito. That was the thing about the Bay Area: sooner or later, you were going to have to cross a bridge, and there was a high probability that an enormous number of cars would also be crossing at the same time.

It felt like she'd been gone years instead of six months, and there was a modicum of pleasure at seeing the giant billboards as the car went through the city toward the Bay Bridge. They passed whatever they were calling the San Francisco Giants' stadium these days off to the right. Even the aggressive girth of the Salesforce Tower was not an unwelcome sight. It was nice in the way things are when you feel dreamy and floaty. The difference between Asteri's sparse landscape and the visual chaos of San Francisco added to the surreal feeling. She had the urge to tell James about it. It took her a full second to realize that wasn't possible. A stab of pain hit her in the gut. There had been a lot of gut-stabbing pain during the flights back.

By the time they were on the lower deck of the Bay Bridge, the iconic cranes of the Port of Oakland looming ahead, some of the magic of being away for a long time had dissipated.

She was home.

The car finally pulled up to her mother's midcentury house. The front door flew open, and her mother shot out. Amelia had the worrying thought that she'd been standing at the window for hours.

"Sweetheart," her mother said as soon as she got out of the car. She enveloped Amelia in an expansive hug, dramatically clinging to her like it was a scene in a play. Any moment now, she and the limo driver would burst into a welcome-home musical number.

"Hi, Mom." Amelia looked at her mother closely. The same red hair as her own—a bit thinner and maybe a shade lighter on top where her mother dyed it—and lots of wrinkles, but her mother looked better than she had in a long time.

Amelia busied herself with getting her pack from the car and thanking the driver. She lugged the pack into the dark, cool cavern of the house, with its arched doorways and long, wide living room that you stepped down into. Huge windows along one wall afforded a fantastic view of the bay and the Golden Gate Bridge, when it wasn't fogged over. Today, the windows were covered by thick shades, shutting out the best part of the day when the sun streamed in and created a comfortingly warm glow. Amelia again had the urge to tell James about it, asking if he could ever imagine covering up windows with this kind of view. There weren't many curtains at the Ria. They were view-spoiled there. Well, James was.

"I've got dinner cooking!" her mother sang, moving into the kitchen. "I bet it'll be a welcome sight after all that nasty airplane food."

"It wasn't bad," Amelia said, still looking at the view.

"Everyone knows airplane food is disgusting."

"I flew first class, so the food was actually pretty good. The company I'm interviewing with flew me home."

"Ohhh, first *class*," her mother sang with a hint of sarcasm. Amelia knew this move. Her mother was going to suggest that Amelia was looking down on her for eating better airplane food than she ever had. Amelia had been home less than five minutes and was already tired of it. "Of course, when *I* flew, I *never* sat in first cl—"

"I'm going to lie down for a bit." Amelia headed downstairs to her old room. All the houses in her mother's neighborhood were built on a hill, so the secondary bedrooms were downstairs along with a big family room, usually paneled in wood. It smelled musty and dank down here, but she noted that her mother had left careful arcs of vacuum marks in the carpet. A little note that she'd worked hard.

Amelia opened the door to her room. Boxes filled it from

when she'd moved out of Micah's apartment. She pulled back the covers on the bed and found a bare mattress: no sheets. Sighing, she got sheets out of the linen closet (also musty) and made up her bed. She lay down and closed her eyes.

"Amelia. Dinnertime." Her mother's voice was soft. Amelia opened her eyes and saw that the daylight had faded into dark. A glance at the clock told her she'd been asleep an hour. Was it possible to feel worse? The kind of worse that came from having only a sliver of sleep when your body needed much more. She got up and went upstairs for dinner.

"Sorry to wake you, but I cooked all this and didn't want it to go to waste," her mother said, indicating a spread of pots and casserole dishes that was far too much food for two people.

"Oh—this is a lot," Amelia said. "I don't know if I—"

"Yes, you can. I made it, and you can eat it. Don't be silly. You're just disoriented from the flight and the time zones."

Amelia stifled a sigh—a move as familiar as breathing when it came to her mother. Her mother liked to gaslight, and it was often easier to stay silent than argue.

"I suppose you'll be seeing your father," her mother said, placing a platter of the biggest meatloaf Amelia had ever seen on the table. It was easily three cows' worth. "As I told you before, he lives in Marin now with a woman named Petunia. We don't talk at all anymore."

Amelia laughed in surprise. "Her name is Petunia?"

"He calls her Tuna, if you can believe that. I was the last to know. He said he was going through a crisis. That was why he moved out and filed for divorce. Right after he moves out, he asks if he can come over to dinner. I said of course. You don't stay married to someone for almost forty years without offering them a nice meal when they want to make a peace offering." Her mother passed a bowl of mashed potatoes so big that it could have won prizes.

"Was it a peace offering?" Amelia asked, confused.

"I was in here making chicken fricassee—you know how he loves that." Her mother wiped her dry eyes, and Amelia had the sense this was a show, carefully crafted for an audience of one—her. "I was going to make Jell-O 1-2-3 for dessert. They don't make the package mixes for that anymore. You have to recreate it yourself with regular gelatin and whipped cream, always supposing you know how to make it. There's a mousse in the middle, which is tricky. You can look it up on the internet, but there's experience and then there's internet recipes. Not everyone can pull off a mousse, but I can."

"Mom."

"He sits down at this table. I serve him, I even use the best plates. He doesn't even pick up his fork. He says, 'Sorry, Chrissie, I'm in love with a woman named Petunia, and I didn't want you to hear it from someone else.' Well, of course I held it together until he left and then I just…fell to pieces. Pieces. Threw the whole dinner out, chicken and Jell-O and all."

Amelia cringed. It was all so theatrical, as per usual. "I'm sorry."

Her mother waved it away, and this, too, was part of the show. Amelia was supposed to agree that her mother was the victim here and her father an evil villain. Her mother would again demur—three times was usually her hallmark—and then she would admit that maybe Amelia was right.

"Mom," Amelia said. Her father had tried to leave before, but her mother had flatly refused to let him go. He had not had a plan in place then—a fatal error. Amelia respected that he'd corrected that this time, because there was no way around her mother without some level of subterfuge.

Her mother covered her face with her hands. "I am a ruin. He has ruined me."

"He hasn't ruined you."

"None of my friends will see me. I'm a social outcast."

"From what? Your weekly mah-jongg club?"

"You couldn't possibly understand how hard it is and how complicated it is."

Amelia tried to hide her eye roll. James had said things were complicated. It was such a general nothing word. "I'm sorry you're sad."

"I don't want him now. Petunia can have him."

Her mother sniffed expansively and looked off into the distance as though she'd all of a sudden made a decision to be stoic. "Of course you'll want to lecture me about feminism now and how single girls get it done and all that, but I'm from a different time, Amelia."

"You're from the sixties. You're not even a boomer."

Her mother glared at her, probably for not playing along. "It's just us single gals, Amelia. You know how it is to lose a husband. It's too bad that you weren't able to make that work."

Amelia clenched her jaw. Her mother had tried so hard to get information out of her as to why she was leaving Greece, and where was James, and why wasn't he coming with her—on and on. "I'm not going to talk about that."

"Yes, fine." Her mother looked mollified, but Amelia knew better. Sure enough, she started in again. "So. Was that a snap decision, to marry that man? Did he hurt you? He probably slept around a lot, eh? Those Greeks. They're notorious."

Amelia stifled a long sigh. "James isn't Greek, and anyway the Greeks are not like that at all. They are, as a people, lovely, and individually all different. Obviously." She pushed back her chair. She didn't have the fortitude to play her mother's games right now. "I need to get some sleep. It's the middle of the night for me, Greek time."

"But I made all this food."

Amelia looked at the massive piles of food and shook her head.

"I had to do a lot of clearing to get your room ready for you. You didn't give me much notice. There was lugging the vacuum cleaner down, and it wasn't easy, you know. I have that hip and the bad knee now—did I tell you I hurt my knee?"

Amelia closed her eyes. "Okay. Thank you. I appreciate everything you've done." She got up and went downstairs, cringing at every creak behind her, sure her mother would follow her and require her to finish attending her one-woman play.

She closed her door behind her and pulled out her phone to text her brother. I am home and it sucks.

The little dots indicating he was replying came immediately.

Oh shit, sorry, sis. She loves to act like she never knew about Dad going and that it blindsided her. I keep my calls to a minimum or else I have to hear the story again.

I don't blame you, she replied. And then, Is Dad really with someone named Petunia? Mom says he calls her Tuna.

Christopher replied, Yes. The whole thing is bonkers. Petunia (I refuse to call her Tuna) is going to want to meet you immediately, so beware when you call Dad. They've already asked me to fly out several times. As if.

Amelia snorted a laugh. Again, the mad urge to tell James about this hit her. He would have thought this was hilarious.

She texted Ella next. She'd thought carefully during the long hours in the air what to tell her. She had decided on: Ella Wu, I am on U.S. soil again. I'm at my mom's. I miss you and love you and want to bring you treats. Partly this is to escape my mother, but mostly it is to apologize in person. And I heard about you calling off the wedding. I'm so sorry to hear that.

She expected no reply as usual, but to her shock, the typing dots appeared almost immediately.

I know. Celia told me you're back.

Ah!

A reply!

Amelia did a fist pump. An actual reply! After all these months! She typed: Can I bring you treats tomorrow?

Ella took some time to reply, the three dots bouncing around for a long time. Amelia held the phone, palms getting sweaty. Then, simply, Yes.

There was no telling what had changed to make Ella reply, but Amelia wasn't going to question it. She lay back on her dusty teenage bed, glad to have something to think about other than the heartbreak of walking away from Asteri and the hotel and Birgitte and Kostas. She couldn't even touch figuring out how she felt about James. She wished it had been different, but she couldn't imagine another outcome. How else could they have left it? An affectionate handshake? Bland best wishes? Jovial waving?

There was no answer that seemed right. She gave in to the time zone and culture shift fatigue and drifted off. Behind her eyes, she saw his face as she left the hotel. He'd stood outside the main door, hands shoved in his pockets, looking deeply unhappy but saying nothing. Birgitte had driven her to the port in her little car, suggesting that it could be too much if James drove her, but in truth, James hadn't offered.

He hadn't said anything at all.

CHAPTER 20

Her mother made an obscenely lavish breakfast the next morning, as though feeding Amelia would make up for all the meals her father would no longer enjoy at her hands. Used to simple Greek yogurt with a dollop of honey for breakfast, Amelia couldn't eat much of the spread. This precipitated a long and tiresome performance from her mother about how she was only trying to make her daughter happy, and how no one was around now to eat her cooking and no one appreciated her anymore, and what was she going to do?

Your mother is having a tantrum because I won't eat her ginormous buffet breakfast, Amelia texted Christopher.

Your mother is a narcissist who lives for your meal refusals so she can be a victim, he wrote back.

Your mother would enjoy a visit from her sweet son, Amelia typed.

Your mother is a grown child who lacks any empathy and seeks to exploit her children at every turn, Christopher answered. Seek alternative shelter immediately.

At last, it was time for Amelia to leave for the city and the interview with Celia and her team. As in the airport, everyone moved too fast, with too much rushing. She wondered how long her slower-paced Greek brain would last. When she got off BART and emerged from the Montgomery station onto Market Street, it was worse. By the time she walked into the lobby of the building, Amelia felt like an elderly person driving too slow in the fast lane of the freeway.

A smiling receptionist with a huge headset greeted her and told her to go up to floor sixty-eight. As soon as Amelia stepped off the elevator, Celia was there to greet her.

"Amelia," she said, holding out her hand to shake. "At long last. I'm so glad. Welcome to Velocity Software."

"Thank you. I'm glad to be here." Amelia followed Celia down a hall with glass-walled conference rooms and large offices filled with people having smiling conversations and looking industrious. Celia showed her into what was clearly the best conference room, with gorgeous views of the bay.

"What can I get you?" Celia asked, stopping at an impressive-looking coffee and tea cart.

She accepted a tea, noting that it was that schmancy French tea she had enjoyed back at Swinck. The tea wasn't easy to find, and as far as Amelia knew, it was only sold in specialty import shops. Celia was definitely trying hard, and Amelia felt flattered and a little amazed.

"I remembered that you liked this brand," Celia said, passing her a whole tray of milk, honey, and crystal rock sugar.

"Thank you," Amelia said. "You remember well."

"So." Celia sat in the seat opposite. "Was your flight home okay?"

"It was great. Thank you for flying me first class."

"You're worth it." Celia smiled. "Velocity is all about strong women who get shit done, and I know your work. You get shit done. That's why I've chased you over these months."

Amelia took a breath. "I appreciate that. But...you've also seen me throw a mug of tea at a colleague's head."

Celia gave a patient kind of smile. "Yes, I did. We've been over this. He wasn't only a colleague, he was a douchebag ex who tried to sabotage you with some terrible code and then tried blaming you for it. I knew exactly why you threw the mug, and then I watched them fire you. Micah was given a minor promotion for getting that software release out. That was when I decided it was time to start my own company. Do I wish you hadn't thrown the mug? I don't really care. He deserved it, honestly. And I know you well enough to know you're not usually a violent mug-thrower."

Amelia dipped her head and nodded. She didn't want to rehash, but she felt vindicated that Celia knew the truth. "I am committed to not being a violent mug-thrower."

Celia smiled. "So. I've taken my code and added all the enhancements Swinck would never let me add, and investors love it." She spread her arms wide to indicate the conference room. "Enough to give me a hundred million dollars to start."

Amelia sucked in a breath. "Wow. That's—insane. Congratulations!"

"Thanks. I want the best project manager working for me. I want software getting released on time."

"What are the terms?" Amelia was already in, but she felt she should probably sound competent.

Celia pushed over a glossy folder. Amelia opened it to find a simple sheet with bullet points. Her salary (a frankly indecent amount), unlimited vacation time, extended sick and maternity leave policies, workspace setup subsidies, and a commitment to a healthy work-life balance on whatever terms Amelia wanted to define.

"I want this place to work for real people," Celia said. "I'm hiring people who know how to work, so you can do your job however you want, whenever you want. I've got a big office down the hall for you, with views on two sides. But I just want you to be happy."

"Wow." Amelia had never been paid that amount of money and had only ever sat in a cubicle.

"And I wanted to let you know that Ella interviewed here for the director of marketing role. A position she got, of course."

Amelia couldn't believe it. She and Ella would be colleagues too?

Celia pushed back from the table. "Let me show you your office."

Amelia followed her down the hall and into a light-filled dream of an office with privacy shades, a couch, and a comfortable desk. The views of Coit Tower and the lower ports were incredible. It wasn't the magnificent cliffscapes of Asteri, but it was a pretty close second. It was beyond anything she'd hoped for. She could live in the city on that salary, probably even buy a place. All kinds of financial security scenarios floated through her mind. Her tax bracket would change. She could retire someday.

Celia stood behind her. "I'm sure you want to think about it."

"I'm sure I want to say yes right now," Amelia said.

Celia laughed. "I won't stop you. But come meet the rest of the team before you decide anything."

The next two hours were spent lunching and chatting with Celia's executive team, all of whom seemed genuinely nice. There was no posturing or poisonous questions designed to catch Amelia out or throw her off. They all seemed briefed on her background and capabilities. And they all said they were happy.

"This is genuinely the best company I've ever seen," said one of them.

"I can't imagine working at any other kind of setup," another said.

"This is the future of software," the third declared.

By the early afternoon, Amelia told Celia yes. There was no point in drawing it out; there was nothing to think about or consider. She wasn't going to negotiate that obnoxious salary for more. This was it. It was a one-way ticket from Greece.

"Listen," Celia said after she stopped clapping her hands. "I know you only just arrived back after several months in Europe. Where are you staying?"

"With my parents—well, my mom. In the East Bay."

"Unless you want to continue with that, we're happy to help with finding housing."

"That's so generous. I'd love to be in the city if possible." The city, while grossly expensive, was busy and full of life, and she sensed she might need distractions if she began to think about what she'd walked away from.

"I have an executive real estate location service on retainer. And we're prepared to pay the first year of rent for you as a signing bonus. I know it can be tough finding a place in the city."

Amelia was astounded. "I—thank you so much." Had she fallen asleep on the plane, and this was all a dream? "Is Ella here? I'd like to say hello to her." Amelia's stomach did a butterfly dance at the thought of seeing her.

"I think she's working from home today. She didn't want to distract you from being impressed by all this and saying yes." Celia laughed the kind of laugh you give when you're winning.

A burst of giddy laughter escaped Amelia's lips too.

Celia clasped Amelia's hands in hers. "And if you need anything else—we'll get it sorted out for you. A car. A Vespa. Whatever."

She wanted to sit in that beautiful office, lean back in her chair, and call James, who would scream on the other end of the line in happiness for her. Amelia pictured the camera of her mind panning back outside the building and around the Bay, a little Amelia in her office window, barely visible.

This was everything.

She left the building floating. Hopefully, with dedicated attention, the urge to tell James everything that happened in her life would be gone in a few days. She'd be enveloped in this new lush life, living a capitalist dream, and he would grow to be a distant memory.

She walked west up California Street toward Chinatown, enjoying the chance to stretch her legs. The feeling of winning the lottery didn't go away. She turned right on Stockton and headed down to Jackson, where the best bakery for char siu baos was. After waiting in a long line, she was able to get six golden-brown buns in a pink pastry box. By the time she arrived at Ella's apartment building south of Market, her feet ached.

Holding her breath, she rang Ella's door buzzer.

Ella's voice came over the intercom. "Yes?"

Hearing her best friend's voice after so long choked her up. She could only eke out, "Ell."

"Is that a pink bakery box I see?"

Amelia looked around. "How do you see?"

"You're on camera, dummy."

Amelia hid a smile. "Yes."

There was a pause, and then Ella's tinny voice asked, "Is it from AA Bakery on Stockton and Jackson?"

"Yes."

Another pause. "You went all the way down there? Did they even have any char siu bao left?"

"They did, and I got six."

"And they actually served a white girl?"

Amelia giggled. "Yes."

Ella buzzed her in, and the sound was the sweetest thing to Amelia's ears. She burst out of the elevator, and Ella was there, waiting. There was a pause in which Amelia tried to read Ella. But Ella held out her arms, and they flew into each other.

"You're so dumb," Ella said into her hair.

"I know."

Ella relieved her of the bakery box, and they went into her little studio. It was tiny but efficiently compact, with things artfully fitting into every possible angle and managing to look cozy rather than cramped. The view of the ballpark and all of Potrero Hill was stunning. On game days, Ella could watch from her living room and see the scoreboard.

On the little kitchen island, Ella opened the box and pulled out a bun.

"Ells," Amelia said.

Ella held a hand out to shush her and took a bite of the bao, her eyes closed in ecstasy. When she was done chewing, she opened her eyes and motioned that Amelia could speak.

Amelia straightened her toes and took a breath. "Obviously I've thought a lot about what to say to you if and when you allowed me to. You know I've apologized a lot in text and email and DM. But what I want to tell you now is that I missed you. I missed everything about you. I adore you because you're funny and gorgeous and brilliant, and I love your laugh and I love the way you think. And I...I want to be better than what I was when I hurt you. Not being there for you was the nastiest thing I've ever done. I'm sorry, Ella. And if you want to accept the bao, but not that, I will understand."

Ella eyed her, her face thoughtful, and for a moment Amelia thought she was going to refuse, or maybe accept with heavy conditions. But Ella broke into a huge smile. "You were a total asshole."

"I know."

"A giant one."

"Yep."

"With hemorrhoids."

Amelia laughed. "Yes."

"But…" Ella sighed. "I realize now—I actually realized it some time ago—that you had to go. If you'd stayed for the wedding, you would not have gone at all."

All of Amelia's organs sagged in relief. "Yes."

"And I called off the wedding, so that would have been a waste."

"Yeah, but on the other side of it, leaving you was terrible, and I wasn't the type of friend I want to be."

Ella studied her. "I think I know that."

Amelia let out a careful sigh. "And I feel horrible that I wasn't here for you when you called things off."

"Yeah." Ella fiddled with the pastry box string. "But—it was okay that you weren't. I might not have called off the wedding if you'd been here."

Amelia watched her, waiting for more.

Ella led the way to the sofa in front of her floor-to-ceiling windows and set the bao box on the coffee table. "If you had stayed, I might have felt pressure—my own pressure—to keep things going, because everything would have gone the way I thought it should have. But I'd been having doubts about Richard for a while."

"You didn't tell me." Amelia ached for her friend, hurtling toward an expensive wedding, the reception booked for a massive banquet in Chinatown. The money, the pomp. Ella had a stunning hand-sewn cheongsam dress for her exact dimensions. It had cost over $10,000.

"I couldn't even tell myself. Your leaving woke me up. It made me realize that things weren't perfect after all, that things had changed. That was when I realized I didn't want to get married. Not to Richard."

Amelia felt awful for her. "I thought Richard was good."

"He was fine. He just didn't set me on fire. Did you know that days would go by when I didn't think of him at all? I would be doing all this wedding planning, and I would realize after the fact that I wasn't marrying myself, that someone else was part of it too. It was like he was an accessory to the party."

"Ouch."

Ella grinned. "But he never complained about it, you know? So when I told him I was having second thoughts, he didn't resist at all. He didn't say, 'Oh Ella, please reconsider, I love you, I want to spend the rest of my life with you.' No, he said, 'Okay.'"

Amelia howled. "Just 'okay'?"

"Yeah! That was it! He didn't fight at all. That was how I knew I'd done the right thing."

James had not fought Amelia either. That was a sobering thought.

"Celia said you were really upset. You quit your job."

"I quit my job because I wasn't being promoted in a timely manner, and this girl deserves fat paychecks and regular promotions." Ella pointed at her chest. "*That* was why I quit. Maybe calling the wedding off made me see that too. Gave me the courage to make other big changes. But I'm doing *fine*. Working for Celia at Velocity has been fantastic, and I'm being paid what I'm worth, which is to say a giant chunk of cash."

Amelia loved her friend's moxie.

"So." Ella took out another bao. "Let's talk about *your* husband and your hotel." Ella raised an eyebrow. "I did get that text. I got all your texts. And I watched the Instagram for the hotel."

Amelia's eyebrows went up into her hairline. "You did?"

"I want to hear all about that from you, but the first thing I want to know is, why are you here?"

"Celia sent—"

"No. Why aren't you with your *husband*?"

Amelia picked at her cuticle. "We were tricked into the marriage. It wasn't real."

"Girl, you know I love a good fake marriage story. It's my favorite kind. Someday I hope to have a husband I have accidentally married, and it will be a love story because you and I love, above all, a good happily-ever-after. Mine will be easy. But I know you."

Amelia stared at her friend, worried.

"I know that you tried to deny your feelings, but now you're hella sprung for this guy," Ella said.

Amelia laughed. She had missed Ella so much. "How would you know that?"

Ella raised an eyebrow and gave her a *come on* look. "We've been friends for a long time. Would you have, at any point, said I was sprung for Richard?"

Amelia cringed, because she most certainly would not have

said that. In fact, she had privately worried many times that Ella was settling for Mr. Boring Man.

"Exactly," Ella said, clearly seeing her face. "We know each other. I know what you look like when you're really into someone. You're sprung for your Greek boy."

"Well, he's not Greek—he's from Oregon. Part Swedish, if that gives you a picture."

"Where he's from has absolutely nothing to do with what I just said. Look at you. You're lighting up."

Amelia was surprised to hear Ella say she lit up when she thought of James. She laughed. "I had feelings for him. But it didn't work out."

"Why not?"

Amelia's phone vibrated. A convenient distraction. She checked it—and it was her mother asking when she'd be home for dinner. Special dinner for my special girl! Spaghetti a la carbonara, she had written. Amelia found the *a la* deeply irritating, because first of all it was *alla* and second, it was sure to be a five-hundred-gallon pot of it, and her mother would be upset if she didn't eat most of it.

"Done avoiding the question?" Ella asked when Amelia put down her phone.

Amelia leaned her head against the sofa. "I can't answer you."

"Because admitting to it will mean going to a place in your brain that you are not allowing yourself to go?"

"Probably." Amelia covered her face and then looked at Ella. "Because my heart is broken, and I was the one who broke it, and I am hiding from the pain of it."

Ella looked at her with such tender sympathy that Amelia began crying. "Stop. Don't. That look."

"You're such a hider," Ella said. "You're a hella hider. You hide from painful things. Remember, oh, I don't know—leaving for Europe for three months to hide from the fact that you'd gotten fired? And then staying on extra to avoid your mother?"

"I went to Europe to escape from the horribleness of what I'd done here," Amelia said. "But staying extra wasn't planned."

"And did it work?"

"Did what work?"

"Hiding from the pain?"

Amelia thought about it. "It did not work hiding from the pain of hurting you. Of course not. But it did work to hide from the whole Micah thing and the work thing. I think."

"About a month after you left, Micah came here with the rest of your stuff. It was only a small box, and he tried to be all, *Hey, Ella, if you're free for a drink* and I was like, *Hey, Micah, here's a foot in your scrotum.*" She used a deep surfer voice that made Amelia snort with laughter.

"Was he actually asking you out, or was he trying to get information?" Amelia asked.

Ella gave her a look. "Girl, he was asking me out! He called me twice after that! Because he is a dirty dog. A D-O-G, Amelia."

Amelia grimaced. "I know."

"I hope you didn't pine over him."

"Not for one second."

"Because you're pining over your husband."

"We're only married in the eyes of the Greek Orthodox Church. It's not legal."

Ella threw her head back against the window and screamed with laughter. "You've lived in Greece how many months?"

"Four."

"And you don't know that the Greek Orthodox Church *is* the legal body there?"

Amelia frowned. "I mean, not—"

"Mmkay, sweetie, come on. Did you sign anything?"

"Just the church reg—"

"YOU ARE MARRIED. LEGALLY."

Amelia scowled.

"Look." Ella put a hand on Amelia's arm. "Whatever, right? You're here now. You have to declare your marriage in whatever country you're living in if you want it to be legit. Don't declare it and you're fine."

"How do you know so much about this?"

Ella waved a hand. "I'm a curious person. I look things up."

Amelia socked her gently. "You looked up my situation."

"I like to be prepared. And what was it like when you left Greece? Between you and James?"

Amelia breathed in. She didn't want to picture his face, those green eyes full of hurt and anger. "It was not good." She told Ella everything—how they'd met, the near sex on the day of their accidental wedding, how they'd gotten blessed, and Takis dying, and then how they had made the hotel work. How they had been friends. About Stavros offering to buy the hotel, and how it was the best possible solution. And James's jealousy over Kostas and the interrupted moment in the driveway.

Ella shook her head. "God. You are *so* dumb, the both of you."

"Well, I'm here now. I've made the choice. And honestly, you can say all you want that I'm sprung or he is, but the fact is, I gave him the opportunity and he declined it."

Ella squinted. "I think there's more to it than that."

"I don't think so, Ells."

Ella gave her another look that said she was an idiot. "From what you're telling me, he's intelligent and sensitive and nice. And he wants you."

"No. He doesn't. He rejected me more than once."

"Why?"

"Why, what?"

"Why did he reject you? There's always a reason. It isn't that he didn't find you attractive or that he didn't like you or that you smell. Well, maybe you smelled—I don't know, but you haven't had an odor issue in the fifteen years I've known you, not even in high school gym, so what was it? What was his reason?"

Amelia gaped at her. "He didn't want to complicate things."

Ella smacked her own forehead and fell dramatically back into the sofa cushions. "Amelia Lang! That is so stupid!"

Amelia shrugged. "I don't know his reasons then."

Ella sat up and pointed a finger at her. "There is a reason though. I'm positive there is. You should figure out what it is."

"It doesn't matter," Amelia said. "I'm here now. And that job is great. Celia is great. That office is great. Right?"

"It is." Ella nodded. "You're going to love the company that she's set up. There are a few hot guys in finance. I know that sounds boring, but maybe one could be a good rebound project."

Amelia took another deep breath. She did not want to think about hot guys in finance. James was a hot guy in finance.

"Good God," Ella said. "You are going to have a hard time of it, Ames."

"I know."

"You're in love with him."

"No, I'm not, and even if I am, I can't think about that now. I have to move on." She gave Ella a pleading look.

Ella reached out a hand and Amelia took it. "Let's go out. Enough of this moping over James. We won't mention him if you don't want to." Ella pulled her to standing.

Amelia gave her best friend a watery, grateful smile. If she had to lose James to get back Ella, maybe it was worth it. As she put her coat on, she didn't think that was quite right. James had been a friend, if not a lover, and she missed his friendship almost as much as she'd missed Ella's. Well then, she thought as they descended in the elevator, she would simply seal off that mental wound and leave it to scar over. James would be the blight that she would slice off. It hurt, but she would heal and stand steady. She had to.

CHAPTER 21

Amelia moved into a small but charming one-bedroom in a Victorian in the Lower Haight. The real estate location company found it for her with expedient attention to detail, and it came fully furnished. It was the same size as the apartment at the Ria Hotel. She wondered if James liked having the apartment to himself. A little nostalgia crept in when she thought of all the little blond hairs from shaving his face around the sink and the incredible amount of flotsam from his pockets that would take over every available surface when he emptied them every night. She wondered if he enjoyed having the whole bed to himself. Spooning a pillow or something.

Work started in her dream of an office. Days were easy despite learning a new company and job, and there were no toxic men to avoid in the conference room and no urges to throw mugs at their faces. Riding up in the elevator to the light-filled office with those ridiculous windows felt next-level. She had peaked. The meetings they had were productive. There were intelligent discussions and collaboration among the staff. Things with Ella weren't perfect—they might not ever be—but they were better, and good, and working together was fun.

At the end of her first week back, she was having trouble believing Asteri hadn't been a dream.

Then November fifteenth came, the date Stavros had given them to decide on his offer to buy the Ria Hotel.

Amelia got in earlier than the others. She liked the quiet of the office first thing in the morning and having a cup of coffee in silence, looking from her insane floor-to-ceiling office window out over the city as it woke. It reminded her of the quiet mornings at the Ria Hotel before guests started making their way up to the top level, when she and James would have that first cup of caffeine together. Before everything got weird. This would be followed by exchanging *kalimeras* and island gossip with Katarina when she delivered bread. Amelia pictured the island and the wind streaming in through the giant green cliffs and the tinkle of goat bells and the lessening of cicada song intensity now that the end of November was near. She missed the shape of things: huge cliffs, flat blue sea, and shaggy, Dr. Seussian cypress trees. It was odd that life could be so utterly different in these two places, that they could occur simultaneously.

She imagined James signing the papers and looking around one last time. Out at the plunging cliffs, at the veranda where they'd spent so much time.

Undeniably, he was better suited to the quiet of Asteri, and she was better suited to this beautiful glass office at the top of the city. And she *was* suited to it: she loved the work. Loved Celia's team. The pressure was lower; the money was higher. She did not have to change gross sheets or run down a million flights of steps every day, risking a broken ankle if you timed it incorrectly or a cat happened to be sleeping on a step, unseen at the last fatal moment. San Francisco was Amelia's home, and there were times in the first few weeks of being back that she couldn't believe she'd ever left it. She met old friends for drinks in Japantown, had garlic-infused dinners in North Beach, and drank swanky cocktails at a drag cabaret in the Castro.

She refused to be one of those people who decided she missed the simplicity of island life and chucked the city and the corporate job and the high salary to go back to Greece. She liked the city and its noise. She liked it all. There was no rethinking it. No mad dashes back across the world to Asteri. That was not how real life went.

Even so, given the significance of the date, she checked the Instagram account for the Ria Hotel to see if there was any mention of a sale or new owner. There were no new photos. The most recent was she'd uploaded weeks ago. No change in contact information either.

The urge to text Birgitte or Alexandra was huge, but she fought it. A scorched-earth policy was best, she maintained, and Ella supported her in this.

"It's the easiest way to get over it, for sure," Ella said. That had been Ella's approach to ending things with Richard, and it had worked. But that had also been Ella's approach when it came to Amelia bailing, so perhaps it wasn't the best advice.

Only occasionally did Ella say Amelia had Sad Puppy Dog James Eyes.

Amelia did not think she had Sad Puppy Dog James Eyes.

But as the holidays approached, the resolution that San Francisco was everything she wanted began to wane—slightly, almost imperceptibly. Amelia caught it in the corner of her eye when she turned from her big office window, wishing for an instant that James was there, in her doorway. Or walking through commuters in the Financial District after work and seeing a tall blond head—nothing like James, but what if? What if it was him? Coming here to try to find her! Or—and this was the most insidious, worrisome type of yearning—in slow moments when she walked through the halls of Velocity Software, a feeling stole over her like fog that whispered: *I miss the whitewashed steps of the Ria Hotel.* Steps? A strange thing to be homesick for.

Maybe it was the reality that friends were nice, but her family consisted of her parents—her mother had already begun making remarks that Amelia was probably too busy to spend Christmas with sad, lonely old her, and her father and his new girlfriend, Petunia, were lobbying hard for Amelia to come spend it with them.

"Are you considering spending Christmas with your father and that woman?" her mother asked every time she called, which was too often.

"I'm not sure yet what I'm doing," Amelia would say cautiously.

"I need my daughter on Christmas. It's hard enough being abandoned by my husband. I expect you to be here."

"I'll try my best." Amelia felt bad for her mother, but everything in her resisted.

Your mother is angling for me to spend Christmas with her, Amelia texted Christopher.

Your mother badly wants to control her adult daughter, he wrote back.

Amelia responded, Your mother would like her hotshot lawyer son who lives in NYC to come visit. She brags about him all the time, especially to her daughter.

Christopher replied, Your mother is not going to get a visit from this hotshot NYC lawyer now or anytime soon.

Amelia arranged to see her mother before Christmas, which would have to suffice. She dutifully made the trip across the Bay Bridge to El Cerrito. Every time she drove up Cutting Boulevard, a heavy lump sat in her chest. Coming home was a feeling fraught with the memories of the deterioration of her parents' marriage, of their fights and blame and manipulation. Christopher had been right to get out when he could. It was no wonder neither of them had married, with that as an example.

Her mouth fell open as the thought hit her.

Had she run away from James because she was afraid to turn out like her parents? Some bell clanged distantly in her mind—she'd had this thought before, in passing, in Asteri. She had ignored it or failed to take the time to delve into it.

"Amelia," her mother said, Eeyore-like, when she came in the house. "I wasn't sure you'd come."

Her mother wanted Amelia to say, *Of course I was coming!* so her mother could then suggest that Amelia was far too busy for sad little old her, and Amelia could insist she was never too busy for her mother. It was a tired game that Amelia didn't want to play.

Instead, she blurted, "When you met Dad, how did you know he was the one? How did you know you were in love with him?"

Her mother stepped back in surprise. "I'm sure I don't know. That was all a long time ago."

"There must have been something." Amelia sat down at the worn kitchen table.

Her mother sat down too, slowly. For the first time, she didn't seem to have an answer. Amelia waited, hands crossed in front of her. She really, really needed to know this.

A silence stretched, and her mother seemed to realize that Amelia wasn't going to drop it. She frowned and said, "I knew from an early age that I wanted to get married and have a family. Your dad asked me out, and we seemed to have a good time."

"Seemed to have a good time?" Amelia repeated. "Like what— he made you laugh? That kind of thing?" James made her laugh. It was one of the things she liked most about him.

"No—well, I mean, we weren't really into comedy." Her mother fidgeted with her hands. "Do you want your Christmas present? Are you hungry?" She got up, clearly trying to escape this questioning.

"What was it?" Amelia persisted. "What made you say yes when he proposed?"

Her mother turned, exasperated now. "Amelia, I don't know what you want me to say. We went out. It was what you did. We dated, he proposed, and we got married."

"But you can't remember a single thing that you liked about him?" She could think of loads of things she liked about James. Everything, really. She liked everything.

"He wasn't bad-looking. And he wanted a family too. What else is there?" Her mother went from exasperated to bewildered.

"There's companionship."

"He liked my cooking. Isn't that companionship?"

It wasn't, and they both knew it.

"Enough about this," her mother said. "I have—"

"I wouldn't want to be married to someone I didn't enjoy being around," Amelia said, more to herself.

"Well, I guess you should have thought about that before marrying that man in Greece." Her mother moved out of the kitchen before Amelia could reply.

There wasn't a suitable reply anyway. Maybe she hadn't seen it in the moment, but she saw it now. She missed James horribly, missed his smell of piney citrus, missed the way he smirked when he teased her, missed the way he said, "Hello, sir" to the lizards when he thought no one was looking. She missed his nerdy tree fetish and his capacity to stare at a bug for long minutes in wonder. She also missed the idea of doing something different, of a second chance at happiness and life and work. Of trying. Of taking the exit ramp off a lonely, unhappy life in which she did awful things like throw mugs at ex-boyfriends' heads, and instead seeing the world and chatting with friends like Birgitte. Of pretending to voice the cats that sat on the steps of the hotel. James assigned a high-pitched British accent to Zeus, a skinny tabby, and Amelia suggested a deep caveman voice for Adonis, an enormous orange cat of low intelligence. They would argue in these cat voices about which room was best for lizard hunting, dissolving into laughter.

Asteri was saturated with color, with life, with taste and smell—yes, there was the smell Alexandra had mentioned, an earthy, rich soil smell that had soaked up sunshine and herbs all summer.

Amelia liked who she was there too. In Asteri, she didn't have to avoid her mother or grapple with increasing irritation when her mother's neediness got to be too much. She could see that in being home, she had fallen right back into the trap of being resentful and—yes—ungrateful about the food and room her mother offered her. Sure, the smothering that went along with it was awful, but Asteri had given Amelia space to breathe and room to see that not everyone's lives turned out the way they wanted them to. Her own parents had started their marriage in Asteri, but it hadn't lasted. For all her mother's faults, Amelia knew now how much this had to hurt. Instead of pushing herself to see past her mother's clinginess, Amelia had slid back into resistance and dislike.

Shame washed over her. For the way she treated her mother and James and good friends like Birgitte and Ella. Instead of admitting that she'd played a part in her misfortunes just as much as anyone else had, she had run away. An incredible opportunity had been gifted to her, a reset, and she was throwing it all away. Again.

Her mother came back into the kitchen and presented her with a slim green box. "It's not yet Christmas, but I wanted to give this to you now."

Amelia looked at her mother and saw, perhaps for the first time in years, a woman who was trying in the best way she knew how—and it wasn't always perfect. Amelia opened the box. It held a small tree branch with black olives hanging off it.

"Oh wow," Amelia said. She wondered if James would have liked this, and if he would think the branch was healthy.

"I went to Sonoma," her mother said. "With my friend Hannah—remember her? Her husband left her two years ago? We bonded over being abandoned. Thought we'd have a nice day out. But it's a long drive to Sonoma, you know, and I didn't care for the traffic. We went to this olive oil farm, and I asked the farmer if we could possibly get an *actual branch* for you. Of course, I had to charm him into it."

"Thank you. It's very nice."

"The farm was out of our way, but Hannah was nice enough to drive there after I said you'd really love something olive-themed." Her mother handed her a flat package, and Amelia unwrapped it to find a T-shirt with *Sonoma Olive Tree Farm: wholesale trees* written on it. Her mother making the connection to olive trees and Asteri was very thoughtful.

"I appreciate it," Amelia said. "It's really nice."

"Now, I've been cooking all day." Her mother turned and pulled out a casserole that was warming in the oven. "I'm trying to be a bit healthier to attract a new man. You can't let yourself go just because you're older and divorced—take it from me, Amelia—so I've made a new kind of lasagna. It has cottage cheese in it."

Amelia accepted the plate from her mother and resolved to eat it, no matter how bad it was. "So is there a man in mind?"

"His name is Gregory." Her mother sat up straighter and gave a little wiggle. "I met him at the grocery store. Eat all of that food on your plate, by the way."

"That's great." Amelia did her best to take a bite. "Here's hoping you actually like spending time with him."

A clatter came as her mother dropped her fork dramatically on her plate. "Not everyone has to live like a prince and princess in a castle, happily ever after, Amelia. Wake up. Rarely do people get that. You have to make do with what you have and be grateful he's not abusive or a cheater or a gambling addict." Her mother's tone had gone hard and bitter.

Amelia felt a surge of resentment rise in her chest. This was the kind of thing her mother did that made it so hard to see that she was human. With effort, and remembering the shame of a moment earlier, Amelia pushed the resentment down. Pushing it down would get easier with time. She would work on it. And she could still disagree with her mother. Amelia did not think she had to *make do*. Not when she had already tasted something better.

The question was whether she had the guts to do anything about it.

CHAPTER 22

A week before Christmas, Amelia sat in her office before sunrise watching the turquoise glow rise over the Berkeley hills. It was her favorite time of the day because it reminded her of the way the sun would rise in Asteri, shining on the water and creating crazy shades of blue that had no names.

It had been almost two months since she'd left Greece.

She played with a little bowl on her desk that held a giant gold paper clip that Ella thought was hilarious and two olives from the branch her mother had given her. Her fingers worried one of the olives, which was little more than withered skin over the pit now.

She wondered where James was—had he gone back to Portland or was he still on Asteri?—and where Birgitte would be spending the holiday and with whom. Kostas, Alexandra, Eleni—had Eleni ever admitted she loved Fisherman Yorgos? What were they all doing? She had no idea. She had simply left the island and never looked back. It was survival, obviously, but it was running away too, and it might have been the dumbest move of her life.

She rolled the olive between her thumb and forefinger.

The thing was, running was tiresome. It got her nowhere and left all the good things behind. The thing she ran from was fear. Before Europe, it had been fear of judgment for throwing a mug at someone's face, and then it was fear that Ella wouldn't forgive her. Then, in Asteri, it was fear of rejection and that she wouldn't be able to handle the pain if James didn't want her.

She sighed.

Her job was exciting, even with the frustrations and rush of getting software out and the inevitable bug fixes. She and Ella saw each other all the time, and there were tons of things to do. She worked a lot, but she didn't mind, because for the first time ever, she enjoyed corporate life.

The olive in her fingers began to disintegrate, the skin coming away in small pieces, revealing the hardened, black pit. She wiped off the bits of olive skin in a tissue and continued turning the pit in her fingers as she watched the turquoise sky over Berkeley deepen into a graduated blue.

She remembered the story James had told her on the day of the wedding—their wedding—about how his grandfather had proposed to his grandmother with an olive pit. It was the kind of story someone would want to recreate with their loved one.

She picked up her phone and opened Instagram, going to the Ria Hotel's account. She was afraid of what she might see—a difference in photos, maybe, which would be worse. But there were photos there, new ones. Photos of young men picking olives. They had been posted in November. A photo of one of her redone rooms, also posted in late November. The most recent post was a photo of the sunset over the plunging cliff behind the hotel. It was dated two days ago, and the caption said, *We have a big announcement in the next few days. Out with the old, in with the new! Stay tuned!* —*J*

Amelia sat up straight. Was it the announcement of new ownership? Obviously that was what "new" meant, right? But James had signed that post. She grabbed her laptop and went to the hotel's website. Previously, the home page had featured a photo of her and James, smiling, sunglasses on, hair windblown, and a short story about how they'd come to run the hotel. Now there was a generic photo of the olive groves and a brief paragraph about how the goal at the Ria Hotel was to deliver an exceptional Greek holiday experience with thoughtful touches. Nothing more.

The urge to see him was so strong that it physically hurt. She wanted to see his face, smell his clean scent, watch him turn out all kinds of trash from his pockets. She wanted to sleep next to him every night and make him smile. To run that hotel with him, making it theirs, making people happy in Greece—both visitors and the locals. She wanted to find out if he wanted her too.

If he didn't, she was strong enough now to handle that, as devastating as it would be.

"Hey. You're in early again." Ella stood in her doorway, a giant coffee in her hand. "Are you doing that thing where you're brooding while staring out your window?"

Amelia laughed. "Yeah."

Ella slid into Amelia's guest chair and slammed her feet on the top of Amelia's desk, crossing her legs. "You're thinking of James again."

Amelia shrugged. She turned the olive pit around in her fingers.

"I think we both know what you need to do," Ella said.

"I don't want to run away from our friendship again," Amelia said.

"You're not. I promise. We're stronger than that."

"I can't just go back. I have this job, this office." She indicated the view with her hand.

Ella snorted. "Yes, goodness knows that happiness in life is only found in a corporate office."

Celia appeared in the doorway. "Ah! Look at you two! In so early. Am I interrupting anything?"

"Not at all," Amelia said as Ella yanked her feet off the desk.

Celia came into the office and walked over to the huge windows. She looked out at the ports, at the bay. "The code release went out without a single issue."

"Fantastic," Amelia said, even though she already knew that.

"Yes." Celia turned to her, smiled, and sighed. "Huge relief, huh? We'll have to have an afternoon happy hour today. You pulled another all-nighter, didn't you?"

Amelia studied the olive pit. "I wanted to make sure it went out all right."

Celia folded her arms and said nothing. Amelia looked up after a minute, confused by the silence. She glanced at Ella, who was watching Celia. She looked back at Celia.

"You're not happy," Celia said. It wasn't a question. She glanced at Ella. "I am saying this in front of you, Ella, because you're her best friend. But if you'd rather not be here for this, I understand."

"Oh, I'm here for it," Ella said. "She's *not* happy."

"I'm happy," Amelia said, making a fist around the olive pit. She squeezed so tight that it cut into her palm. "You've built a great company and I love it here. I'm happy I get to contribute. I'm just tired."

Celia watched her, and Amelia was beginning to feel uncomfortable. Was this a dressing down or not? Was she in trouble?

"She married the guy in Greece," Ella said. "She's pining for him."

"Ella!" Amelia squealed. She hadn't wanted all their friends to know because of the inevitable questions.

"The guy with the hotel?" Celia asked.

"Oh yeah," Ella said. "They weren't in love when they got married. It's taken her months to admit how she feels. Now she's afraid of going back because she thinks she belongs here or something."

Amelia closed her eyes against the words, as though that would make Ella and Celia go away.

"Is he still in Greece?" Celia asked.

Amelia gave the smallest of shrugs. "I don't know."

"Oh," Ella said. "Listen to that sad voice."

"Amelia," Celia said, her tone full of sympathy, which Amelia had not expected. "Listen, and think carefully about this. Maybe you should find out if he's still there and if he feels the same way."

"This is really not a conversation—" Amelia started.

"What I learned," Ella interrupted, "from canceling my own wedding, is that if you're not happy, you have to go *make* yourself happy."

"Were you happy there?" Celia asked.

"It wasn't without its issues." But as Amelia said the words, she pictured the plunging cliffs, the bright expanse of sky, the tinkle of sheep bells, the simple food. Running up and down white-washed steps and always, always lighting up when she caught sight of James, because she liked being near him. The good friends—intensely good—and how much she enjoyed talking with them, sharing meals with them, helping them.

"Look at that face," Ella said, not unkindly. "Look at those puppy eyes."

Amelia said nothing.

"I appreciate that you tried to make a go of it here," Celia said.

"I haven't said anything!" Amelia said. "I'm still here!"

"This is just a job," Celia said. "It's just an office. You've done amazing things here. You've set up an entire system to manage all our projects. We'll be fine. But you need to do what's important for you."

Amelia looked between Celia and Ella. "Are you—am I being let go?"

"No way." Celia walked over to the desk and picked up the giant gold paper clip. "You're a great team member, and I have no regrets about flying you back here. No regrets at all. But it took a lot to pry you out of Greece, and there's probably a good reason why it took so much."

Amelia studied her boss. Celia knew what she was doing, had always been one step ahead of the management team at Swinck, always seemed to see right into everyone's soul and intuit what the situation was. It was one of the things Amelia admired about her. She did and said nothing without careful intent, and Amelia realized Celia was telling her to go. If she wanted.

"I…I don't know," Amelia said.

Celia put the paper clip down and went to the door. "Think about it." She disappeared down the hall.

"Wow," Amelia said when she was gone.

"Seriously," Ella said. "She's good."

There were sounds of more people arriving; it was still early, not yet eight o'clock, but the team liked to get in early on code release days in case things hadn't gone well.

"What does James look like?" Ella asked into the silence.

"My friend Alexandra said he looks like Alexander Skarsgård, but that's not true. He's Swedish-looking, blond, tall, lean. That's about the extent of the similarity."

"Hmm." Ella rubbed her chin. "That's very white boy."

"It is," Amelia agreed. "He has green eyes, and he's very nerdy. He carries the most enormous amount of stuff in his pockets, picking up interesting things as he goes about his day. I was tempted to start an Instagram account dedicated to his pocket contents. You know, like those mudlarking accounts, the people who comb through the Thames in London and are always finding bits of amazing old treasure? His pockets were like that. He had shells and things and old skeleton keys—it was just so cool. I could totally picture him on his daily walks through the olive groves, picking up neat things. He's nice to animals. And he always knows what to say to visitors and how to engage them. He used to get into these long conversations with guests on the most esoteric topics. It was so cool. He's full of interesting facts, and I loved talking about ideas with him. Like, did you know that lovely, earthy smell after it rains is called petrichor? Or that Article 301 of the Turkish Penal Code says that it's a crime to insult Turkey or the Turkish government or any of their national heroes? Which makes it really hard to be Greek."

Ella gave her a long pointed look.

"What?" Amelia asked. "You're going to say I'm hung up on him again."

Ella laughed. "Woman. You are *sprung.*"

"I'm not," Amelia grumbled, but it was a foregone conclusion. She ached for him.

"Think about it," Ella said quietly. "Please. We'll survive this time. I promise you."

———

It took the rest of the day for Amelia to realize what Ella and Celia already had.

She had gone about her work. Attended meetings, nodding thoughtfully, and occasionally contributed. She had eaten lunch with Ella and had a midafternoon vanilla decaf latte with extra foam.

By 5:00 p.m., the need to get back to Asteri was like a throbbing ache. She shouldn't have left in the first place. An inexplicable urgency accompanied the pull, as though she had very little time. She thought about what to do first. She would have called

Birgitte, but it was the middle of the night in Asteri, so she texted her instead: Did James sell the hotel? She hit Send and then sat back in her chair, feeling breathless.

Her heart felt like it was going to catapult out of her chest.

It was a familiar feeling. And she resolved to ignore it, because running was what she did. It was her personal brand. But she hated it. She ran from place to place and person to person, and she'd left a trail of unhappiness wherever she landed. The best person to talk to was her brother, Christopher, the champion runner, the one who'd made his escape first. But for him, running away to New York had solved all his problems.

She reached for her phone and texted him. Can you chat or are you doing big shot lawyer things?

His reply, as always, came almost immediately. I am always doing big shot lawyer things, for I am a Big Shot Lawyer.

But then he called her using the video app.

"Hey," she said.

"Hey you," he said. He was walking on the sidewalk, and the lights of a building shone behind him in the New York evening. He wore an expensive-looking gray suit. "What's wrong? The materfamilias bugging you?"

"Always. But that's not my issue." She swung around in her desk chair so he could see her view: her own San Francisco lights.

"Nice window," he said. "What's wrong?"

"I'm worried that you ran away from your problems here."

His face cracked into something like a smile. On him it was more of a pained grimace. "I ran from our self-centered parents.

And it's worked out nicely. Why are you asking me about it? Wait. I know." He looked up at something and then looked ahead, crossing a street. "You feel like you *also* run from your problems." He tapped his temple. "See? Big shot lawyer brain."

"I *do* run from my problems."

"Then stop it. Shit hurts. That's how life is. There's a lot of living in that hurt, you know? Hurting is how you know you're alive. I mean, obviously, that's true for joy too. They're two sides of the coin. Dude, I'm not in New York City because of Mom. I wouldn't give her that kind of credit. I'm here because I want to be."

Amelia bit her lower lip and smiled. "You're such a hardened New Yorker now."

"Yeah." He breathed out the word. "Are you having a hard time settling into the fast lane again after being a goat farmer or whatever in Greece?"

"It's different."

"I don't even know why you came back. Didn't you love the guy there or something?"

She smiled at her brother's ability to both assess the heart of things while simultaneously making the heart seem inconsequential. "I don't know that I would say that—"

"Please stop wasting my valuable time and admit you love him. I'm headed into a contentious client deposition." He stopped walking, standing in front of an office building.

She laughed. "It's eight in the evening for you. You're not working."

"That's what you think. Say it. Go."

"I think there could be feelings there of...strong regard."

He laughed. "Strong regard! Who says that? You love him!"

"If I go back, I'm just running away from here then."

Her brother gave a dismissive snort. "The way I see it, you've tried both things out, and now you know what you really want, and we both know it's the goat farmer in Greece. Get back there. If you're clever, you can make it before Christmas. Everyone loves an arrival before Christmas. It'll be like that movie *Love, Actually.* Can't stand that one, but everyone else loves it. I gotta go. Client's waiting on me."

"Because you're a big shot," Amelia said, but the words lacked the jokey tone she'd tried for. Instead they sounded sad.

"Ooh, listen to my little sister. Be sad for like fifteen minutes, okay? Then go feel what you're trying to avoid feeling. *That* is life. I guarantee you'll be glad you did, and then you'll never want to run again. You have my full support. And trust me, it'll be fine. Call me again if you want to talk through the logistics."

She nodded, unable to speak or she'd start crying.

"Love you." The call ended with that little *do-do* sound. Amelia put her phone down and took out the olive pit, rolling it in her palm.

Her phone lit up with a text in her international calling app. Birgitte. I'm fine too, thanks for asking.

Amelia found that her face was half smiling, half crumpling with tears.

A follow-up text from Birgitte arrived: Although it is three a.m., I will answer your demanding American text, because I am an excellent friend. He asked Stavros for a month to figure things out. Stavros is giving him until the end of the year, if that information is useful to you.

The implication was clear: he was still there. She pictured James sitting across from Stavros at the big table on the veranda, asking for more time. Her heart ached for that veranda, for that view, for the wind in her hair. And to be there sitting next to James as he told Stavros no.

"Amelia." Celia was in her doorway.

Amelia looked at her, eyes unfocused, rolling the olive pit.

"All right," Celia said. She came into Amelia's office and closed the door. "You're good, Amelia. But this is a business. All I ask is that you give me a heads-up as to your last day so I can plan."

Amelia gaped at her. "I'm not—"

"Yeah, you are. Block some time on my calendar tomorrow, and let's chat about the possibility of remote work. I don't want to lose you, but your face is already back there, and I need to know."

Amelia stared at her, knowing she was right. Celia smiled once, quick, and then walked away.

CHAPTER 23

Amelia's flight from San Francisco to JFK was delayed by over four hours, which meant she missed her connecting flight from JFK to Paris. She spent the night on the grimy carpet of the airline gate in New York, nodding in and out of sleep. When she finally got on a flight to Paris, there was no luxurious first-class pod, which she regretted as the kid behind her kicked her seat repeatedly. Except it wasn't a kid; it was a man whose knees were too large for the space. He gave her an apologetic shrug and then shoved his knees into her kidneys again.

She arrived in Paris wide-eyed, sleep-deprived, and her middle aching only to find that her flight from Paris to Santorini was canceled. She parked herself in a worn chair in the terminal as she waited for her new flight to be called. A woman walked past at one point and tripped, spilling a large iced coffee all over Amelia and her bags. Her phone took the brunt of it. Amelia madly tried to dry it off, but it had been soaked and the screen did a weird jagged thing and went black. The coffee spiller kept walking with barely an apology.

"Do you have—" Amelia tried to ask the gate attendant but couldn't think what she needed. A bag of rice?

In Santorini, at last, customs held her up. "Step over here," the customs agent told her after looking up her passport in the computer. Maybe she was flagged for overstaying her visit without a visa the last time. She stepped to the side and waited impatiently. If the afternoon ferry was running to Asteri, she was going to miss it. It had taken her almost a week to extricate herself from the Bay Area and pack up. Now it was December 23. She had time, if James was deciding before the end of the year, but the impending holiday wouldn't make it easy.

After all the other passengers from three flights had been processed through customs, Amelia was allowed to resume.

The customs agent tapped a lot of things into his computer. She shifted her weight from foot to foot and sighed heavily. He looked up at Amelia. "*Ypomoni.*"

"Yes, patience, I know."

"Oh, you know this?" The customs agent looked at her with interest.

"I was on Asteri for a while. Running the Ria Hotel."

The agent's face broke into recognition. "I know the Ria Hotel. My cousin is married to Yorgos Faragolis, you know him?"

"Ah…" She needed a better description. "What does he do?"

"He catches the calamari."

Calamari Yorgos! "Yes, I do know him. He's nice. He's good at what he does."

"*Kala.* Ria Hotel is good, yes? Open soon. Big changes."

A sliver of worry went down her spine. She should have texted

Birgitte that she was coming. That was an oversight, and now her dead phone wouldn't allow it.

Maybe she should have contacted James directly. Too late now.

The customs agent finished with her, waving her through with no issues. She picked up her bags to find a taxi, but there were none—the rest of the passengers had gotten them, and it was almost Christmas, so things were slower as a result. She waited forty-five minutes before one of the airport employees took pity on her and called a cousin, who appeared almost two hours later in an ancient car and a disinclination to take her to the ferry port.

He tsked. "Ah, no. Port closed now. No more ferry until after Christmas."

She closed her eyes in exhaustion. "Let's at least check. Please go to the port."

The driver got behind the wheel with what felt like excessive slowness. "You take ferry?"

"Yes, to Asteri."

"Hmm. Asteri."

Last time she came through here to get the ferry to Asteri, her taxi driver and ferry ticket guy had been outright dismissive of Asteri. Now, he was undecided. That was progress.

As they drove through Santorini, Amelia couldn't help but experience a thrill and a sense of impatience all at once. The car drove through the town of Mesaria, which looked slightly run-down because the bigger plain buildings contrasted with the charming little snow-white cliff-hangers like in Fira or Oia. Nonetheless, it filled her with excitement because she was here, in Greece, on her way home. And finally the port, which had a collection of rental car businesses with actual modern cars in stock alongside catamaran rentals and accommodation centers. Everything was quiet and closed up tight, with holiday decorations in the windows. But a small ferry waited at the dock, its engine churning the water. Amelia spilled out of the taxi, shouting, "Wait!" and waving her arms. One of the men working the ferry leaned against the railing, smoking, and regarded Amelia with some interest.

"*Perímene! Parakalo!*" she yelled, asking him to please wait. The man gave a small shrug that she understood well enough: he would wait as long as she could get her ticket in time. She ran to the ticket booth and asked for a ticket to Asteri.

By some incredible luck, the ticket man sold her a ticket.

She had finished paying for her ticket and was bending over to pick up her bags when she was pushed from the side.

"Pardon, pardon," a man said, stumbling. He was obviously drunk and looked like he'd spent a few nights sleeping at the port. He fell into her and toppled her bag, spilling its contents all over the cement. She madly scrambled to scoop them back in the bag before finally making her way to the ferry, where the guy on the ferry was unlatching the wooden plank connecting it to the dock. He had *seen* her.

"I have a ticket!" she yelled.

The man stopped and, cigarette dangling from his mouth, appeared to be deciding whether to reconnect the plank or not. He decided not, and let it go. The ferry, freed, began moving away.

Amelia uttered a stream of expletives. "I literally have a ticket!"

She spewed all the Greek invectives she knew, which only got her a disappointed head shake from the jerk on the ferry.

She sighed and went back to the ticket office. "He just left."

"Ah," the ticket agent tsked. "It goes to Ios."

Amelia sighed. "I thought you said it was for Asteri."

"No, there is no ferry for Asteri."

She had definitely asked for Asteri. "When does the ferry come for Asteri?" She crossed her fingers hard, hoping it wasn't late next week. After New Year's.

"Tomorrow. You lucky."

"But tomorrow is Christmas Eve." The guy at the airport said there wouldn't be any more ferries until after Christmas.

"No, is okay. Ferry tomorrow to Asteri."

She was in no position to argue so she handed over the ticket she had just bought for Ios, apparently, to exchange it. If the ticket guy had the nerve to tell her it was nonrefundable, she was going to lose her shit.

Of course it was nonrefundable. She did not lose her shit but had to employ birthing-style breathing techniques to calm down. She turned and looked around for a taxi to take her to some hotel, always assuming there were hotels with vacancies. Naturally, the accommodation stations were closed.

She was preparing herself for the reality of hauling her huge bags up the switchback road to the top of the cliff and walking to Fira herself when a man leading two donkeys ambled into the square. She ran to him and asked for a ride up the cliff, which he thankfully agreed to.

In Fira, she found one of the few open hotels. She had blisters on her feet, and her arms felt like they were going to detach from their sockets after hauling her bags around the narrow cobble-stoned streets. The hotel reception clerk gave her a look of undis-guised disgust—she surely smelled like donkey.

"I don't suppose you can spot me any rice?" Amelia asked. "My phone got wet."

The clerk raised an irritated eyebrow, which Amelia did not think was necessary, and said nothing.

Amelia sank into a hot bath once in her room. She missed the Ria's rooms. Tomorrow couldn't come soon enough, but she couldn't sleep. Jet lag descended on her like a fog. She stared at the ceiling for most of the long hours of the night, managing only a few hours of sleep. Not her best Christmas, but then, it was better than shuffling between her mother's house and her father's new condo where she'd have to face him and Petunia.

In the morning, she groggily headed back to the port. She was sure they would tell her there was no ferry, but luck finally shined on her, and although she inexplicably paid more for her ticket today, she got on the ferry bound for Asteri. The ride would take three hours.

Ominous purple clouds circled overhead as the ferry departed Santorini, and the water looked rough. Fifteen minutes into the journey, Amelia was introduced to the deeply unpleasant sensa-tion of seasickness for the first time in her life, along with the intense desire to puke. If she had been religious, she would have thought God was playing a joke on her.

"If you're feeling seasick, do not throw up," an elderly German advised her. He wore a jaunty cravat at his neck and appeared hearty and happy. "You'll never stop once you start."

But she did start, over the railing into the sea, and he was right—she didn't stop. She spent two and a half hours with her head hung over the railing, being soaked by sea spray. She puked everything that she'd ever eaten over her entire lifetime. She puked parts of her she didn't know she had. There was nothing left except sand and grit—and that came up too. The clouds covering the sun made it cold, so while she puked, she shivered.

At last, the ferry slowed and positioned itself against the old dock in Asteri. Amelia had planned to watch the approach to Asteri carefully, drinking in the island and everything she'd missed, but she could barely raise her head. They were going to have to punt her off the boat like a football. The old man who helped people off the ferry did not recognize her.

"Feel better?" the German asked. They stood on the cement with their bags. Amelia was trying to stop the world from spinning.

"Not really," she said. "Are you...staying at the Ria Hotel?"

"No, no, the Ria is not open. Off-season. I am staying with a friend on the south end of the island."

Car Rental Yorgos shuffled over to them, eyes bright. "Amelia! Ameliaoula! *Tikanis!*"

She teared up a little at the recognition and told him she was fine and asked about his mother.

"Come, I give you car," he said, scooting back into his rental kiosk. "Best car."

THE SECOND CHANCE HOTEL 321

The car he ended up giving her was James's old car, the blue one with broken windows.

"Ah?" he asked, pleased with his prodigious memory. Amelia could tell she was supposed to be pleased too, so she pretended as best she could.

"I would like a car," the German told Car Rental Yorgos behind her as she walked to James's car with the keys.

"Ah, no," he told the German, giving him the spiel about it being too much, too long, and besides, it was the off-season. She had worked hard to get Car Rental Yorgos to change that tune in order to be more accommodating to the increase in tourists. By the time she'd left in November, some progress had been made, but it appeared he had reverted to his old ways in her time away.

"Would you like a ride?" she called to the German.

"Yes, thanks. Splendid." The man strode toward her and deposited his bags into the trunk. For a moment, Amelia was lost in the past, picking up guests and taking them to the Ria. The disorientation was sharp.

"I apologize for my driving," she said as they started up the cliff, even though she knew the car and the road fine. "I'm still not feeling great." She was also on three hours of sleep.

"Think nothing of it," the man said kindly.

By the time they were at the top of the cliff, the switchbacks on the road had made Amelia nauseous again. She stopped at the crossroads, got out, and puked into the scrub grass at the side of the road. Nothing came up except bile that burned her esophagus. Tears of frustration streamed down her face. This wasn't how she envisioned coming back. She turned to ask for help—to tell the kind German that she was sorry, but she didn't think she should drive any further—only to see him scooting over into the driver's seat. Her eyes couldn't believe what she was seeing as he turned the car on, put it in gear, and drove past her.

She didn't have the energy to yell after him.

The car headed in the direction of the main town and south beaches. He couldn't get far on an island that was the size of a postage stamp, but all of her bags were in the car, including her phone and laptop. And she had no idea where his friend lived. Kind German, her ass. She rolled back and sat down, head pounding. Seasickness was the worst, because it didn't appear to end after getting on land. The ground felt like it was moving on waves.

Then it began to rain.

For several long minutes, the only sound was the wind and the gentle fall of the drops on the ground. Amelia reveled in the comfort of the quiet.

The whine of a Vespa coming from the direction of the town roused her. She willed herself not to puke again and scooted away from the road to avoid being run over, because that was exactly what her luck would have happen here.

The Vespa stopped at the crossroads.

"Ameliaoula?"

She looked up to see Kostas staring at her in disbelief.

"Is it you?" he asked.

"Yeah." Her face felt like it was streaked with dirt, rain, and maybe some snot.

"What—what happened? Why are you here on the road?"

She wanted to get up but was afraid to. "A German stole my car and my bags."

Kostas waited, clearly expecting more, but she had nothing more.

"Okay." He got off the bike and came to help her up. "Are you sick?"

"Yes." Her stomach lurched.

He helped her stand and seemed to dither. "What—where can I take you?"

She sighed, because it was so much effort even knowing where to begin. "I need to lie down."

"Okay. I help." He helped her onto the Vespa and then climbed on in front of her. He turned it around and went back in the direction of the town. The journey was only minutes, but she wasn't sure how she stayed on or remained conscious. She threw up again, hanging over the Vespa, apologizing in her head for splattering the tail end of the bike.

Then she was in a bed that was blissfully, wonderfully stationary. The room was cool and dark, and that was all she asked from life. She closed her eyes again.

When she woke, she was unsure what time it was. She felt a million times better and sat up with clarity. It was dark out, so clearly late.

She looked around the dim room and thought she was probably in Kostas's apartment above his taverna. It was neat enough but smelled like a man: a little musky and grassy, not unlike a barnyard.

She swung her legs out of bed, recognizing a pounding in her head that was likely the result of dehydration. Kostas had left a bottle of water next to the bed, and she gratefully drank it.

Going carefully, she made her way out of the room and downstairs. Colorful holiday lights were strung along the open walls of the taverna, and a few of the dedicated island drunks sat at the bar. At the end of the bar, Birgitte and Kostas stood talking quietly. They stopped when they noticed her.

"Well," Birgitte said. "You look like shit."

"Merry Christmas to you too," Amelia said. "I feel better than I did though. Which is something."

"So," Birgitte said. "You are back."

"Thank you for texting me the information." Amelia gave a half smile.

Birgitte sniffed. "You left it until the last moment, as usual."

Amelia was too exhausted to go into all that had happened trying to get here. "I'm sorry. I'm going to do a lot of apologizing while I'm here."

"Yes," Birgitte agreed. "You will. Your bags are behind the bar. And the car you rented is parked over there." She pointed vaguely.

"The German returned it?" Amelia couldn't think straight.

"No." Kostas snorted. "Birgitte went after him and got it all back."

Birgitte scoffed. "We cannot allow old men to treat our locals badly."

It was one of the loveliest things Amelia had ever heard Birgitte say. She was *their local*. "Thank you. How did you find him?"

"I know everyone on this island." She gave Amelia a once-over with a grimace that suggested some of Amelia's seasickness might still be on her. "You need a shower and more sleep. Then you go to the hotel tomorrow. But the car has a flat tire now, and something is wrong with the brakes. Not safe to drive."

Amelia waved this away. She could walk to the hotel if needed. "Please tell me what happened with James and Stavros," Amelia begged. "Is James selling the hotel?"

"It was a rather difficult situation. People were anxious. They didn't know who to side with—James, whom they like, but whom you left all on his own, or Stavros, who is Greek. Of course, as an honorary Greek, I was torn."

Amelia gritted her teeth. "I'm surprised you didn't side with James for being half-Swedish."

"Ah." Birgitte raised an eyebrow. "And that proved to be of interest."

Amelia wanted to scream but didn't have it in her. How? Where? What happened?

"You will see tomorrow," Birgitte said.

"Birgitte." Amelia grabbed her arm and Birgitte turned to her. "I really am sorry. Thanks for getting my stuff back. I missed you."

"I missed you too. Tell no one." She weaseled out of Amelia's grip. "And *god Jul*, which is *happy Christmas* in Swedish, which I translate for you because you are an ignorant American. Of course, in Greece we say *kalá Christoúgenna*." She walked away into the dark *plateia*.

"You are hungry?" Kostas asked.

"No. Thank you. Still recovering." Amelia downed the water.

"You go back upstairs, sleep. Feel better." He did not suggest that she might like company. He simply patted her arm and directed her to the steps. Even though she had had a long nap earlier and didn't think she could possibly sleep with her mind racing as to what she would find at the hotel tomorrow, she felt drowsy as soon as she laid her head on the pillow. The rain had cleared, and the stars were visible from the window. How bright they shined here, how utterly massive they seemed in the sky. She wondered, just before she fell asleep, how she ever managed to walk away from them.

CHAPTER 24

The clouds had returned with force overnight, and Amelia woke to a downpour. It was her first storm on Asteri. She was glad she had not made the crossing on the ferry today. Looking at the angry gray sea made her slightly nauseous again.

She took a shower in Kostas's small bathroom and dressed in a long-sleeved shirt given the cooler weather—another first for her here. Downstairs, the rain had stopped—temporarily, judging by the bruised clouds—and Kostas was receiving the morning bread order from Katarina Yagapololis. Katarina screamed when she saw Amelia and pulled her into a viselike embrace.

"Ahhh, Amelia!" she yelled, rocking her in her arms. "*Kalá Christoúgenna!* It is nice surprise. I am so happy you are back. This time you stay!"

Amelia carefully evaded answering, but there was no denying how lovely it was to see Katarina.

She seemed to attract everyone's attention after that. A stream of people who had provided goods or work for the hotel seemed to find her, covering her in hugs and kisses and general goodwill and holiday wishes that Amelia wasn't sure she deserved. It was ten o'clock before the stream of well-wishers died down.

Kostas slid over a cutting board and a knife and a pot of Asterian thyme honey. Amelia cut herself a slice of heavenly bread and closed her eyes. Nothing came close to this, not even Boudin sourdough. It was as though Asteri was baked into it, the yeast in the air here distinct.

"Thank you," she said. "For everything."

"You are always welcome, Ameliaoula. And you see now how everyone loves you." He gave her a kind, pleasant smile that she'd never seen before. It made a nice change from the wolfish, flirty look he usually gave her. Maybe he felt bad about before. "Let me know when you want to go up to the hotel, eh?"

The idea of her roaring up on the back of Kostas's moped did not create the picture she wanted. "You know what, I'll walk since the rain has stopped. I need the space and fresh air after last night."

Kostas raised his eyebrows. "But it is five miles. It is Christmas. And the rain will start again soon."

"I can handle it."

Kostas promised to bring her bags up later. She started up the road to the hotel, breathing in deep the smell of petrichor—that earthy, pungent after-rain smell James had told her about. Shoots of lime-green grass lined the road, and sheep, fat with wool, waddled on precarious stick-thin legs next to the road. Birds twittered and goat bells drifted across the fields. She loved this place with all her heart, even while missing the bustle of downtown San Francisco. She was not naive. Asteri was small and didn't hold the number of opportunities that San Francisco did, but both things could be true. It was possible to love and live on a small Greek rock, an island so tiny that it didn't even show as a pinprick on Google Earth, and still keep a leg in the big city. She suspected that it was necessary to keep perspective of both realities in order to avoid romanticizing the other too much.

She was two miles away from the hotel when she heard the noise. It was a cacophony of animal noises. She rounded a corner, when a sea of white fluff made her stop in the road. More sheep than she'd ever seen, bleating in such a chorus that it hurt her ears. There had to be hundreds of them, filling the roadway so completely that they stretched far into the distance with no end in sight. Amelia looked around but did not see a shepherd.

One particularly large ewe took a few steps toward Amelia, as though she might hold the answer to the sheep jam.

"Get out of the road!" Amelia told it, more to give an outlet to her frustration than any hope of human-ovine discourse.

"Bahhh," the sheep said.

Amelia remembered the story Alexandra told her about tons of sheep blocking the road for days. Days! She didn't have days. She could try to weave through these fluffy jerks, but she would be knocked off her feet.

She surveyed the stepped land. Which way to go? Either way would take her on a long circuitous route through olive groves and farmland, and God help her if she ran into anyone she knew. She would be bound by the requirements of Greek etiquette to sit and join the host for a drink, especially on Christmas.

Decided, she began to hike up the hillside to the west. A cold, clear breeze ruffled her hair as she trod carefully down sodden goat paths, her shoes filling with mud. The bottom of her pants got soaked. She wondered if this was all in vain—if her arrival wouldn't matter. She had not stopped to think about what she would do if James was less than pleased to see her or flat-out didn't want to run the hotel. Both were fair feelings. Staying on in Asteri and running the Ria Hotel alone weren't ideal.

But she realized she wanted to do just that, James or no James.

She hadn't thought about that before, which was interesting. Could she run it herself? If she did, there was no way she could keep doing her job in San Francisco. She wanted to do both things: work for Celia and mastermind code releases, creating tons of Jira tickets, *and* update rooms and play hotelier. Responding to the urge to see the hotel again, her feet picked up the pace. Instead of dodging ankle-turning rocks and tree roots, she hurtled straight through them, desperate now to get there.

At long last, she recognized Olive Grove Yorgos's little house, low and whitewashed but with long, narrow windows that looked like eyes. She passed his olive grove and went on toward the little cemetery and the dead olive grove. But something was off. The dead, withered old trees weren't there. She stopped, looking around to get her bearings. The rise of the cliff that held the Ria Hotel was just ahead. The terra-cotta roof tiles of the hotel peeked over the hill. But the dead grove was gone. In its place were dozens of new plants. Little baby olive trees in paper cones to keep them upright and protected from the wind.

Her heart pounded. If these new trees were an initiative from Stavros's group, then she might be too late. She remembered James saying it would be incredibly expensive to replant this grove. There was no way he'd made a sudden pile of cash after she'd left that would have paid for this replanting.

The rain began again as she hurried on to the Ria Hotel, up to its round driveway. She had imagined this moment many times over the past several months, but she would savor the sight later. It did not look open. The door to the reception area was locked, and the whole place couldn't have looked more dead. The rain increased to heavy, hard drops that hurt as she went around the side to the stairs that ran down the length of the hotel's terraces, taking care not to slip on the wet steps. All of the doors and windows were closed and shuttered. It was, by all appearances, a hotel in dormancy.

There was no sign of James. Not even a table with an empty glass on it. She wished she could text him, but her stupid phone was still waterlogged.

She went down each level, adrenaline racing. The terraced courtyards were empty, the deck chairs covered by tarps. No scraggly cats sitting on steps, paws tucked under their bodies; they would all be hiding from this deluge. The goat trail leading down to the cove was the last place to check, but why would he be at the cove in this rain? She sighed, dithering, not sure what to do next.

It was fruitless to go down to the cove, but she started down the path anyway. She wanted to see the sliver of beach, even in the rain. And there was nowhere else for her to go just now.

She was soaked through by the time she got to the final big boulder. She rounded it—

And there he was.

James sat on one of the flat rocks that bordered the sand, drenched through but eyes closed and looking as though he was enjoying it. The exact picture of her idea of him: easygoing, open to life, even in rain like this. Everything she was not. Was he an apparition? Had she conjured him because this was the last place to look? He certainly wasn't signing any papers or dressed for a business transaction here on the beach. His hair was slightly longer, and his biceps stood out as he leaned back on his arms. He was an absolutely beautiful man, which of course she'd always known, but the surge of attraction she felt surprised her. And it wasn't only his gorgeousness. She wanted to hear him talk about the bugs on the island and about olive trees in that gentle, patient, yet confident voice of his. She wanted to have that first hot cup of coffee with him in the early morning, discussing the day and the needs of the guests. She wanted to be anxious and upset at having to clean a bathroom for the twenty-second time and have him soothe her by saying it was better than sitting in Bay Area traffic. And then retire to the cozy apartment at night, slide into bed next to him, and sneak peeks at his hotness. She wanted him to spoon her in his sleep and watch him in profile as he looked out over the cliffs and sea, with the sun on his face. She wanted to laugh with him and tease him and be teased.

She loved him.

This was what her mother had missed with her father. The

camaraderie, the fun, the intimacy whether there was sex or not. The inside jokes, the looks, the smirks. The weight of what she had done hit her, harder. She had walked away from him and never given him the opportunity to explain anything. He had been put in a terrible position with Stavros and even Magda and Angry Yorgos. She had walked away like she *could*. And here he was, taking responsibility, being himself, sitting in the rain and meditating or whatever—just being *him*. His face seemed peaceful. He looked relaxed, happy even, in the rain. Not like the stressed, scrunched-up faces he had when she was here, which she'd caused.

"James."

He didn't hear her. No head-turning, slo-mo fantasy sequence. She had to walk closer and talk louder over the rain. "James."

His eyes flew open and he stared at her.

"Really?" he asked.

Her breath caught. Oxygen did not move in her body. She drank him in, watching his eyes widen and skitter over her. What was he thinking? Was he angry? The urge to run, to hide her shame, was enormous. She could easily turn around and run up the goat path now, disappear back into her life in San Francisco.

But she was not going to run away again. If he wasn't happy to see her, that was just something she'd have to deal with. "Yes. Really."

He pushed himself off the rock to standing. "I'm not dreaming this?"

"I am not a siren from the sea."

He made to step off the rock, but she stepped forward to meet him, stepping up onto the wide flat rock beside him.

"You're soaked," he said.

"So are you." She laughed. "Why are you down here in the rain?"

He studied her face and then smiled, the expression slow and delighted. "Why are *you* down here in the rain?"

"For—the hotel and—" She didn't know how to articulate the enormity of it without sounding corny. No option but to say it. "For you."

His expression was unreadable. She wished she knew what he was thinking.

"I texted Birgitte," she babbled. "She said Stavros gave you until the end of the year."

He looked up at the sky, rain hitting his face and streaming down, then back at her. "I can't believe you're here."

"I'm here. I hope I'm not too late."

He gave a sad smile, which made her heart jolt in panic. "Stavros's company claimed I was taking resources from the island by running this hotel. They made a complaint to the Power Transmission Operator—you know how they handle the submarine power line between the islands? They looked at the hotel's usage and agreed that the hotel had been a huge draw on Asteri's power since we took it over."

"That's because Takis had no guests! We filled it with people!" Amelia couldn't believe it. "We had to run washing machines! Guests needed light! And food!"

"I know." James shook his head. "Stavros's company apparently gave them a plan saying how little power they would draw in comparison."

"James. I'm so sorry that I left you to deal with all this." She wiped the rain out of her face.

"One could argue I pushed you away."

"But I did the worse thing. I ran away when you needed me the most. That's what I do. Did. Trying not to anymore." Tears threatened to fall, but she held them back.

His eyes met hers, steady and serious. Under that gaze, she felt a little breathless. The wind whipped her hair around, blowing wet strands into her mouth. He reached out and tucked a sprig of hair behind her ear.

"If you're feeling guilty about leaving, don't," he said. "I don't blame you. I think we—we needed some space, probably."

Maybe the situation would have been impossible whether she'd gone or stayed. Their friendship always seemed to be seasoned with something more, but they hadn't known how to cross the divide. It might not ever happen now, and she would have to come to terms with that. At least this trip back to Asteri wasn't wasted. It was worth it to hear him say he forgave her.

"But," he said. He ran a hand through his hair, the rain splattering through his fingers. Her heart sang at seeing the familiar gesture. "I am so glad you're back."

Her heart had its landing gear in position for takeoff and was sailing down the runway. Now it was climbing, pushing, into the air.

"James," she whispered.

"I was sitting out here on this rock and thinking how I would act differently if I got a second chance at something like—" He stopped and shook his head.

"Like?" *Me, me, me, me,* her brain sang in a suspiciously Ella-like voice.

"Like you," he said.

Ah. Her arms broke out in goose bumps.

He reached out, his fingers brushing hers, and the touch was like a spark. She moved close as their fingers slid across each other's knuckles, hands, arms, and up—and then she was in his arms. He held her against him, wrapping his arms around her so that they were closer than skin. After a long moment of delicious comfort, she craned her head up. Their lips met, tentative, then assured.

Then urgent.

Their mouths told stories, celebrated a homecoming. He tasted of sun-drenched grapes, and of the slightly mineral air, and of the sea. He tasted like Asteri. When they broke for the air they badly needed, he whispered, "Is this okay?"

"Yes." It came out barely audible. "Totally." The withheld tears finally hit her eyes. This felt *so* good. It was obscene how good and right he felt. What the hell had she been doing all this time? How could she have walked away from this man?

He wiped rain—or maybe it was a tear—away from her cheek with his finger. "I don't want to assume anything."

"I know." She was barely listening. His thumbs drew down the sides of her face, making her feel wobbly. Heat and desire were taking over. Where was that shoulder she wanted to lick? Right there.

"I'm sorry." His thumb traced her lips now. "For all of the tension. For being a jerk when you left. For not telling you how I feel about you before you walked away. For saying it was complicated. It was only complicated because I didn't know how to deal with what we were, or weren't, and with you leaving maybe forever."

She thought about the rejection, of how it felt when he left their apartment. "I was never sure about us. You pulled away, and then you'd come closer, and then pull away again."

"And I'm sorry about that too." His eyes were pools of emerald green. "I didn't think I was ready to fall in love with you because I'd just walked away from my fiancée and a wedding. I didn't think I could be ready so soon, especially under our unusual circumstances. I thought if I pushed you away, it would protect both of us."

Her heart ached with the possibility, with the hope.

"But," he went on, "I realized over the past month that I was a complete idiot. I have zero feelings for my ex, and I couldn't be happier that I walked away from a wedding that was all about her. That relationship has been dead and buried—*permanently* buried—for a long time."

She snorted at the burial reference. "That's what happened to Ella too, it turned out. She called off her wedding because it was just a fancy party and not actually about them loving each other."

"Exactly." James looked relieved. "It turned out, I didn't even like my fiancée very much. Especially not compared to how I feel about you. But it took you leaving for me to see that."

She involuntarily shivered under his hands. "I feel the same way about you. It took me kind of a while to figure that out and

I'm annoyed at myself for that, but I just…you are it, man." She felt wobbly at admitting it, vulnerable and new.

"You have no idea how hard I've fallen for you." He kissed her again, and they were like drowning people, nipping each other's lips, exploring, mouths open. The rain ran around them, inconsequential. She grabbed at him, at his neck. He whispered, "Slow down."

"Can't."

"I need you to slow. I want to savor this. I've been waiting for this for so long." He skittered kisses down the side of her neck, telling her all kinds of things with his lips.

She laughed. "I was an idiot."

He dropped his smile and took her face his hands. He looked at her, his focus intense. "Amelia. Please. Look at me. *I* am the idiot. I've wanted you from the start, and I pushed you away."

Her mind ran at a hundred miles an hour trying to process this. "I get it."

"And I—" Hand through hair! "I adore you. I tried to tell myself that being friends was better than nothing. But I actually looked forward to cleaning the worst messes in this hotel, because I knew you'd be there with me. I couldn't wait to get into bed at night, just to be near you."

She shuddered out a sigh that was at least ten percent the comfort of being in his arms. (Fine, ninety.) "I liked cleaning up horrible messes too, for the same reason."

"I pretended I didn't have hangovers," he said. "In that first week with you. So I could be up and about when you came out of your room. I hid the pain."

"I *knew* you were too chipper." She grinned and he caught her smile with his mouth. He trailed a fingertip down her jawline, over to her nose. She wrinkled it, not breathing. "You spooned me every night. I never told you."

"I did not!"

"You did. And I liked it."

His hands slid down to her shoulders, over her back. It felt delicious. She could smell his skin, his musk, some indescribable mixture of clean laundry and him and sunshine—and the rain. She ran a few fingers down the back of his neck. He closed his eyes, pushing his head back into her hand. The hand on her back dipped, rubbed, grasped, traced goat paths along her skin. He ran a hand through her hair, cradling her head. Desire surged through her, and she pressed against him, kissing his jawline. He sighed. He lowered his mouth to hers and gently bit her lower lip.

"James."

"Yeah."

"I don't want to do this and end up hurting you."

"Believe me, same."

He breathed in, and there was a small groan from the back of his throat. He pulled her down to the rock, onto his lap, into a puddle on the rock. She didn't care. She moved so she straddled him, pressing against him as much as she could, every pleasure point on her body roaring for more. He nosed into her neck, sending an intense shiver down that side of her body, and dragged his lips up to hers. They were absolutely going to have sex right here on this rock in the rain. She couldn't wait.

But a ferocious wave slammed the shore and sent a spray of frigid seawater on them.

"Maybe we should go up," he said. "To drier places."

She nodded, and she accepted James's hand to get off the rock. Another wave hit the rock and sent a river of water over it. The storm was gaining.

They worked their way up the goat path, her hand in his. It was difficult going. The dirt had turned into slick mud, and they had to scramble for purchase several times. At last, soaked and exhausted, they made it to the top.

Amelia suddenly felt shy. Being on the level ground of the hotel somehow felt different from the wild cove, where anything went. This was real up here. Would he change his mind?

"What?" he asked.

She was suddenly aware of how wet they were—and cold and uncomfortable. "Is it this easy?"

He stared at her, eyes roving her face. She wondered if he hadn't understood her meaning, but then he said, "It is to me."

"I mean, too easy? Too—I don't know."

"Amelia. Look at me." His gaze was fierce. "It took us how long to get here? No, it isn't easy. And it may not be easy from here on out. But I want to try."

The certainty in his voice told her everything she needed to know. She pressed close to him, luxuriating in his warmth against the storm. "I do too."

"I remodeled the apartment a little," he said into her ear, running a thumb over her knuckles. "After you left."

She couldn't imagine why he would do that when he wasn't staying. "That's—wow. I spent a lot of time imagining changes to that place."

"Want to see? It also has the advantage of not being in this rain."

They climbed the stairs again to the top, passing Zorba hiding in an alcove that was not as sheltered as he would have probably liked. The cat sat, eyes closed, hunched against the rain. Waiting it out. Such a tough guy, like this hotel. At the top, Amelia was ready to collapse, but she followed James to the apartment she'd missed so much.

He pushed open the door and stood shyly aside.

The sitting room now had a big bright window that looked out over the ridiculously picturesque cliffs. Big cheerful leafy plants flanked the window. It totally transformed the room. Light streamed in, even through the dimness of the wet day, brightening a new white sofa with a modern coffee table and two chairs. A small kitchenette had been installed in the far wall, with an electric kettle, microwave, and mini fridge. The kettle and fridge were both retro turquoise and looked incredibly chic.

"Oh, wow." She sucked in a breath. "James."

"You like it?" He handed her a towel from the bathroom.

This was the kind of remodel she'd wanted to do so badly here. It made it not only livable, but cozy and inviting. A place to truly live.

"I don't understand why you did this. Stavros and whoever he picks to run the hotel are just going to come and live here." She looked around the room with longing. *She* wanted to live here.

"I guess that's up for discussion."

Something in his voice, some teasing note, made her snap her eyes to his. "Did you tell him no?"

He gave her a cheeky grin. "It's a long story, but I've had recent intel that suggests signing might not be in the cards."

She stepped over to him, reveling in his closeness and the fact that she could touch him like this. "Yeah? What's the intel?"

"You're in my arms."

She made a scrunched-up face, and he kissed it away.

The kiss was a gateway drug. Desire rippled down her belly, and she could tell from the way his hands were roaming that he felt it too. This time they let it take over. Their mouths scrambled to kiss, to find bare skin. She peeled off her sodden shirt, which he assisted with, and they slid out of the remainder of their wet clothes. She could not believe she had lied to herself that this wasn't what she wanted—that they were only friends and partners and nothing more, and that it could possibly stay that way. For months she had told herself this lie, appreciating that he always gave her room, noticing that he made sure she was okay in any situation. She'd slept next to him and worked beside him as a friend, cooked for him, watched him, witnessed his personal habits, and loved it all—even his astonishing assortment of pocket jetsam. He always had a few shells and olives in there.

The olive!

"Wait," she said, already regretting removing herself from his arms. She grabbed her pants and felt for the olive pit, holding it out to him.

He peered at it. "An olive pit."

For a moment she thought she'd gotten it wrong, that the story he told her about his grandfather proposing to his grandmother was made up, but he turned those vivid green eyes on her, and they were serious and a little wet.

"I wanted to propose to you with this," she said. "If you... wanted that. James—"

"We're already married." His eyes did that thing where he managed to convey both laughter and love. "And I would like to consummate it. Soon."

"But I want to marry you for real. I know we haven't known each other for long, but I want—I want..."

He covered her mouth with his.

"Amelia," he murmured against her mouth.

"Yeah." She applied her lips to his jaw, his ear, his neck. *Can't talk, call you back later.*

"I don't..."

She was afraid he was going to say that despite all the smoochy-smooing, he didn't want to be married, or that they should wait a bit and see how this went. That would be the sensible course of action.

"I wanted to ask *you*," he said. "But yes. I will marry you for real."

She pulled back a little. "I might not want kids. I didn't even want to get married. I was antimarriage. Are you okay with that? You can back out. Now's your chance."

He stared into her eyes in a way that gave her delicious chills and said, "I don't know if I want kids either. I have to be with someone I love first in order to decide."

"Well, I'm right here."

"Good." He guided her into the bedroom, lowering her onto the bed. The rain slammed against the window. She arched up to meet his skin, thrilling as he gave a little groan into her mouth. He trailed a finger down her shoulder and slid along the length of her, slowly, so that their skin touched in every possible place. His hands slid down, low, between her legs, making sure she was ready. When she was squirming with need—a little mewl might have escaped her, but she would tell no one—he paused.

"James," she whispered. Chills that had nothing to do with having been in the rain rippled up and down her body.

"Yeah?"

"Stop teasing."

In response, he kissed his way down her body. After an interminable time that she didn't think she'd survive, he reached into the bedside drawer and got a condom. She made a mental note to ask him later why he'd stocked them. She hoped it was because he was wishing she'd come back. He moved over her and slid inside her. She briefly lost her mind. He increased his speed, holding her tightly against him. Her lips moved but no sound came out.

"You want me to slow down?" He *did* slow down. He stopped moving.

"No," she hissed. "I don't want it to stop. Don't. Don't stop."

"We can do this forever."

"Fine." She was going to tip over and fall down a deliciously deep hole. "Good. Let's."

He adjusted his angle and tilted her hips, and then, leaning into her neck, gave a single deep thrust that pushed her over the edge. She gripped him, rolling with every wave of pleasure that hit her. She saw stars that were clearly not on the ceiling. The ends of her toes felt it. She might have yelled; she had no control of her mouth. On the downhill slide, she saw him close his eyes and speed up, and he was coming, clutching her to him. When it was over, they lay heaving and warm, the pattering rain outside providing an ambient soundtrack.

They lay on the bed she'd spent months in. He held out his hand and she took it, reveling in the warmth of his hand, of the way his fingers wrapped over hers. There was a lot to talk about, think about, and understand. But for now all of that could wait.

———

Staying in the hotel without guests reminded Amelia of that happy first week with James, when they were learning about each other and constantly laughing. Amelia could see how spending the winter months this way would be nice.

The storm had spent itself, and peeks of sun shone through the dispersing clouds. They sat on the veranda upstairs, towels spread on the chairs, feet up on the low wall separating them from certain death over the cliff edge, looking out over the still-gray sea. Zorba lay magnificently at their feet, ears flicking. Amelia had been catching James up on her time in San Francisco.

"And you want to leave all that behind?" he asked. "That's a great job."

"No. I don't want to leave it behind. I like my work. I like the company." She reached over and hooked his pinky finger with hers.

"Hmm. How does that work with Asteri?"

"I don't know." Celia had asked her to work remotely, but Amelia meant it—she liked San Francisco too.

"I want to be wherever you are," James said.

Her heart squealed and ran around in circles. "Yeah?"

"Yeah. And if you want to be in San Francisco in your fancy-schmancy job, I would like to come with you."

"I want to be here. And there. I want to run the hotel with you. I love it here. And I want to spend part of the year in the States, with you. Celia said I can oversee overnight code releases from here, where it's our daytime."

"That could work. We could go back in the off-season," he said. "Since the Ria Hotel is closed in the winter."

She gazed at him, amazed all over again that they were here, that they were having this discussion. "I might like that. But I want to hear about you and what happened after I left."

"After you left—"

"And I'm sorry about that—"

"I know—me too, but let's not dwell. It actually turned out to be good." He paused, breathing in as though to get his bearings. "As I told you, Stavros tried to make it a problem with the power company. But I got a small loan from my parents to replant the olive grove below the hotel, which also covered the remodel of the apartment. Olive Grove Yorgos helped, and the power company was satisfied I was reinvesting in the island. I even gave them a fancy presentation last week about how much energy it would offset over the years by reducing carbon emissions. One grove won't offset the whole hotel, but the numbers looked good and they were impressed."

"I saw that! I saw the little baby trees! You presented all that? I'm so proud of you."

He looked back out over the expanse of sea in front of them. She loved looking at his face in profile. "And because I had remodeled the apartment, I showed that I was reinvesting in the hotel."

"Why do the apartment though? Why not a room or the kitchen?"

He sent her a sly look. "Because I thought you might like the apartment."

A thrill zipped through her body.

"But there was still the visa issue," he said. "I told my mom about that, and she thought of the Swedish citizenship angle, since her parents are Swedish. She still holds a Swedish passport. That qualifies me for one, so I applied. And I got it. My EU citizenship is now approved and pending, and I won't need a visa any longer. That satisfied the council here too."

"Wow." Her mind scrambled to keep up. "You solved all the problems. Are you—did you still want to sell?"

He sighed and looked out at the cliffs for a long moment. "I didn't want to do this alone. Stavros was offering a lot of money."

Her heart twinged. He'd turned down a lot. "I'm so, so sorry I left."

"Amelia." He took her hand across their chairs. "Please don't feel bad for leaving. I think we both needed it in order to figure things out."

"But what if I didn't come back?" She let him pull her out of her chair and settle her onto his lap.

He nuzzled her neck, trailing small kisses down her neck and making her squeal with pleasure. "Then I'd be an olive grove farmer in Oregon. And I still might have come to San Francisco to see if you'd have me."

"Really?" She pictured him charging into Velocity's chic sixty-eighth floor of Velocity's offices, running along the hall until he found her office.

"I was starting to make plans to go. But Birgitte told me that you'd texted her. She was fairly sure you'd make your way here. As usual, she was right—but for God's sake, let's not tell her that."

"You knew." She laughed into his cheek.

"I *hoped.*"

Shivers of joy jolted through her. She held on to him, arms around his neck, and decided she wanted to stay like this forever. "The past few days were horrible."

He pushed a lock of hair away from her face. "I spent my time making sure my new olive trees were doing okay and rehearsing what I would say if you came back."

"Oh yeah?" She leaned into his neck. "What did you decide on?"

"A lot of this." He kissed her, his lips soft and lazy.

She told him about all the delays and accidents, and about the German and then the sheep and the long walk through the country-side. "And this morning when I got up, everyone in the *hora* came to say hello and welcome me back, and I was hoping that it worked out, otherwise it was going to be extra hard to leave if you didn't want me."

"Oh, I want you," James breathed. "You're well-loved here, and not just by me. You think you run away from things—"

"Not anymore." She squeezed his legs with her thighs.

"Everyone asked about you, all the time. I heard a mouthful from Katarina and Eleni, and Fishmonger Yorgos. Not to mention Kostas and Birgitte and Olive Grove Yorgos. Birgitte's been the worst pill imaginable." He laughed. "She hasn't let me forget for one minute that I let you walk away."

"You didn't *let* me. I walked away on my own."

"We both did," he said quietly. He ran a hand down her back that said the days of being hurt were behind them.

"It was nice of Birgitte to be worried," Amelia said after a minute.

"You're a friend to her, and she was upset you left. As were many people. Everyone. The whole island."

She lowered her head into his neck and breathed in. They were in that heady, wonderful space where they'd realized their feelings for each other, and they'd started having sex and wanted to have it all the time.

His arms tightened around her, and as though he read her mind, he murmured, "How about right here in front of this view?"

"Yes," she whispered. "Let's."

He helped her wriggle out of her shirt. "By the way, as my wife, you can have Swedish citizenship."

She met his eyes and his lips. He ran his hands up the sides of her face, up under her hair, around her head. The sensation made her shoulders tingle in the most enchanting, light-headed way.

"You have it all figured out," she whispered.

"I wanted to be ready."

"That's pretty cocky," she whispered. "I could have moved on. I could have been boning a guy in my office."

"But you weren't." He breathed into her, nuzzling his nose into her neck and sighing with what sounded like contentment. "You weren't."

CHAPTER 25

Amelia moved down the worn stone steps cut into the land, made smooth and dark with decades of use. Her dress was too long for the shallow steps not to be a tripping hazard, but that couldn't be helped now. It wasn't a real wedding dress, but the train was long, and that pleased her, because this was the only wedding dress she ever intended to wear. She looked up to see the assembly of guests in the orchard. Most of the island had showed up. The roasted lamb might have been an enticement, since everyone liked a celebration. Her heart squeezed every time she thought about the good wishes from everyone they saw. Birds sang all over the grove. The spring March air was deliciously sweet, even after the delight of holing up with James through the winter.

A hand appeared on her lower back. "Ready?" he asked.

"Yep." She turned and nestled her head in the crook of his neck. What she really wanted to do was ditch the reception and go back to the Ria and have loads of hot monkey sex. The way he trailed his hand down her arm suggested he did too.

"Come on." She took his hand, and they made their way down

the steps from the church, where a teenager named Photography Enthusiast Yorgos had finished taking their post-wedding blessing photos.

The church was not the one where they'd gotten married the first time. Amelia hadn't wanted to go back there, given the negative associations with Takis's death and the trickery of their vows. She wanted to start somewhere new. So they had their marriage and shiny Greek gold wedding rings blessed in the tiny blue-domed beauty they'd found in the middle of Olive Grove Yorgos's land, where the priest was less cranky. They renewed their vows—or, more accurately, stated them properly this time, with intention.

"When are you guys opening the hotel for the season?" Ella asked them. She had arrived several days ago.

"Beginning of May," Amelia said, fingering her new wedding band. "We're already booked out until July." Pedro, who was still doing tweaks for their online presence—but being paid for it now—had made it so guests could get notified by email when bookings were open for the season. And they had staff now: a full-time housekeeper, a dedicated handyman named Handy Yorgos, and Chef Stefanis, whom they stole away from a popular restaurant on Crete after his good friend Kostas assured him that Asteri was up and coming and he'd have his own kitchen.

"Hmm," Ella said. "I was thinking of staying a bit longer since Celia doesn't mind where we work."

Working remotely for Celia had turned out to be easier than Amelia anticipated. It had its challenges, but these were overcome with video calls, and Amelia had proven her worth when she caught a major bug in a piece of code overnight (Greek daytime).

"Always room for you here, Ella," James said.

"Don't worry about me," Ella said. "I have places to stay."

Ella had hit it off with Olive Grove Yorgos. He was a charmer, Amelia agreed. Ella had been here a week and had not spent a single night at the hotel.

Christopher held up a glass of wine. "To the happy couple," he said, and everyone yelled, "*Yamas!*"

Amelia left James's side to give her brother a hug. She still couldn't believe he'd come all the way here. He couldn't believe it either, he said. But as long as their parents weren't coming, someone had to represent the Lang side. In typical warring fashion, her mother said she wasn't coming if her father was, and her father said he wouldn't come if her mother did, so neither would book a ticket. For the first time, Amelia felt sympathy for her mother and told her that she would love it if she would visit in a few months. This was the right thing to say; her mother was delighted. Her father sent a long email saying that marriage was hard, and if Amelia and James didn't enjoy spending simple quiet time together, then that was a sign and Amelia should think twice about committing herself to James. This was clearly about Amelia's mother. Amelia loved spending any kind of time with James, talking or not. She felt confident they were escaping whatever trap her parents had fallen into.

"To the future of the Ria Hotel!" James's mother called, and everyone yelled "*Yamas!*" again. His parents were everything

Amelia could have hoped for as in-laws. Admittedly, compared to her parents, the bar wasn't high. His mother had hugged Amelia right away and told her how happy she was to welcome her to the family. James's father had been shyly delighted, saying how happy he was to finally have a daughter after three boys.

"Do you consider naming the Ria Hotel to something else?" Birgitte asked. "Because Ria was Takis's wife."

"We've branded the Ria Hotel all over the internet," James pointed out.

"Whatever." Birgitte waved this away. "You should call it the Secret Love Hotel. Guests will like the intrigue."

Amelia grimaced. "Sounds like a pay-by-the-hour dive."

James laughed. "We could install some mirrors on the ceilings."

"Yorgos Hotel," Angry Yorgos called from where he was tending the roasting lamb.

"Asteri Luxury Resort," Kostas supplied.

"I like Alexandra Resort," Alexandra said. "Too long though. Alex Res, perhaps."

"To save time," Birgitte said, and they laughed.

"We can't change the name." James shook his head.

"How about the Accidental Hotel," Ella said.

"I like Ria because it's an ode to love that takes its time," James whispered in Amelia's ear, pulling her close. She nestled against him and softly exhaled.

"Can you please wait a little longer to have sex?" Birgitte scoffed. "We have the lamb to eat."

"Eh, let them have the love," Angry Yorgos said. His rage when it came to Amelia and James had reduced so significantly that some people had started calling him Magda's Yorgos.

With Amelia's hefty salary, they had been able to undertake further renovations and pay Angry Yorgos and Magda more than half of what they needed to make Takis's grave permanent. The rest would come over the next two years. At the hotel, they had fixed several structural issues, expanded the kitchen into a gorgeous, light-filled space with new high-end appliances that rivaled Birgitte's and increased space in the reception area. They had also added another room to their own apartment. Amelia had plans for a fountain to be installed somewhere, as soon as she figured out where.

Old Port Yanni began to play the bouzouki. People dispersed, clearing the area for dancing. Birgitte and Kostas were the first two out on the dance floor, and everyone else soon joined. Shepherd Yorgos and a few builders approached James to toast him, and they went across the grove to swig back some potent ouzo shots.

Ella sidled up to Amelia. "He *does* look like Alexander Skarsgård."

"Again, he does not."

Ella sighed happily.

"You like?" Amelia asked.

"I like that you're in love and you're here, and that he loves you. I like that you're having sex. And I like that *I'm* having sex too."

"Your parents would never approve of Olive Grove Yorgos."

"Of course not. But I'm never getting married. I've decided it's too fraught."

Amelia nudged her with her shoulder. "I said that too, you know." She held up her hand with the shiny gold ring.

Ella shook her head. "Right, but it took a drunken mistake to do it."

"You never know. Drink up. You may find yourself married and owning a thriving olive farm in the morning."

Ella pretended to consider it, making Amelia laugh. She looked around the grove, taking in all her friends and family, wondering again if this was a dream. Who ended up this lucky? James caught her eye and gave her a tiny private smile. Now he was in conversation with Dimitri Lykaios, who exported olive oil and honey from Asteri. They would be talking for a while.

But when she refilled her glass and turned again, there was James, next to her.

"I don't want to stand next to anyone except you," he said into her ear.

"I agree to those terms," she said, nestling into him.

Birgitte sailed by, twirling in circles from Kostas's spin, whooping. It was not only their wedding celebration, but also St. George's Day. Church bells rang in the distance. Everyone had brought a dish to share. Tables lined the edges of the olive grove, covered with lamb cooked in vine-leaf nests, pork with sweet wine and capers, and handmade sweets like loukoumades and delicious nutty halva. The late afternoon would morph into a cool evening with a black-orange sky. Every day would be this way until it gave way to the heat and lazy cicada drone of the summer.

Amelia looked forward to the changes of the months ahead,

and the challenges too. She and James would tell all their guests how they met and fell in love. Someday when they were old, they would tell some scraggly travelers who were hurting, who were done running but didn't know it yet, how they had gotten here. They would tell them of how their friendship settled into love over citrus-scented days and against this landscape of sparse, simple beauty. And with any luck, they would swindle them into taking over the legacy of the Ria Hotel.

BIRGITTE'S POTATO MOUSSAKA

//

Once you make this delicious dish, you will wonder how anyone in their right mind would ever use eggplant instead of potatoes. Typically, potatoes are part of this anyway, but here we just omit the offensive eggplant.

3 tbsp unsalted butter

3 tbsp all-purpose flour

FOR THE MEAT SAUCE:

2 tbsp olive oil

1 medium onion, chopped

4.5 lbs potatoes

1 lb ground lamb

1 lb ground beef

1/2 cup red wine

5 ripe tomatoes skinned and finely chopped, or use a 28 oz can of San Marzano canned skinned tomatoes

1 tbsp oregano

3 tbsp tomato paste

salt

pepper

2–3 cloves of garlic, chopped

1 tbsp ground cinnamon

FOR THE BÉCHAMEL SAUCE:

3 tbsp unsalted butter

3 tbsp all-purpose flour

3 cups milk (whole milk is best)

Salt and freshly ground pepper

1–2 tsp nutmeg

2–3 egg yolks (optional; this makes it creamier but isn't strictly necessary)

1 cup grated kefalotyri cheese (substitute pecorino or parmigiano reggiano if you can't find kefalotyri)

STEP 1: PREPARE THE POTATOES.

1. Peel the potatoes and cut into thin coins. Fry them in a little oil until lightly browned, or parboil in boiling water for 5 minutes. If parboiling, drain and set them aside.

STEP 2: PREPARE THE MEAT SAUCE.

1. Heat 2 tbsp of olive oil over medium heat, and sauté the onions until translucent, 10–12 minutes.

2. Add both ground meats and continue to sauté until lightly browned.

3. Add the wine, tomatoes, oregano, tomato paste, salt, and pepper, and bring to a boil. Cook until as much liquid as possible is absorbed; avoiding too much moisture will make for an easier bake. Stir in the garlic and cinnamon. Mix well. Let the mixture simmer lightly.

STEP 3: MAKE THE BÉCHAMEL SAUCE.

While the meat sauce is simmering, make the béchamel.

1. In a large saucepan, melt the butter over medium heat. Once melted, add the flour and stir until there are no lumps. You may opt to heat the milk while the butter melts to make the stirring easier, but the milk can also be added cold.

2. Increase the heat to medium. Add the milk in small batches, stirring constantly with a whisk so it absorbs fully before adding more.

3. Stir until the sauce begins to thicken; it should be creamy but not too thick. Remove from heat and stir in salt, pepper, and nutmeg.

4. If using egg yolks, beat and stir into the sauce. Remove from the heat and set aside until ready to use.

STEP 4: ASSEMBLE THE MOUSSAKA.

1. Preheat the oven to 350°F (180°C). Lightly oil a 5 qt baking dish.

2. Layer the potato slices on the bottom of the dish. If you want to layer them in a scallop pattern like Birgitte told Amelia to, you can, but this will quickly become pointless.

3. Spread the meat mixture evenly on top of the potatoes. Add the cheese.

4. Cover with the remaining potato slices and pour the béchamel sauce evenly over the top.

5. Bake for 40–50 minutes. Let rest 10–15 minutes before cutting. The dish is best if served warm, not hot.

READING GROUP GUIDE

1. Do you think Amelia was right or wrong for ditching Ella's wedding to go to Europe?

2. Have you ever lost your temper at work? What were the repercussions?

3. Are you a person who runs away from your life problems, or do you confront them head-on?

4. Why do you think Amelia was so reticent to return to her life in San Francisco?

5. During the dinner party, Birgitte proclaims that "everyone is a little broken." What do you think she meant by that? Do you agree with her statement?

6. Amelia realizes that part of why she was holding herself back from her feelings for James was because of what happened between her parents. Did your parents' relationship (or that of someone else important in your life) ever have an impact on your own relationships?

7. If given the chance, would you run a boutique hotel on a small Greek island?

8. Each of the Yorgoses on Asteri has a distinct job: Blue Tavern Yorgos, Mover Yorgos, Feta Yorgos, Plumber Yorgos, Olive Grove Yorgos, Fisherman Yorgos, Kiln Yorgos, Calamari Yorgos, Oyster Diver Yorgos, Car Rental Yorgos, Photography Enthusiast Yorgos, Handy Yorgos, and Shepherd Yorgos. If you went to live on a Greek island, which Yorgos would you be?

9. If you had a second chance at a completely different life than the one you're living today, would you take it? Or would you keep your current life?

A CONVERSATION
WITH THE AUTHOR

How did the idea for this book come about?

Several years ago, I was sitting in my car in traffic on Highway 80 in Berkeley, and I heard a story on the radio about a couple who had gone to a remote island for their honeymoon. They made great friends with the hotel owners and ended up buying the hotel from them after one very drunken evening. This real-life couple stayed and made a go of running the hotel—business was bolstered by the news story. What a life change! I couldn't stop thinking about this idea. I have also always loved the marriage of convenience trope it's one of my very favorites, so when I put a sudden accidental marriage together with accidentally acquiring a hotel, this story was born.

Tell us about your connection to Greece, and why you set this novel there.

My mother and I moved to Santorini when I was almost ten. We stayed there for a few years, off and on. I learned some Greek, enough to get by, and we lived in a villa overlooking the caldera in Thira. It was the eighties so the music was great and the island far less developed and touristy, the way it is today. Then, you had to visit a telephone office to make a phone call, and if someone had a VCR, that was special. There were a lot of wonderful things about that experience, as well as challenges. It was unorthodox and it was great, but I'm ultimately grateful to have lived abroad and on one of the most beautiful islands in the world, where I got to know the secret nooks and crannies. As a result, I wanted to set a novel in Greece using what I knew of it. A Greek island is the perfect setting for drama.

What was the most fun scene to write?

One of my favorites is the scene with Ella toward the end, when Amelia is trying to make amends. She woos Ella with char siu baos (barbecue pork buns) from a real bakery in Chinatown—AA on Stockton and Jackson Streets, which indeed has delicious buns on offer. My wonderful mother-in-law, Theresa, confirms it is the best, and she grew up in Chinatown. Personally, I would be susceptible to apologies made with pork buns.

I also enjoyed writing the trials Amelia has trying to make her way back to Greece. I had a lot of fun throwing every obstacle at her, all the while knowing she was going to make her way back to James.

What do you think is next for Amelia and James?

Amelia and James are going to face some challenges as they dedicate themselves to the hotel. There will be a lot of visitors and new characters to get to know. It won't be easy to live on a small, relatively isolated island most of the year. Maybe they'll do a lot of traveling, or maybe they'll face a natural disaster and have to rebuild. The Aegean is a hotbed of volcanic activity, after all.

What's your advice for new writers?

Keep going. The writing process can feel overwhelming at first. Many writers are tempted to delete the words they have because they're not perfect. But writing is an iterative process, and it takes time and lots and lots of editing. Every published author has gone through years of trial and error. You won't get anywhere if you quit.

Do you ever get stuck while writing? How do you work your way out of it?

If I'm having problems with a scene, I picture it like reversing out of a dead end in a maze—that direction didn't work, so you back out to the main path and take another one. Sometimes it requires other perspectives, like trusted beta readers. The scene in which Takis dies and leaves Amelia and James the Ria Hotel was a hard one to write, because dying and leaving strangers a hotel when they've just gotten married is a tall order to pull off. For that scene, I tried a bunch of different paths. Ultimately, the path is the one that feels the best for the characters and the story.

ACKNOWLEDGMENTS

As many people know, Greece is a wondrous place. I spent a few years on Santorini in the 1980s as a kid and saw its sun-kissed hopes and dreams, silhouetted against its actively volcanic caldera. A Greek island is a place to explore and soak and breathe. Perhaps this is what makes it a perfect backdrop for drama. I chose to set this story on the fictional island of Asteri (ἀστέρι), which means *star* in Greek and is the base from which we derive English words such as *aster* (a starlike flower) and *astronaut* (a star sailor). I imagined Asteri to be like one of the smaller, less developed (and thus less touristy) islands in the Cyclades, like Anafi or Kimolos. The Asteri of my imagination is much more like the Santorini of the 1980s in the off-season, when it was quiet and belonged again to the island locals.

There are so many special people who helped this story on its way. Thanks to my agent, Melissa Edwards, who patiently read several terrible story pitches from me, but when I sent this one, said, "I'd read that in a heartbeat!" Melissa, your guidance, knowledge, and partnership along this journey are incredibly appreciated. To my editor, Erin McClary, thank you for being a friend and a reader as well as an enthusiastic editor. You get me so well that you looked up the specifics of rigor mortis. To the entire team at Sourcebooks, thank you for the love and care you take preparing my books to meet the world—including Cristina Arreola, Heather VenHuizen, Molly Waxman, Danielle McNaughton, Stephanie Rocha, and Jessica Thelander.

To Kristen Lippert-Martin and Denise Logsdon, thank you for your feedback and being truly excellent in all ways. You're my sounding boards and my wise Sherpas. (And Denise, thank you for overlooking egregious typos and other horrors in the first read of this one. I know it must have hurt.) To Mike Chen, thank you for always having my back. To Mónica Mancillas, the bestieoula who shares with me a childhood spent abroad, including Greece, thank you for the insightful feedback and peeing-my-pants laughter on a near constant basis—I know that makes it sound like my pants are always wet, but I assure you they aren't. To Meredith Schorr, Dianne Freeman, Bea Birdsong, and Catherine Arguelles, thank you for providing a sanity check on early chapters, and to all my #TeamMelissa siblings, my goodness, you are the very, very best friends and supports.

Thank you to my mother for the recipes, and for being excited about all the book stuff. Thanks to Sisalee, Shannon, Lisa, Erika, Rob, and Amy for your support always. And thanks to Ken and Matthew and Tim for making me laugh and being my loves every day.

ABOUT THE AUTHOR

Sierra Godfrey is originally from Santa Cruz, California, but has lived all over the world including Santorini, Greece. Now she resides in the foggy San Francisco Bay Area with her family, which includes a dog, two cats, and a turtle, all of which seemed like a good idea at the time. Her first novel, *A Very Typical Family*, was published by Sourcebooks.

ALL FAMILIES ARE MESSY. SOME ARE DISASTERS.

"I loved this. I couldn't put it down. Engrossing, satisfying."
—KJ DELL'ANTONIA, *New York Times* bestselling author of *The Chicken Sisters*

A VERY TYPICAL FAMILY

A Novel

SIERRA GODFREY

Natalie Walker is the reason her older brother and sister went to prison more than fifteen years ago. She fled California shortly after and hasn't spoken to anyone in her family since. Now, on the same day her boyfriend steals her dream job out from under her, Natalie receives a letter from a lawyer saying her estranged mother has died and left the family's historic Santa Cruz house to them—but only if all three siblings come back and claim it together.

Natalie arrives home expecting to sign some papers, briefly see siblings Lynn and Jake, and get back to sorting out her life in Boston. But Jake, now an award-winning ornithologist, is missing. And Lynn shows up with a teenage son. While Natalie and her nephew look for Jake, she unpacks the guilt she has held on to for so many years, wondering how (or if) she can salvage a relationship with her siblings after all this time.

A Very Typical Family navigates the messy yet warmhearted journey of a family struggling to find one another again. Written with delightfully dark humor and characters you can't help but cheer for, this debut from Sierra Godfrey will have you reveling in the power of family and second chances.

"Atmospheric and uplifting. A great recommendation for fans of Marian Keyes and Emily Giffin."
— ***Booklist*, STARRED Review**